Dragon Captives

Also by Lisa McMann

» » « «

THE UNWANTEDS SERIES

The Unwanteds

Island of Silence

Island of Fire

Island of Legends

Island of Shipwrecks

Island of Graves

Island of Dragons

» » « «

THE UNWANTEDS QUESTS SERIES

Dragon Captives

Dragon Bones

» » « «

FOR OLDER READERS:

Don't Close Your Eyes

Visions

Cryer's Cross

Dead to You

LISA McMANN

THE UNWANTEDS QUESTS

Dragon Captives

Aladdin
NEW YORK LONDON TORONTO SYDNEY NEW DELHI

ALADDIN

An imprint of Simon & Schuster Children's Publishing Division

1230 Avenue of the Americas, New York, New York 10020

First Aladdin paperback edition February 2018

Also available in an Aladdin hardcover edition.

For information about special discounts for bulk purchases, please contact Simon & Schuster Special Sales at 1-866-506-1949 or business@simonandschuster.com.

The Simon & Schuster Speakers Bureau can bring authors to your live event. For more information or to book an event contact the Simon & Schuster Speakers Bureau at 1-866-248-3049 or visit our website atwww.simonspeakers.com.

Book designed by Karin Paprocki

The text of this book was set in Truesdell.

Manufactured in the United States of America 0421 OFF

6 8 10 9 7

This book has been cataloged with the Library of Congress.

ISBN 978-1-4814-5681-4 (hc)

ISBN 978-1-4814-5682-1 (pbk)

ISBN 978-1-4814-5683-8 (eBook)

To my faithful Instagram friends: Your love and support of the Unwanteds world means everything to me. Thank you!

Contents

Tragedy in the Jungle

Thisbe Stowe glided through the vines in the dim light, with her twin sister, Fifer, right behind her. They were far deeper inside the jungle of Artimé than they'd ever ventured before. Much farther than their brother, Alex, the leader of the magical world, would allow. There were horrible living statues and creatures here that would attack them, he'd said. Creations carved from stone or molded from clay and brought to life with strong magic in the early days of Artimé. Not all of Artimé's creatures were dangerous, but the ones banished to the jungle most certainly were.

As the girls crept forward to a small clearing, Fifer spied an entrance to a dark cave some distance away. She jabbed Thisbe with her elbow and pointed excitedly at it. They'd never come across something like this before. Thisbe paused to look, trying to discern between shadows and crevices, and watching for any sign of danger. Sensing none, they started toward it.

Each footstep crackled. Every now and then, Thisbe hesitated and put her hand up for silence. They stopped and listened, then continued on. When Thisbe heard a rustling that wasn't theirs, her heart quickened. She turned sharply to see if Fifer had heard it too. The look on Fifer's face told her she had.

The noise grew louder. Nearer. A few treetops began to waver, letting slivers of bright sunlight in before the branches covered the girls in shadows again. Something was coming, and it was definitely big.

"Maybe it's the rock," whispered Fifer. The enormous living rock that roamed about the jungle, watching over its creatures, was nameless, at least to these visitors.

"Maybe," said Thisbe, sounding doubtful. "Come on." She pushed forward, periodically looking back to try to see what was following them, but she couldn't make out anything in the low light. As they moved, the noise from their pursuer stopped. Thisbe glanced at Fifer. Perhaps it hadn't detected them.

Fifer peered in the direction of the cave, dying to know what was inside, but her nerves got the better of her. She gripped Thisbe's shirtsleeve. "It's too dangerous. I think we should go back."

Thisbe nodded. But how? They'd have to go past the thing making noise in order to get back to the safety of Artimé's lush grounds. "This way," she whispered, pointing in a different direction. "We'll go around and take the tube home."

The rustling started again, and Fifer strained her eyes toward the noise. Would they be able to see the creature before it saw them? "Do you think it could be Panther?" she asked anxiously. Panther, carved from ebony-colored stone, had become slightly tamer in recent years than she'd once been, but she was still unpredictable and dangerous.

"Panther doesn't make the trees move. Shh." Thisbe headed away from the noise, stepping carefully, but there was no possible way to be silent.

The rustling behind them began again, then turned to loud crackling noises. Trees swayed. Their pursuer grew nearer.

"It's following us," said Thisbe in a harsh whisper.

Fifer took Thisbe's hand and looked back as the outline of the enormous creature finally emerged from the shadows. She froze, then gasped. "Scorpion! Run!"

Thisbe's heartbeat pounded in her ears. *The scorpion!* They were going to die. She abandoned the plan and ran for her life, dragging Fifer with her. Behind them came the sharp clap of splitting trees. The ground trembled under their feet. The giant clay scorpion was in mad pursuit and gaining ground rapidly. Hunting them.

The girls lurched and staggered as fast as they could over the uneven ground, but there was no way they could outrun the magical creature. No way for them to reach safety. Trees groaned and thudded to the jungle floor around them, their roots bursting from the ground and spraying dirt high into the air. Vines flew up in all directions as the scorpion closed in. Fifer could hear the sharp clicking of its pincers getting louder. "Thisbeee!" she screamed.

From a different direction there appeared a smaller, shadowy figure, too far away for Thisbe and Fifer to figure out what it was. "Look!" shrieked Fifer. "Over there!"

"Oh no!" Thisbe cried. "This way!" They changed course and barely slipped away from the scorpion, but it turned and followed. Seconds later the girls heard a third enormous-sounding creature thundering toward them. Could there be more than one scorpion in the jungle? No one had ever mentioned it. The girls were surrounded.

"Up this tree!" Thisbe cried, ripping her hand from Fifer's sweaty grip and leaping for a low-hanging branch. She swung and caught her foot on the trunk, then scrambled up as fast as she could. Fifer followed, the noises around them growing louder still. "Hurry!" Thisbe said, climbing higher. She held her hand out to pull Fifer up.

But it was no use. The scorpion slid to a stop below them. It gripped the tree with one of its pincers. Then it snapped the trunk in two, sending the top portion with the girls in it falling through the air and crashing to the jungle floor. The girls lay stunned, the wind knocked out of them.

The sounds from the other two approaching beasts grew more distinct. Suddenly a piercing scream filled the air, coming from one of the creatures.

"That's Panther!" Fifer managed to say as she tried to catch her breath. She struggled to get to her feet. "Come on, Thiz!" The scorpion was clipping branches and batting them aside, trying to get to them.

"I can't—I'm stuck!" Thisbe's ankle was caught under the tree. She yanked on it, then tried pushing the tree trunk off her while wildly looking around. "Watch out!"

Fifer turned an instant too late. The scorpion, moving steadily toward her with its poisonous tail raised, knocked her flat with its pincer. Then it pinned both girls to the ground with its spindly front legs. "Help!" Thisbe screamed. They stared at the horrible monster, who was looking down at them with all of its creepy eyes. It swished its tail, knocking over more trees in the process.

Just then a large black panther came bounding into sight, her chiseled stone jaw opened wide, emitting a piercing scream. Was she coming to help the twins? Or help the scorpion eat them? One never knew with Panther.

"Let us go!" Thisbe struggled and fought to free herself. But neither Fifer nor Thisbe could escape, and with the scorpion's feet pressing hard on their chests, it was getting harder and harder to breathe.

As the third creature came running toward them, making the ground shudder, Fifer began screaming in a strange, almost melodious manner. Hundreds of birds swooped in and flocked to the trees around them, but they did nothing to help.

Thisbe closed her eyes and gagged at the sight of them. A familiar pulsing began in her stomach, and it rose up like bile to her throat. As the panther jumped over the girls and slammed into the giant scorpion, knocking it off balance, a garbled, uncontrollable shout burst forth from Thisbe.

Sparks flew from the girl's fingertips and slammed into Panther's flank. The creature's scream stopped abruptly. With a loud crack and a horrible thud, the black stone beast hit the ground, split completely in two. She didn't move.

"Oh no," breathed Thisbe, horrified.

"Panther!" screeched Fifer. She slammed her fists against the scorpion's thin leg, trying to break it so she could roll away. She thought she heard a crack.

The scorpion reared back in anger, pincers clicking and tail swishing. Thisbe yanked on her leg to free it, and both girls scrambled out from under the creature just as the third pursuer drew near and rose up, flapping its wings and taking to the air. The scorpion swiveled and whipped its tail around, swiping at the girls. Thisbe and Fifer leaped and dodged the stinger, then tried to run. A shadow hovered over them, making the jungle even darker and harder to navigate. The scorpion took another swing, its aim dead-on.

Before it could connect, two sets of claws grabbed the girls and lifted them up into the air, and with a loud roar, the third pursuer carried them off. The scorpion slid to a stop and watched, a sinister hiss dying in its throat. Frustrated, it slammed its tail into a tree, then skittered away to its cave in the darkest part of the jungle, leaving the unmoving pieces of Panther's stone body on the ground.

A Fight

When the girls realized what had just happened, they looked up at the enormous winged-cheetah statue that carried them.

"Oh, thank goodness it's you," said Fifer. She slumped, feeling like all the bones in her body could fall out through her dangling arms and legs.

Thisbe remained rigid. She watched the trees getting smaller below her, and her stomach, still in knots from the scorpion attack, twisted tighter. Her mouth went dry and she covered her eyes. "Please don't drop me," she whispered. "Please don't drop me."

"I won't drrrop you," came the snarly reply. "Even though you deserrrve it. Alex is going to be verrry upset. You put yourrr lives in terrrible dangerrr! You'rrre lucky I was therrre orrr you'd be eaten by now. And you destrrroyed Pantherrr!"

"I didn't mean it, Simber," Thisbe whispered, feeling awful in every possible way. "I didn't try to hit her."

"Do you have to tell Alex?" Fifer asked. Now that they were safe, her fear of the scorpion turned immediately into fear of what Alex would say to them. He was going to be so disappointed.

Simber, built from sand and hardened into stone with magic, was the head mage's closest confidant. A low growl rumbled in his throat as he tried to control his anger—Panther was a special friend of his. "Of courrrse I'm going to tell him. Pantherrr was trrrying to save you, and you killed herrr!"

Thisbe's eyes flew open. "It was an accident, I swear! I wish I'd hit the scorpion!"

"Well, you didn't!" The giant cheetah's disgust was evident in his voice.

"I wasn't even trying to do magic," Thisbe moaned. "It just came out like it always does." Tears sprang to her eyes. "I'm really sorry. Isn't there any way . . . ?" She wanted to ask if there was a way to fix Panther, but she didn't quite dare, in case the answer was no.

Simber didn't reply. Like Alex, he'd heard the girls' excuses before, way too many times.

Fifer shot Thisbe a sympathetic look. "Sorry," she mouthed.

Thisbe nodded, still hanging stiffly from Simber's claws and trying desperately not to move so he wouldn't accidentally lose his grip on her. She swallowed hard and shut her eyes again. Both girls remained silent, agonizing internally over their fate for the rest of the journey to the Unwanteds' mansion, knowing their brother was going to be so mad he'd probably send them back to the scorpion's cave.

A short while later, the nearly identical girls stood in the grand office of the head magician of Artimé, staring at the floor in front of Alex's desk. Thisbe's short black curls were flipping every which way. A small dead leaf and a few tiny sticks from the jungle were entangled within, unnoticed. Fifer nervously smoothed her long black waves away from her face, picking out the remnants of the jungle floor and putting them into her pants pocket. Nearby, the sand-colored cheetah statue sprawled on the floor, taking up a huge amount of space. His wings were folded in, his eyes narrowed, and his angular jaw set more sharply than usual.

Alex Stowe, wearing a multicolored robe, came in through a magical door at the back of the office and strode quickly toward them. He was the second ruler of Artimé, having been forced to take over the magical world at the age of fourteen, when Marcus Today, the original mage and creator of the secret world for Unwanteds, had been killed. Now in his late twenties, Alex had been wizened by countless challenges. His face wore a weary expression.

Fifer lifted her eyes to look at him, then swiftly averted her gaze. Alex rounded the desk and stopped. He placed his right hand on it and leaned forward to study his sisters. His left arm dangled limply, withered and useless. "What did you do this time?" he asked warily. He glanced at Simber, then back at the girls.

Thisbe frowned hard at the ground. Fifer looked sidelong at her, then spoke. "We went into the jungle."

Alex's expression hardened. "How far?"

"Far."

"Obviously you escaped alive and well," said Alex in a measured tone, "and I'm glad about that. But you know you're not supposed to go there. It's dangerous."

Fifer nodded.

"So . . . what happened?" Alex sounded like he expected to hear something dreadful.

"We ran into some trouble," Fifer hedged.

Alex sighed. "I could've guessed that. Just spill it, will you?"

"We would have been fine if you'd just let us take Magical Warrior Training—"

"Don't start," Alex warned.

Fifer sighed. Thisbe remained mute, so she plowed forward, telling Alex everything that happened. When she got to the part about Thisbe's crazy spell that had broken Panther in two, Alex stiffened. His brown eyes flared. He turned slowly to glare at Thisbe, his face beginning to burn. In a dark voice, he thundered, "You did *what*?"

Thisbe lifted her chin. Her eyelashes were wet. "I didn't mean to do it," she said, her voice trembling. "I couldn't stop it." Desperate, she stepped toward him. "Aaron can fix her, can't he? He can put her together again. It's not much different from her losing her tail and him putting that back on, is it?" Aaron was the girls' other brother and Alex's identical twin.

Alex fell back heavily in his chair and covered his face with his good hand, letting out an exasperated breath. "That's beside the point!"

Thisbe shrank back but immediately grew defensive. "No, it isn't. Not if he can fix her." She frowned. "And you don't have to yell about it. It's not that bad." Alex always made too big a deal of everything.

"Not that bad?" Alex sprang to his feet. "Do you seriously still not understand? How many times will you accidentally fire off a deadly spell before you kill another *person*, Thisbe? Someone who *can't* be brought back to life?" He shook his head, looking exhausted. "When is this nightmare going to end?"

Thisbe's eyes narrowed. "So now we're your *nightmare*? Way to make us feel like true Unwanteds, Alex. I thought you were against that."

Alex gave her a hard look. "You have no idea what being declared Unwanted really feels like, and you never will."

Thisbe pursed her lips and looked at the floor. "Sorry."

Fifer stepped in and tried again, addressing her brother in a calm voice. "Maybe if you would just give us component vests and let us start Magical Warrior Training, we could learn more about our magic and how to control it. It's not like we can help it, Alex."

"No," said Alex sharply. "You're not old enough. And besides, I'd be a fool to give you *more* access to magic when you can't handle the kind you've already got. You both need to learn self-control first, and that's not something anybody can teach you—though I've certainly tried. You have to actually care enough to do it yourselves!" He turned away in frustration and started pacing.

Thisbe's eyes sparked in anger. "Well, you don't have to be so mean! We're doing our best, but sometimes we just can't—"

"Thisbe, stop!" Alex shouted, silencing her. Then he lowered his voice. "Take a few breaths and cool off before you accidentally almost kill *me* again."

"But—" Thisbe's mouth clamped shut. His words stung. She would never want to do that. She never wanted to kill anyone. It was the most horrible ability she could imagine, and she was stuck with it.

Fifer flashed Thisbe a look, trying to get her to stay quiet. This was far from over. They still had to see what Alex was going to do to punish them, and she didn't want Thisbe making it worse.

But today the girls had finally exceeded the patience of their beloved brother. He began muttering like a madman. "Tried and tried since *you* were two years old to teach *you* . . . to help *you* . . ." He began gesturing at the ceiling. "The whole community is fearful every time one of *you* gets upset. I've done everything I could think of. Practically changed this entire world for *you* two—moved Magical Warrior Training to Karkinos so *you* wouldn't learn anything new, ordered people to stop doing magic if they see *you* around . . . All to protect *you*." He ripped his hand through his dark brown tangles. "And they've all done it very graciously, just so *you* could be raised near me in the mansion and be like the other kids. But *you* don't appreciate any of their sacrifices. You never have."

"That's not true," Thisbe interjected.

But Alex wasn't listening. He worked his jaw angrily. "I

wanted to send you to another island for a while just to give everybody here a break, but that would put others in danger. And you two just don't seem to care. You're twelve years old, and you still sneak out and put yourselves in these precarious positions without a thought for anybody else. I can't take it anymore! I really can't." He lowered his head as if he'd given up and pinched the bridge of his nose. "Why can't you do something *good* with your uncontrollable magic for once? Do you always have to be so destructive?" He stared at the wall for an uncomfortably long time.

Thisbe bowed her head, thinking about Panther and feeling like the worst person in the world.

"We're really sorry," Fifer said quietly. "We're going to do better. We promise."

Alex exploded again. "You're always sorry afterward! But sorry can't fix everything! Sorry doesn't bring Panther back to life." He slammed his fist against the back of his chair and cringed in pain, making him even angrier. "The only thing that'll keep Artimé safe is to lock you both up until you actually care enough to learn self-control!"

Fifer and Thisbe looked sharply at their brother, their

faces slack with shock and fear. Did he really mean that?

Simber sat up and emitted a low growl, startling Alex and pulling him out of his enraged rant. He turned quickly toward his sisters, seeing the pain in their eyes, and his anger fizzled. What had he just said? He replayed the words in his mind. Then he pressed his lips together and flexed his stinging, throbbing fist. In a resigned voice, he said, "I'm sorry—I really lost it. Why don't *you* two get dinner and head up to your room? We'll talk more later."

Thisbe hesitated, as if she were about to protest.

Fifer touched her shoulder. "Come on," she said.

Thisbe's expression flickered, but she turned toward the door, and they quietly walked out.

When they were gone, Alex slumped into his chair and let out a shuddering sigh that would tug at the hearts of all the loyal people of Artimé, if only they could hear it.

But, except for Simber, they couldn't. So Alex bore the burden alone.

Taking a Toll

"What did I just say to them?" Alex wearily asked Simber. He felt dazed.

"You told yourrr sisterrrs that you wanted to lock them up," the winged cheetah said drily.

"Forever? I didn't say forever, did I?"

"No, it wasn't quite that bad."

Alex leaned forward over his desk and put his head in his hands. He remained still for a few moments, digesting everything. "I can't believe I said that," he said, his voice muffled. He sat up. "What in the world has happened to me? Some days I really don't know. Thisbe . . . she just sets me off when she throws the 'Unwanteds' term around—as if she has *any* idea what it was like for us. . . ." He trailed off. Years ago in the adjacent land of Quill, where Alex and Aaron and many of the other Artiméans had grown up, being creative had been a crime. If children were caught singing, inventing something, telling a story, or even drawing in the dirt with a stick like Alex had done, they'd be declared Unwanted and sent to the desolate outskirts of Quill to be killed. Little did the Unwanteds know that Mr. Marcus Today, the man who was supposed to be putting them to death, had created a secret magical world to hide the Unwanteds in. Instead of killing them, Mr. Today taught the Unwanteds to use their creativity to do magic. But just because they'd been rescued at the last minute didn't make the experience any less frightening or horrible. It wasn't something to make light of.

"Thisbe is still learrrning how farrr she can push things with you," Simber said, abruptly breaking into Alex's thoughts. "Trrry not to be too harrrd on yourrrself. The past ten yearrrs haven't been easy."

Alex was quiet, reflecting on the more recent time of peace in Artimé. He cradled his left arm, staring at its ugly uselessness until his eyesight blurred. Then he blinked and gazed blindly out the window at the lawn and the sea beyond. "Tomorrow is the annual Day of Remembrance," he said. "Ten years since the last battle, when Queen Eagala did this to me." Alex narrowed his eyes. He didn't want to think about her or how she'd ambushed him—it always made him bitter. She'd ruined his life . . . and in turn, he had ended hers. He fought off the memories of the evil queen and tried to fill his mind with more pleasant ones. Like those of Pan, the dragon ruler of the sea, and her young, who'd come to help Artimé when all had seemed lost.

"Ten years," Alex repeated, almost forcefully, "since we made magical wings for the young dragons. They'll be having their growth spurt about now, I imagine." Idly Alex wondered if the young dragons would be back for their new larger wings soon, since he hadn't been able to create ones that would grow with them. He'd told them to return to Artimé when the time came to replace the small wings. "Do you remember them?"

Simber nodded, and Alex went on, his voice subdued. "I can't believe how quickly time has passed. Sometimes those battles feel like they happened yesterday. And sometimes . . ."

He shook his head listlessly. "Most of the time," he corrected himself, "I barely remember what it was like to be that Alex, leading Artimé against our enemies. To have that kind of energy. I was so young. So stupid, half the time. But . . . brave, too. Setting out to save everyone and everything." He got up and walked around the desk, absently perching on the corner of it like Mr. Today had often done.

"You'rrre still prrretty young."

Alex gave Simber the side eye, noting that at least he didn't say Alex was still stupid. But he didn't say he was brave, either. No matter. Those two pretty much canceled each other out anyway.

"I used to be so . . ." He swallowed hard and couldn't find the word. *Creative. Skilled. Talented.*

Generous.

Kind.

He let his left arm flop at his side. "And now . . . I'm nothing."

Simber frowned and remained silent for a time. "Do *you* still trrry to do magic orrr drrraw with *yourrr* good hand?"

"No." Alex laughed bitterly. "Not drawing, anyway. Magic only when I have to. Who could have predicted that I'd hit my peak for both at age seventeen?" His chest constricted. He slid off the desk and walked to the window. "And it's just so painful now, you know? To see myself powerless while the girls are so . . . so bursting full of potential. Way more potential than I ever had. But their magic is so dark and so different from everyone else's—we don't have a clue what they're capable of. And for me to try to raise them when I was just a kid myself . . . I didn't know how hard that would be.

"And now they won't listen to me. They don't remember what it was like back then—they think magic is all a big game. When I was twelve, there was no such thing as a game." He thought back to when he and Aaron were his sisters' age. Aaron had been looking forward to university, but Alex was awaiting death. Knowing his parents would just allow that to happen. He'd felt so abandoned.

"Thisbe and Fifer don't understand," Alex murmured, his voice anguished as he floundered in the memory. "Life, death . . . They've never been forced to survive—not really. Not with someone always there to rescue them from their reckless escapades. They don't respect death. Not like the rest of us." He fell silent.

"I would imagine you'rrre grrrateful they don't have to grrrow up in a society that sends its crrreative childrrren to theirrr deaths." Simber brought his paw to his mouth and bit at a claw. He glanced sideways at Alex.

"Of course I am. I wouldn't wish that experience on anybody. But . . ." He closed his eyes briefly. "I don't know. I'm just . . . I'm afraid for them. For all of us. I mean, what if . . . ?" He trailed off, imagining what it would be like if the kinds of attacks they'd experienced ten years ago happened today. Would the new generation of children in Artimé be able to fight the way they needed to? How could they, when they hadn't experienced the desperate, urgent desire for survival? But even more importantly, would Alex be able to lead them? He knew the answer to that already, and it scared him to death. He wasn't fit to charge into battle. Not anymore. Not in his condition. He'd lost all confidence in that years ago.

"You don't sound like the Alex I used to know," said Simber.

A lump rose to Alex's throat. He swallowed hard, and this time, when the tears came, he let them. "That Alex died along with this withered arm."

Simber rested his paw on the floor and looked at the young

man he'd been loyal to since the death of Marcus Today, the mage who'd created him. He'd watched Alex struggle time and time again. And now it seemed like he was giving up. "That Alex is still inside of you," Simber said quietly. "You can brrring him back if you choose to."

Alex shook his head, too disheartened to speak. After a minute he blew out a breath and said, "Tomorrow, for the Day of Remembrance, I'm going to stay in my living quarters so I can meditate on everyone who sacrificed so much for Artimé. Maybe that's what I need to do to find my way out of this funk." He looked at Simber. "Can you get word to Aaron about Panther, and let the girls know not to disturb me? It'll be good for us to have a little break from each other anyway, after today. Tell them I said not to kill anything." He frowned. "No, don't tell them that. That's horrible."

"I wasn't going to," said Simber. "I'll take carrre of them and Pantherrr. You focus on taking carrre of yourrrself." He got up and went to Alex's side. "Maybe you'll rrrediscoverrr some semblance of yourrr old self in yourrr memorrries." He paused, looking troubled. "I rrreally hope so."

"Maybe." Alex ran a hand over Simber's sleek side and gave

him a little scratch behind one ear. He knew it wouldn't happen. He'd buried the old Alex. There was only one person who could bring him out, and it didn't happen often. "I wish Sky were here."

"I know." Simber gave Alex a sympathetic look, then exited the office. Alex went and sat at his desk, and opened one of the books he'd been studying. He tried to read it but couldn't concentrate. Eventually he gave up and turned in for the night. Today had been brutal. But tomorrow, with all its memories, would be even worse.

The Day of Remembrance

The next morning, on the annual Day of Remembrance, Thisbe and Fifer sat down on the lawn outside the mansion with their best friend, Seth Holiday. Seth was thirteen, and he wore his new magical-component vest, which was an important piece of gear given to all thirteen-year-olds when they began Magical Warrior Training.

Fifer admired it, trying to ignore the jealous twinge she felt. She wondered what components were in his pockets, but the flaps were down so she couldn't see them. No matter—he'd show the girls later in secret. Fifer traced the perfect stitching on his shoulder with her finger. "Would you maybe let me try it on sometime?"

Seth hesitated. Part of him wanted to let her, but part of him didn't. "Well," he said, "I would, but I don't think that's allowed."

Fifer persisted. "You're not allowed to show us your spell components, either, but you've done that before."

Seth's pale cheeks flushed. "I—I . . . That's not quite the same."

Fifer sighed. "Oh, all right. It's fine," she said. "I get it." She dropped the subject and began to tell Seth what had happened the day before in the jungle, when something caught her eye. She paused mid-sentence and focused on it. "Look," she said, pointing to the west, where a creature was flying low and cumbrous over the sea toward them. "What is that?"

Thisbe and Seth looked where she was pointing, and as the creature got closer, it became frighteningly clear what it was. "It's a dragon," Thisbe said in a hushed voice.

"Is it one of the young dragons?" asked Seth.

"I don't know."

The dragon landed in the water with a violent splash. Flames and smoke pulsed from his nostrils. His chest heaved, and his ice-blue iridescent scales shimmered in the sunlight.

Then his long, ropelike tail lashed and twirled, propelling the beast toward the shore.

"He's coming here!" said Fifer, alarmed. The twins exchanged a glance and jumped to their feet. Not wanting to get into any trouble with large scary creatures today, they started running to the mansion. "Simber!" Fifer yelled. Thisbe joined in. "Simber!"

Seth stared slack-jawed at the creature, then scrambled after the girls, a beat behind them as usual.

Simber came thundering toward the girls from the great dining hall, making the marble floor shake. "What's the prrroblem?" he roared. But before they could answer, Simber saw for himself through the window. The dragon was propelling himself toward the mansion. In the sea, far beyond him and coming from the other direction, a black speck grew larger by the second. The growl died in Simber's throat. "Oh. I see." He looked at the girls. "Fetch yourrr brrrother. We have guests."

"But—but you said not to bother him today," said Thisbe, a little breathless.

Fifer nodded but seemed unsure.

Seth interrupted. "If that's one of the young dragons,

wouldn't Alex want to know? It's been ten years. Maybe—"

"It's a *drrragon!*" the large stone cat growled impatiently. "I don't carrre what I told you. Go get him!" That sent the three of them charging up the grand staircase two steps at a time without another word.

When they reached the top, they headed left across the open balcony, running past the various residence hallways all the way to the end, to a secret hallway that housed Alex's living quarters and office, and a variety of other rooms. Only a small percentage of Artiméans had the distinct magical ability to see and access the secret hallway, including Fifer and Thisbe. The girls turned sharply and disappeared through what seemed to be a solid wall, while Seth, lagging behind, stopped short and waited anxiously for their return. His breathing was ragged after the strenuous climb—he preferred to avoid stairs at all costs and regularly used the magical tube system to get places. But when the twins went somewhere, he usually followed. He always had, for as long as he could remember.

His blue eyes strained anxiously after Fifer and Thisbe, but he was unable to see anything other than a large mirror on the wall, which left him stuck standing there alone with his reflection, feeling awkward. He desperately wished that he could join the twins and be part of the elite group, but even though he'd started Magical Warrior Training, his magic wasn't strong enough *yet*—and it might never be. He always felt like he was missing out on something great.

After a moment he glanced over his shoulder at Simber, who had apparently grown impatient waiting for Alex and was going outside to greet the visitors. Seth frowned, then dug through the pockets of his component vest, thinking maybe he ought to be armed, just in case this dragon wasn't actually the *right* sort. His fingers trembled when he thought about it, but he located a string of scatterclips and held them tightly in one hand, only a little afraid to use them. His hand started to sweat, so he wiped it off on his pants. "Hurry up," he muttered. He didn't want to be the only one prepared to fight.

Soon Thisbe and Fifer burst through to the balcony again, nearly plowing over their friend. Trailing them came Alex, his robe flapping loosely behind him. His right hand reached out to the handrail, while his left remained hidden inside his sleeve.

Seth regained his balance and ran after them. By now the people of Artimé had heard the kerfuffle. They began gathering at the windows and in the frame of the enormous open door to see what was going on. Fifer, Thisbe, Alex, and Seth reached the bottom of the stairs and headed for the exit but got caught up in the crowd.

Lani Haluki, a young woman with long, straight black hair and olive skin, appeared in the doorway of a nearby classroom on the main floor. She paused a moment, watching curiously. Then she rolled to the nearest sea-facing window by using a belted contraption that magically propelled her forward, since her legs were paralyzed. She took in the scene, her orange eyes shining, then turned quickly to flag down Alex. "They're back!" she called out as he drew near. "One of them is, anyway. The ice blue is named Hux, as I recall. And look—Pan is coming too. Do you see her? She must have sensed Hux's presence returning to our waters and set out to greet him." Her voice contained an undisguisable thrill. "Maybe we'll get to witness their reunion. Come and watch!"

But Alex didn't seem to share her excitement. Instead of joining her, he weaved forward through the onlookers, following after Thisbe and Fifer as they forged ahead and pushed their way to the doorway. Once outside, the girls and Seth went down the path near the sea, but Alex halted and lifted his hand to shield his eyes from the sun. His expression flickered as he observed the dragon approaching. "Girls!" he barked. "Get back inside. That's a *dragon*!" Incredulous, he watched them running foolishly toward the water. Had they forgotten yesterday already?

The twins and Seth stopped running and turned together, guilty looks on their faces.

"What's his problem?" asked Seth out of the corner of his mouth.

"Tell *you* later," muttered Thisbe. Reluctantly they inched back to Alex and the mansion door.

"Dragons," Alex repeated, giving them a look. "Fire breathing. Carnivorous. Please tell me *you* grasp the severity of this situation?"

"But it's one of *our* dragons, isn't it?" asked Fifer meekly. "It seems safe."

"Inside," repeated Alex firmly, and the girls moved to the threshold directly behind him. Seth trailed after them, even though he didn't have to.

Lani Haluki watched the interaction between Alex and the

girls from the window and frowned. She rolled to the door and slipped in and out among the Artiméans who'd gathered. She went past the girls and Seth, past Alex, and headed to the lawn near Simber.

Thisbe and Fifer hung on to the doorframe and watched Lani. "Lani and Simber will protect us," Fifer said. She bit her lip nervously—would Alex start yelling again?

"Please, Alex," added Thisbe. "Can't we go back out?"

Alex turned sharply and silenced them with a look. Then he turned back to the water. The approach of the dragons on this Day of Remembrance made the painful events of the past come alive again for him, and they were all too jagged and real. He trained a discerning eye on the ice-blue dragon's wings, which he'd helped construct and bring to life before the final battle. Despite being marked with scars, they were still beautiful, though clearly too small now to carry the beast for much longer. It was just as Alex had predicted. He was certain that Hux must've remembered his promise to make larger wings—why else would he return?

A lump rose to his throat, and he glanced down at his left arm. It had been his spell-casting arm, but now he was unable to grip a single magical component with those fingers or perform any component-less spell with that hand. Chances were Alex wouldn't be able to keep his promise to the growing creature—not now. Not without help. After a moment he turned slowly and glanced through the open door into the mansion, watching as more people of Artimé descended from their rooms, and he wished for the familiar sight of the woman he loved. *Sky would know what to do*, he thought. But Sky wasn't here.

"Please, Alex," said Thisbe again, and that brought him back. She grabbed her brother's wrist and hung on him. "Come on. Nothing fun like this has ever happened before."

Alex took in a measured breath and gave her a grim smile, refusing to argue with her out here in front of everybody. Something in her expression made him catch his breath. Her serious look resembled their mother's in that moment, with her rare black piercing eyes and exotic features. His sisters would never remember that look—their parents had been killed by a falling wall in Quill when Thisbe and Fifer were barely a year old. Their mother had died protecting the girls.

"Sorry to break it to you," he said lightly, pulling out of Thisbe's grasp, "but danger isn't fun. However, if you want to do something useful, why don't you and Fifer zip over to the Island of Shipwrecks and find Aaron. See if he'll come. Hux won't be able to fly much longer without new wings. And I'm . . . I can't do the job properly." He lifted his chin almost angrily when he said it, then strode toward Simber and Lani and the visitors.

Thisbe sighed. Neither she nor Fifer made a move to get Aaron. They looked on in awe as the beautiful black coiled water dragon, Pan, came ashore. The renowned ruler of the sea was dedicated to tirelessly guarding the waters that surrounded the seven islands of their world. She also kept a protective eye on its sea creatures, including Spike Furious, who was Alex's own magically intuitive whale, and Karkinos, the giant crab island who lived just offshore, among others.

The two dragons touched snouts, and the witnesses around them held their breath as the larger black dragon nuzzled the adolescent ice blue. They spoke in a strange language of their own. But the conversation didn't sound soothing or lovely in any way. It sounded harsh and panicked.

As Alex and Lani approached them, Hux turned. The young dragon was trembling. Thisbe, Fifer, and Seth hopped off the step and crept forward so they could hear.

"It's nice to see you as always, dear Pan," said Alex. He turned to the ice blue. "And you, Hux. A heartfelt welcome back." He hesitated, then held his fist out for the dragon to sniff, as he'd done years ago. "You remember me, don't you? Are you here for new wings?"

The ice blue bowed his head in greeting, and when he spoke, his words were soft. "Greetings, Alex," he said. "These wings have served me well until recently. You are correct—they are too small now for me to fly very far. But . . . I'm afraid new wings are not the only things I need." He looked at his mother, whose solemn face had taken on an expression of deep concern.

"Oh?" asked Alex, his voice immediately guarded. "What else can I do for you?"

"I . . ." Hux faltered and dropped his gaze. "I hate to ask it, coming here after all these years."

Pan nudged him. "You must tell Alex what you've just told me," she said, her voice regal. "He will answer in truth."

Alex studied the dragons, growing warier by the second.

Hux raised his head, giving Alex a sorrowful look. "I've been sent here to . . . ah, that is . . ." He trailed off, then snorted, unintentionally sending sparks shooting from his nostrils and singeing the leaves of a nearby willow tree that hung over the water. "I need you to come with me to the land of the dragons."

Lani looked at Alex.

The head mage blinked. "You . . . I'm sorry. What?"

"Please. Come with me. I wouldn't ask if it wasn't for a reason of grave importance."

Even though he'd been wondering for years where the land of the dragons was, Alex was already shaking his head. "I don't think that's going to be possible. I'm sorry."

"But you must come," implored Hux.

"Why?" asked Alex, growing irritated. "Explain yourself."

Hux closed his eyes and gave a ragged sigh, as if he'd been through a battle. Everyone around them became quiet, waiting to hear his response. Finally the dragon opened his eyes and looked at Alex, completely dejected. "Because if you don't come, my sister Arabis the orange will be killed."

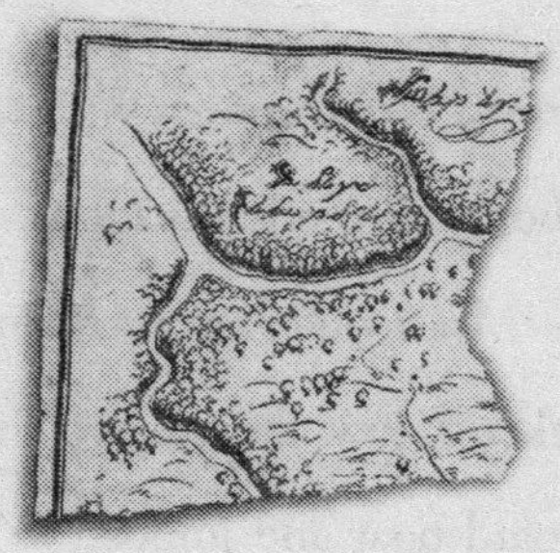

The Dragons' Plight

As Alex began firing questions at the dragon, Thisbe glanced at Fifer and Seth, her eyes wide. Her bangs blew up off her forehead in the breeze. "Arabis the orange," she whispered. "She's the one who gave us rides when we were little, right?"

Seth nodded. Although he'd only been three at the time, he remembered a little more about the final battle and the dragons than the girls did, as they'd barely been two when it had happened. But they'd all heard the stories dozens of times.

The three edged closer, weaving among the thickening

crowd of Artiméans who continued to gather as word spread about the visiting dragons.

Meanwhile, not far off in the lagoon, the twins' former caretaker, Crow, drew up to the sandy shore standing on a sleek board boat and jumped to land. He tossed his paddle in the sand, then pulled the smooth, shiny board out of the water and left it next to the paddle. Then he started jogging up the shoreline toward the gathering. When he drew close, he spied the girls and made his way over to them.

"What's going on?" he whispered. "That one's Hux, isn't it? Where are the rest of them?" Crow's long, dark brown hair was pulled back in a knot at the nape of his neck, and his brown skin glistened with spray and sweat. Once a scrawny boy from Warbler who had escaped Queen Eagala's reign, he was now twenty-three and had managed to put some muscles on his tall, slim frame. But his personality remained unchanged. He was a gentle homebody who didn't apologize for avoiding the art of magic. He just didn't care for it, unlike nearly everyone else in Artimé.

"Yes, it's Hux," said Fifer. "He told Alex and Lani that Arabis the orange will die if Alex doesn't go with him! Shh."

They listened.

"I'm not sure I understand," Alex was saying. "Who could possibly be powerful enough to kill a dragon? Perhaps you should start from the beginning. What's happened to all of you?"

"I'm sorry. I shall explain." The dragon's voice wasn't as deep as the children expected from a dragon, but it was definitely loud enough for them to hear. "Several years ago," Hux began, "shortly after we left this world of the seven islands and made our way to the land of the dragons, we were captured and taken as slaves—all five of us."

Lani gasped. "What? How?"

"Slaves?" exclaimed Alex. "I thought the wings were supposed to keep you safe as you journeyed there."

Hux nodded his oversized head as Pan looked on, anguished. "They were. But they didn't. Well, they got us there safely, but . . ." He glanced at Pan, who gave him a warning look. Pan had always been very secretive, and it appeared that she was going to continue to be that way.

"And only you've escaped?" asked Alex.

"No," said Hux impatiently. "I haven't escaped at all. As I said, I . . . I've been sent to fetch you."

Alex shook his head, puzzled. "What? Why? Sent by whom?" He glanced at Lani, who appeared as puzzled as he.

"Our wings are failing now that we are growing too heavy for them, you see," said Hux, looking rattled. "Some of us are already completely grounded. Well, all of us, except me. If we can't fly, we are useless to our master, and by that logic, we ought to be killed. Since I'm the smallest and still able to fly, I convinced the Revinir to send me to fetch you so you can make new wings for me and the others."

"The Revinir?" asked Alex. "Who is that?"

"The one who took us captive. The most powerful being in the land of the dragons. Even the king serves under the Revinir's rule." Hux swung his head around to look behind him, as if he were afraid the being would somehow magically appear. With his neck outstretched, Fifer and Thisbe and the others nearby could see striped scars on the bare patches of his skin where the scales had worn away.

Puzzled, Lani stepped in. "Are you saying that the land of the dragons is ruled by someone other than . . . dragons?"

"It is now, I'm afraid," said Hux. "If I don't return with Alex, Arabis will be killed first. Then the others, too, I'm sure." He looked imploringly from Alex to his mother and back to Alex again. "And then me, when my wings are useless."

The crowd whispered.

"Please help us, Alex. We need you to create new wings for us—all of us."

"Why—so you can continue being slaves?" Alex asked. "Don't you think that's a little bit crazy?"

The dragon flinched. "It's better than the alternative."

"And what happens if I *do* accompany you and make new wings for everyone? Do you believe this Revinir overlord will allow you to freely take me back home? And then expect you to return to be enslaved again?"

Hux bowed his head, looking miserable. "I'm—I'm afraid I can't predict that. I imagine the Revinir will threaten the lives of my siblings until I return from that trip as well. But I will do everything in my power to get you here safely."

Lani reached out and put her hand on the dragon's neck. "I believe you will," she said.

Alex frowned. "Something's very troubling about all of this." For the first time in the conversation he sought out Simber. He held the giant cat's gaze for a long moment, numerous untold conversations happening in that one look. The cat's face reflected Alex's skepticism, making the mage even more reluctant to help.

Thisbe and Fifer exchanged a fearful glance. The beloved dragon from their past was in danger of being killed, and it didn't seem like their brother was going to do anything for her. For the first time in their memory, here was an adventure for Artimé. A chance to help, being handed to them. A chance for the girls to witness their brother's magical power instead of being hidden from it. To see his generosity in action instead of just hearing stories about it. And Alex wasn't having it.

To Fifer and Thisbe, this was sadly predictable—the Alex they knew was overly cautious and seemed to hate adventure. But the stories about the old days had painted a different picture of him. Compared to those brave tales, his hesitation to help seemed strange. But all of those stories had happened before Alex's devastating fight with Queen Eagala of Warbler. And before Thisbe and Fifer had become, well, a menace to society. Alex wasn't that person anymore, partly because of them. As if they were thinking the exact same thing, the two exchanged guilty looks.

“Al,” prompted Lani.

Alex glanced at her, a flash of agony in his eyes before he looked away. “Lani, I don’t know about this. It’s not that simple. And it feels like a trap. If I get involved . . . we’re asking for trouble. There’s no guarantee I’ll make it home again.” He shook his head again. “I can’t do that to my sisters or to Artimé. Not this time. Besides . . .” He glanced at his arm, then said quietly, “You know.”

Lani shook her head, as if refusing to decipher his intended meaning. “Let’s at least talk about it,” she said.

“Well, of course we’ll talk. I can do that much.” Alex sighed and looked sadly at Hux and Pan. “But I’m going to be brutally honest. I’m not sure I can help you.”

Hux didn’t hide the alarmed look on his face, but Pan bowed her regal head. “We understand,” she said. “Perhaps it was too much to ask.”

“You must never be afraid to ask,” said Lani.

“I’ll think about your request,” Alex promised, “and we’ll fashion new wings for Hux tonight. I’ll give you my answer in the morning. You are both welcome to remain here as long as you like.”

Hux seemed unable to speak in that moment, so Pan spoke for him. "Thank you," she said in a soft voice. "We'll take to the lagoon until you've had a chance to consider my children's predicament."

Alex's face flickered. Pan most certainly felt as passionate about her children's safety as he did for Fifer's and Thisbe's. He hoped that meant she would understand his position. He nodded to the dragons, ending the discussion. Then he turned around and marched through the crowd as people stepped aside to get out of his way. Catching sight of his sisters, Alex gave them a disapproving glance. "Did you fetch Aaron like I told you?"

Thisbe's eyes widened. She grabbed Fifer's hand. "We're going right now," she said. Leaving Seth stuck in the crowd, the girls ran ahead of Alex into the mansion and darted up the stairs to the same magical hallway they'd gone down before.

The hall was wide and tall, with huge wooden beams and a dark wood floor. They ran past two mysterious doors, the contents of which perhaps only Alex knew, then past the doors to Alex's living quarters on the left and the Museum of Large opposite it. When they neared Alex's office on the left, where they had gotten yelled at the previous day, they turned right instead, into the little kitchenette across from it. From there they went straight for the large glass tube in the corner. They squeezed inside it together, and Fifer pressed the blue button in a row of colors.

Instantly the girls' world went dark for a second or two. And when it became light again, they were looking upon a completely different landscape. Indeed, they were on a completely different island, far from home—it would take several days' journey by ship to get here. How they loved the convenience of magic.

While Quill, with Artimé on its southern border, made up the middle island of the seven in this world, this one was called the Island of Shipwrecks, and it was the easternmost island of the narrow triangular chain. This island had once been ruled by a constant hurricane. Back then it had been stark and ugly, but now the sun shone six days out of seven on a maze of rock structures, with blooming flower beds and gardens all around. And there were no signs of shipwrecks anywhere, but the girls knew there had been several once upon a time. There were still some under the water that they had explored many times.

Fifer and Thisbe stepped out of the tube and ran down the path toward the rock structures. "Grandfathers," Fifer called out melodiously, sweeping one particularly wavy lock of hair out of her face. It bounced back annoyingly. "Are you home?"

Thisbe, who was quite a bit less musical than Fifer, hollered for her brother. "Aaron! Where are you?" They continued on and soon entered a large covered stone shelter, which held a maze of rooms. Automatically they turned down the hallway that led to the greenhouse, where they knew they were bound to find someone. There, hunched over a box of strangely colored gourds, was Alex's identical twin.

Aaron looked up at the noise, and his smile spread and lit up his tired eyes. He set down the two gourds he was holding and opened his arms wide. The girls went to him to give him a hug. Before he could ask what had brought them there, they began talking over one another.

"Were you able to fix Panther?" Thisbe asked anxiously. "Please say yes."

"You've got to come quickly!" said Fifer. "The young dragons are back!" Impatiently she wet her fingers and tucked the obstinate lock of hair behind one ear, securing it this time.

"Whoa," said Aaron, laughing a little. He addressed Thisbe first. "Yes, I just came back from fixing Panther."

"So she's okay?" asked Thisbe anxiously.

"She's perfectly alive and almost as good as new. You made a clean break, so she went back together pretty seamlessly. Ha-ha. Get it? Joke."

Thisbe grinned. She still felt terrible about hitting the beast, but Aaron almost always made her feel better about everything. "Thank you so much," she said, relieved.

"Now what's this about the young dragons?" asked Aaron, turning to Fifer.

"Only one, actually. Hux, the ice blue," said Fifer. "He says the Revinir is going to kill Arabis the orange."

"Alex needs you to help with Hux's wings," said Thisbe. "Can you come?"

"You've got to help us save the dragons, Aaron!"

Puzzled as he was, Aaron waited for them to finish. When they quieted, he spoke reassuringly. "More excitement in Artimé? That's a rare treat. Let's go see what it's all about."

He dusted his soiled hands on his pants and started making his way through the stone structure. The girls moved quickly to keep up with his long strides. As they neared the exit, Aaron stopped at the mouth of another hallway. He shouted down it, "I'm running over to Artimé again! Back soon."

The only reply was the startled cry of a newborn, followed by a woman's sigh.

Living Life in Peace

"Whoops." Aaron cringed and stopped outside the stone entrance. "Still getting used to this. You go on ahead," he said to his sisters. "Tell Alex I'm right behind you. And . . . I'll pick up some supplies on the way."

"Hurry!" said Thisbe.

"Bring the baby with you," Fifer suggested.

"I will likely do just that," said Aaron. "See you in a bit."

Thisbe and Fifer headed outside and ran to the tube, then whizzed back to the mansion. By the time they made it downstairs, they found the various leaders of Artimé rushing about.

Among them was the beloved, albeit strange-looking octogator named Ms. Octavia, the art instructor, who had an alligator head and an octopus body. Her fake glasses sat askew on her long snout. When she walked, her eight tentacles moved in a rhythmic, almost hypnotic pattern that made her appear as though she were skimming the ground.

A few flower petals floated through the hallway outside the octogator's classroom, stirred up by the scurrying. The girls followed Ms. Octavia toward the room and found Seth hanging on the doorframe, looking in.

"What's happening?" asked Thisbe.

"They're starting on the new wings," said Seth. "Where's Aaron?"

"Coming," said Thisbe.

Fifer added, "He woke up Daniel so he went back to get him."

"Oh." Seth sniffed. He had two younger siblings and wasn't impressed with babies.

Not far inside the room, Crow overheard their conversation and looked up from an enormous, colorful pile of flower petals, from which he was carefully plucking the light blue ones. "Oh good," he said. "I'll watch the baby while Aaron does whatever magical junk he's got to do over there." Crow pointed his elbow toward the large table at the center of the room, where Ms. Octavia, Lani, and Alex stood.

At the word "magical," Fifer and Thisbe instantly turned to see if they could catch someone doing something. The two had had an uncanny ability from a young age to learn new spells easily just by witnessing them, which was why Alex had tried so hard to keep people from doing magic near them. Still, the girls had learned to sneak around to catch mages in action, unaware.

As children they hadn't known when it was proper to use those magic spells. Now, of course, they knew better. And they had pretty good control of the learned ones. It was the uncontrollable magic that came from deep inside them that was the problem—and that problem was a big one, obviously. So Alex stubbornly continued shielding them. It was most annoying.

The twins watched as Ms. Octavia spread out a large sheet of paper in front of her. With two of her tentacles, she swiftly drew a plan for the wings while Alex stood by, pointing out a few changes that he wanted the octogator to make.

Thisbe sidled closer to the table to get a better view of what the art instructor was doing, while Fifer and Seth helped Crow dig for more light blue petals.

A few minutes later Aaron strode in, his son Daniel wrapped in a blanket in one arm, apparently asleep again. Aaron had several long, thick vines draped over his opposite shoulder. They dragged behind him on the floor.

"What are those vines for?" Thisbe whispered to Fifer.

Fifer and Seth shrugged. They all watched as the brothers greeted each other and Alex filled Aaron in on everything that had happened. The two young men had once been nearly impossible to tell apart, but it was easy enough for people to do so now. Alex was rarely seen without the colorful robe of the head mage. He wore his dark brown wavy hair longer than Aaron, who kept his cropped short. Up close, Aaron had a distinct scar between his eyebrows and another on his forehead from a shipwreck some months before the big battle. And Alex, of course, had lost the use of his left arm.

When Crow, Seth, and Fifer finished sorting through the pile of petals, they gathered up the light blue ones and carried them over to Alex and the others, who were talking earnestly about the structure of the wings. Thisbe tagged along so she could get an even closer look at what they were doing. So far, no one had done any magic.

Still holding the baby, Aaron struggled to lay out one of the vines on the table. Crow set his load of petals down on a free work surface nearby and offered to take Daniel so Aaron could use both hands. Aaron gratefully passed the baby to him and bent low over the table, artfully sculpting the vines according to the outline of the dragon wings.

Thisbe, Fifer, and Seth hung around for a few more minutes, watching. Silently they wondered if Alex would start talking about the potential journey with Hux to make wings for the other dragons, but the adults were intently focused on the task before them and didn't discuss it.

Soon Fifer and Seth grew bored and went outside to the lawn. Thisbe lingered a few more moments, hoping to catch some magic in action, but then Alex noticed her watching them. He raised an eyebrow and shooed her out of the room. Reluctantly Thisbe went outside too.

Most of the people of Artimé had dispersed by now to do whatever they normally did on the Day of Remembrance. Some spent a few moments in the hospital ward to thank Henry Haluki and Seth's mother and the other healers, or remember a friend or loved one who'd spent their last moments there. Others paid their respects at the new memorial fountain at the far end of the lawn, where the giant rock from the jungle had once shielded all the orange-eyed children and the twins and Seth from the pirates and Queen Eagala's warriors. Thisbe had a slight memory of that because of Fifer screaming and destroying a huge flock of Queen Eagala's magical eye-pecking ravens, which went up in a cloud of smoke. Ever since then, Fifer had been able to call flocks of birds to come to her . . . but unfortunately she hadn't figured out yet what to do with the birds once they came. Thisbe shuddered thinking about them. Only two things really freaked out Thisbe: heights, and Fifer's creepy, useless birds.

As they strolled along the shore of Artimé, Thisbe and Fifer told Seth about what had happened in the jungle. Seth didn't seem sorry to have been at Magical Warrior Training during that adventure.

They stopped at their favorite spot to sit and looked out over the sparkling sea. The two dragons had retreated to the lagoon at the edge of the jungle to wait for Alex's decision and Hux's wings, so the children were quite alone. Thisbe sprawled out on the lawn and plucked a long piece of mint grass to chew on. Fifer sat down a bit more carefully on her left, and Seth followed Fifer's lead, not wanting to get grass stains on his vest.

"Do you remember the dragons from before?" asked Thisbe. "From when we were young?"

"I remember the stories about them," said Fifer. "But I'm not sure if I actually remember *them*. Or being with them."

"I do," said Seth. "We stood right down there by the water and watched them swim and fly around. What about you, Thiz?"

Thisbe shook her head. "Sometimes I imagine I do—I can see the stories in my head almost as if they were real. But all I can actually remember about those days were those awful black ravens attacking us. I was *severely* traumatized. I hate birds."

Fifer whooped uncharacteristically at the mention of the ravens—she'd ended their existence with a scream, or so the story went. After her whoop, the children heard the distinct tinkling of glass. Fifer cringed. "Oops. I was trying to call the birds."

"Please don't," said Thisbe, rolling her eyes.

One of the mansion windows opened and a perspiring chef from the kitchen leaned his head out. "Fifer, please!"

"Sorry!" said Fifer. "What did I break?"

"Two hundred water glasses," said the chef, glaring.

"Is everyone okay?" Fifer asked meekly.

"This time, *yes*."

Fifer knew the chefs would never stay mad at her or Thisbe. The two had been helping out in the kitchen since they first came to Artimé as nameless one-year-olds. They would spend hours with Crow sending up room service meals and snacks through the tubes to the people of Artimé. And the girls never got mad or upset working in the kitchen, so the chefs had little to fear . . . other than occasional exploding glass when they least expected it.

"I'll come in and clean it up," Fifer offered.

The chef waved her off with a dish towel. "Just try to stop doing it," he blustered, and closed the window, continuing to grumble.

Seth leaned back on an elbow, eager to continue the conversation. "Is that all you remember about the big battle, Thiz? You don't remember killing the pirate captain?"

Thisbe frowned. She hated having that image in her head. Hated how she couldn't stop thinking about it when people brought it up. And it was an especially tender topic after what had happened yesterday with Panther. "No," she said tersely. "I was two."

"Well, you did it, you know."

"Yeah, Seth, I know."

Seth's face grew puzzled. The twins lapsed into an uncomfortable silence, looking at the sky. Around them colorful platyprots repeated snatches of conversations they'd overheard around the grounds. "I know, I know, I know," said one nearby. It exploded into giggles. The three friends barely noticed, having grown up surrounded by them.

"So . . . what's the matter?" Seth asked Thisbe, feeling uneasy. He could argue with Fifer and not feel too bad about it, but he didn't like it when Thisbe was mad at him. And not just because she might accidentally blow him to bits with her crazy killer magic.

She looked at him crossly. "Nothing."

Fifer rolled to her side and wrapped a protective arm around her sister's waist. "Nothing," she echoed. She hardly realized she'd said it, for the two often echoed each other without intending to. But both girls knew what was wrong. Thisbe didn't like talking about the fact that she had killed someone—an actual human—at the age of two. She didn't even like *thinking* about it. It made her feel weird . . . and really very awful. She'd also nearly killed others in her younger years, including Alex, almost effortlessly with magic that was beyond her control. It was terribly unsettling, but it just happened sometimes when she didn't want it to . . . like with Panther.

As she thought about it, Thisbe didn't really blame Alex for being strict, even though it made her feel bad that he didn't trust her. And it wasn't at all fun that he'd had to stifle the twins' creativity and magical abilities for the safety of the people, but she could see why it had been necessary when they were younger. Even though stifling creativity went against everything Artimé stood for, it had seemed a fair enough trade when lives were at stake.

But now they were the same age Lani had been when she came to Artimé and began to learn magic. Fifer had begged their brother incessantly to let them start Magical Warrior Training early, alongside Seth and the other thirteen-year-olds. She kept arguing that Florence, the Magical Warrior trainer, could help them figure out their strange brand of dangerous magic and learn to control it. But Alex kept digging his feet in, saying they had to take responsibility for their actions and learn self-control first. Besides, he often argued, becoming a mage in the traditional sense brought with it a whole slew of problems, one of which was being forced to grow up really fast and make some very difficult decisions. It had happened to Alex, and he didn't wish the same thing on his sisters. In fact, it almost seemed like he'd rather they didn't do any magic at all. Ever.

But that was impossible. So even though the girls weren't supposed to practice the few odd noncomponent spells that they'd picked up by observation, they did it anyway, in secret. And now that Seth had earned his component vest and was learning what all the different components were for and how to use them, Thisbe and Fifer couldn't wait for him to teach them.

At least that would give them something to do. Because Thisbe and Fifer were bored out of their skulls. They'd done everything nonmagical they could possibly do on a small magical island. They were expert swimmers since the age of four and could hold their breath underwater for seven minutes like the other mages. They'd been good gardeners since they were six thanks to chief healer Henry Haluki, and their adopted grandfathers—Ishibashi, Ito, and Sato—three old shipwrecked scientists with whom Aaron, Kaylee, and Daniel lived on the Island of Shipwrecks. The girls were pros, thanks to Aaron, at inventing unnecessary machines that cluttered the hallways of the mansion, and experts at riding Simber despite Thisbe's fear of heights, thanks to the winged-cheetah statue himself taking pity on the bored girls. And they had pretty good knife skills after chopping thousands upon thousands of vegetables alongside Artimé's chefs.

They had also explored every inch of the land of Quill, which took up the larger, northern part of the island that was adjacent to where Artimé's mansion, lawn, and jungle were situated. Quill was much less desolate now than it had been when Alex was growing up. Before the final battle, it had been destroyed by a terrible fire, but Alex had rebuilt it magically, so there were lots of rocks and cliffs and a beautiful lighthouse to visit. And it was no longer ruled by a tyrant, so it was safe to go there. Now, Lani and Henry Haluki's father, Gunnar, was in charge, and he continued to slowly impress upon the people of Quill that there were much smarter and more humane ways of being a great nation than sending creative children to their deaths.

The girls had also visited Warbler Island to the west, where

Queen Eagala had once tormented her people by taking away their ability to speak and marked them as slaves by changing their eye color to orange. There were lots of caves and tunnels there, but Thisbe and Fifer had been in all of them. Warbler was where Sky was now, helping her mother, Copper, who'd stepped in to lead the people after Queen Eagala's death.

They'd been to Karkinos, the crab island, many times—only when Magical Warrior Training was not in session there, of course—visiting with the unusual legendary creatures who lived there, like the sea monster named Issie, who had been searching forlornly for her baby for over seven hundred years. Thisbe and Fifer had helped her search, to no avail.

And the girls had been to the Island of Shipwrecks through the tube countless times to visit Aaron, Kaylee, and the grandfathers. And while there was a lot of weird collected junk to investigate inside the rock structures, and some shipwrecks underwater to look at, it could only keep Fifer and Thisbe satisfied for so long.

They wanted more. They wanted to do magic without having to hide it. They wanted to figure out exactly what strange, incredible things they were capable of and actually practice them, not stifle their abilities. Why wouldn't Alex see that they were ready?

Thisbe chewed her mint grass thoughtfully. Despite her deep longing to do magic freely for once in her life without getting yelled at, she still hated that she had the ability to kill someone. And she would never, ever purposely use that kind of magic again, now that she understood it . . . if she could help it. The incident with Panther had scared her. The creature was too close to human. And even though Panther was okay now, Thisbe couldn't stop feeling terrible about it.

She had to make up for it somehow. "Why can't you do something *good* with your uncontrollable magic for once? Do you always have to be so destructive?" Thisbe cringed, remembering Alex's words. Maybe it wasn't possible. But if it was, they had to prove it to him.

How to do that was another problem. Lying here on the grass, thinking things through, Thisbe was starting to understand Alex's point—she needed to figure out how to control her natural magic so he could trust her. And she needed to do something *good* with it for a change. Something Alex would be proud of, instead of angry about.

Thisbe sighed. She would talk to Fifer about all of this later, when Seth wasn't around. Maybe doing something good really was the answer to earning Alex's trust . . . and making up for the accident with Panther. Maybe it would even lead to better control.

Maybe.

But for now the dilemma remained. The two most magical people in the history of Artimé were completely untrained, stifled by a stubborn brother who seemed nothing like the adventurous leader they'd heard so many stories about, and reliant upon their own devices if they were ever going to see some excitement. They could only handle lying around being good for so long before something had to be done about that.

As Thisbe, Fifer, and Seth wrestled with their thoughts, Thisbe turned her attention to the dragons in the lagoon, who awaited Alex's answer. Sadly, she had a feeling she knew exactly what that answer would be.

Weighing Risks

That night at dinner, Fifer and Thisbe saw Alex sitting with Lani and Samheed Burkesh, who was the theater instructor. The three were deep in conversation, no doubt talking about whether to help Hux.

At a long table nearby, Henry Haluki, Lani's younger brother and the chief healer of Artimé, sat with a young man of a similar age named Thatcher. With them were a group of new Unwanteds who'd been sent to Artimé from Quill. Even after peace had come to the island and magic had covered Quill, some of the people there still insisted on purging their creative offspring once a year, cutting ties with them and sending them to Artimé. The practice had troubled Henry horribly, so he'd set out to make the transition less traumatic for the newcomers. From the time he and Thatcher were barely twenty, they began adopting Unwanteds, and now they had quite a large family.

The twin girls also spotted Seth sitting with his family across the room. They waved to him but headed to Alex's table.

"I thought you'd take dinner up in your living quarters because of the Day of Remembrance," Thisbe said to Alex, interrupting the conversation. She and Fifer greeted Samheed and Lani. Both girls eyed the empty space next to Lani, wanting to sit there. Fifer was closer, so she casually slipped into the seat, giving Thisbe a triumphant look.

Thisbe sat down between Samheed and Alex. "What are you talking about?"

"We're talking about what to do with Hux," said Lani. "Whether to help him or not."

Alex flashed Lani an annoyed look, but she stared Alex down. "The girls are old enough to hear this. They're not babies anymore, Al. They're the same age I was when we fought our first battle."

"True," said Samheed.

"You were nearly thirteen by the time the battle began," Alex pointed out. "They're just barely twelve."

"A few months' difference," Lani scoffed, and waved him off. "And they're a lot more mature than I was at their age. Lighten up. We're just talking about what to do. It's a teaching moment, right, Sam?"

Fifer and Thisbe exchanged a glance but stayed silent. Samheed did too, but he wore a strained smile that conveyed his tolerance of Alex and Lani's frequent spats, and he wisely refused to jump into the middle of it.

Alex gave up and continued the conversation. "Well, I'm decided. I wish we could help them—I really do. But it's too dangerous. I can't go with Hux."

"I disagree," Lani said vehemently.

"Of course you do," said Alex, looking tired.

Lani leaned forward. "Since when do you refuse to help anyone who came here asking for it? That's so unlike the Alex I once knew. What if, way back when, you'd decided it was too dangerous to rescue Samheed and me on Warbler Island? We'd still be stuck there, thorn necklaces and all, with your favorite person, Queen Eagala, in charge. And the pirates would have captured all the sea creatures by now and taken over these islands, including Artimé, I'll bet. You'd have never found Sky's mother, or been able to save Karkinos, or met Ishibashi, or even rescued Aaron so we could overthrow Gondoleery Rattrapp if *you* hadn't taken that first daring step of saving us." She shook her head, exasperated. "I know we haven't met anybody in a long time who needed help, but what's stopping *you* now?"

Alex glared at her. Then he lifted his useless arm and let it fall to the table with a startling thump. "What do *you* think?" he muttered.

"Great." Samheed closed his eyes briefly. "Here we go again."

"Besides," said Alex, ignoring him, "I can't make the wings alone. I can't do it at all. Aaron might be able to . . . ," he began, but shook his head. "No. He can't draw well enough—he'd need either me to guide him or Octavia there to sketch the wings. But that's beside the point. He won't risk it."

"Won't he?" asked Lani. She looked around the dining room. "Where is he, anyway—did he go back home already? I didn't have a chance to hold the little monster." Lani's face grew sad for an instant, then cleared.

"Yes, he went back. And no, he won't go anywhere—not

with Kaylee and the baby needing him right now. Not with the grandfathers counting on him. There are just way too many uncertainties. We don't even know where the land of the dragons is or how to get there."

"Why don't you ask Hux?" asked Samheed.

"I did. But dragon law forbids him from telling me." Alex narrowed his eyes, looking even more skeptical.

Lani sighed. "So you're going to let five young, beautiful dragons be killed because of your bum arm. You still haven't gotten over that? Wow. I'm really disappointed in you, Alex. If I could do the drawing and that kind of magic, I'd go myself."

"It's more complicated than that. You heard Hux—he said the dragons are slaves. And when I went out later to measure him, he told me that this Revinir person uses them to transport people and goods, which is why he wants their wings fixed. But it gives me a bad feeling. If the dragons are slaves, do you really think the Revinir will let one of them go free again to bring me home? I don't buy it."

Lani stared hard at Alex, thinking. "The Revi— What is it again?"

"Revinir."

"The Revinir could hold the same threat over the dragon that brings you back, I suppose, to guarantee it returns."

"That's what Hux said," Alex admitted. "But if they can all fly again, with wings more their size, it seems like they'd have a better chance of making a break for it. They're *dragons* after all. How hard can it be to fight off this ruler person? Can't they just torch the crud out of him?"

"That's a good question," Lani said finally. "Maybe the Revinir isn't a person."

"Well, that just makes it even more uncertain. And I have the twins to think about. They've already lost their parents—there's no way I'm going to risk abandoning them." He frowned, then glanced at the girls. As much as they frustrated him, he loved them fiercely, and now that he had them in his life, he would always choose them above anything else. He never wanted them to feel like he'd felt when he was their age.

"Of course that's a good reason," Lani conceded. "Especially since we don't really know who we're dealing with."

They ate thoughtfully for a moment; then Alex swallowed and set his fork down. "Look," he said, softer now. "I'll test Hux's new wings tonight to make sure they're working properly. Then I'll attach them in the morning so he can go back, or fly free, or whatever he decides to do. And I'll rack my brain all night to come up with a safe way to do this. And if I think of something, I'll be the first one to say let's try it. But there's no one else available who knows how to do the magic. So . . . ," he said gently, "we'll just have to do what we can, and hope for the best for the other dragons."

"But, Alex," Lani began.

Alex shook his head. "No. I'm sorry. That's the end of it. I have more important things to take care of. Like these two." He glanced at his sisters. "I'm not willing to risk anyone's life for it. Not this time. I . . . I've already lost way too much."

A Story to Remember

The finality of Alex's decision led to a tense silence at the dinner table, which lasted until Crow walked up. He joined them like he often did. Automatically sensing the tension, he didn't speak at first other than to nod his greeting. But soon the air became exceedingly uncomfortable, and since Crow didn't care for uncomfortable moods, he cleared his throat. "Did Aaron and Daniel go back home?"

"Yes," said Alex.

"Oh." His gaze swept the faces around him and rested again on Alex's. "Any idea when Sky's coming back?" Not only was

Sky the love of Alex's life, she was also Crow's older sister, and the two were very close.

"Not soon enough," muttered Lani.

Alex glared at her.

Crow caught Thisbe's gaze, and his eyes widened. His lips twitched with mirth, as if asking, "What have I stumbled into this time?" Thisbe returned Crow's look with a dramatic paranoid stare, while Fifer shook her head the slightest bit to warn him.

"Sky . . . and *Scarlet*," Alex said with a slight emphasis on Scarlet's name and a side-eye glance at Crow, "will be gone a few more weeks. Last I heard, they're about halfway through rejuvenating and repopulating the Island of Fire, and Sky's figuring out how to control the island's core temperature and maybe stop it from plunging underwater so often. Honestly, I still don't understand why anyone would want to live there. But that's beside the point, I suppose, as some clearly do."

"Well then," said Crow, his face warming at the mention of Scarlet, who was originally from Warbler but had come to Artimé as a refugee. Crow had had a crush on her ever since he saw her swish her long blond hair while masterfully throwing a spell years ago. But he was too shy to do anything about it other than reach out in friendship. "That's not much fun for us, is it. But I suppose my mother is enjoying spending time with Sky."

"I suppose." Alex set his fork down loudly.

"Okay . . ." Crow made a face at Fifer and quickly changed the subject. "So . . . girls, what story would you like us to tell on this Day of Remembrance?"

Nearly everyone at the table had forgotten the tradition of the day because of the excitement brought by the dragons' dilemma. The twins sat up straighter, and both of them immediately launched into thinking about which story they wanted to hear.

Thisbe and Fifer already knew well enough that Alex had been the head mage of Artimé since he was fourteen, when the former head mage, Mr. Marcus Today, had been killed by Aaron—that was back when Aaron was evil. It was a story filled with battles and sacrifices and love and hatred and good and bad, and most of all magic. A story that would take weeks or months to tell in full, and which Lani had taken great care to write down in the years following—seven volumes worth in all. The people of Artimé often spoke of moments they especially remembered, and those stories had become legends over time.

Thisbe and Fifer loved to hear about how Aaron had once been very bad and had killed Artimé's beloved Mr. Marcus Today, because it was such a horrible story. It seemed so unreal and impossible when they thought of their loving brother and this peaceful land they lived in, that they sometimes forgot it was true. It occurred to Thisbe that if Aaron could have changed so much since those days, maybe Alex could have too. Unfortunately, Aaron would never tell the story, and Alex didn't like to—he said it still hurt to think about and he wanted to forget it.

But once in a while, when the girls could find Sky alone, Sky would tell it to them. She'd explain that Aaron had become the ruler of Quill, and how, when he'd killed Mr. Today, all of Artimé had disappeared because the world couldn't exist without a head mage running it. Every last one of the living statues and creatures, like Simber and Ms. Octavia and Florence, had immediately ceased to be alive. Simber had plunged headlong into the sea. The girls knew how horrible that must have been for the great cat, for Simber abhorred water of any kind. It made him extremely cranky, and nobody wanted to be near Simber when he was cranky.

Sky had also told them how she and Alex used to sit on the roof of the gray shack—the same shack that now rested in the Museum of Large—and try to figure out the magical clue Mr. Today had left Alex that would help him bring Artimé back. "That time was terribly difficult for your brother," she'd told them.

"Is that when you and Alex fell in love?" Thisbe always asked, for the question seemed like it should be part of the story.

"Not quite," Sky always answered, playing along with a sly grin.

It had been hard for Aaron, too, Sky had told them, though she hadn't really known him then. Fifer couldn't picture her kind, gentle brother Aaron killing anybody. He was ashamed of it, he'd said once. His biggest wish was that he could go back to Quill when he and Alex were ten and take the blame for drawing in the dirt, for he had broken the law in Quill too—he just hadn't been caught. That way both brothers would have been declared Unwanted and sent to their deaths, and they'd have magically found themselves in Artimé together. And maybe Aaron wouldn't have done so many things he regretted.

But unfortunately, they hadn't known Artimé existed back then. And even more unfortunately, that's not how it happened.

It was a shocking story. But that wasn't the one Fifer and Thisbe wanted to hear that night at dinner.

"Tell us about the end of the world," said Thisbe, her eyes bright.

"Yes, the giant waterfall!" said Fifer.

"Oh, my aching head," said Crow with a groan, "that was the worst."

"It was a rough ride," Samheed admitted.

"It's all your hero Lani's fault," Alex told the girls, and he darted to one side quickly to avoid the smack spell Lani flicked at him from across the table. Thisbe caught her doing it and made a mental note of how Lani had flicked her fingers.

Alex continued. "She found a map of our seven islands that had an extra piece of land on it to the west, and since we were out that way, convinced us all that we should go in search of it."

Lani leaned in. "That's not exactly how it happened," she

said. "But yes, we all *as a group* decided to go in search of this land, and we found ourselves being pulled toward a tremendous waterfall. We couldn't escape the current no matter how hard Spike and Simber and the squirrelicorns fought it. Soon we plunged right over the edge! We headed down it at top speed, turning and twisting and speeding along, the crew bouncing and slamming into things, thinking we were all about to die—"

"And then we turned sharply again and went upside down for a long time," Crow interjected.

"Yes," said Lani, "and we finally found ourselves thrown backward, going *up* a waterfall on the other side of the world, out beyond where Aaron lives now. Only back then we didn't know where we were. It was a horrible ride. We're lucky we didn't all die." She nodded her head toward the table where Seth sat with his mother, Carina Holiday, his two young half siblings, and a man named Sean Ranger, who'd become a part of Seth's family a few years after Seth's father had been killed in Artimé's first battle. "Sean's broken leg was reinjured quite seriously. Simber had to take him home."

Thisbe scrunched up her nose. "Why didn't you all just jump on Simber's back in the first place and let the ship go over?"

"There wasn't room for everyone," said Alex, perking up a little. "And a loyal group sticks together through the tough times. Even Simber and the squirrelicorns rode the waterfall, dragged over the edge with us as they held the ropes. Simber could have let go and flown home, but he wasn't going to abandon us."

"And Alex could have gone with Simber," Samheed said quietly, "but he stayed with the ship as well."

Thisbe listened, her face solemn. That was pretty brave of Alex. He had done a ton of good things with his magic. She glanced at him. He was staring at his plate, deep in thought.

Fifer nodded emphatically. "That's like you and me," she said, looking at Thisbe. "Loyal. Kaylee says we're besties."

"Besties?" asked Alex, looking up. "What does that mean?"

"Best friends," said Fifer with authority. "Like her and Aaron, and Carina and Sean, and Thatcher and Henry, and Lani and Samheed, and you and Sky. Sometimes in love, sometimes not—that part doesn't matter. Besties is one of the weird words from her world."

"Ah," said Alex. By now they were familiar with Kaylee's unusual words and phrases. Kaylee Jones had come from a different world, a place called North America, and had found herself here after sailing through a terrible storm in the Dragon's Triangle. And so far, no one had found a way back there.

"What happened then?" prompted Fifer, although she knew.

Alex continued. "Right. Well, we floated for a bit, but were soon caught in a hurricane and our ship wrecked—"

"And you met our grandfathers," said Thisbe, who loved the three old men dearly. They were scientists whose ship had also wrecked, though many years before the Unwanteds found themselves there.

"Yes, and then—"

"Aaron got kidnapped by pirates, and you rescued him and fought off evil Gondoleery Rattrapp!" said Thisbe, hopping away from the table and beginning to act out the fight scene.

"Very nice footwork," said Samheed, amused.

Just then, Thisbe sliced the air with her hand, and the movement somehow magically cut a rather large slit in the table and broke Samheed's plate in two. Thisbe froze. "Oops."

"Be careful!" said Alex.

"She didn't hurt anyone," Samheed said quietly.

Alex ignored him. "Maybe you'd better sit back down when we're talking about fighting people. We don't need *another* accident."

Thisbe had heard dozens of similar statements in her life. She bit her lip, and her body sagged. There went trying to do something good with her magic. "Sorry," she muttered. She slid back into her chair. Lani shot her a sympathetic look.

"But then, the big battle," prompted Fifer, eager to move on. "And the dragons came and helped, right? They helped *so* much. Artimé never would have succeeded without them." She closed her lips, looking a little smug.

Now Lani's mouth twitched.

Alex gave Fifer a look. "Yes," he said abruptly. "And that's the end." He tapped his empty plate and utensils and they folded in upon themselves until they were so small they disappeared. "And now I'm going to repay the dragons by making Hux some new wings to replace the old ones I *already made* as a favor—a giant favor—to them. So I'd say we're even."

"Oh, Alex," Lani said, shaking her head.

"Don't start. Not today." Alex softened. "Please."

Lani softened too. She understood many of the emotions Alex was struggling with, thinking of all the losses they'd experienced when they were barely older than Thisbe and Fifer. Today was not a day to bicker. "All right," she said. "Fair enough."

They dispersed on that somber note. Samheed and Lani held hands, him walking and her rolling in her contraption to the tubes in the entryway. Crow got up to join Henry and Thatcher and their children at the long table. Alex slipped away to Ms. Octavia's classroom to test Hux's wings. A few moments later Thisbe and Fifer followed, sneaking into the room behind him to watch . . . and to learn.

A Daring Plan

Alex lit a single small lamp in Ms. Octavia's classroom near the tables where the two shimmering ice-blue wings lay. He studied them. He rarely did magic anymore, other than simple spells like flicking on a highlighter in a dark corner of the Museum of Large or sending a seek spell whenever he couldn't find his sisters and wanted them to come home. A seek spell merely required him to hold an artistic item created by the person he was seeking. Concentrating on that item would send a ball of light at top speed in the direction of the missing person. When it reached its destination, the light would explode into an image of the creation, thereby cluing in the recipient as to who sent it. So it wasn't hard for Alex to do that spell. But any magic that involved throwing a component, like scatterclips or clay shackles or heart attack, was no longer in his repertoire. He didn't even carry those components with him these days. It was too embarrassing when he missed.

He wasn't very worried about pulling off the spell that would bring the wings to life, though, despite it being one of the more difficult spells he'd ever known or done, because it required concentration above all. And Alex had plenty of that.

Thisbe and Fifer crept silently closer, staying hidden behind statues and tables. One of the statues, a grumpy ostrich, opened an eye to look at them and frowned. Thisbe held a finger to her lips, pleading silently to the bird not to give them away. The ostrich fluffed his stone feathers, annoyed, but didn't reveal the girls' presence. Fifer decided she'd better keep an eye on him anyway.

They slipped behind Ms. Octavia's desk and peered around it—Thisbe in front, Fifer looking over her shoulder. Thisbe was close enough to witness everything Alex was doing. She watched, enthralled, as her brother ran his hand skillfully, lovingly, over the enormous wings. Alex and Ms. Octavia had designed them, Aaron had built their frames with jungle vines, and then they'd all covered the frames in cloth. On top of that they'd layered flower petals thickly in rows and dotted the wings with actual dragon scales that Alex had collected from Hux earlier.

The wings didn't look real. Not yet.

Alex inspected both wings carefully, looking for any part of the construction that might weaken them. When he was satisfied that they'd been perfectly put together, he double-checked the measurements and compared them to the diagram that Ms. Octavia had sketched. He took a moment to admire her work, and a twinge of jealousy passed through him—that had been his job in the past. Then he reached into his robe pocket and pulled out a small pencil, and began working some figures on the paper in the horrendous scrawl of a child.

In the back of his mind, he thought about the terrible twist of fate that had landed him here. All his life Alex had been wildly, predominantly left-handed, until that final fight with Queen Eagala. She'd ruined his arm with her sword, and in return he'd given her a death sentence by sending her ship hurtling into the underwater volcano of the Island of Fire. It had felt like a win for him at the time. But in the years since then, facing his disability, Alex wasn't so sure. And while he'd made attempts at writing, drawing, and performing magic right-handed, he'd been vastly disappointed with the results. Over time he realized that his best days had come . . . and gone. The highlight of his career as head mage had happened in his teenage years, and life had rolled downhill from there.

He often tortured himself by thinking back to the time shortly before the final battle when he'd actually sketched a dragon that had lifted off the page in 3-D—something no artist in Artimé had ever done before. Not even Ms. Octavia. Now he knew that *that* had been his creative shining moment—the height of his artistic ability. At age seventeen, his art was cruelly, permanently snatched away from him. Now his right-handed drawings looked worse than those of Aaron. Absolutely terrible. And Alex's accuracy casting thrown spells with his right hand was less than 50 percent. It was unacceptable. And mortifying for the leader of the magical world.

After the final battle, he'd spent hours every day holed up in his living quarters, trying to improve that nondominant throw. Trying to draw simple things. But the more he'd tried, the more he'd failed, and the more defeated he'd become. Until one day he finally admitted it to himself, and to Sky: He'd never, ever be the same again.

Without his art, he felt like he'd lost his identity. With the loss of his magical abilities, he felt like it was only a matter of time before he'd have to give up his role as head mage. Granted, he could do the job well enough when they were at peace. And peace was wonderful. He didn't want any part of another years-long war. He was older and wiser now. Artimé and Quill got along for the most part. The seven islands remained allies—well, all except for the Island of Graves, but the saber-toothed gorillas that inhabited it kept to themselves. Life was as easy as it could be under the circumstances.

Alex had his young sisters under his care. While they'd ended up giving him a lot more worries than average children might have, he loved them very much. And he was willing to sacrifice almost anything to keep Artimé calm for their sakes, so they wouldn't have to face all the pain and loss he had faced at their age. They'd already lost their parents—they wouldn't lose their brothers, too. Not if he could help it. Even if it meant the young dragons' lives would remain at stake. "I wish I could do more," he muttered as he finished measuring. "But this is all I have to offer. At least I can do this much."

Thisbe and Fifer exchanged a silent glance from their hiding place. Little phrases from earlier kept coming to Thisbe's mind. *Why can't you do something* good . . . ? *No one else can do the magic.* A hint of an idea began to form.

Then Alex breathed in suddenly, deeply, and blew the air out. "Enough of that." He took a few more cleansing breaths, and then rested his right hand on one of the wings. He closed his eyes and concentrated for several moments, imagining the wing taking flight. He pictured it sparkling in the sun, flowing with ease, and as light and free as the petals that adorned it. He focused, letting the images fill him. And finally he spoke a single word. "Live."

The wing began to move.

Alex did the same to the other wing. Thisbe watched, enthralled. Fifer kept an eye on the ostrich and plotted their escape. When both wings were moving successfully on the tabletop, Alex smiled grimly. And then he went back to the first wing, placed his hand on it, and began singing the most ridiculous song Thisbe and Fifer had ever heard.

Had Alex gone mad?

But no—when the silly song was finished, the wing ceased to be alive. Alex did the same to the second wing, putting it "to sleep" as well.

When both wings were still, Alex turned out the light, then walked past the hidden girls and out of the room.

Long after he was gone, Thisbe and Fifer remained behind Ms. Octavia's desk, discussing what they'd seen. And then Thisbe pressed her lips together. "Fifer?" she whispered.

"Yes?"

"Do you remember when Alex was yelling at us, and he said he wished we could do good things with our magic instead of only bad?"

"Yeah," Fifer said miserably. And then, slowly, her eyes widened. She looked at Thisbe solemnly. "Do you mean . . . ?"

"I—I don't know. What do you think about it?"

"It seems like it might be pretty difficult."

"Yeah." Thisbe dropped her gaze.

Fifer thought hard. "But maybe . . . maybe this would make up for what happened with Panther."

Thisbe let out a breath. "I think . . . maybe . . . it would."

"And then he'll let us take Magical Warrior Training and we'll get our component vests!" Fifer's heart surged. She reached out and squeezed her sister's arm. "Let's do it. Okay? I'm in."

Thisbe looked up. "Really?" A thrill fluttered in her chest. "We can't let Alex catch us."

"We'll set out at midnight, after he's gone to bed."

Thisbe nodded. "And Seth?"

"He'll come too."

Thisbe was quiet for a moment as doubts crept in. She knew they'd have to fly on the dragon's back. But how high? She cringed, angry with herself that this was the thing that scared her the most. "Are you sure we can do it?"

Fifer laughed out loud, startling the ostrich. She made a face, then leaned forward, her mind made up. "Of course we can. Haven't you heard? We're the most naturally talented mages Artimé has ever seen. We'll fix all the wings and be back before Alex even knows we're gone."

Sneaking Off

The moon was high in the night sky when Thisbe propped herself up on one elbow and peeked under the curtain. The outline of the two dragons filled the lagoon. She turned to her twin across the room. "Are you sure, Fifer?" she whispered. "Alex will be so mad if he finds out."

Fifer's eyes shone in the darkness. "He'll get over it once he hears about the good stuff we've done." She climbed out of her bed and slipped on some clothes. "I wish we had our component vests *now*," she grumbled, but then her face brightened. "We'll have them soon enough, though."

Thisbe fell back onto her pillow and rested there a moment,

then hoisted herself to the floor and started getting dressed. "What about Seth?"

"We'll send him a seek spell."

"You know how to do that one?"

"How hard can it be? Kitten did it once and she can't even say the right word."

"Don't you need something Seth created in order to do it?"

Fifer patted her pocket. "I've got that scene he gave me—the one that he wrote in Samheed's class. That should do the trick." She hopped onto Thisbe's bed and drew the curtains aside. Then she put her hand on the glass windowpane, concentrated, and whispered, "Release." The windowpane disappeared. Fifer looked over her shoulder. "Ready with the rope?"

Thisbe frowned, then reached behind the wardrobe and grabbed a rope. "Can't we just go the normal way?" she asked. Even though she'd climbed down the side of the mansion a dozen times or more, her stomach flipped at the thought of it.

"You mean so Desdemona sees us and reports us to Alex's blackboard? I don't think so." A blackboard was like a magical host in the living area of each apartment. Each personality delivered messages, kept an eye on the residents, offered help, guidance, and sometimes attitude, and some even shared gossip from the other blackboards. "Plus," Fifer went on, "we'd have to walk right past Simber."

Fifer had a point. Whenever the girls found themselves in odd predicaments, their blackboard, Desdemona, was a major tattletale—Alex had demanded she report any hint of the twins' shenanigans to him as a condition of their living on their own in the girls' hallway. And there was no way Simber would keep a secret from the head mage of Artimé.

"Not the back door either?" Thisbe pleaded.

"The chefs will see us. Come on, Thiz," Fifer said impatiently. She glanced at her sister and turned sympathetic. "Look, I know you're scared. But you have to do it. It's the only way."

Thisbe sighed. "All right, fine. Catch me if I fall?"

"I'll turn you into a bird so you can soar to the ground," promised Fifer.

"Ugh. No thanks. Can't you just catch me?"

"Sure," said Fifer, growing impatient again. "Just hurry up."

Thisbe tossed the coiled rope to Fifer, who, balancing on the sill, attached one end of it to an invisible hook outside the window, which one of the girls had installed years before for the first of many escapes.

As Thisbe put on her boots and tied them, Fifer slipped out and rappelled down the side of the mansion. Thisbe reached for her backpack and, not knowing how long they'd be gone, quickly stuffed it with their canteens and a few snacks they had in the bedroom. She climbed onto the bed and peered out the window at the ground below. With a grimace she grabbed the rope, took a breath, and swung out, hanging suspended above the ground from a dizzying height. She found her footing against the mansion wall and began descending. A few feet down, she stopped, and with a shaky hand, cast a new glass spell in the opening.

Once on the lawn, Thisbe breathed a sigh of relief. Now that the scary part was over, she grew excited for their adventure. Muttering a spell under her breath, she released the hook's hold on the rope so it landed in a heap at her feet, then coiled it up and put it in her backpack.

Nearby, Fifer was concentrating on the bit of script that Seth had given her. She held it pinched between her fingers, and when she felt ready, whispered, "Seek." A startling flash of light exploded from the paper and shot up to the second level of the mansion and in through a window, leaving a softly glowing line behind it. The girls waited breathlessly as the line began to fade, hoping Seth was sleeping lightly enough that he would notice the spell before it was gone.

Finally their best friend appeared at the glass. The girls waved frantically and jumped up and down, and after a moment Seth saw them. He waved back, then disappeared. A few minutes later he exited the back door of the mansion and closed it softly behind him. He was wearing his new component vest, its pockets bulging. Fifer smiled approvingly.

"What's this all about?" he whispered. "How'd you do that seek spell?"

"Never mind that," said Thisbe. "Did anybody see you?"

"Just the night chefs. They don't pay much attention to me."

"Let's hope not." Fifer scowled. "We need to move before Simber finds out what we're doing out here. Come on." She took off running across the lawn, toward the jungle. Thisbe and Seth jogged behind.

"Where are we going?" whispered Seth.

Thisbe glanced sidelong at him, her backpack jouncing on her back. She flashed a mischievous grin. "We're going to rescue the young dragons."

The Adventure Begins

"First we need vines," Thisbe said softly. Now that her fear of climbing out the window was a distant memory, her boldness returned, and she headed into the dark jungle. "Lots of 'em."

"What for?" asked Seth, following her. He smoothed his component vest absently as he tromped over the uneven ground. His vest was the one thing he had that the girls didn't have. And he knew they wanted one, especially Fifer. It gave him a little bit of confidence, which was a feeling he wasn't particularly accustomed to having around the twins.

"For the wings," said Fifer, bringing up the rear. "Like

Aaron brought yesterday." She began grabbing at the nearest vines and yanking them down. "Come on."

Seth grabbed a vine and tugged at it until it came loose, then threw it over his shoulders. He reached for another.

"These aren't as thick as the ones Aaron brought," said Fifer.

"They'll have to do," said Thisbe. "We don't have time to be picky."

They gathered as many long vines as they could carry, and then Fifer led the way to the lagoon. It was hard to be silent with the vines dragging over the jungle floor behind them, and they startled some platyprots along the way, but the colorful parrots with platypus-like bills, feet, and tails only ruffled their feathers and settled again.

Pan saw them coming. Very little happened in the seven islands without her knowledge. "You are Alex's sisters," she said in greeting.

"Yes," said Thisbe and Fifer together. Fifer added, "And this is Seth Holiday."

"Carina's young?" said the dragon. She looked down her broad snout at him, the whites of her eyes reflecting the moonlight.

Seth nodded and took a step back. He was more than a bit awestruck by the creatures.

"Did Alex send you?"

Fifer began to answer truthfully, but Thisbe spoke faster and louder. "Yes," she said. "We can help you with . . . with whatever you need." She clamped her mouth shut.

Fifer and Seth remained silent. Their hearts raced as Pan stared into Thisbe's eyes for a long moment. Thisbe refrained from the urge to shrink into a tiny ball, and she tried desperately not to flinch.

"You are very small," said Pan.

The three children stared ahead, and at first they didn't know how to respond to that observation. Then Thisbe said, "We are also the best mages in Artimé."

Hux snorted fire and eyed Thisbe. He swung his head around to sniff her. She trembled but held her ground.

"This one killed the captain of the pirates," said Hux. "I remember the story. She was only a baby."

Thisbe grimaced. "That's right."

Seth started to point out that she was actually two years old, not a baby, but then thought the better of it and stayed quiet.

Pan lifted her head. "I remember as well. And the other female eliminated the raven spell." She gave her first indication of approval and backed off, allowing Thisbe a second to breathe and wipe away the nervous sweat that beaded on her forehead.

Hux swung his head around to face Seth. "What have *you* done?" he asked with a growl.

Seth stumbled backward. "I—I—nothing much, I suppose," he said, his voice pitching higher with each word. He'd never done anything noteworthy—not like Fifer and Thisbe. He could feel the heat from the dragon's breath and waited for fire to burst forth and burn him to a crisp.

"We need him to carry the vines," said Fifer.

"Yes, carry the vines," echoed Thisbe. She promptly pulled the vines from her shoulders and plopped them onto Seth's. Fifer did the same, until Seth staggered under them.

His shoulders began to ache. "I can do magic too," he said, a little grumpily. Did the girls really mean that? Was that the reason they wanted him along—to hold their junk?

"Yes, he can," said Thisbe. "He keeps track of the spell components, as well. He's . . . very handy."

Hux frowned but moved his face away, to Seth's great relief.

"I'm not sure I can carry all of you," the dragon said. "Has Alex created my new wings?"

Fifer and Thisbe glanced at each other, trying not to reveal their panic. They'd forgotten about that. There was no way for the girls to get the huge wings out of Ms. Octavia's classroom without being detected. And even though Seth could go in and out of the mansion at all hours more freely and invisibly than the girls could, he would certainly look suspicious carrying the wings outside. Even the night chefs wouldn't overlook that. They'd have to leave without the new wings, and quickly. Every minute they stood out here was a minute they could get discovered.

"We'll make your wings as soon as we get to your land," said Fifer. "But aren't you in a hurry to get there? I'm so worried about Arabis. What if the Revinir changes his mind, or thinks you aren't coming and decides to kill her?"

Hux's face clouded. "Of course I'm worried. It's all I can think about."

"Then we mustn't waste any more time," said Thisbe. "You're really strong. I believe you can carry us easily. And like Pan said, we're very small."

Pan nodded at her son. "You can swim the distance until you must fly. That will save your wings."

Thisbe found herself nodding profusely. "Excellent idea," she said under her breath.

"How far away is the land of the dragons?" asked Seth.

"I cannot say," said Hux. "It is against the dragon code. But you'll learn the answer soon enough." He eyed the three children, sizing them up to determine if he could take them on his back while flying with too-small wings, then looked at his mother. "I believe I can do it," he said.

Pleased, Pan regarded him regally. "Go swiftly, then."

Hux nodded. "You'll search . . . for us?" he asked her in a quiet voice. "Like I told you? There has to be another way."

"If there is, I will find it," said Pan, nuzzling him. "My love to all of you until then."

The children glanced sidelong at each other, not knowing what the dragons were talking about. But Alex had always said that dragons were more secretive than most creatures, and Pan got angry if you asked too many questions, so they didn't dare inquire.

Hux turned in the water and unfurled his tail, making a

bridge for the children to climb aboard. The girls took back their vines so Seth wasn't quite so overloaded, and they made their way onto the dragon's back. When they were seated and properly holding on, Hux said good-bye to his mother, then swirled his tail in the water, and they were off, heading westward over the glassy sea.

Rough Waters

It was hard to get used to sitting and hanging on to a dragon, but Hux offered a suggestion. "At the base of my neck there's a bit of a flat area between it and my shoulder bones. Some of the scales are worn away there from all the cargo I've carried, so it'll be less slippery for you. The three of you should be able to fit."

Thisbe, Fifer, and Seth felt around Hux's muscular back for it. Fifer nearly tumbled in. "Found it," she said, her voice muffled as she rolled. "It's like a shallow bowl." Soon the other two joined her, and they discovered that Hux's neck shielded them from the wind there as well, which made the ride even more comfortable.

As the friends got settled and coiled their vines, Hux sped across the water using his ropelike tail as a propeller. By the time they looked back, the lights of Artimé were small behind them, and the reality of the task before them became imminent.

"Are you sure we should be doing this?" Seth asked quietly. He was less excited about the venture now, after what the girls had said about him. "My mother will explode if she finds out."

Thisbe and Fifer flashed him a sympathetic look. Carina Holiday was as sharp and tough as they came. She was a true warrior if there ever was one. But she was kindhearted, too.

"Just think how proud of you she'll be once she's done being mad, though," said Thisbe. "It's exactly like something she'd have done."

Seth remained troubled, but he nodded slowly. "I guess so." He looked up. "Do you suppose we'll be back by morning?"

Of course neither of the girls knew how long it would take to get to the unknown land. If Hux knew, he either wouldn't answer because he was sworn to secrecy, or he wasn't paying attention to their conversation.

There wasn't much that the three of them could see in the dark, though there was a bit of light from the stars and moon above. After an hour or so, cramped up in their little pod, Fifer shifted and sighed. "I don't think we'll be back by morning. Warbler is still a long way off, and I'll bet we have to go past that and the Island of Fire to get to wherever we're going. Maybe we ought to try to sleep."

Since the excitement of the adventure was waning, the others agreed. One by one they drifted off. When they awoke, the sun was shining brightly at their backs. Warbler Island was behind them, and the volcanic Island of Fire was a safe distance away. Clearly Hux knew enough to skirt far around it, since it could plunge underwater at any moment and suck them all down with it.

Fifer twisted around and squinted at the sun. The morning brought new worries with it. "Well, they probably know by now," she said, trying to sound upbeat.

"Yep," said Thisbe, ignoring the uneasy feeling in her stomach. She ran her fingers through her hair, causing the loose curls to stand up wildly. "So, how are we going to . . . you know . . ." She lowered her voice. "*Make them?*" She pointed a thumb at Hux.

"The wings?" whispered Fifer.

Thisbe nodded while Seth scooted closer so he could hear.

"Just like Alex and the others did. You were watching, weren't *you*?"

"Yes. But what if Alex was right?" Thisbe's uncomfortable feeling grew, and doubts kept working into her thoughts. "What if the Revinir won't let us go home after we're done?"

"Pfft," said Fifer. "What would anybody want with a bunch of kids like us?"

Seth laughed uneasily. "Yeah," he said, "good point." He looked ahead of them as they sped along, not noticing the Island of Fire's rumbling or the molten lava it spewed as it grew small behind them. He tried not to choke on his nerves. "I've never been this far west before. Have you?"

The girls shook their heads. "There's nothing out here," said Fifer.

"This is where Karkinos used to be," said Seth. "But he moved nearer to us to help fight the big battle."

"And so Talon and Florence could be together," said Fifer, sighing.

"Gross," said Thisbe.

Seth caught Thisbe's eye and nodded in agreement, then blushed, his cheeks turning dark red in an instant. Thisbe didn't notice. She hitched herself up so she could see around the dragon's broad neck. But there was nothing but water in front of them.

Seth's uneasiness grew as the day wore on, but he didn't share it. After a while, Thisbe pulled out the few snacks she'd brought along. They ate ravenously with little thought for the trip back home, which would no doubt take just as long.

"I wonder how we'll get to the land of the dragons," mused Fifer. "We'll be the first ones to know out of all of Artimé."

"Yes," said Thisbe, growing more enthusiastic at the prospect. "I hope it's exciting."

"I hope we don't go plunging down the waterfall," muttered Seth.

"That has to be where the flying part comes in," said Fifer. "Flying on a dragon's back? I can't wait!"

Thisbe choked down her fear. "It'll be even better than flying on Simber," she said, trying to convince herself. "As long as Hux stays pretty low, that is."

"Oh," said Seth, his chest tightening, "I can think of a few ways it could be a lot worse."

"You're not helping," Thisbe muttered.

"Sorry." But Seth couldn't help imagining all the things that could go wrong with a dragon whose wings weren't strong enough to carry himself, much less three riders. All Seth could do was to try to tamp down his worries, not panic, and be brave . . . as brave as the two who accompanied him. It wasn't easy. But then again, being best friends with these two never had been.

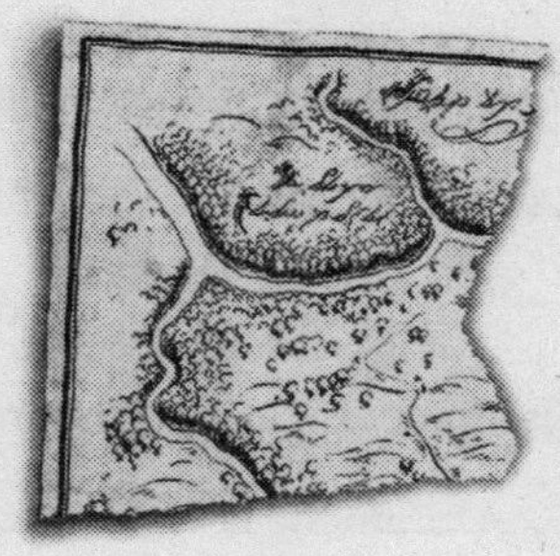

Artimé on Alert

Back in Artimé, Carina Holiday was the first to discover that her son wasn't answering his blackboard. Her first thoughts sprang to the twins, and she wondered if the three of them might be together.

She summoned Binh, her apartment's blackboard. A man's face pushed out of the screen, its contours intricately detailed. Binh wore a wary expression, not unfounded, for Carina and Sean's rambunctious youngsters weren't always gentle with him. His eyes darted around the room before he relaxed. "Yes?"

"Call Desdemona, will you, please?" She wanted to find out from Thisbe and Fifer's personal blackboard if they were in their room, or if there might be some sort of mischief afoot. "Ask if the girls are there."

"Sure," Binh said. "I'll return shortly." He shrank back and disappeared, leaving a shimmering blank space in the blackboard.

A moment later, in the girls' living area, Desdemona surfaced and looked around. She didn't see them. The door to their bedroom was closed, as was the exit door that led to the hallway. She hollered out their names, but if they were asleep, Desdemona wasn't able to rouse them. She melted into her screen and reported her lack of findings.

Binh resurfaced. "No sign of them."

"Thanks anyway," Carina said, turning away, and tried to decide what to do. She suspected the three were up to something. After all, she'd always been adventurous, so it was the least she could expect from her son. Plus, Fifer and Thisbe were always getting into trouble, and they often dragged Seth into it with them. With a sigh, she left the younger children in the apartment with Sean and went in search of her eldest.

She checked the lounge, the library, the theater, and the dining room with no luck. Then she went outside to check the lawn and even ran down to the lagoon. There was no sign of anyone there—not even the dragons.

"Well, that's suspicious," Carina muttered. Frowning, she returned to the mansion, fighting a barrage of emotions. She knew it would only be a matter of time before Seth ventured out without telling anybody. Her generation of Unwanteds wouldn't have thought twice about it, since they didn't have parents there to worry about them. Back then, Mr. Today had made it clear that the children could freely come and go from the mansion at any hour, and they had done so regularly. Even today it wasn't a big deal to see people wandering the lawn or the mansion's many extensions in the middle of the night. It was a rite of passage when a kid got his own room, she knew. But it didn't make her worry any less.

Back in her apartment, she filled Sean in on what she'd discovered.

"Oh dear," said Sean, trying to gauge Carina's level of concern. "Are you . . . worried?"

"I'm not sure," Carina admitted. "Kind of."

"We all did it," Sean said quietly. "He'll be okay."

Carina turned and gazed out the window. "I know. It still feels unsettling."

"Want me to search Quill?"

Carina shook her head. "With the dragons gone, I'm pretty sure I know where he and the girls are." She sighed. "And the worst part? Now we've got to tell Alex."

Sean groaned. "Those poor girls—Alex will be angry as usual. I'm sure all three of the children are perfectly fine. They'll turn up eventually, like we always did."

"I'm sure they will. But dragons . . ." Carina pressed her lips together. "That makes me nervous." They gathered up the younger children and went down the hall to the balcony, then to the secret hallway to alert Alex. Sean stayed back with the children, who couldn't get through the wall, while Carina, who could, ran to Alex's living quarters. She pounded on the door.

A moment later the door swung open, and Alex, bleary-eyed, stared at the woman. "What's wrong?" he asked.

"Have you seen Thisbe and Fifer?" asked Carina.

"Not since dinner last night. Why?"

"Seth's missing. Desdemona says the girls aren't answering. And . . . the dragons are gone."

Alex squinted. "What—gone? But I haven't given Hux his new wings yet."

"That's all I know, Alex," said Carina, running a hand over her spiky hair to smooth it. "What happened yesterday, exactly? Seth was telling me bits and pieces over dinner, but we didn't get the full story."

Seeing Sean waiting on the balcony with the children, Alex grabbed a fresh robe. "Let's go." He maneuvered his arms into it and secured it at his neck as the two left the secret hallway. Alex greeted Sean, then shared the events of the previous day. He told Sean and Carina about his decision not to go with Hux, fearing it was too risky.

"Oh. I see." Carina turned abruptly to take her daughter from Sean, trying to hide her disappointment in Alex. But it wasn't easy. She broke away and headed for the girls' residence hallway, daughter in tow. "I'm going to check the twins' bedroom. You check Seth's."

"Got it," said Sean.

"She's mad at me," remarked Alex.

"Yep."

While Carina went down the girls' hallway to pound on

Thisbe and Fifer's door—the door exclaiming in surprise at the intrusion—Sean and their young son went with Alex to Seth's room. They found it empty.

"Well, that explains it," said Sean as he and Alex left the boys' hallway. "Of course they've gone with Hux. You really do smother those girls so much, Alex. I'm surprised they haven't run off before."

Alex was taken aback by the harsh, judgmental words, though it was fairly common for Sean Ranger to be perfectly frank with his friends. "I do not smother them," he said defensively. "They're dangerous. I have to be careful."

Sean shrugged. While they descended the sweeping mansion staircase, Alex fumbled in his pocket to come up with the tiny pebbles he'd made Thisbe and Fifer paint for him so he could send a seek spell to them at any time. He sent off two of them, one to each girl. Two little balls of light shot from his fist and out of the mansion, zipping westward.

By now they had arrived at the front door, where Simber stood.

"Have you seen Thisbe and Fifer?" asked Alex, breathless.

"Or Seth?" asked Sean.

"Not the girrrls," said Simber. "I saw Seth arrround midnight heading forrr the kitchen, but he does that everrry so often. I didn't think much of it."

"They're missing," said Alex. "All three of them."

"Did you happen to see Seth go back upstairs?" asked Sean as Carina came down the steps. He quickly filled Carina in on what Simber had seen.

"No, but I wasn't paying attention. And I did my rrrounds shorrrtly afterrr, so I might have missed him. Orrr perrrhaps he went out the back doorrr."

"You didn't stop him?" said Alex, his voice pitching higher.

Simber harrumphed. "Of courrrse not. I'm not anyone's babysitterrr. He's gone out at night beforrre, as most of the childrrren like to do once they have theirrr prrrivate rrrooms." He glanced from Sean to Alex to Carina. "You all did it too."

"I know," said Alex, agitated. "You're right. I didn't mean to accuse you. It's just that . . . if they went with Hux, they have no idea what danger they are in for. We have to find out where they've gone. We have to go after them!" He glanced at his arm. "Someone does, anyway. Someone who can actually fight in case there's trouble."

"I'll go, of courrrse," said Simber in a grim voice. "Who would you like to accompany me?"

Alex looked at Carina with a question in his eyes. She was one of Artimé's strongest warriors and spell casters, as well as an adept healer. More than almost anyone in Artimé, Alex trusted Carina Holiday with his life. "Will you?" he asked.

Carina needed no urging. "Of course I'll go. I want to be the first one to yell at Seth for doing something so foolish." She frowned, as if trying to forget the multitude of risky adventures she'd taken part in over the years. "We should take someone else with us, though, shouldn't we, Sim? Henry, maybe."

The stone cheetah growled his agreement.

"That would leave us without a chief healer if you both go," Alex pointed out.

"Right, right," said Carina, thinking hard. "What about Thatcher, then? Or Scarlet?"

"Scarlet is at Warbler, working with Sky and Copper," Alex reminded her. "But Thatcher is a great choice. We'll ask him."

"Perfect. I'll send Spike to find Pan," said Carina, shoving her daughter into Sean's free arm, then looked up at him. "You're okay if I leave for a few days, right?"

"As if that matters," Sean said fondly. "I only feel sorry for Seth when you get ahold of him."

"As well you should." She pecked him on the lips, then ran outside to call for the intuitive whale. Spike Furious, who Alex had created and brought to life from an old whale skeleton, had strong traits like speed, intelligence, and the intuition to sense approaching danger. She was also the best at finding Pan, who could be anywhere in the vast waters.

When Spike appeared offshore, Carina gave her the instructions. Moments later the whale was off to track down Pan and bring the mother dragon back to Artimé so they could question her and begin their search for the children.

"Now I need to pack some supplies," said Carina as she and Sean went back to their apartment down the family hallway.

"And load up your component vest."

"It seems so strange to do that. Like old times. I feel pretty rusty."

Sean nodded. "I can imagine. But it'll all come back to you."

"My aim is off. I haven't practiced or sat in on a Warrior Training class in I don't know how long."

"You'll be fine. You probably won't have to fight."

Carina laughed. "You're right. I think I got a little carried away there. Let's hope there's no fighting necessary, and most of all that the kids are safe, of course. That would be ideal."

Sean thought he heard a hint of wistfulness in Carina's voice when she talked about the old days. But wisely he held his tongue.

When Spike and Pan arrived that evening, Alex went outside to have a talk with the dragon. "We need to know where they've gone," he said.

At first Pan was adamant. She couldn't give Alex the information. But when she realized the children had misled her and Hux, and that they really hadn't been given permission to help, she relented. "Simber is the only one who can get there safely. I will tell him," she said. "No one else needs to know."

"I'm the leader of this land," said Alex, voice raised, "and my sisters are in danger. You must tell me!"

Pan regarded him. "I'm very sorry your sisters lied to me," she said coolly. "I wish they hadn't done that, for they've put my young in danger now too with their foolishness. And I know you will never understand the ways of dragons. But know this: I will be giving Simber secret information. And that act violates the dragon code. It is grounds for my execution." She paused as the words sank in, then softened a little. "I'm doing the best I can for you, but the fewer I tell, the better."

"But Carina and Thatcher will find out, won't they?" Alex said. "I mean, obviously they'll be able to see where they're going."

"They won't find out from me," said Pan. "And that is what is important here."

Alex fumed. He wished Sky were there to talk him through this terrible feeling of helplessness. But she wasn't, and he had to deal with it. Finally he let out a heavy sigh. Simber was the protector of them all, and he knew he could trust the enormous stone beast. "All right," he said. "Just . . . find them. Please."

When Carina and Thatcher were nearly ready to depart, Pan came ashore and took Simber aside. After a short conversation where Alex assumed she was telling him how to find the land of the dragons, the two creatures parted. "You must promise never to repeat my words aloud," said Pan as she returned to the water.

Simber promised.

Not long after, Carina and Thatcher said good-bye to their loved ones. They tied their provisions to Simber's back. And soon they were off to rescue the runaways. When they were out of sight, the others trickled back into the mansion, leaving Alex standing on the shore alone.

To the Rescue

Thatcher and Carina rode on Simber's back into the night, heading west as Pan had instructed. They were almost a full day behind Hux, and Simber couldn't move nearly as fast as a dragon could swim or fly, so they'd constantly be losing ground. Carina tried not to think about that. She was a seasoned adventurer and skilled fighter, though there hadn't been much adventuring or fighting lately. And even with the worry for her son's well-being in the forefront of her mind, the old familiar thrill in her gut kept pushing its way back, trying to be noticed.

The wind sliced through her light brown hair, and it batted

a bit of ruddy color into her pale cheeks. Her muscles pulsed as she hung on to the flying cheetah, and in her mind she went over the contents of each of her component vest pockets. She hadn't had to be this sharp about spell casting in many years, and she didn't want to appear rusty.

Thatcher, like other Warblerans, didn't use a last name. He wasn't new to fighting, though he didn't have the extensive experience that Carina had. He was in his mid-twenties and had assisted Artimé in the final battle as a teenage refugee. That war had left its mark in the form of slowly fading scars on his forehead and cheek. Thatcher and Henry Haluki were partners in all things, including helping to raise the Unwanted children that continued to make journeys into Artimé from Quill.

Thatcher had very few qualms about working with a bunch of frightened thirteen-year-olds, but on board Simber, his stomach flipped. He hadn't spent much time on the beast's back in the past and had always maintained a respectful distance from him. But now the two were forced into a much closer relationship. He sat in front of Carina at her insistence—it just felt a little more secure up there, she explained. He shifted now and then, trying to overcome his fear of sliding right off

Simber's slick stone back. In contrast to Carina, his black hair barely moved in the wind. He wore it meticulously sculpted in corkscrew coils, which stood up naturally most of the time, whether it was windy or calm. His dark brown skin shone with nervous sweat for the first several minutes of the ride, but the wind soon took care of that.

"So, Simber," said Carina, leaning forward, "is the other land on Lani's map actually the land of the dragons? And is the secret to fly over the waterfall rather than ride down it?"

"I didn't say that," growled Simber. "I'm sworrrn to secrrrecy."

Carina wasn't deterred. "I admit I've wondered it ever since the young dragons left us. I couldn't think of another way for them to leave this world, and after the scientists and Aaron and Kaylee explored every inch of these waters and came up with nothing, there really wasn't any other method that I could think of."

"I've thought it too," Simber said. "I brrrought up the subject with Alex, but he wasn't interrrested in explorrring anything afterrr his injurrry." The cat paused. "I'm surrre you'rrre not surrrprrrised to hearrr that."

"No."

After a moment, Thatcher broke the silence. "I wish I'd known Alex better before the battle. To a Warbler kid like me, he was bigger than life. I was so surprised back then when he knew my name. I still remember that moment."

"There's a lot the same about him now as then," said Carina. "But he's become very cautious. The battles hurt him in more ways than just physically, I'm afraid. And the stress from the girls' destructive abilities must be exhausting."

"Do you ever worry about Seth being around them?"

"Not really," said Carina, but a shadow crossed her face. "I think he figured out how to adapt to stay safe."

Thatcher glanced over his shoulder. "How?"

"He learned pretty early on not to make them mad at him. Ever." Carina smiled grimly.

"Oh." Thatcher faced forward again. "Have you talked to Alex about it?"

"No. He doesn't need anything else to worry about. He's a dear friend, and I'd do anything to take away some of his burdens if I could."

"Of course," said Thatcher. "We all would."

Simber nodded grimly. Artimé was fiercely loyal to the young mage who had seen them through years of fighting and brought them safely to the other side of a devastating war. And while Alex wasn't the only one with a life-altering injury, he seemed to be the only one who hadn't been able to pull out of the funk it had created. He'd lost so much. His mentor, Mr. Today. His best friend—and Sean's sister—Meghan Ranger. His parents, and all the people of Artimé he felt responsible for, like Mr. Appleblossom and Liam Healey, and his blackboard, Clive. At least he had Sky to help keep his spirits up . . . though it was harder right now with her away at Warbler.

Simber, Carina, and Thatcher flew on steadily into the night, their minds filled with battling emotions of fear over the disappearance of the children, anticipation of discovering a new land, and sorrow for Alex, who'd been so drastically changed from the man he should have become.

A Perilous Flight

By morning the sea had grown rough. Thisbe, Fifer, and Seth bounced along in the hollow on Hux's back, and they could hear the pounding of the rapids and the waterfall looming ahead of them—it sounded just like Crow had described in the story the other day. Thisbe's heart leaped in fear and anticipation. "Look," she said, pointing to the cloud of mist that rose up in the distance. "There it is. The end of the world."

The dragon addressed the children. "I'll be taking flight shortly," he said. "You'll want to hold on to the folds of my neck. And try not to grab my wings. I need full use of them if we're going to make it. And I should warn you . . . it may be a bit of a rough ride. Perhaps you can use your vines somehow to help secure yourselves."

The girls and Seth moved to their knees and began to search for ways to use the vines. "Try looping one around Hux's neck," suggested Fifer. But it was impossible to reach all the way around and grab the end at this high speed—it just got blustered about in the wind. They looked for other ways to attach the vines, but Hux had no spines sticking up anywhere to hook them to.

"We can keep ourselves together, at least," said Thisbe, awkwardly knotting one end of the vine around her waist. "Tie yourself to this." She tossed the other end to Fifer.

"What about Seth?"

"I'll do one for him, too." Thisbe tied a second vine around her waist and handed the other end to Seth. Soon all three were connected with Thisbe in the middle.

Fifer looked skeptical. "I'm not sure how this is going to help."

"I don't know either," admitted Thisbe, "but at least we're doing something. I can't stand just sitting here any longer thinking about Alex and how mad he probably is by now. He's sent like eight seek spells already. At least now if something happens, we'll all be together." She didn't mention that she was also trying to keep her mind off the fact that they'd be airborne soon.

Just then, a ball of light reached them and exploded into a picture of the ugly painted pebble Thisbe had made for Alex a million years ago. She sighed.

Fifer ignored it. "Nothing's going to go wrong," she said firmly.

Seth's mouth went dry. This was really happening, and there was nothing he could do to stop it.

Just then the dragon's wings unfurled and he stretched out his neck, upsetting the children.

"A little warning next time might be nice," Seth said under his breath. Quickly they regained their balance.

"You must hold on tightly now!" shouted the dragon, peering into the mist. "Don't let go, or you'll be lost in the scrolling waterfall. You'll most certainly drown if you don't die from the fall. Once we're over the waterfall, there'll be nothing below."

Nothing? The children's eyes grew wide.

"Oh my," whispered Thisbe, trying not to sound terrified. She hadn't really thought much about what they'd be flying *over*. Or how high they would be above whatever it was. But having nothing at all below them? *Nothing?* She gripped the dragon's loose skin as her sister and Seth did the same, and she tried not to throw up.

With a violent lurch, the dragon's spinning tail propelled them up out of the water. His wings stretched out wide and began to flap, making for a constantly moving perch for the kids. He stayed low. Mist and churning seawater splashed up and soaked the three passengers while they hung on, eyes stinging and breath hitching over and over. Soon Hux rose higher into the air, his movements growing more and more fluid, yet every muscle in his back rippled beneath the children.

Seth gasped as he adjusted to his new, unstable seating arrangement, and tried desperately to see where they were going. But the mist was as thick as a cloud, and he could barely even make out the shape of Hux's head in front of him.

"Don't look down," Fifer reminded Thisbe.

Thisbe groaned. "Yeah, thanks for the tip." As they rose higher, the nearly fearless girl closed her eyes and pressed her face against the dragon. She tried not to think about how high they'd be after they went past the edge of the waterfall.

"How much farther?" Fifer asked the dragon, even though she knew he wouldn't tell her.

"Hold on," he said instead, panting a bit but remaining steady. "Don't let go."

They obeyed, Fifer peering up and around the side of Hux's neck, and Seth, a bit more cautiously, doing the same from a slightly more crouched position. His breathing turned to little fearful gasps of air. He tightened the vine around his waist, then grasped a thicker fold of dragon skin, all the while trying and failing to take a slow, smooth breath.

Hux gained altitude as the roaring sound of the waterfall pounded in front of them. The thundering noise grew louder and louder until all of them could feel it rattling their insides. Thisbe clenched her teeth to stop them from chattering and stayed as still as she could, trying not to look down.

Hux's breathing became labored, and small bursts of flames burned circles into the fog in front of them. His wings beat the air, emitting small thunderclaps with every forceful downward flap.

"Look!" Fifer exclaimed, pointing at the roiling white water below them rushing off the edge of their world. Even more mist rose up. They'd heard so much about this, but to actually see it was wondrous and breathtaking and horrifying all at once.

"Whoa," said Seth. His heart fluttered as he struggled for breath. He was having trouble focusing. Thisbe stole a peek at the grand view below, then moaned and squeezed her eyes shut again.

Hux powered onward through the mist, concentrating, seeming to focus on something in the distance invisible to the children. His chest heaved with effort. The children, while small, added enough extra weight to Hux's back to make the journey significantly harder than it had been without them. And every day Hux had been growing a little bit larger. Soon he, like his siblings, would be flightless. But now he had one and only one thought and goal in mind: to make it to the dark cliffs of Grimere that loomed on the other side of the chasm that split the worlds.

A Tenuous Landing

The harder Hux pumped his wings, the thinner the mist grew. But before it cleared completely, Fifer felt the creature losing steam and altitude. "Come on!" she yelled. "You can do it!" Her shouts seemed to bolster her own spirits more than it spurred him on. She glanced at Thisbe, who was hanging on so tightly her hands shook. Or perhaps they trembled with fear. Thisbe was a rock when it came to most things, but she'd never conquered her hatred and fear of high places. Fifer, on the other hand, loved the thrill of being high up and had a hard time understanding anyone who didn't feel the same way.

Ahead of them the mist seemed to turn gray, and the air chilled considerably. A cold wind blew up from below, making Fifer shiver. It seemed to give Hux a bit of momentum, though, so she was glad for it despite the discomfort. She squinted ahead, wondering what they were flying toward. Wondering how far Hux had to labor to get them there. Hoping the dragon had it in him. She sat up a little, trying to be lighter.

But Hux's breath became even more labored and his wings seemed to falter, taking an extra second, then two, to make their full rotation up and down. Almost imperceptibly at first, and then noticeably, they began to drop in the air with each upward flap before Hux's wings pulled them back up again, not quite as high. Soon the drops were enough to cause Fifer's stomach to flip.

Seth and Thisbe felt it even more. Seth threw a helpless look Fifer's way but stayed quiet and focused on breathing—he couldn't speak.

"It's going to be okay," Fifer said, recognizing his glassy-eyed look—this wasn't the first time she'd seen Seth like this. She lifted her chin bravely. "Hang in there, Sethy."

He nodded and almost smiled at the use of her childhood

name for him. He flashed the word "okay" in Warbler sign language, even though he was feeling far from okay.

Fifer turned back to Hux. She wished she could help the dragon, but there was nothing the children could do but hang on.

The mist grew even darker and the air colder. Rain began to pelt Fifer's face. Soon Hux's gasps took on a thick, sickly sounding rasp. The rain increased, and then a wall of it swept over them, drenching the children. Hux dropped several dozen feet in the air with the weight of it and wasn't able to regain altitude.

Once Fifer could clear the rain from her eyes, she realized they'd left the rising mist of the waterfall behind them. The thundering sound had lessened, and Fifer quickly faced forward again. With a gasp strong enough to get Thisbe and Seth to look up, Fifer stared at the sight that emerged before them. The dark cloud morphed into a giant black cliff that jutted up in thick, needle-shaped points against the sky, some so far above them that their tips were lost in clouds.

Upon the biggest, thickest needle's point was an enormous stone fortress, and a small river that met its end and fell off the side of the cliff. A smattering of village houses painted the valley below in pastel colors. Several other smaller fortresses and villages could be seen all along the cliff, and the vast land appeared to go on forever beyond them, with no sea anywhere in sight. Fifer had never seen anything like it. Having come from the world of seven islands with water all around, she didn't realize a place with so much land could exist.

As Fifer stared on in awe, Thisbe peeked from between her fingers. Seth's jaw dropped, and he momentarily forgot his panic and managed to take in a few good breaths. His hold on Hux loosened as he strained to see more. But Hux was quickly loosing steam. They began to drop lower and lower into the chasm the closer they got to the cliff.

Fifer sat up higher. "Hux?" she called out anxiously. "Everything okay?"

The dragon couldn't answer. His too-small wings tried pumping harder and faster, but they became more and more jerky and uncontrollable in their movements.

Fifer glanced down, and now she could see there was no water below her—they'd left that behind to wrap around their world. She looked back over her shoulder and saw their world suspended in the air, with mist and water flowing around the edge. There was nothing below them—nothing but space. Now her own stomach lurched. She watched the drops of rain from her soaked hair drip off and fly out into the chasm, falling, falling, out of sight below her. Falling until they surely evaporated somehow. She began shivering in earnest. The thought of slipping off the dragon's back now struck a deep fear in her that she'd never felt before. Perhaps it was the knowledge that there was nothing below them that made it seem so much more frightening. If she fell . . . what would happen? Would she just keep falling . . . forever?

Hux jerked in the air. "Hold on!" he gasped, stretching and straining his neck, as if that would help lift his falling body. The back end of him began to drag. The children gripped harder as their once flat surface became an inclined plane.

"Help!" squeaked Seth as they jerked and faltered again, falling ten or fifteen feet. The boy whipped his head around wildly, desperately, gasping for air. "Are we . . . going to . . . make it?" As the cliff loomed closer, they looked up at the possible places to land, and all three began to wonder if there was any way Hux would be able to clear the sheer wall.

Fifer moaned. "We're all going to die!"

Hux snorted in effort and exhaustion, unable to utter another word. He arched his neck and back, and began bucking in the air and propelling his tail wildly, trying everything to gain height so he could land safely. But the best he could do was to head straight for the solid cliff wall.

Frozen in fright, Thisbe didn't utter a sound. She only held on for dear life while Seth and Fifer watched in horror as the jagged rock wall came into focus. The nearest valley was far above them. They weren't going to make it.

Hux flailed, his short dragon legs rotating as if to climb magical air steps, his wings straining to pull his heavy body and cargo up, up, up, but barely making progress. He put his head down and gave one more burst of effort, clawing at the wind, his front end flying up and his back end falling even more. His tail twirled angrily, but it didn't seem to help much. With a shuddering lurch, he let out a blast of fire from his mouth.

Seth's hands slipped loose. He screamed. His upper body flew wildly backward, and only his knees still pressed a fold of dragon skin between them. "Ahh!" he cried out as the cliffs danced and jiggled sickeningly around him. His fingers raked the air as Fifer shouted his name.

Legs outstretched and wings wild and out of control, Hux hit his giant pronged claws hard against the side of the cliff. The dragon scrabbled and scraped, trying to find something to hold on to, but he slid downward at a sickening pace, his claws screeching against the rock. Seth lost his grip and fell, screaming, until the vine rope reached its limit, jerking Thisbe backward.

Thisbe couldn't hide her face now. With every bit of strength she could gather, she lunged upward to reach the top of Hux's wing and managed to get her elbow hooked over it. Seth dangled in the air over the vast nothingness, screaming until his breath failed him. He fainted and was quiet as the whole party slid down the face of the wall.

Fifer shrieked and clung to the dragon, trying to throw her leg over its other wing. Finally Hux managed to sink his claws deep enough into the side of the black stone. There was an excruciating jolt as the falling dragon came to a sudden stop. Fifer lost her grip and flew off, and in an instant Thisbe was the sole anchor for the other two attached to her by tenuously tied vines. Fifer swung wildly at the end of hers and slammed into Seth. The last of the extra vines they'd brought along slid off the dragon and squirmed like worms in their infinite fall.

"Hux!" Thisbe screamed, hitching her elbow and holding on as tightly as she could, but she felt herself slipping. She dug into the dragon's wing and wrenched herself up. Her arms trembled.

Then the awkwardly tied vine knots, which tugged painfully hard at Thisbe's waist, began to slip.

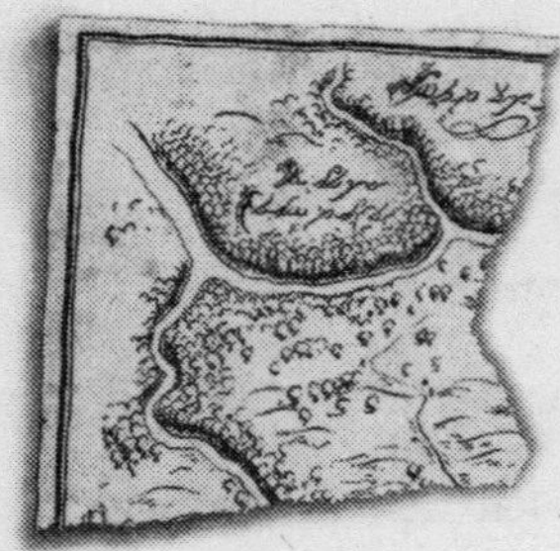

The Black Cliffs of Grimere

Still heaving for breath, but with all four sets of claws firmly gripping the cliff side, Hux swiveled his head around and looked down. He opened his mouth and swiftly bit down on the vines that hung below Thisbe's waist, careful not to sever them, and lifted up. With the weight of the other two off Thisbe, the girl shakily climbed up to a safer spot on Hux's wing as he pulled the vine higher. His tail, which had ceased propelling, swept up from below them all and coiled to make a platform. He brought it up beneath Fifer. Fifer continued flailing until her feet sensed the dragon's tail below her, and then she melted onto it, trembling but safe. For the moment at least.

Hux raised his coiled tail up, catching Seth on the way. Seth regained consciousness just as Thisbe scrambled up the dragon's shoulder. She went around his neck to the other side so that if she or the others fell, the vine would catch around Hux's neck.

Once they were all safe, they took a moment to catch their breath and tighten their vines, and then Thisbe fearfully looked upward. The vines had saved them from certain death. But the cliffs stretched to the sky. How were they going to get up there? It seemed impossible.

When Hux had rested for a moment and could speak, he instructed Fifer and Seth to climb to his wing and drape themselves over it as Thisbe now did on the other side. He needed his tail for the climb.

They obeyed—there was no other option. And in a most violent and jerking fashion, Hux loosened one clawed foot from the rock and found a new hold higher up. He did the same with each leg, using his tail for balance and to feel around for more footholds.

They made a bit of progress. The process was painstaking, and the dragon's body shook with concentration and strain. Every now and then Hux made a lasso with his tail and threw it up into the sky, trying to catch on to any sort of rock jutting out to help ease the climb.

Inch by inch, foothold by foothold, the ice-blue dragon and his passengers scaled the side of the black cliff, until finally they were close enough for Hux's tail to reach and encircle one of the smaller, narrower needlelike points. After a minute's rest, Hux called out to the children.

"Hold on now like never before," he said wearily. "I'll fold my wings around you to help keep you close to my body. This is not going to be easy."

The children did what Hux told them to do, and then the dragon tested his tail's grip around the needle to make sure the rock was secure and wouldn't break off. Next he began to wind his tail around the base of it. When it held fast, Hux scrabbled and jerked his way up the wall as fast as he could go, the kids flopping around and trying to hold on, screaming at every heart-stopping move. When they approached the top, Hux wound the slack of his tail around the needle, then let go and lunged to try to get a claw up and over the edge of the precipice. He slid back and his claws scraped along, not catching anything. They free-fell for an excruciating second until his tail caught, and they jerked to a stop upside down.

Thisbe shrieked and dug her fingernails into the dragon's skin. Hux grunted and pulled himself up by the tail the rest of the way, until finally he could heave his body up between the crags to level ground.

With a giant shuddering exhale of relief, Hux loosened his wings around the children. They flopped limply onto the land, their bones and muscles feeling like rubber. They had never been more glad to touch land than they were at this moment. At last, they were safe.

"I thought we were going to die," said Fifer, choking up now that the danger had passed. "The vines saved us." She let out a sob.

Thisbe could only nod in response, trying not to imagine the outcome if they hadn't been tied together—it was too overwhelming. She stared numbly at the sky and gripped the uneven ground. Her body wouldn't stop shaking. She closed her eyes and a tear slipped out.

"We almost didn't make it," said Seth. His voice shook, but the realization of how close they'd come to falling forever into the abyss filled him with horror and wonder. He thought of his mother and how sad she'd be. How she'd search for him and wouldn't be able to find him—not even a trace of him or a hint of what had taken place. "They would never know what happened to us," he whispered. His face crumpled and tears poured from his eyes.

Fifer swallowed hard. Her throat was horribly parched and ragged from screaming, but she was alive. She'd never been this close to death before. Even in the jungle, the girls always knew in the back of their minds that Simber had to be somewhere nearby, ready to get them out of a scrape. But there had been no safety net like that here. She let her head fall listlessly to one side, feeling the precious ground rolling beneath it, and she reached for Thisbe's hand and took it. She didn't want to think about all the bad things that could have happened anymore.

Once the three friends had a chance to rest, stop shaking, and regain control of their senses, they sat up and untied the now worn-out vines from their waists. Throwing the remains aside, they looked around. They were perched on a black, rocky precipice. Far above them was the majestic fortress. Less than a mile down the hill below was a lush, green glen with a village. "Where are we?" Fifer asked, turning to Hux.

Hux was slumped on the ground, completely spent. His eyes were half-closed. Perhaps it was his complete exhaustion that led him to finally disclose some information. "The black cliffs of Grimere," he said dully. "We're headed up there." He pointed his tail toward the highest, biggest cliff, where the fortress was planted just below a wispy cloud. The sand-colored stone structure was a stark contrast to the cliff on which it stood.

Thisbe spotted the river that ran near the castle and poured off the side of the cliff into the abyss, and was reminded of their severe lack of provisions. "Is there anything to drink around here?" She shivered, still wet from the journey. And though she had no appetite at the moment, she knew they'd be hungry soon.

Hux snorted fire. "In time." He closed his eyes, pained. The journey had taken a terrible toll on him.

"We should have given him the wings before we left," said Fifer in a low voice, looking guiltily at the others.

"We couldn't," said Thisbe. "Besides, we didn't know how hard it would be. He said he could do it."

"At least we made it," said Seth. "I was afraid we weren't going to."

"You were afraid all right, I'll give you that," muttered Thisbe.

Seth frowned. "Be quiet. You were cowering quite a lot yourself." He kicked a stone as Fifer looked at the other two, perplexed by their petty arguing. They were all exhausted from the ordeal.

Hux began to snore, making the three turn at once toward him.

"Oh great," said Thisbe. Now that she was on solid ground, her fear dissipated and she realized just how thirsty she was. She eyed the village and could barely make out movement in the very center of it. "Do you think it's safe to go down to that village? I want to find us something to eat and drink."

"Why wouldn't it be?" asked Fifer. "It looks like lots of other people are heading there. Let's all go."

"No," said Thisbe. "Somebody has to stay with Hux so he doesn't think we abandoned him."

"Well, I'm going with you," said Fifer. "Seth, you stay here."

"Okay." Seth didn't think he could walk quite yet anyway, and he certainly didn't mind having someone else do the scrounging around for food for him. He glanced at Hux, who had smoke drifting up from his nostrils. "Hurry up, though."

The twins set off down the hillside. There wasn't a path, so they picked their way over the moss and rocks and around the boulders as quickly as they could.

Seth watched them until they were out of sight, then got up and walked to the edge of the precipice, peering toward the seven islands. He could see a tiny glimpse of the big waterfall every so often when a bit of fog and mist cleared, but then it was hidden again. No wonder the people of Artimé hadn't been able to find this world. While it really wasn't all that far away, it was nearly impossible to see. This definitely explained the map with the extra piece of land on it that Lani had found years before, which was on display on one of the walls in the mansion outside her classroom. And now Seth and the twins were actually standing on that land. He couldn't wait to tell Lani that it really was here after all—they just had to fly over the waterfall to get to it.

Hux snorted in his sleep, making Seth jump. Quickly he backed away from the edge of the cliff and turned to look up toward the various castles on the mountainside. Only a few high points remained bare. From this angle and distance, he could see that the strange, stalagmite-like perches were a bit larger than they'd appeared from Hux's approach and weren't nearly as needlelike as he'd first thought—they were simply narrow at the east end that faced the world of the seven islands.

Seth focused on the biggest castle. The cloud that had hung above it earlier had moved on, and now Seth could see the fortress's majesty more clearly. It was enormous, with more than a dozen turrets of varying heights. The sand-colored stone seemed to sparkle in different places when the sun caught it, as if it had been coated in a light dusting of jewels.

Seth couldn't quite see the grounds around the castle. But he imagined it was the kind of place that would surely have a moat and a drawbridge and creatures called horses, like in the plays he was studying in theater class and the stories his mother had read to him when he was a little boy—and which he still loved to read now. That sent a chill of excitement down his spine. But then, thinking of his mother, he cringed. He'd been gone so long already. She was going to be furious by the time they got home. But at least he was alive, and she wasn't searching endlessly for him for the rest of her life—that would be a good selling point, he decided, when it came time to explain. The thought cheered him.

Seth directed his gaze to the various villages he could see around him. They were all quite similar, with a circular town center surrounded by pastel-colored houses with orange-tiled roofs. In the middle of each town was an open patch of land. People appeared to be traveling on foot between the villages. At the moment, most of the people were going toward one particular place—the village nearest him, where the girls had gone to get food and water.

Just then Seth heard a slow rumble in the distance. He looked up toward the castle, but the sound wasn't coming from there. Much farther inland, beyond a great forest, a trail of black smoke rose up to form a cloud, then began drifting away. Seth puzzled over it, wondering what it was. But he soon forgot it when the dragon stirred and nearly rolled over him. He scooted out of the way.

Once fully awake, Hux looked around and realized the girls were gone. "Where did they go?" he demanded.

Seth shrank back. "To the village to find something to eat and drink," he said. "They should be coming back soon."

Alarmed, the dragon heaved himself to his feet and stretched out his neck, trying to spot them. "They must return immediately!"

"But we're all really thirsty," Seth said. "Humans have to eat and drink pretty often, you know."

Hux swung his head down to look Seth in the eye, so close that Seth could feel the heat from his nostrils. The dragon snorted impatiently, spraying something hot and sticky onto Seth's neck. Seth scooted back, grimacing and flinging his arm up to wipe it away.

The dragon didn't seem to notice. "Better to be thirsty than for them to be seen out there in public. If anyone gets a good look at those girls, they'll be captured and sold to the highest bidder. You must go and get them."

Seth stared. He'd never heard anything so ridiculous in his life. "What are you talking about? They're coming right back." He peered down at his vest to make sure none of the hot dragon . . . *whatever* . . . had gotten on it.

Hux wasn't interested in discussing it. "NOW!" he roared.

Before the sound of the dragon's voice faded, Seth was on the run, heading down the mountain.

Glen Freer Market

Thisbe and Fifer peered over a boulder at the edge of the village and saw a sign a short distance away. "Glen Freer Market," read Fifer.

"Sounds friendly," said Thisbe. People scurried about through the narrow streets and alleyways. They went in and out of small, pretty houses, pushed carts down the road that ran along a short length of the cliff, and led young servants loaded with goods toward the center of the town square. Most of the servants wore plain, light-colored clothing and tall black boots, while the ones directing them were more colorfully dressed. The place seemed safe enough.

Stealthily the girls followed one overladen cart of fruits and vegetables, falling in step behind it and walking nonchalantly like the townspeople, trying not to stand out despite their different style of clothing. When the cart hit a bump in the road, a few pieces of fruit shook loose from a crate and fell to the road. The girls quickly picked them up and stuffed them inside their shirts, making their chests look suspiciously lumpier than usual, but no one really seemed to be paying attention. Or so they hoped.

They kept on after the cart, and soon they could hear the noises of the market. A little farther along, the narrow road opened up to a large square with vendors all around. Townspeople went from stall to stall, trading for goods or purchasing items using small gold rocks. Thisbe and Fifer, wide-eyed, took it all in.

"How do you know how many rocks to give?" whispered Fifer.

"No idea," said Fifer.

The servant pulling the cart came up to an empty stall and stopped. The girls slipped away and snuck down an alley, then ducked into a doorway to figure out what they were going to do. They nodded at some men who walked by and pretended to be casual. One of the men frowned at Thisbe and narrowed his eyes. But they continued walking.

Fifer's attention was focused elsewhere. "Do you hear that?" she whispered after the men passed.

Thisbe listened and heard the distinct sound of rushing water. Quickly the girls darted out and followed the noise to the end of the alley. There they reached a grassy bank and found a stream. A water mill stood in the middle of it, its moss-covered blades turning slowly, lifting the water up and around. The twins filled their canteens, taking plenty to drink, and then refilled them so they and Seth would have some once they returned.

"How are we going to get more food?" Fifer asked. "We don't have any of those gold rocks."

"We'll have to steal it." Thisbe twisted the cap tightly on her canteen and put it back in her rucksack. Then she fished the fruit out of her shirt and put that into her bag as well.

Fifer pulled her fruit out too, looked at it longingly, then placed it gently into the rucksack on top of Thisbe's.

Suddenly there was a scurry of footsteps behind them. Before either one of the girls could turn, they heard a man's voice.

"There they are," he said. "That one's been caught before!"

As Thisbe whirled around in surprise, she felt a strong, calloused hand reaching over her mouth, then a scratchy cloth placed over her nose that had a sickly sweet smell. She tried to scream.

"Ah, see?" the man said triumphantly to his friend, who had snatched Fifer. "Both of them! Now that makes for a lucky day!"

"I'll say," said the friend gleefully.

Thisbe didn't comprehend what the men were talking about. She reared back as hard as she could and tried kicking her captor, but try as she might, she couldn't connect. She twisted and struggled, but she was stuck fast. She gasped for breath, the horrible sweetness from the cloth permeating her nose and throat, and traveling into her brain. She felt a strange fuzziness creep in and take over her, making the market sounds seem distant and growing ever fainter. Her sight blurred. She fought to keep her senses, fought to shout or at least think of some magical spell she could say to stop them, but she couldn't speak. Her mouth couldn't even form a single word. With one last, limp struggle, everything went black and she slumped forward, unconscious.

The Most Magical Ones

When Thisbe opened her eyes, her cheek was pressed against the cold, stone ground. Drool dripped from the corner of her lips. She wrinkled her nose, coughed, and sat up, wiping her mouth on her sleeve. She remembered her rucksack and looked frantically for it, and found it nearby—nothing had been stolen.

Fifer was lying next to her. The last glimmers of another of Alex's seek spells faded in the air in front of her. It only made Thisbe feel more helpless. The memory of the capture and that sickly sweet smell made her feel ill. Nothing was what she'd expected—this adventure was not fun at all. In fact, it was terrible. She sniffed and held back her tears. She had to be strong and get them out of here . . . wherever they were.

The sounds of the marketplace grew clearer. Thisbe looked around, her head still feeling foggy. They were in a small, prisonlike cave, with three rough walls hewn from natural stone. The fourth wall, which locked them in, was made of bamboo bars going in a crosshatch pattern. Thisbe crawled forward and looked around. She could see out to the market square a short distance away. Occasionally someone walked by and peered in, curious. One tough-looking woman spat at Thisbe and muttered, "Tough luck, thief."

Thisbe recoiled, but when the woman continued walking, she scowled at her. "It was only a few pieces of fruit! Sheesh." She shook the bars, found them to be frustratingly secure, then crawled over to Fifer and touched her leg. "Fife. Hey. Wake up."

Fifer groaned and stirred. She opened her eyes and squinted at the stone ceiling. After a minute, she asked, "Where are we?"

"Not far from the marketplace, but we're stuck in here. We have to do something." She went back to the bars and glared at a man who looked inside. He hurried on. She gripped the bamboo with both hands, and with as much concentration as she could muster, whispered, "Release."

Nothing happened.

Fifer got to her feet and went over to where Thisbe stood at the bars. "Plug your ears," she said. "Lemme see what I can do."

Thisbe quickly put her hands over her ears, and Fifer, hoping to break the bars, emitted a high-pitched whoop that sounded musical, though it was awfully loud. From the marketplace they heard the sound of glass breaking, followed by a burst of angry voices. But the bars remained intact. A second later they could hear a fluttering noise.

"Crud, here come the birds." Thisbe quickly ran to the back of their little prison and ducked down in a corner. She covered her head with her arms as a swarm of birds flocked to Fifer, some of them coming inside the prison.

Fifer looked at them. "I wish you'd do something besides stand there," she muttered. They stared back. Finally Fifer shooed them all away. "They're gone," she called.

Thisbe got up and returned to Fifer's side. "I hate those things."

"I know. I wish they were more useful. What other spells do we know? Anything that can help us?" Fifer thought through the magical spells they could do. "The glass spell won't do us any good in here."

"Neither will invisible hooks." Thisbe quirked her finger anyway and pointed at the wall. A spark shot out and supposedly an invisible hook attached itself to the wall, though neither girl felt like going to feel around for it.

"You know," said Fifer, "those hooks might have come in handy on the side of the cliff."

"Hmm," said Thisbe. She wasn't used to thinking that way—most of the time she was trying *not* to do magic. But throwing out a few hooks might have actually been something good . . . if only she'd thought of it. Another missed opportunity. But then she frowned. "I doubt these little hooks would be strong enough to hold a dragon."

"Yeah, you're probably right. Plus, he wouldn't have been able to see them." Fifer thought some more. "What else can we do?"

"Well," said Thisbe with a little shudder, "I suppose I can try to kill someone if we get really desperate." She hated the thought of it but remembered how they'd been captured. Perhaps she should have used the boom spell then. But she was glad she hadn't, now that she knew she was alive . . . and just stuck.

"What about the shatter spell?" Fifer suggested.

"Lani said that only works on people, and she also warned me never to do it because it almost cost her Alex's friendship when they were doing *Perseus, Perseus*, their first play together."

"We're not trying to keep anyone's friendship."

"True, but I don't see how it helps."

Fifer scowled. "I'm trying it on the bars anyway."

"Fine. Go for it." Thisbe folded her arms and stepped back while Fifer held on to the center bars and closed her eyes. After a long moment of concentrating, she whispered, "Shatter."

Nothing happened.

Fifer opened her eyes, and her face fell.

Thisbe emitted a hollow laugh, trying to mask her growing fear that they might never escape. "For being the most magical people in Artimé, we sure can't do very much."

"Because nobody will teach us. It's not our fault. Maybe we aren't the most magical yet. But we will be. Everyone says so."

The two contemplated silently for a few minutes.

"Well," they said at the same time.

"You go ahead," said Fifer.

"I was going to say we could send Seth a seek spell."

"That's what I was going to say. I don't like it, though." Fifer scrunched up her face. Neither of them wanted to ask for Seth's help. But he might have components in his vest that could break down the barrier. "I suppose there's no other option," she said reluctantly. "No use being stupid about it. We're turning into stubborn Alex."

"Ugh," said Thisbe.

Fifer reached into her pocket and pulled out the folded page of the script Seth had given her. She closed her eyes and sighed, then tried to concentrate on it. But before Fifer could say the word "seek," Thisbe laid a hand on her arm. "Wait a second," she whispered. "Look. Out there to the left."

Fifer opened her eyes. Not far outside their prison, near one of the vegetable stands, was a boy about their age who was staring at them. Like many of the people they'd seen so far in the village, he had medium brown skin and wavy, shiny black hair. It was strange for the twins to see people who had similar features to their own. The boy wore a ragged, lightly patterned shirt that looked like it had once been beautiful, but now the sleeves were ripped off and the colors faded to a pale hue. His tan pants were tattered and barely reached below his knees. And unlike other servants, he was barefoot. When Fifer stared back, the boy narrowed his eyes and lifted his chin defiantly.

Thisbe frowned. "What's his problem?" she muttered to Fifer.

Soon a girl, taller but with similar features and similarly dressed, joined the boy and began to berate him for not following her. He pointed to Thisbe and Fifer and said something the twins couldn't hear. The girl and boy started angrily toward the prison.

Fifer and Thisbe shrank back. These two didn't seem like they were about to rescue them, that was clear enough. "What's happening?" whispered Fifer.

"I don't know."

The girl began to yell at Thisbe and Fifer in a different language, as if she expected them to understand her. She waved her hands wildly, pointed at the boy, then imitated an explosion.

Fifer gave Thisbe a side-eye glance. "I think that boy figured out we caused the glass stuff to break," she said from the corner of her mouth.

"Pretty sure you're right," said Thisbe. She put her face up against the bars. "I'll clean it all up if you let us out of here," she said to the girl.

The girl stopped speaking, frowned, and looked puzzled. "You speak the language of the dragons and our people," she said, and now the twins could understand her clearly, though she had an accent that sounded uncommon to them. "Where do you come from?"

Thisbe and Fifer didn't dare respond. The girl drew closer, peering into the shadow of the prison. She tugged at the boy, pulling him along and pointing at Thisbe's hair, then uttered something in her original language that made him stare. Slowly his lips parted, and his eyes grew wide. "Thief," he whispered.

"Look closer," said the girl.

The boy obeyed, but the twins stepped uncertainly into the shadows again. "What are you looking at?" asked Thisbe, growing annoyed. "If you're not going to let us out, then go away."

The two onlookers didn't respond. They peered into the shadowy prison at Fifer, and the girl pointed at her, saying something rapidly to the boy. An unsettled look crossed his face. Slowly they backed away from the cage. And then they ran.

"That was really weird," said Thisbe. She returned to the bars to watch them go. "They're obviously not going to help us. Are you ready to try the seek spell?"

Fifer came back to Thisbe's side, craning her neck to see where the boy and girl went, but they had moved out of sight. She still gripped Seth's scene page in her hand. "I suppose." She sighed. "Okay, well, here we go." She closed her eyes and let out a breath, trying to concentrate.

"Wait," Thisbe said again.

Fifer opened her eyes. "Now what?"

"I just remembered there's one spell we haven't tried. And now might be a good time to practice it."

"There is?" Fifer thought for a moment. "What is it?" she asked, and then, "Oooh." She eyed the prison bars, then glanced at her twin. "Do you think it'll work on *that*?"

Thisbe shrugged. "Why wouldn't it? We might as well try."

“I wasn’t paying enough attention,” said Fifer, stepping back a little fearfully. “You do it.”

“Gladly.” Thisbe’s black eyes sparked with hope. If she could pull it off, this would be the biggest spell she’d done so far that didn’t happen by accident . . . and it could get them out of here.

She shook out her wrists, then rubbed her palms together. Then she moved to the center of the bars and placed her hands in the very middle. She closed her eyes and cleared her mind, remembering how Alex had taken his time with it. She focused on what she wanted to happen, since she wasn’t quite sure what else she should be thinking about. She let herself relax completely, and then, when she was good and ready, she whispered the magic verbal component. “Live.”

More Than She'd Bargained For

The bamboo bars began to move. They pulsed so gently at first that Thisbe wasn't quite sure it was happening. She opened her eyes but didn't let go. "I think it's working," she said.

"I'm not sure how it'll help us," said Fifer, cautious but skeptical. "But good job," she added. "First try. That's pretty great."

"I just did what Alex did. Maybe if these bars get enough movement, they'll crack, and we'll be able to break them open wide enough for us to squeeze out." Thisbe released her hands as the bars began moving more. "Come on," she pleaded to them. "Really live. Live like you mean it!" She backed away, and their prison door began to sway in and out, straining at the edges where it was attached to the stone cave.

"Whoa," said Fifer. "I think it heard you."

"Just be ready. If it pops out, we're going to have to run for it." Thisbe didn't take her eyes off the bars. The bamboo grid began to billow, and suddenly the top right corner of it worked its way out of the stone. It waved this way and that, and with a series of little pops, the grid came loose one bar at a time along the top and several rows down the right side of their prison.

The girls took a few more steps back, and Fifer's eyes grew concerned. "This thing is a lot more active than Alex's wings were," she said. "What did you do to it?"

"I don't know."

"I think you turned it into a monster." They inched backward until they were up against the back wall. As the bars popped loose and the freed section became larger, the grid began to fan wildly. Soon the bottom right corner popped out. The bars began twisting and curling, trying to loosen the rest of it, almost as if it were alive. It made broad swipes inside the prison, forcing the girls into the corner farthest from the opening.

"We have to get around it," said Thisbe, a bit breathless.

People in the market noticed what was happening. A wave of panic spread through the area.

"I think we might be in trouble," said Fifer. The bamboo grate flailed dangerously close, and the girls flattened themselves against the rock.

Another corner broke loose. "Now!" shouted Thisbe, grabbing her rucksack and shoving her sister forward. The bars curled out, and the girls made a break for the opening. Fifer managed to get out safely, but the bars twisted and came back before Thisbe could escape. They caught her and knocked her flat. "Ouch!" she cried, and scrambled along the prison floor. "Help!" She dove for the opening. Fifer grabbed her sister's hand and yanked her out of the way.

Thisbe got to her feet, and the two girls ran into the alley, then stopped short to look back. Finally the bars broke loose from the last corner. The people in the marketplace ran away screaming, and the grid, filled with exuberant magical life, wiggled and tumbled and chased after them. The girls looked around desperately, trying to get their bearings, and searched for the way out of the maze of alleyways so they could get back to the mountain. The grid circled around and began pursuing the twins.

"Oh no—it's following us!" said Fifer.

"Run uphill!" shouted Thisbe. The girls finally found their way out of town. They kept going, starting up the mountainside, and didn't stop until they were a quarter of the way back to the dragon. They rested for a moment to catch their breath, looking back over the village, and realized the grid hadn't followed them very far, for now it was terrorizing the marketplace. Carts and tables were overturned, and produce was spilled everywhere, getting trampled by the stampede of people trying to escape the strange, living wooden structure.

"I guess I didn't quite know what I was doing there after all," Thisbe admitted.

"At least we're safe."

"That's for sure."

"I hope it doesn't hurt anyone."

"Me too. I feel bad about the mess." Thisbe cringed. She didn't think this was the kind of magic Alex had in mind for her and Fifer either. Was it even possible for her to get it right?

They watched a moment longer, and then Fifer gasped and pointed. There, in the center of the chaos, grabbing armloads of food, was a figure with a very familiar gait. He was moving almost without being able to see overtop his stash of goods, yet he continued to scoop up everything he could. Fifer leaned forward and squinted. "Is that—? Yes! It's Seth!"

"Oh no," said Thisbe, catching sight of him. "What's he doing? He needs to pay attention and get out of there. He's running straight toward the grid!"

Unable to help, the two watched in horror as Seth realized his error a second too late. He sidestepped and slipped on some trampled fruit. His armload of stolen goods went flying, and he flopped down in front of the pursuing prison door. A moment later one corner of the bars hooked Seth by his shirt and took him on a ride into the air. Then it slammed him into the ground and dragged him around again in the same manner as it rolled through the square.

"Seth!" the girls cried out, forgetting all about needing to escape. They knew they had to do something. There was no way Seth could survive that kind of ride for long. Without another word, both girls ran back down the mountain toward the village to rescue their friend.

Saving Seth

"How do we turn it off?" Fifer shrieked as she and Thisbe ran toward Seth. "Can *you* just do a release spell?"

"Alex sang that ridiculous song—remember?"

"Do you know the words?" asked Fifer. Their voices jiggled as they ran.

"I didn't pay very close attention to that part," Thisbe lamented. "I figured we wouldn't ever have to shut down the dragon wings once we had them going."

"Same here," said Fifer. They lost sight of Seth and the

grid monster they'd created, but the cloud of dust rising up over the square told them where they were.

The townspeople had scattered by now, abandoning their booths and their precious goods—and Seth—to spare their lives. When the twins rounded the corner that led to the square, they saw Seth flipping around upside down, his legs kicking wildly as he rummaged in his component vest pockets for a spell that would free him or stop the grid. "Release!" he cried over and over as he searched, but the prison bars kept moving. Components fell out of Seth's pockets and littered the square every time he went upside down.

"Come on!" Fifer ran nimbly over the cobbled ground, careful to avoid the mashed produce so she didn't end up on her back like Seth had.

Thisbe followed in her sister's footsteps. "What are we going to do? Can't you call the birds in?"

"What good would that do? They'll just fly around and do nothing and leave again. They might even swoop in at Seth—who knows? I wish I could do more than just call them. Maybe if you had made a giant birdseed monster come alive, they could do something about it."

Thisbe thought about her glass spell but couldn't see how that would help matters. She didn't want Seth slamming into a glass wall, that was for sure. And she didn't think her death spell would help in this situation either, even if she dared try it. That one only worked when she was piping mad. Right now she was scared. And even if she could manage to do it, she didn't think it would kill a piece of bamboo. Besides, she didn't want to accidentally hit Seth with it.

Most everything else magical she and Fifer had done had happened randomly and often unexpectedly, and they'd rarely been able to re-create those spells unless they had a good idea of how to do it. Alex had been especially careful to caution the people of Artimé not to let the girls see them do any noncomponent magic, because they'd be sure to imitate it, which is how Thisbe had learned the glass spell.

"He-e-elp!" said Seth. The word came out in gasps as he seemed to spot the girls.

Thinking maybe she was the only one who could release the spell since she'd been the one to cast it, Thisbe ran ahead and shouted with great authority, "Release!" She even managed to touch a piece of the prison bars before it moved out of reach, hoping that might help. But the structure kept going as if nothing had happened.

"Just hang on, Seth!" cried Fifer.

"Sing the song, Fife!" urged Thisbe.

"I told you I don't know it!" Fifer yelled back. "Why don't you sing it?"

"Singing is in *your* studies, not mine!" Thisbe said. "That means you're supposed to pay attention to those parts."

"Now you're just making up rules!" said Fifer, but she felt guilty for not writing down the song Alex sang to get the wings to stop moving. Thisbe was right. Singing was her thing. And even if they'd never officially talked about which of them would be best to learn the different varieties of magic spells, it seemed logical that Fifer would handle the singing ones.

"Stop arguing and do-o-o-o something! Please!" Seth called out again.

"We'll just have to grab him when he comes around again and pull him off," said Thisbe.

The twins eyed the moving structure, trying to predict

where it would go next. When it came charging toward them, they flinched identically but held their ground. "Reach out your hands, Seth!" Fifer called.

Seth did it—or at least he tried—but he was awfully dizzy. When the rolling structure of sticks drew near, the girls grabbed Seth's hands and leaped out of the way, pulling him with them. He hit the ground with a sickening thump, his face slamming onto the pavement. Luckily some squashed tomatoes kept him from hitting it too hard.

Fifer and Thisbe took a fresh grip on his hands and pulled him along over the smashed produce, slipping and sliding, as the giant tumbleweed headed off in a different direction. When they were a safe distance away, they let go of Seth's hands. Thisbe glanced around warily, making sure the men from earlier hadn't spotted them.

Seth sat up, disoriented, and together all three watched as the prison grate roamed down an alley, heading straight for the cliff. Soon it threw itself over the edge and was gone.

The children breathed a sigh of relief and looked around the square. It seemed like a hurricane had come through it. Thisbe caught sight of a couple of villagers hiding behind a flipped table. She narrowed her gaze as she realized it was the boy and girl from earlier. She caught the boy's darting glance and held it, but he made no move to do anything. He only eyed her fearfully. After a minute or two, when Seth decided it was time to try standing up again, Thisbe forgot about the strangers.

Seth was covered in slime. Part of a smashed tomato clung to his cheek as he got up; then it slid off and hit the ground with a splat. "Well, I have to say *that* was terrifying." He wiped his cheek on his sleeve and checked his front teeth to make sure they were still in place. His body ached. "How exactly did all of this happen?" He examined his component vest, and his face fell. It was covered in sticky goop.

"Tell you on the way," Thisbe said, growing cautious again now that the grid was gone. "Let's get out of here before the creeps who captured us come back. Are you okay?"

"Good enough to walk," said Seth, trying not to cringe at every step.

The three of them set off the way they'd come, through the backstreets and up over the rocks, forging a path to the dragon. They moved slowly to accommodate Seth's turned ankle and various unnamed injuries. As they went, Thisbe kept watch over her shoulder while Fifer told Seth the story of their frightening capture and imprisonment, and the magical experiment that ensued and went horribly wrong.

"Hux was pretty mad when he found out where you'd gone," Seth said. "He told me you were in grave danger, but I didn't really believe him. I'm sorry."

"Clearly he was right," muttered Thisbe. "We know that now. But did he say why?"

"No. He just told me to get you."

Thisbe flashed him a judgmental look. "So once you got to the village to rescue us from grave danger, you decided to steal food instead."

"Hey," said Seth defensively. "I haven't eaten since yesterday and I was starving. I was going to find you. Besides, the place was chaotic." His gaze landed on her bulging rucksack. "You don't happen to have any water in there, do you?"

"Yeah." Thisbe pulled out one of the filled canteens. "Here."

Seth stopped to take a drink. Fifer put her hand up to shade her eyes and looked toward the cliff where they'd landed. "We should be getting close. Do you see Hux anywhere?"

"Maybe he's hiding," said Seth, capping the canteen and handing it back to Thisbe. "He seemed afraid to go down to the village. Which is really weird, since this is supposed to be the land of the dragons and all."

"Hiding?" asked Thisbe. "Where's a dragon supposed to hide on a mountainside? And why would he be afraid of anything?" She put the canteen away and they set off again.

They continued hiking up the mountain, growing more and more unsure of where exactly they'd landed with Hux. The ice-blue dragon was nowhere to be seen. They trekked for hours, combing the area, looking around giant boulders and quietly calling out Hux's name.

When night began to fall, they grew frantic, but they knew they'd traveled more than far enough to find him. Where was he? They didn't want to believe the truth—Hux was gone.

To the Rescue

While Fifer, Thisbe, and Seth were wandering aimlessly around the black cliffs of Grimere, Simber was only just coming upon Warbler Island. He spotted a familiar white boat skimming the waves offshore. "Therrre's Sky," he told Carina and Thatcher. "I'll drrrop down to let herrr know what's happened."

Sky noticed them soon enough, and she slowed the boat a little to match Simber's speed. "Where are you off to?" she shouted, and put her hand above her eyes to shield the sunlight. Sky's auburn hair was streaked with natural highlights, and it flew wildly in the wind. Her light brown skin was darker than usual and peppered with freckles from spending so much time on the water between Warbler and the Island of Fire.

Carina explained everything to her.

Sky listened with alarm. "Do you need me to go back to Artimé?" she asked, her brow furrowing. "Or come with you? Is Alex okay? I'll bet he's panicking."

"He's a little upset," Carina said. "But he's all right. I think you can stay here and keep working with your mother. It'll probably do Alex good to stew about it alone for a bit. And Aaron's not far away by tube if he needs help."

"Is everything else all right? How is Kaylee? And the baby?"

"Kaylee and the baby are doing wonderfully," said Carina. "Everything else is exactly the same as when you left. Artimé and Quill are sleepy as always." She paused. "How is your project?"

Sky glanced in the direction of the Island of Fire, which wasn't visible at the moment. "It's going well. Scarlet has been a big help," said Sky. "We've turned the old broken underwater glass cage into a feeding station for sea life, and we've completely redone the gardens inside the reverse aquarium to resemble Ishibashi's greenhouse. And," Sky said, a gleam in her eye, "I'm *so close* to figuring out how to stop the island from plunging underwater. I can feel it." She took on a faraway look. It had been her mission for years to figure out the mysterious scientific workings of the volcanic pirate island. "I almost got pulled under the other day, though. I thought life was over for me."

"Didn't you feel the island trembling?" asked Thatcher, who had never been on or inside the underwater island, but who'd heard plenty about it.

"Barely," admitted Sky. "That's part of the problem. As I've been working on changing the climate inside the volcano, the tremors have lessened, and they don't offer as much warning as they used to. I was so wrapped up in my work—thought I had more time. Thankfully Scarlet was in the boat and saw the water rippling. She scooped me up at the last second and got us out of there." Sky patted the control panel. "If this thing wasn't magic, I don't think we would've been able to get away from the suction."

Carina looked alarmed. "Be careful, please," she murmured. "We need you."

"I will, believe me," said Sky. "Don't mention that to Alex, all right? He's always so . . . so worried. You know? I don't want to give him anything else to fret over when his sisters and Seth are missing."

"Speaking of them," said Simber, "we rrreally should continue."

"Right," said Thatcher. "Let's keep moving. We've got a long flight. Nice seeing you, Sky. Say hi to Scarlet for me."

"I will."

"And . . . for Crow," Thatcher added with a half smile.

Sky grinned. "You got it." She turned back to Simber. "Stop by and let me know once you've found them, will you? If you think of it, I mean."

"Of courrrse we will," Simber promised.

Soon the trio was on their way again, with the long night stretching out before them. They were only a third of the way to the waterfall that marked the western edge of their world . . . and there was no telling how much farther they'd have to go beyond it to find the land of the dragons.

Lost and Alone

While Thatcher and Carina were gearing up for their second night balancing on the back of a stone cheetah, Fifer, Thisbe, and Seth found themselves alone in a foreign world with no way to get home, or even make contact with home. And after their experiences earlier in the day, they were feeling more than a little jumpy.

They hadn't thought to bring any seek spell items from Alex or the others in Artimé—Fifer only carried a single created item from Seth with her, which did them no good now that he was sitting right next to them. Yet every few hours

Alex sent seek spells to the girls from Artimé. Being unable to respond was just one more thing that made them feel helpless, and they were quickly veering toward hopelessness, too. The reality of their predicament hit them like a door slamming in their faces—first came stunned silence, then painful realization, then a terrible sense of dread.

"No one knows where we are," said Fifer. "No one. We're going to die out here, and they'll never find us." Her lip began to quiver, and a tear escaped one eye. She batted at it fiercely but didn't trust her voice to say more.

Thisbe hated to see her sister so upset. Even though she felt the same way, she tried to hold her worries inside. "It's going to be okay," she said grimly, though she couldn't imagine how. Using the last bit of daylight, she scoured the mountainside, hoping to catch a glimpse of the ice-blue dragon. Surely he was too big to disappear completely, but it seemed he had done just that. He wasn't anywhere—not up the mountain toward the castle, not in the valleys in between or by the forest farther inland, not down the mountain toward the little village of Glen Freer, which was now in shambles.

"Hux said our plan was to get to that castle," Seth said.

"Maybe he went ahead . . . without us? That hardly seems smart, though."

"What if he was captured?" asked Fifer, sniffling. "What are we going to do?"

Thisbe paused her search, thinking aloud. "Well, the other dragons are probably hanging around that castle, right? I mean, that's why Hux brought us here, to fix their wings, so if the castle is where he said we need to go, Arabis and the others would be there."

"I suppose," said Fifer, and Seth nodded.

"Then all we have to do is find one of the dragons and make new wings, and have him take us home. It doesn't have to be Hux."

Seth and Fifer looked at Thisbe as they ran the proposed solution through their minds. Fifer wanted to believe it would be that simple. "I guess that would work," she said, though her tone was doubtful. Ever since she and Thisbe had been abducted, frightening what-ifs had filtered into Fifer's thoughts. Fears she'd never even imagined before were suddenly piling up, poking at her to notice them.

This experience had been nothing like she'd expected—it wasn't glamorous at all, like the stories Lani and Alex and the others had told. It was awful. The twins and Seth couldn't trust anyone here. They were wandering around aimlessly without a place to sleep, without decent food or enough water. And Hux had abandoned them.

Fifer began to wonder if Alex had been right about this trip being too risky. It certainly felt that way now. And she couldn't stop worrying about getting back home again.

She sat up, unable to keep her worries inside. "But, Thisbe, the dragons are slaves. Do you still believe the Revinir will let one of them take us home after we're done making new wings? Or is he going to maybe . . . I don't know . . . take us as slaves too? Like those men in Glen Freer tried to do?"

Thisbe's expression darkened. "Well," she reasoned, "the Revinir sent for somebody to fix the wings. So he needs us. He's not going to do anything to hurt us." *At least . . . not right away*, she thought.

For once, Seth was less worried than the twins about something. "Seriously—what would the Revinir want with a bunch of kids? We're not anything special."

Thisbe tried not to feel insulted. "Well, whatever. It doesn't matter anyway. We don't have any other options, do we? We can't sit on this mountain forever. The dragons are our only way home."

The knot in Fifer's stomach tightened a bit. But she swallowed hard and tried to sound upbeat. "So we should just go up there and . . . find them?"

"Exactly," said Thisbe with more confidence than she felt.

"It looks awfully steep," said Seth, who preferred flying to climbing, especially after the bamboo-grid incident had left him limping. The moon, rising behind the castle, made it glow in the night sky. The high ground was far off with a few valleys in between, and the climb would be steeply uphill a good portion of the way. "It's going to take us forever to get there."

Thisbe frowned. "I guess I'll go get us some more food, then." She rummaged through the rucksack and took out what they'd stolen so far, stacking it on a flat rock. Then she pulled out the canteens and handed them around. "Let's eat and drink what's left. I'll get more."

"You're not going alone," said Fifer. "And we shouldn't leave anybody alone on this mountain, either. We need to stick together from now on."

Thisbe agreed. The three wearily went back down the mountainside again. In the dark, the town square was sparsely lit by torches around the perimeter, and the streets around it were unevenly illuminated by lights coming from house windows. Most of the townspeople had cleaned up their stalls by now, and the carts and tables were gone. But on the outskirts of the square in the dirt and bushes, the children found a few pieces of produce and some crushed loaves of bread. They snatched them up.

Once they had picked up everything edible, stuffing the rucksack as well as all of their pockets, Seth remembered his lost magical components. He ran back into the square where he'd been turned upside down by the prison grate and got down on his hands and knees, feeling all around, trying to find some of the components he'd lost. He managed to locate a bundle of scatterclips and a blinding highlighter, which could also serve as a light if they needed it, and a few preserve spells, which seemed completely useless at the moment, as he had nothing of value that needed preserving. He kept them anyway.

When Fifer heard a rustling sound down an alleyway

near her, she fled toward the others and whispered harshly, "Someone's coming. Let's go!"

Seth abandoned his search and shoved what he'd found into his vest pockets, and then the three of them snuck away to the river to fill the canteens again. As Fifer bent down to fill hers, they heard a crackling noise somewhere in the darkness.

"We should hurry," murmured Thisbe, looking around wildly, fearful that the men from earlier might come back. They hadn't seen anyone outside—and now many more of the house windows and apartments above the shuttered shops were lit up. Shadows passed in front of them as people went about their evening rituals. Smells of dinner cooking wafted out and made the children's stomachs growl, which in turn made them even more homesick.

They drank their fill from the river, capped the canteens, and tried to clean Seth's sticky clothes and hair the best they could. Then they headed back up the mountain, glancing over their shoulders now and then as they went. It was slow going without much light to help them find their way—they counted on the moon to guide their journey and keep them from stepping too close to the edge of the cliff. A faint boom echoed from far away, like the one Seth had heard earlier, and an angsty animal's howl broke their concentration. The children tried not to think about what sort of strange animals or creatures they might encounter without warning.

After a time, the sky grew cloudy and the moon became veiled, making it even harder for the children to see. Seth, who was leading at the moment, tripped over a rock and went sprawling, coming to rest in an open area. He muttered under his breath and sat up, rubbing his sore ankle.

"Why don't you use your highlighter?" urged Fifer.

"I don't want to waste it. Let's just camp here," he said crossly. "I'm tired and hungry."

"Good idea," said Fifer.

Thisbe wrinkled up her nose at the other two, knowing they couldn't see her doing so, and said nothing. She wanted to keep going. Their limited water wouldn't last them long, and they had no idea where or when they'd find more. But she was tired too, so she didn't argue.

There wasn't much they could do to make a camp, since they had no gear, so they just sat down on the smoothest ground they could find. Once they settled and had a little something to eat and drink, they began wishing for blankets, but those weren't to be had. At least their clothes were dry, though they were a bit stiff and scratchy from all the seawater they'd soaked up. One by one, huddled together, Fifer, Seth, and Thisbe dropped off to sleep.

They had no idea anyone was watching them.

The Other Children

When Thisbe opened her eyes at dawn and remembered where she was and why she was lying on the ground, she immediately reached for her rucksack. It felt strangely lighter. She sat up and opened it, then gasped. The canteens were there, but the food was gone.

She looked at Seth, wondering if he was to blame, but she didn't think he would have eaten all the food and left none for the girls—he wasn't a horrible person. Besides, he was lying in almost exactly the same position he'd been in when they went to sleep last night.

It couldn't have been Fifer. She was fond of food, no doubt, but she'd never do something like that. Thisbe scanned the mountainside, wondering if one of those strange animals they'd heard howling was responsible. But how could an animal open the rucksack without destroying it?

And then she spotted him. Sitting on a small boulder several yards away was the boy from the market. He was eating a piece of fruit—*their* fruit—and he cradled several more pieces in a sling made from his ragged shirttails.

"Hey!" Thisbe shouted, scrambling to her feet and stumbling over the uneven ground toward him. "Fifer, Seth, wake up! Let's get him!"

The boy whirled around and instinctively threw the core at her, hitting her in the shoulder. His eyes widened, almost like he couldn't believe he'd done it. Then he took off running.

"Stop!" yelled Thisbe again as Fifer and Seth roused to see what was happening. "Give us back our food, you thief!" She ran after him.

The boy stopped and turned. "No, *you* are the thief," he challenged, with an accent similar to the girl he'd been with the previous day. He started coming toward her, glaring, his face iron hard in the morning light.

Thisbe began to protest, but she had to admit the boy was right. They'd stolen the food—even if it had been trampled and would never sell. "We're both thieves, then," she said amicably. Fifer and Seth caught up to her and stopped.

The boy stared at Thisbe, surprised by her candor. The corner of his mouth tugged upward, but he forced the iron gaze back on his face and looked at the three who watched him. Then he frowned and tossed a loaf of smashed bread at Thisbe, who caught it. The boy turned and slipped lithely between the rocks, heading up the mountainside.

"Wait," said Thisbe. She shoved the bread at Fifer and ran after the boy. "Where are you going? What's your name?"

He kept walking, though he slowed a little. "Doesn't matter."

Thisbe caught up to him. "I'm Thisbe."

The boy stared straight ahead. "Dev."

"Why doesn't it matter? Your name? I think everyone's name matters."

At this, Dev sighed and picked up his pace. "I have to go.

You'd better stay hidden, magical thief Thisbe, or you'll go right back to that jail. They'll be looking hard for you today. And you're not difficult to spot, if you know what I mean."

Thisbe frowned. "I don't have a clue what you mean."

"You're not from here." Dev said it matter-of-factly. He started jogging.

Thisbe ran after him. "Wait, please. I need to know if there's more water up the mountain. We have to get to that castle."

"You don't want to go up there." Dev stopped short, and Thisbe bumped into him.

"Sorry," she muttered. She looked up at him, expecting him to say sorry too, but instead his face froze as he saw her up close and in the sunlight for the first time.

His lips parted, and he emitted a soft gasp. "Oh," he said. "Shanti *was* right."

"Oh, what?" Thisbe demanded. And then she noticed his eyes. They were black like hers.

Friend or Foe

Dev's demeanor changed. "How did you escape?" he asked softly. "Are the others . . . like you?"

Thisbe tilted her head in wonder, too consumed with her own thoughts to answer him. "You have black eyes," she said. "I've never seen anybody with black eyes before, except Fifer. Well, my mom had them, but she's dead, and besides, I don't remember her."

"Not many people have them." Dev dropped his gaze, confused. "But . . . I don't understand." He glanced at Fifer and Seth, who were coming toward them. "Who's Fifer?"

"My twin," said Thisbe, shrugging a shoulder toward her. "That girl there."

"Is the other one your master?"

Thisbe snorted. "Seth? Of course not. Why would he be?"

Dev took a step back, keeping a wary distance between himself and the strangers as Fifer and Seth approached. He studied the newcomers, and then looked back at Thisbe, his face still a puzzle. "Who cut your hair? Someone in Grimere?"

"What a strange question. Why does that matter?" Thisbe's hand flew to her short wavy locks, which were sticking up a bit wildly from the night's sleep on the ground. She smoothed them down, though normally she quite liked them to be a crazy mess. They sprang back as soon as she let go.

"I cut it," said Fifer defensively. "And I think it looks very nice."

Dev studied the twins, and slowly the confusion left him. "I see," he said quietly. "You're identical."

"Obviously," said Fifer. "Except for the hair." They stood in awkward silence for a moment.

"So is there water up the mountain or not?" prompted Thisbe. "It's not a difficult question. You seem like a smart person."

"Of course there's water," Dev shot back. "How else would the villages up there survive? Don't you have any common sense? The river snakes around that way," he said, pointing away from the cliff toward the edge of the forest, then up the mountain. Slowly he brought his hand back down to his side, then narrowed his eyes and tapped his lips thoughtfully. After a moment he turned back to Thisbe, though he didn't quite look her in the eye. He shifted, then said, "I can guide you to the castle if you want."

Fifer and Seth nodded profusely. "Yes, please," said Fifer. "That would be great."

But Thisbe raised an eyebrow. "I thought you said we don't want to go there."

"Alone, I meant," Dev muttered. "Without a guide. Like me."

Thisbe dipped her head, but the boy refused to look squarely at her. "I'm not so sure that's a good idea," she said.

Fifer sighed. "We need help, Thiz."

"No we don't. We're fine. All we have to do is walk. We can't miss it." Thisbe turned toward the castle. "Come on."

"But what about our food?" asked Seth. "He's still got it."

"Forget the food." Thisbe started up the mountain. "We'll

make do with the bread." Reluctantly, Fifer and Seth followed her. Seth gave Fifer a silent, miserable glance. She patted his arm.

"Wait," Dev called after them. "It's dangerous up there." He ran nimbly past Seth and Fifer and caught up to Thisbe. "I . . . I insist on guiding you. You don't have to pay me. I've got to go that way anyway. Shanti is expecting me."

Thisbe stopped and turned. "Is she the girl you were with yesterday?"

"Yes."

Thisbe wasn't sure why she was feeling uneasy. She looked up at the castle in the far-off distance. It didn't seem quite as simple to get to as it had at first glance. There was no path, and the rocks seemed impassable in many places, with cliffs and steep climbs everywhere. She forced back her trepidation and studied the boy. This time Dev caught her gaze and held it. There was something about him that drew Thisbe in, despite her suspicion. Perhaps it was his black eyes that made her trust him.

And the truth was they needed him. Badly. "All right," said Thisbe finally. She smiled.

Dev didn't smile back. He turned his face away and didn't waste any more time. He started up the mountain past her. "Come on, then," he said gruffly, "before I change my mind."

Thisbe shook her head, more puzzled than ever. "Change your mind? You've already done that. First you wanted nothing to do with us but to steal our food, then you ran away, and then suddenly you wanted to lead us to the castle. And now you're threatening to change your mind? Well, go ahead and do it, then. Like I said, we don't need you." They tromped farther. Thisbe went on. "I suppose next you'll disappear and leave us stranded somewhere. And that would be completely fine. But I guess we'll let you walk with us for now. Though you're being awfully sneaky."

The barefooted boy snorted but didn't respond. If he was surprised that Thisbe was so perceptive, he didn't let on. And Thisbe's uneasy feeling pushed its way back to the forefront of her mind.

It was frustrating. There was something totally intriguing about Dev, more than just his black eyes and the fact that he knew the way to the castle, that kept Thisbe at his heels. Her mind brimmed with questions. "Why did you call me a thief yesterday when we were in that prison? And why did you ask who cut my hair?"

Dev plowed ahead. "Where are you from?"

"Artimé. Answer my questions."

"Artimé? Where's that?"

"Over there," Thisbe said, pointing her thumb east toward the mist on the other side of the bottomless cavern.

Dev gave her a scrutinizing glance. "You mean the Seven Islands? Are you serious?"

"Yes, of course I am. Now *answer me*." Thisbe kicked a stone angrily. It hit Dev's leg by accident.

"Ow!" said Dev. "All right, all right. If a thief gets caught in one of the villages of Grimere, the townspeople cut his hair short as part of the punishment. That makes thieves easy to spot so the villagers can beware in the marketplace."

"Oh. Well, that's not why mine is short." Thisbe hesitated, unsure what to think about that strange practice, and realized that must've been why all the men and women she'd seen there wore their hair to their shoulders or longer. "Who is Shanti?"

Dev hesitated. "She's my . . . friend." He darted up a steep part of the mountainside and around a boulder, then stopped and waited so the others could catch up. "If you're from the Seven Islands, how did you get here?"

Thisbe opened her mouth to answer, but then her suspicions kicked in again. If the dragons were in trouble here in their own land of Grimere, did she want to mention them? She closed her lips and thought it through. Perhaps if she told him, he might know where Hux had gone. "We flew," she said cautiously. "Somebody gave us a ride. How big is Grimere?"

Dev narrowed his eyes at her. "It's all the land you see. Why?"

Thisbe didn't bother to answer as Seth, panting, reached them. Dramatically he flopped over a waist-high rock and lay there, sweaty face pressed against it, gasping for breath.

Fifer joined Thisbe and Dev. "How long will it take us to get there?"

"Depends," said Dev, eyeing Seth. "A couple days if this keeps up."

"It's very steep," panted Seth. "And don't forget I twisted my ankle."

Thisbe had forgotten all about that. "I'm sorry, Seth. We can slow down if you need us to."

"Where's Hux, anyway?" Fifer lamented. "He could get us there in an hour."

Thisbe gave her a sharp look as Dev raised an eyebrow.

"Hux?" he asked, an odd expression on his face.

"Never mind," said Thisbe. "Let's keep going."

Dev led them higher and higher through the day. The landscape grew more desertlike, but lush valleys could be seen not far away. Nobody spoke much. They wanted to conserve their energy and water. Every now and then Dev called out "Watch your step here!" or "Be on the lookout for . . ." Whether it was sidewinders, tarantulas, or poisonous centipedes didn't really matter to the Artiméans. They'd never seen any of those creatures before, and they were extremely wary of anything that moved.

Finally, in the heat of the day, they reached a spot where a river curved toward them and they could stop to rest under a scraggly tree. Dev crouched a distance away from the others and, once he drank from the river, pulled the pieces of fruit he'd taken from Thisbe's rucksack and laid them gently in his lap. He began eating the first one without a word.

"That is so rude," exclaimed Fifer, wiping the sweat from

her face and leaving a dirty streak in its place. Seth was too exhausted and thirsty to register Dev's actions.

Thisbe glared at Dev, not bothering to hide her contempt. She thought about attacking him to get their food back, but instead she divided up the remains of the stale, crushed bread and passed the pieces to Fifer and Seth, careful not to spill any crumbs on the ground. They probably wouldn't have found this bend in the river without Dev. Thisbe supposed he deserved some food since they weren't paying him for guiding them. The three Artiméans ate and drank in silence as they rested under the tree, all of them continuing to wonder where Hux could have gone, and why he'd leave them.

After a time, Fifer looked up. "Remember that story that Alex and Sky tell sometimes about how they left the Island of Shipwrecks in the hurricane?"

"Yeah," said Thisbe. "Why?"

"How did they get to the ship?"

Thisbe thought for a moment. "Magic carpet components, wasn't it? Sky weaved them from seaweed, and Alex and Lani and Samheed instilled them with magic—or something like that."

"Yes! That's right—I remember now." Fifer turned to Seth. "Do you have any of those components?"

Seth shook his head. His blond hair was streaked with sweat and his face was red from sunburn and exertion. "Florence hasn't taught us that one yet. Besides, I think it's only a temporary spell. I wouldn't trust them to get us across the gorge, much less beyond that to the nearest island."

"Crud," said Thisbe. Fifer's face fell. The three watched Dev finish off his second piece of fruit, and their mouths watered as they imagined its juicy goodness. After a minute Thisbe turned away and went to fill the canteens. As she knelt on the bank, she heard a commotion from Seth and Fifer behind her.

"Whoa!" hollered Seth. "What the—is that a sidewinder?" He jumped to his feet in record time. A long snake slithered sideways toward him. He shrieked and leaped into the scraggly tree, making the brittle branches crack under his weight. The snake continued on the ground past him, heading toward Dev.

"Look out!" shouted Fifer.

Dev hopped up. "Get back!" he cried. The snake approached and struck out, narrowly missing him. He staggered to one side, off balance, trying to dodge the thing.

Thisbe stared, frozen. And then, without thinking, she ran straight toward the snake. It darted out, this time elevating its front end to strike at Dev's thigh. Thisbe pointed at it. "Boom!" she cried.

As Dev twisted and spun around, trying to get away, the snake's head froze in midair. For a split second it hung there. Everyone held their breath. And then the snake exploded into dozens of pieces that went flying far and wide.

From the ground, Dev watched in horror and disbelief.

Thisbe's face wore a stricken look. The boom spell. She'd done it on a living thing for the second time in her life. After a moment, she began to breathe again.

When the others understood what had just happened, Fifer caught her sister's eye and went over to her. "Nice one," she said gently. "You did good. You okay?"

"It just happened," Thisbe muttered. "I didn't think about it." The memory of Panther came flooding back, and she turned toward the river to hide her emotion. She didn't like to hurt any living creature, but she'd done it again. She'd used her magic destructively. Maybe she just wasn't capable of doing what Alex wanted her to do. But at least she had good instincts, and that was worth something, wasn't it? As much as Dev annoyed her sometimes, she didn't exactly want to see him die. So Thisbe's destructive spell had actually managed to save someone this time. She stared at the water, perplexed.

Dev slowly pushed himself to a sitting position, his face betraying his fear. He looked all around, as if he thought the magic was an illusion and he was still trying to figure out where the snake had truly gone. But only the little pieces remained, scattered across the area.

Fifer watched Dev as he began to comprehend what had happened. After a moment, he glanced guiltily at Thisbe, but she wouldn't look at him.

"Thisbe saved your life," said Seth, stating the obvious with contempt as he eased his way out of the tree. "The least you could do is thank her. And give her that last piece of stupid fruit."

Dev, still dazed, got up and staggered over to Thisbe. He stood there for a second, then cleared his throat. "Thanks," he said quietly. "I didn't see that one coming."

"You're welcome," Thisbe said, a bit stiffly. She put the caps on the filled canteens and loaded them into the rucksack.

"You want me to, um, carry that for you?" asked Dev.

Thisbe laughed contemptuously. "Are you kidding me? No thanks. You'd probably run off with it." She picked it up to swing it on her back, but Fifer took it from her and slipped it on.

"My turn," she said.

Dev looked at the piece of fruit in his hand. Slowly he held it out to Thisbe.

She grabbed it from him without hesitation, took a big bite out of it, and began chewing. Then she handed it to Fifer. "'et's go," she said, her mouth full.

Dev stared at her for a long moment as if she completely mystified him, and then he turned toward the castle and they all began walking again.

A world away, Simber, Thatcher, and Carina passed over the Island of Fire, all of them eager to see if they could detect any changes that Sky and Scarlet had made to the exterior of the island. Simber dropped lower as Carina pointed to one of the skylights, thinking she saw something through it.

Without warning, the volcano belched out a fireball of lava, striking the great cat's wing. Simber began spinning out of control, making a nosedive for the water. His passengers flew off, and one of his wings slammed into Thatcher before they all plunged wildly into the sea.

A Temporary Setback

Simber hit the sea at top speed, and, luckily, the water helped slow him down. He righted himself, feeling a bit dizzy, and managed to angle his body and wings toward the surface before he lost momentum, keeping him from sinking all the way to the bottom. He began to flap mightily, struggling to get out of the disgusting liquid that he had such fierce hatred for. Once he broke through, he flew up and shook his body hard, trying to get the drops of water off him. He quickly examined the wing that had been hit, finding it no worse for wear. The burning orange lava hadn't been hot enough to destroy him—only the hottest blue and white flames could do that.

He began to look around for his riders. "Carrrina!" he growled, scanning the water for her. "Thatcherrr!"

"I'm here!" called Carina, waving so the cat could spot her. "But I can't find Thatcher!"

"Does he swim?"

"Yes. He's as good as any of us." Carina whirled around as she treaded water, trying desperately to spot him. "Thatcher!" she called.

Simber soared over the area, his careful eyes taking in everything they could.

Carina dove underwater to search better. As she floated near the island, she thought she felt vibrations pulsing through the water. They seemed weaker than the last time she'd been here, and at first she wondered if she was imagining them. But then they happened again. Immediately she struck for the surface, her heart racing. When she emerged, she yelled, "Simber! The island is trembling! It's going to sink!"

Alarmed, Simber stopped combing the waters and flew over to Carina. He dipped a wing down low, and she grabbed on to it as he went by. He flipped his wing up, launching Carina onto his back as if they'd practiced dozens of times. She scooted up on his back and grabbed him around the neck as she caught her breath. "Any sign of him?"

"None," said Simber. "Did you see wherrre he landed?"

"I was in a spiral—I don't even know where *I* landed."

"Same herrre." Simber flew low to the water. "We'rrre going to have to go underrr. Rrready?"

"Ready." Carina took a deep breath. As they plunged underwater, Carina held on as tightly as she could. Like countless others, Carina and Thatcher had learned to exercise what Ms. Octavia called underwater breathing, which allowed a person to hold their breath for six or seven minutes at a time if necessary. It worked great if you were planning on doing it. But there were no guarantees when plunging underwater came as a surprise.

The Island of Fire shook again, sending slightly stronger vibrations through the water. Feeling them, Simber propelled himself even harder with his wings, his eyes and ears on high alert for any sign of Thatcher.

Carina felt the tremors too and squeezed Simber's neck harder. She knew they didn't have much time before they'd have to get out of there. If they didn't, they'd get sucked down with the force of water as the island sank and they'd be dragged to their deaths. *Where is Thatcher?* Carina tried to open her eyes so she could help look for him, but her eyelids weren't willing to cooperate against the pressure and speed.

When Simber took a wild turn, Carina could only hope it was because he had spotted the young man. But a sensation of her world brightening made her realize they were headed upward. At the same time, the water pulsed again, and soon Carina felt a deepening suction tugging at her, nearly ripping her body off Simber's. She tightened her grip, dug her heels into his flanks, and hung on for dear life.

Seconds later Simber and Carina burst from the water as the volcano plunged below the surface, dragging millions of gallons of water and everything else floating nearby into its empty maw.

They circled and circled as the water crashed below, Simber's senses on their highest alert possible, and Carina staring at the churning water until it felt like her eyes would pop out. Before she could fully catch her breath, Simber made a sharp turn in midair.

"Hang on!" he cried, and soared like a bullet back down to the roiling surface, claws outstretched. With a frustrated roar, he swooped into the whirlpool of water like a giant hawk that had spotted its prey. They hit the water hard, and then Simber turned sharply toward the sky and rose up. This time, hanging from his claws, was Thatcher's limp body.

A Major Setback

There was nowhere for Simber to land. Flying out of harm's way, he gripped Thatcher tenuously by the back of his shirt, which was ripped enough already to cause Simber great concern that he'd lose the young man again. Once they cleared the dangerous area, the great cat slowed his speed and moved closer to the surface of the water so that Carina could jump off and pull Thatcher to safety if he dropped. Soon Simber hovered low enough that the tips of his wings, and Thatcher's feet, splashed in the waves.

"I'm going in," said Carina. She dove into the water and quickly surfaced. Simber turned around and glided back toward her. She held her arms out. "Okay, drop him right in front of me!"

Simber released Thatcher, who slipped into the water feet-first. Carina caught his wrist, pulled him toward her, then wrapped her arms around his chest. She flipped to her back and slipped under Thatcher, keeping his head as high as she could, and began to tread water, waiting until Simber could swing around once more and rescue them. As she did, she wrapped her arms around him and pressed hard on his chest, trying to get him to breathe.

Simber turned around, then came back and made a shallow dive in front of them. He slid underneath the two and lifted them up as steadily as he could.

Once she felt Simber below her, Carina righted herself and dragged Thatcher's body along so he rested securely on Simber's back. All the while, whenever she could, she worked on reviving him. After a few moments, the young man began coughing wildly, spewing seawater everywhere. He gasped for air.

"Thank goodness," Carina breathed. "That was close."

» » « «

The ordeal had been exhausting, and once Thatcher came to life and could support himself, Carina sank back between Simber's shoulder blades. "I think he's okay," she called to the cheetah.

"Sounds that way," said Simber, relieved now that the danger appeared to be over.

Thatcher continued to gasp and cough, and then rolled over to his stomach and lay there, chest heaving, water dripping off him.

"You'll be all right in a bit," Carina said. "Hurts, though, doesn't it? Is this your first near drowning?"

Thatcher shook his head and coughed more.

"Well, good—you know how it goes, then. Are you ready to continue?"

This time Thatcher nodded.

"Do you want something to . . . ?" She trailed off, looking to the tail end of Simber where they'd strapped their supplies—food, water, and extra components. The crate was gone, lost in the chaos. "Oh no!" she cried. Her hands flew to her component vest, which was still stocked with components, but she didn't have even a drop of freshwater on her. Nor did Thatcher.

"Simber, I'm afraid we've lost the supplies. The crate is gone."

Simber turned his head sharply to see for himself, while Thatcher lifted himself up between violent fits of coughing to look too.

The cheetah growled in frustration. He scanned the sea, but there was no sign of the crate floating on the waves. "I'm surrre it went down into the volcano when it submerrrged," he said. He shook his head, angry with himself. "It was foolish of me to fly dirrrectly overrr the volcano like that. I'm sorrry."

"It's not your fault," Carina said. "You were taking the shortest route. And besides, we wanted to see Sky's progress. I'm the one who told you to go closer."

"But we can't continue ourrr jourrrney without supplies," said Simber. "Can we?" He certainly didn't need any supplies to survive, but the humans' needs were sometimes baffling to him.

Carina was silent. She knew freshwater was the most important thing they lacked, and it was probably even more crucial for Thatcher than for her, after the ordeal he'd just gone through. She searched Thatcher's face. "What do you think?" she asked him. "Be honest."

He sat up. "I don't know," he said, his voice raspy. "We've come this far already. How much farther is it?"

"We're more than halfway to the waterfall, but we don't know what distance we have to go beyond that to reach the land of the dragons." She turned back to Simber and laid a hand on his neck. "You don't know the answer from what Pan told you, do you? I mean, I know you're sworn to protect the dragon code, or whatever, but this is kind of important."

Simber hesitated. "I don't know exactly. But I don't think it's farrr beyond the waterrrfall."

"So that's . . . what? A full day's journey without water. Assuming we can find some once we get to where we're going."

"We could go back to Warrrblerrr and rrrestock."

"That's nearly as long a journey in the wrong direction, also without freshwater." Carina pressed her lips in a tight line, contemplating, and looked at Thatcher again. "We're going to have to do without either way. What do you say? I think we may as well soldier on."

Thatcher wiped his face on his sopping shirt as he thought through the scenario. His throat ached, and his mouth felt disgusting after all the seawater he'd taken in. But he was feeling a little stronger. Going back to Warbler would delay them severely. Plus, it wouldn't bring the drinking water much sooner than if they continued on. "I'm worried about the kids," he said. "I can make it if you can."

Carina studied him. "If you're sure," she said. "Obviously I'd like to keep going and find my son."

Thatcher swallowed hard and nodded. He hadn't had to sacrifice like this in a long time. But he'd given his all before, in the final battle, and he had the scars to prove it. If he could survive that, he could make it through this. "Land of the dragons it is."

Carina clasped Thatcher's hand in a show of gratitude, then turned to face forward. She patted Simber's neck. "Onward, my friend. Full speed ahead."

Simber flapped his mighty wings, rising higher off the water and picking up speed. The battered and bruised rescue team was on its way once more.

A Night Visitor

Thisbe, Fifer, Seth, and Dev continued their journey to the castle through the sweltering afternoon and into the evening. Everyone had unanswered questions running through their minds, but Fifer and Seth followed Thisbe's lead and didn't say much about what they were doing or why they wanted to do it. And Dev had questions of his own. Occasionally he cleared his throat to ask, but he always backed down. He knew they were mad at him, and he knew why—their growling stomachs were complaining loud enough for him to hear. But they didn't have the first clue about his motivation.

Not that Dev was about to reveal it. He had too much at stake now.

Finally, under the cover of darkness and with the castle looming closer than ever, they made camp in an open area. "The river's not far," Dev told the others.

"Why don't we set up camp by the river, then?" Fifer asked.

"To keep out of the way of the wild animals that come out to eat and drink at night. Plus, we want to stay off the plant life."

"Why?" asked Seth. "Wouldn't it be softer to sleep on?"

Dev pulled a few sticks together and began to build a fire. "That would kill the plants and leave the animals hungry."

Again Thisbe puzzled over their guide. Every time she wanted to hate him, he did or said something surprisingly kindhearted. "You like animals?" she asked.

"I like to eat," he answered truthfully.

"Oh. I thought for a minute there you actually had a heart." Thisbe sniffed and turned away. But the simple mention of eating sent her stomach growling fiercely. "I'm going to get some water," she said.

"Wait," said Dev, pulling a flint from his ragged pocket.

"Let me get this started and I'll go with you." He struck the flint near the kindling a few times, and then blew furiously. The sticks caught fire. When he was sure it would continue burning, he looked at Seth and Fifer. "Don't let this go out."

"Um, okay," said Seth. He glanced sidelong at Fifer, and the two exchanged a bewildered look. They'd never had to tend a nonmagical fire before and had no idea what to do, but not wanting to appear stupid, they went along with it as if they had.

Dev rummaged through another pocket and pulled out a box the size of his palm. He slid it open and, using the firelight to see, selected a hook that was attached to some fishing line. "Okay, Thisbe the thief, let's go to the river."

"You can stop calling me that now." Thisbe grabbed the canteens and followed Dev. When they reached the riverbank, Dev cautioned Thisbe to be quiet. "Let me catch one before you fill your canteens," he said. "I don't want you to scare them away."

Thisbe frowned, not sure if she should feel offended, but she'd spent enough time in water to know how easy it was to frighten fish, so she determined it wasn't a slight. She hung back silently, watching him as he balanced on his haunches. He slid something on the end of the hook and lowered it into a still section of the water, which resembled a miniature lagoon like the one in Artimé.

Dev remained incredibly still. When he finally jerked his arms sharply and stood, it gave Thisbe a fright, but she soon realized he held a big, shining, flopping fish on the end of his hook.

"You can go ahead and fill your canteens now," he said.

Thisbe did so. "Is that enough for all of us?" she asked, eyeing the fish and trying not to watch as Dev took out a pocketknife and put it out of its misery.

Dev laughed. "No. It's enough for me. I didn't think you cared for eating animals."

"We eat fish," said Thisbe, indignant.

"What's the difference?"

Thisbe wasn't sure. She thought for a second. "The land animals where we come from are mostly magical creatures. I couldn't imagine eating them." She would gladly take a platyprot egg right about now, though. She glared once again. "So you're not going to share that fish?"

"No."

Fury bubbled inside Thisbe. "Well, can I at least borrow that hook and line from you?"

Dev carefully unthreaded the hook from the dead fish's mouth. "Sure." He handed it to her. "But you probably won't catch anything now. They've all scattered."

Thisbe made a frustrated noise and took the hook and line. But she had nothing to use as bait. It was useless, but she didn't know how to admit it without feeling totally idiotic. At least she was trying. That was more than what Seth or Fifer was doing.

"So, that was magic you did," Dev said.

"What?"

"When you killed the sidewinder."

"Oh, that. Yeah."

"Your land is magical?"

"I guess you'd say that." Thisbe dunked the hook in the water a few times.

"Why don't you just make some magical food, then?"

"Why don't you shut it?" asked Thisbe sweetly.

Dev stared at her. "I'm going back. Don't lose my hook." He hesitated. "And don't get eaten."

"By what?" asked Thisbe, whirling around.

Dev shrugged, an evil smile playing at his lips. "Dragons. This is their land, after all."

"That would probably be the best thing that could happen to me right now," Thisbe said.

Dev shook his head slowly. "You are the strangest person I've ever met."

"And you're the rudest," said Thisbe, waving him off. "Go on. Go away." She turned her back on him, more determined than ever to catch something with her baitless hook.

After a minute she could hear Dev shuffle back toward the fire. She squatted and folded one arm around her knees to warm herself against the evening chill. It had been so hot all day, and now it was cold. She missed Artimé's perfect climate. She missed Alex and the mansion, and all the comforts of home. And she began to wonder about what Alex must be thinking. Was he worried? He must be—he'd sent enough seek spells. How foolish it was for her and Fifer and Seth to run off like that, thinking they'd be back by morning. She cried over her sorrows for a moment, knowing that would make her feel better. Then she pulled up her empty hook, splashed water on her face, and took a few deep breaths. There was nothing she or any of them could do but to find a familiar dragon, give it new wings, and let it take them home. There was no use feeling sorry for herself. And wherever the dragons were, there was probably food, too. They just needed to get a good night's rest and start moving again in the morning. The castle wasn't far away now. They were so close she could almost smell dinner cooking.

Thisbe's stomach rumbled again, and she realized she *could* smell dinner cooking—Dev's dinner. She got up and went back to the camp area. There she made a spot to lie down, faced away from Dev and the others—who were looking just as put out as she—and willed herself to fall asleep. And it must have worked, because hours later, she awoke to the sound of Dev screaming.

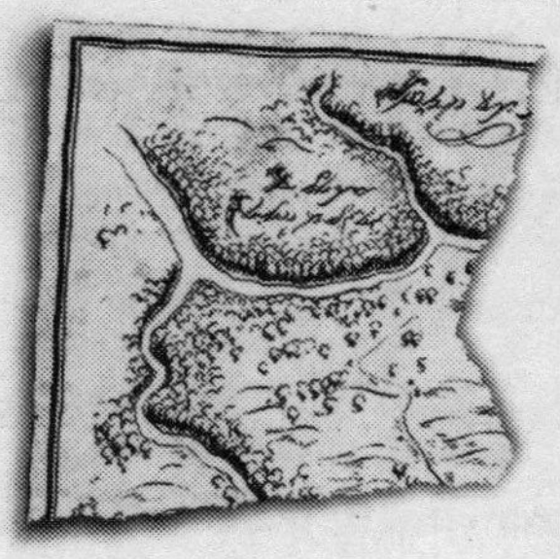

In the Middle of the Night

Dev's shouts caused a chain reaction of screams from everyone else, though the twins and Seth had no idea what they were yelling about. It was a shock to be pulled so abruptly from a deep sleep into defense mode. All of them scrambled to their feet before they could even think straight, ready to fight the first thing they set eyes on.

In an instant they had their answer. A roar, followed by a large burst of fire, woke up the night. The flames revealed Hux the dragon, which silenced the screams, at least momentarily. Though their hearts still pounded, the three Artiméans sighed with relief, but Dev wasn't on the same page as them at all. He merely took a breath and began yelling again to run. He scrambled to his feet and fell back down again in his haste. The other children couldn't get a word in edgewise to let Dev know there was nothing to worry about—they were safe.

Thisbe took a bit of satisfaction in watching Dev panic. He deserved it after his selfishness with the fish. He began scrambling away on his hands and knees. Soon the dragon had enough of Dev's noise and picked the boy up in his teeth. Hux laid him on the ground, then held him in place with one of his front feet.

"Be quiet!" said Thisbe, going over to them. "Do you want to wake up the whole world?" Now that the panic was over, Thisbe was just annoyed.

"How do you know this boy?" growled the dragon.

Dev stopped yelling. His face became more and more confused. "Why aren't you afraid?" he asked Thisbe.

But Thisbe wasn't paying attention to Dev. She stared angrily at the dragon and threw her hands up in the air. "Where have you been? Maybe you could start by telling us why you abandoned us." She was feeling all kinds of emotions at once simmering under her skin, and she wasn't sure what to do with them. "We came here to help you!"

Fifer saw how agitated Thisbe was and went over to her sister's side. "It's okay," she whispered in Thisbe's ear. "He's here now." Fifer knew better than anyone that if Thisbe got too worked up, nobody was safe, and there was no telling what could happen.

Thisbe clenched her teeth and tried breathing through her nose. She didn't want to make anything bad happen either—not really. Though she was pretty mad at the moment.

"You really shouldn't startle her," Seth told Hux. He'd been on the receiving end of Thisbe's wrath when he'd stolen her beach sand shovel at the age of six. He'd nearly lost an eye from it. He knew better than to make her mad.

"Just . . . I'm fine," Thisbe muttered. She didn't like being talked about like this. She looked at Hux and explained. "Dev is our guide. He's taking us to the castle so we can find the—"

Fifer nudged her, reminding her they hadn't actually told Dev why they wanted to go to the castle.

"Anyway," Thisbe said, "to the castle. He's leading us. But now that you're here to take us the rest of the way, you can kill him if you want to, since he's kind of a jerk." She didn't really mean it, but it was fun watching Dev squirm.

Dev's eyes widened in the glow from the fire. He knew Hux well enough. Each of the dragon's claws were as big around as his forearms, and the points were very sharp. One false move and they'd pierce him through. He pushed aside the thoughts of his crumbling plan and gathered his wits, knowing he had to survive first before he could profit in any way from this little journey. Not that profit was on his mind at this moment—he just wanted to live to see the morning. "Thisbe," he choked out, "you know I've been helping you. If you'd tried going this route alone, you'd be dead by now."

Thisbe sneered. "Like you almost were before I saved you?" She knew she wasn't being very kind. He had led them to water, and if she was being honest, she wasn't sure they'd have been able to find that on their own. And it was true that the young Artiméans were terribly unseasoned at figuring out how to live on their own means. Back home they'd traveled around a lot to the various islands, but they'd always had a comfy bed to return to every night, and they'd never had to think about where food and water would be coming from.

"Please," Dev begged. "Let me up. I—I can help you. I'm sure I can. I know every part of this land. I'll fish for you. I promise. And . . . and I'll go without." He tried not to struggle, and for a moment, feeling weak and defeated, he closed his eyes and awaited the sharp claw to pierce his chest.

But something Thisbe and Fifer both heard him say made them pause. He knew the land. The girls looked at each other. "Hang on a minute," Fifer said to Hux, and pulled Thisbe aside. She spoke in a hushed tone. "I've been wondering how we're going to make the dragon wings without those vines we lost on the journey across the big gap of nothingness," she said. "We need other materials too, like flower petals. Where are we going to find that stuff? Maybe Dev can get it for us."

Thisbe frowned. Fifer had a point. "All right," she conceded. "I guess we can use his help. Besides, he has to travel in the same direction we're headed. If we just let him go, we'll still be walking together, and that'll be awkward."

"Very," said Fifer. "So we agree?"

"Of course we do," said Thisbe with a little smile, feeling calmer now.

"You can let Dev up, Hux," said Fifer. "We've got a job for him."

The dragon complied, and soon Dev was rolling to his side and staggering to his feet, breathing a huge sigh of relief.

Thisbe introduced them. "Dev, this is Hux the ice-blue dragon. Hux, this is Dev . . . the most annoying person in the world."

Hux and Dev looked at each other for a long moment, which seemed strange. Thisbe's eyes darted from one to the other, trying to read their expressions. After an excruciating moment, Hux nodded slightly, and then looked away. "We already know each other."

Thisbe took in a breath. "What? How?"

"Not very well," said Dev, dropping his gaze.

"That's not true," said Hux. "You are as much a slave to the Revinir as we dragons are."

"I am not," said Dev hotly. "I serve the princess and no one else. Except the prisoners. But that's because the princess wants me to."

Hux snorted fire. "And who do you think controls the princess?"

Dev was quiet for a moment. And then he laughed bitterly. "No one. Or she and I would never have been down in the glen messing around on market day."

Hux snorted. "Think what you want."

"The king, then. But hardly." Dev clenched his jaw in defiance, but it was useless and stupid to argue with the dragon.

"And who controls the king?"

Dev spun around and marched toward the river, and didn't answer.

"Hey!" Thisbe yelled. "Where do you think you're going?"

"To catch your stupid fish."

Thisbe looked at the others, puzzled. "It's the middle of the night."

"So what?" Seth interjected. "I'm starving to death. Let him go, please." He shook his head as if he still couldn't believe he was part of this disastrous adventure, where they had to fight for every bite to eat and drop of water to drink. He pressed on his soft stomach as it snarled. He'd think twice about doing something like this again. But somehow the girls always talked him into it. Maybe one day he'd be brave enough to say no.

Dev disappeared into the darkness.

Thisbe turned toward the fire. "You should have killed him when *you* had the chance," she muttered to Hux, then stoked the embers and added some sticks to the fire like she'd seen Dev do. *A slave,* she thought, staring at the glow. *What a horrible place this is.*

The dragon lowered himself to lie down on the ground. "I couldn't, even if you'd wanted me to."

"What do you mean? Why not?" asked Fifer.

"It is because of what my mother taught us. And what her mother taught her, for generations—thousands of years. It is so strong a teaching that it is ingrained in our being."

"Wait. What is, exactly?" asked Seth, not sure he was following the conversation.

"Our line of dragons must not kill anyone who is more good than evil. It's part of the code."

Thisbe snorted. "And how do *you* tell? Is it because you are both slaves to the Revinir?"

"No. It has nothing to do with that."

"Well, I think you might have made a mistake with Dev."

Two tiny trails of smoke rose from the dragon's nostrils.

"There is no mistake. I can tell with full certainty: He is not more evil than good."

Seth tilted his head. "So he's more good, you're saying."

The dragon hesitated. "I would not say that, either."

Fifer was truly confused and wasn't sure if they were supposed to trust Dev or not. "So . . . what is he?"

The dragon paused for a long time, and then finally said, "He is exactly half-good and half-evil. And each side of him is fighting to take over." His ears twitched, as if he were listening for Dev to return. "Only time will tell which side wins."

The Trek to the Castle

The dragon hesitated as the children soaked in the information about Dev. And then he added, "You must never tell Dev this, for he doesn't know it himself, and he must shape his own life. Just as I will not tell you what percentage good or evil you are, for it could alter the person you are destined to become."

Fifer's eyes widened. "Thisbe and I are probably the same, though. Right, Hux?"

Hux said nothing. He looked away.

Thisbe stared at him. "You mean we're *not* the same?"

"Your brothers were quite different from each other," said Hux. "*Quite*. There was no difficulty for us, even as young as we were back then, in telling them apart." That was all he would reveal. "I'm weary—I've said too much already. Don't ask me any more about it."

"But where have you been?" Fifer asked Hux. "You still haven't told us. And why did you abandon us?"

"I could ask the same question of you," accused Hux. "You shouldn't have left me. I could tell something was happening down in the village. When people began to scatter and some of them ran in my direction, I had to take to the forest to hide. If the Revinir gets word that I've been seen on the loose near a village, my life is over, new wings or not."

Fifer frowned. "But why are you in so much danger? Isn't this supposed to be the land of the dragons?"

"It used to be. That has all changed in the years since we arrived."

Thisbe stared. "That's horrible! The Revinir must be pure evil."

"Ninety-nine percent," said Hux, being candid again in his

weariness, and under the cover of darkness. "Or so the story goes. I've never been close enough to get an accurate sniff. And I'm perfectly happy to keep my distance."

"So, back to the story—you were hiding in the forest?" asked Seth, eager to hear what had happened.

"Yes."

"Why didn't you find us at night?"

Hux's eyes narrowed as Dev appeared out of the darkness, carrying three fish. "I was otherwise disposed," he said, staring at the boy. "Ensnared, you might say." He didn't elaborate. Dev didn't look at the dragon. Silently he held out the fish to Thisbe.

She took them, and Seth jumped to get sticks so they could cook them over the fire.

"Once you're finished eating, we'll continue traveling," said Hux. "We cannot waste any more time. I've been gone too long already and I fear . . ." He didn't finish the sentence, but the girls and Seth knew what his fear was. It was their fear as well. Arabis's life depended on them.

They ate quickly, then doused the fire and refilled their canteens. Soon the humans, except for Dev, were riding on Hux's back. Dev ran alongside as best he could in the dark, but no one offered to give him a ride and he didn't ask for one.

"Okay, Dev, you said you knew this land really well," said Thisbe. "We need vines and flower petals. Where can we find those things?"

Hux answered before Dev had a chance to. "There are no vines here like the ones you were carrying earlier."

Fifer and Thisbe looked at each other in horror. "No vines?" they said together.

"I'm afraid not," said Hux. He turned to Dev. "Would you agree?"

"No vines that I know of. Unless you're talking about ivy. The forest has plenty of that."

"No. Ivy isn't nearly strong enough." Fifer knitted her brow. "Is there anything else?"

"Branches from a young tree might do," murmured Thisbe, thinking about all she'd learned about plants from Henry Haluki and the grandfathers. "They'll bend but they won't break."

"We have plenty of green saplings," said Dev, huffing alongside them. He seemed less obstinate than before. Perhaps because they were finally on their way again. Or perhaps because Hux's claws on his chest had put things into perspective. Needless to say, he was being helpful—for the moment at least.

By dawn they reached the last valley before their ultimate ascent to the castle. This valley was the greenest, lushest one they'd passed through, and the forest area grew large and close around a village a little bigger than Glen Freer. The river emerged from the woods and split into two, surrounded the village, making an oval shape around it, then joined up once more on the other side. A small wooden sign on the outskirts of the village read SOUTH GRIMERE.

"It's so funny how there are all these villages on one piece of land," remarked Seth.

"And this land is so big," Fifer added.

"Doesn't seem funny to me," said Dev.

Thisbe rolled her eyes at him. "Yes, you're right, Seth," she said. "It's different from home."

At the mention of home, all three children from Artimé shifted uneasily. They'd been gone for days now. Maybe people at home would understand. Even Alex had slowed the frequency of sending seek spells—perhaps he was getting used to the girls being gone. They could only hope as much. But deep down they knew a lot of people would be very upset with them when they returned.

If they returned.

A ball of fear rose to Thisbe's throat. *What if we can't actually fix the wings?* She swallowed hard and tried to shake the thought. She and Fifer had always been able to do magic they'd witnessed. Sure, this spell was one of the hardest ever, or so everyone said, but Thisbe had already used it once to make the prison grid come alive. So they were good, right? Once they had the supplies they needed, the magic would be easy. And they would be doing a very selfless thing. It was exactly what they needed to do. Thisbe took in a sharp breath and sat up, feeling newly determined. It felt a little bit like when they'd first set out on this journey, only now her determination had a gritty, dark edge to it. There was a lot at stake—they'd found that out the hard way. She leaned in and spoke quietly. "We have to prove to Alex . . . We have to get it right."

Fifer and Seth nodded. Fifer knew by now that this

adventure was far from glamorous. And if they were ever going to make it home alive, they couldn't mess this up. Beyond that, if she and Thisbe were ever going to get a chance to learn more magic, they had some major changes to make in themselves that wouldn't be easy. Everything was riding on the girls accomplishing the task before them. Everything.

Hux and Dev remained oblivious. But all was soon forgotten as they entered the forest.

When Hux had gone in as far as he could without uprooting trees, Thisbe slid down his side to the ground. The other two followed her, and they began to search in the weak morning light for the right kinds of flower petals and trees.

To keep herself from worrying too much, Fifer began humming a difficult song she'd learned in her music class as she walked around. After a minute, Fifer stopped humming. She looked at Thisbe. "Maybe we should practice on Hux before we get to the castle, so we can *prove* that we can make wings?"

Thisbe nodded. She'd been worrying about this as well. What if, after all this, they weren't able to actually make the wings work? It would be better to discover it here rather than in the presence of strangers who could potentially hurt them.

After much searching, they gathered enough soft branches and flower petals to create one set of wings. But they didn't have any cloth to cover them.

"We'll figure that out," muttered Fifer, who was already eyeing giant palm fronds to use instead.

Just then they heard an eerie, forlorn cry in the distance, coming from the direction of the castle. Everyone stopped in their tracks.

"What in the world was that?" asked Seth.

Hux rose up on his back legs and roared in return, so loud it nearly split everyone's eardrums. Then the dragon turned to look at them, fire in his eyes. "That was Arabis. We must go immediately. There's no time to waste."

The Castle Grimere

Thisbe, Fifer, Seth, and Dev stared at Hux. "But we haven't—" Fifer began.

"NOW!" roared the dragon.

The four moved quickly to obey. They gathered up all the supplies they could carry and shoved them into the hollow on Hux's back. At the last second, and without invitation, Dev hopped on as well, certain that the dragon was planning to run faster than he could keep up. And he was determined to be there to hand over the twins. After all his trouble in getting them here, he wasn't about to miss his opportunity.

Thisbe turned and eyed Dev, and he quickly lowered his

gaze, guilt poking at him from all directions. Then Hux lurched, and Thisbe had to face forward to keep her balance and help hold on to the supplies. At a surprisingly quick pace, the dragon moved through the forest, plowing down trees when necessary, then headed up the mountainside's rocky terrain toward the castle. At one point he attempted flight, but his feet barely lifted off the ground. His wings were no longer strong enough.

The glory of the glistening castle lay before them, foreboding despite its beauty, for the Artiméans didn't know what to expect from the people inside—people who kept dragons and humans as slaves. It was reassuring to know that they'd be safe, since the Revinir had sent for them. Fifer, who had draped her body over the sticks to keep them from sliding off, kept stealing glances at the majestic structure whenever she was stable enough to do so. She wasn't old enough to remember the old, gray palace that had once loomed over Quill where the lighthouse now stood, but she'd seen drawings that Alex had done before his arm had become unusable. This castle looked nothing like that. If anything, it more resembled the mansion, but it was a supercharged version of it in every possible way. The towers were taller. The windows immense. The main doorway was so vast that, when the iron portcullis was raised, a dozen Simbers could fly through at once.

The castle Grimere was surrounded by a moat, which they'd seen from the neighboring peak. It became visible again as they climbed. Eventually they could hear the sound of the rushing river and the waterfall that slipped off the cliff on the back side of the property.

Thisbe focused on the waterfall for a moment. "The water just falls to nowhere," she murmured, and for a second she nearly felt sorry for it—for how useless and forlorn it seemed. She had come to appreciate water in a great way these past few days, more than she'd ever given thought to before. It made tears spring to her eyes. But then she blinked hard and turned her attention back to the castle.

Now they could see the lines of soldiers surrounding it. They wore dark green uniforms and carried swords like the ones that lined the walls in Artimé's theater, as well as crossbows and a variety of other weapons the children had never seen before except in books. Seth eyed the soldiers nervously, and his fingers immediately went to his vest pockets, but his few components would be no match.

Thisbe saw him. "We won't have to fight," she said quietly in his ear, feeling nervous too. "They need us, remember?"

"Yeah," said Seth, but the worry never left his face. He pulled his hand away and gripped the dragon tighter.

Once the soldiers spotted the dragon coming, they began lowering the drawbridge over the moat and raising the iron portcullis.

Hux was breathing hard, but he wasn't slowing down. Whatever that mournful sound was that Arabis had made, it had scared Hux severely, and that put Seth, Fifer, and Thisbe even more on edge. Was Arabis okay?

Hux's direct path finally intersected the winding road that led to the castle, and the ride became a little smoother. The dragon followed the road to the drawbridge, and when he saw the guards waving him down, he skidded to a halt. Several of their precious flower petals flew up in the wind. Fifer squeaked in protest, trying and failing to grab them, then regretfully watched them go. She glanced at the guards, who were staring at her, and quickly settled back down, a wave of fear passing through her. None of them appeared friendly.

The soldier who seemed to be in charge apparently

recognized Hux, to no one's surprise, but she scrutinized the children's faces. "Who are these children with you?"

"They are the magicians from the Seven Islands," said Hux.

"And me," said Dev, straightening up. "I'm delivering them to the princess. The girls, I mean. Officially."

Thisbe looked sidelong at him and whispered harshly, "What are you talking about?" Dev had been acting more and more sneaky lately. He was definitely up to something, but she couldn't figure out what it was. She addressed the soldier. "We're not here to see the princess, ma'am. We're here to fix the dragons' wings."

"Right," Dev mumbled. He slouched again.

The woman studied the girls, looking them in the eye for a long moment. But the expression on her face didn't give away her thoughts. She raised a brow at Dev. "Hmm. Interesting."

Fifer glanced at Dev too, her suspicion growing. "What's going on?" she demanded.

Dev stared stonily ahead. "Nothing."

Thisbe and Fifer exchanged a suspicious glance. But their worries were interrupted by Hux.

"We must hurry," the dragon said sharply. "The orders came from the king."

"Fine, then," said the soldier, and she waved them in.

Hux wasted no time. He thudded over the drawbridge and headed straight inside.

"They let dragons inside the castle?" asked Seth in a low voice, which hitched as they bumped along. But it was clear they did, for the other guards stood aside and let Hux through.

As their eyes adjusted, Fifer's lips parted in awe. The entryway was bigger than the entire mansion in Artimé. The ceiling rose up to a dizzying height, and jeweled light fixtures lined the walls, sparkling. The floor was made of vibrant green stone that had been polished smooth, making the dragon's claws slip and clack as he moved along. The ivory walls contained intricate carvings that looked very old, yet were impeccably maintained. It must've taken skilled artists centuries to complete all that work. In spite of their trepidation, the three Artiméans marveled at it.

But the most unusual thing about the castle entrance was the pair of white-and-gray-striped tigers. They were adorned with rich-looking fabric that lay across their shoulders and backs like capes, and they wore delicate headpieces with pearls and diamonds that hung between their eyes. The tigers paced the back wall of the entryway, but they weren't loose—they were secured around their necks by long, thin, flexible metal chains.

One of the tigers snarled at Hux as he went by. Hux roared back, but the tiger showed no fear. Hux continued toward them, making Fifer worry there'd be a confrontation, but then the dragon turned to the right at the back of the entryway and went through an enormous arch, leading to a wing of the castle. Just as they were about to enter through a similar-size doorway, a girl's voice from behind halted Hux in his tracks. "Stop, dragon," she said.

Hux stopped.

Dev's face lit up. He jumped down, while Thisbe, Fifer, and Seth turned around to look at the girl. Clearly a princess, she was dressed in shimmering clothes and wore a small beaded headpiece that dripped jewels across her forehead, similar to what the tigers wore. She walked casually to one of the tigers and petted its head, barely looking at it.

Dev ran over to her. "I'm back," he said in a low voice.

"And I'm bored to death." She looked at the dragon, who seemed to be waiting for permission to continue on. Her gaze moved to the three children on his back. She put a finger to her lips and studied them. "Are they the ones . . . ?"

Dev smiled. "Yes, Princess. And I'll need you to inspect them, if you please."

The princess looked puzzled. "What? Why? Was I right?"

"You'll see." Dev looked around nervously. "Please."

"Of course." She moved fluidly over the malachite floor, her gown sweeping along with her, and approached the dragon. "You made it just in time, Hux," she said in a scolding tone. "You'll thank me for holding off the execution."

"Thank you," said Hux meekly, about as undragonlike as Thisbe could imagine. Briefly Thisbe wondered why Hux didn't just blow fire and burn up everyone who kept the dragons captive. But something else held Thisbe's attention. It was the princess, but not her beautiful clothing or her elegant stance. It was her voice. Her face. They were familiar.

The princess looked curiously from one twin to the other, and now that they were in bright light, she saw something she hadn't been sure of before. "Oh my," she whispered. She turned toward Dev. "Well done."

It was then that Thisbe finally figured out what was so familiar. The princess was the ragged girl who'd been with Dev in the village.

The Dungeon

D*ev said the girl's name earlier*, thought Thisbe. Shawni? No. It was Shanti. But why had she been dressed like a servant? Like Dev? Did this mean that Dev was secretly a prince?

"Soldiers," said the princess. She clapped her hands.

Immediately two men and two women in green uniforms appeared.

"Accompany the party to the dungeon so they can fix the dragon wings. When they are finished, make them . . . more comfortable."

The four soldiers obeyed.

The princess looked at Hux and frowned. She called after the soldiers, "And get his muzzle on right away. There's no reason for this carelessness."

"Yes, Princess," said the four in unison.

"Excuse me," said Thisbe, trying to sound bold. "What's happening?"

The princess eyed her with contempt, and Dev stepped forward. In a harsh voice he said, "Thieves do not address Princess Shanti." But he wouldn't look Thisbe in the eye.

"Look," said Thisbe, feeling heat rising to her cheeks. "Where we come from, people cut their hair if they want to. Not because they're thieves. Besides, *you're* a thief yourself, Dev. Why isn't your hair short?" She hesitated, waiting for the princess to apologize or at least appear to understand.

But the princess stared stonily. "Get them out of here."

Before the visitors knew what was happening, the soldiers prodded Hux through a doorway and whisked Thisbe, Seth, and Fifer after him, down a winding stone ramp. As they descended, the air turned damp and chilly, and the lighting became sparse. Near the bottom, the beautiful green-stone flooring ended abruptly and turned to dirt. The ceiling was low enough that Hux had to stoop way down in order to fit. He kept moving with the soldiers. The children followed.

As they reached the bottom of the ramp, the area opened up into a huge, dimly lit dungeon. More soldiers appeared and roughly slapped a muzzle over Hux's face. The dragon didn't struggle at all, which left the children mystified. Perhaps his refusal to fight like a normal dragon had been in the terms of agreement to save Arabis's life. Or maybe, after ten years of being enslaved, Hux didn't have any fight left in him. The three friends observed, silent and cautious, not wanting to talk about anything until there weren't any soldiers around to hear them.

There were a few small, high windows with bars over them. Blocks of sunlight streamed in. The children looked around the vast dungeon area, and it was only seconds before they realized they weren't alone.

Lined along one wall, inside enormous stables, were the other four dragons that the children hadn't seen since they were very young. Nearest them was Drock the deep purple, then an empty stall that was presumably Hux's. Then Ivis the green, Yarbeck the purple and gold, and at the far end by the outer wall with the windows, Arabis the orange. All of the dragons were stuck so tightly in their stables that they could hardly move, and their snouts were constrained by similar muzzles to the one Hux wore.

The soldiers forced the children to one side, taking their supplies for the wings and throwing them to the ground. Then they whipped poor Hux until he backed into the empty stall, and they continued whipping him even though he was doing exactly what they told him to do.

"Stop!" cried Fifer. "What do you think you're doing?"

"Leave him alone!" shouted Thisbe. "Can't you see he's doing what you're telling him to do?"

"Besides," Fifer continued, "we need the dragons outside of their stables. How else are we supposed to work on them?"

Seth ran over to the other dragons. "Are you all right?" he asked them. "Arabis! Do you remember me?"

But Arabis didn't answer because she couldn't. None of them could. Their mouths were locked shut by the muzzles, which Seth could now see were also attached to the walls of each stable. The dragons could only emit strange yowls through their clenched jaws, and they could hardly move their heads.

"Fix the wings!" barked one of the soldiers, making Seth scramble back to Fifer and Thisbe, who cowered near the supplies. The man turned to the other three soldiers, who were attaching Hux's muzzle to the chains in his stable. "Go stand guard at the ramp."

The three finished the job and moved out of sight to the end of the ramp as they were told. The first soldier stood over the children, looking at their strange organic supplies. "What is this junk?" he muttered. "This better not be a trick."

"We're going to need more supplies," said Fifer, trying to appear unfazed. She clenched her fists in front of her to show that she wasn't messing around, though she knew there was no way she'd win in a fight—not with three other guards nearby.

"Tough luck," said the man. "Make do with what you have."

"No, seriously," Fifer said, starting to panic. "We can't do it without more sticks and petals. And we need some cloth, too."

"You are not to leave the dungeon."

Fifer looked at the man, knowing that however difficult the soldiers were going to be, the twins had to figure out how to do this or they were all done for. "Okay, well," she said in a measured tone, "that servant boy Dev knows what we need. You could send him out to get it."

The soldier frowned.

Thisbe stepped in. "Can't you at least ask whoever's in charge, please?"

The soldier slammed his thumb against his chest and snarled, "I'm in charge. And I do not negotiate with thieves."

Boiling mad, Thisbe shoved her hands in her pockets to keep them from doing any unintended magic. "Enough about the hair thing! I. Am not. A thief." She stepped toward him and tried to look threatening, even though the top of her head barely came up past his shoulder. "Do you want us to help you or not?"

Immediately the soldier pushed Thisbe against the wall. He pulled a dagger from his belt and pressed the point to Thisbe's chest. "Don't move," he said menacingly. Without turning, he called to his fellow soldiers, "Take the thief away."

Thisbe's eyes widened as two soldiers rushed in and grabbed her. "What are you doing? Stop!" More soldiers came rushing in.

"Let go of her!" shouted Seth, running at them.

Fifer rushed to her twin's side and tried to pull her free. "You leave her alone!"

The soldiers yanked harder. Thisbe's eyes sparked dangerously. "Get away from me!"

The other soldiers grabbed Fifer and Seth and pulled them back while the two holding Thisbe dragged her to the ramp and began to ascend it. "Help!" Thisbe screamed. "Stop!" Little jets of fire burst from her eyes and hit the wall, leaving two smoldering divots behind. Thisbe screamed. She'd never done anything like that with her eyes before. Abandoning her quest to do good with her magic, she attempted to replicate that spell, aiming her eyes at the soldiers. But try as she might, she couldn't do it again.

In desperation, Fifer screeched. Birds flew in through the tiny dungeon windows, but as usual, all they did was flutter about. The soldiers batted them away and kept dragging Thisbe, who dug in her heels to no avail.

"Stop!" she cried out, her voice ragged. Part of her desperately wanted to shout the word "boom" and kill these creeps. But she couldn't make herself do it. The results of that spell had been traumatic enough when she'd killed the venomous snake, much less Captain Baldhead back when she was two. She couldn't bear to kill these soldiers no matter how much she hated what they were doing to her. Besides, more soldiers came rushing in, and she wouldn't be able to kill them all. If she managed to destroy one or more of them, what would they do to her then? She'd be a thief *and* a murderer. Alex wouldn't be the only one wanting to lock her up if that happened. Surely they wouldn't let her go free, and right now, all she wanted to do was make it home somehow. She wrenched her arms, but the soldiers held her fast. "Back off!" she shouted desperately, flicking her fingers the best she could, hoping something else would happen. Fiery sparks flew out of them, hitting the soldiers in the face.

The men and women dropped Thisbe and began pawing at their stinging faces. Thisbe tried to run, but the next group of soldiers grabbed her and picked her up.

"We need Thisbe to stay here so she can do the magic!" Fifer was shouting from the dragon dungeon. "Bring her back this instant!" The head soldier held her, kicking and screaming. Next to her, Seth landed a well-placed kick and managed to break loose from his captor. He rushed after the larger group, searching desperately inside his vest pockets as he ran. He pulled out a few scatterclips and sent them flying. They snagged one soldier, dragging him backward and stacking another behind the first, and pinned them to the wall. But it wasn't enough. There were too many soldiers. Soon he was recaptured and held tightly.

"Just fix the wings, Fifer! You have to!" Thisbe yelled out as the soldiers dragged her higher up the ramp. "Then we can all get out of here!"

Fifer stared after her. She felt like she was being torn down the middle, half of her body being wrenched away, and she was helpless to do anything about it. How could she function without Thisbe? They'd never been apart before.

Fifer thought about her life stories. How their mother had died saving her and Thisbe when they were only one year old. The townspeople of Quill had brought them to Aaron at the palace, but Aaron had been abducted by the pirates. Gondoleery Rattrapp had taken over and ordered them to the Ancients Sector. Then Liam Healey had risked his life and stolen the girls away, and they'd been on the run in the freezing cold for days with no food or water. He'd brought them to Artimé.

She thought about how the girls had been together inside the giant rock during the final battle. How Fifer had stopped Queen Eagala's evil birds, and Thisbe had killed the pirate captain because he was kidnapping Fifer.

They'd lived peacefully in the mansion since then. And through all of it, they'd been together. Through every traumatic event, the twins had been side by side. And now, horribly, everything was changing.

Fifer barely noticed when the soldier let her go. Magical Warrior Training, her component vest—neither of those held any place in her thoughts anymore. She sank to the ground, then looked at Seth, who looked back at her solemnly and didn't say a word. They both lowered their heads. Thisbe was gone. And Fifer couldn't do this job without her.

Seth and Fifer Improvise

But Fifer didn't have a choice. She blinked back the tears, sucked in a sharp breath, and stood up. Then she very deliberately straightened her clothes and gave the soldier one last look of hatred as he moved back to join the others at the bottom of the ramp. Inside, Fifer was scared to death. What were the soldiers doing to her sister? Where were they taking her? But she knew she had to step up and make this happen . . . without the supplies they needed.

"What are we going to do?" Seth asked in a low voice.

"I don't know." Fifer turned and knelt on the cold floor. She straightened the sticks and started to gather up the flower petals that hadn't been damaged in the scuffle. She sniffed once and shivered in the damp room. "Let's look around, I guess. Maybe we can find something down here to use for the cloth covering."

Seth and Fifer began looking in the shadowy corners of the low-lit dungeon and discovered a narrow hallway that led to many more open dungeon rooms—some of which had actual prisoners chained to the walls by their wrists. The children didn't get far before they saw at least ten soldiers patrolling the maze of hallways and yelling at the prisoners.

"At least they didn't put Thisbe in here," murmured Fifer. "Whoa, look out—soldiers coming this way." The two turned around quickly and went back to the section where the dragons were.

By the exterior wall near Arabis, Seth spotted a stack of swollen burlap sacks marked DRAGON FODDER. Next to the filled sacks was a small pile of empty ones. "Can we use these sacks for the cloth part of the wings?"

Fifer went over to examine them. "They're better than nothing. I think they'll work. But I'm still not sure what we're going to do without more branches." She looked up at Arabis the orange, whose neck curved uncomfortably in the too-small stall and whose pained eyes watched Seth and Fifer from above the muzzle.

Fifer spied a few widely spaced, rusty iron rungs built into the wall between the stalls. She used them like a ladder and climbed up to stroke the dragon's neck. "I wish you could tell me why they keep you locked up like this. And what happened to make you captives in your own land. It doesn't make any sense."

Arabis blinked.

Fifer wished she'd asked Hux more questions when he'd had his muzzle off. But she doubted Hux would have answered—he'd already seemed uncomfortable with the amount of information he'd given them. Dragons had so many secrets.

Almost as if Arabis could hear Fifer's thoughts, the dragon snorted. Fifer gasped in surprise. Medium-size dragons were pretty intimidating, even if they were friends of Artimé.

When Arabis had settled again, Fifer climbed up higher and slid along the top of the thick stall door so she could examine the placement of the dragon's existing wings. She remembered that Alex and the others had done some sort of mathematical equation to determine what size the new wings needed to be, but Fifer and Seth didn't have a clue what the formula was. She tried to remember how big the new wings were compared to the long tables they sat on in Ms. Octavia's room. They'd stuck out over the edge in both directions, she recalled, but that was about as much as she knew. They were huge. And Fifer's materials were limited. It seemed impossible. Plus, how were they going to get the old wings off? She hopped back down and went over to where Seth sat, counting the sticks.

"There's absolutely no way we can do this," Fifer lamented. "We need ten giant wings. That's practically a whole forest full of branches."

Seth frowned as he studied their meager supplies. He looked up at Fifer, and then he glanced at Ivis the green, who was the dragon nearest him. "What if . . . ," he began, then stopped.

"What?" asked Fifer.

Seth shook his head as if he were embarrassed to say it. But then he thought some more and said, "Why do we have to make entire new wings? Why can't we just, you know, add on to the existing ones?" He cringed, expecting Fifer to laugh at the idea, for he wasn't normally the one of the three to come up with a smart solution to a problem. Not that Seth didn't have ideas, of course. He just didn't often have a chance to share them, what with the twins always scheming a step ahead of him. And under normal circumstances he was perfectly happy to let them do the plotting and take the lead. But Thisbe was half of Fifer's masterful brain, and with her gone, Seth felt a little bolder about making a suggestion.

Fifer tapped her lips thoughtfully. It was such a simple plan that she was surprised she hadn't thought of it. But would it work? She scrunched up her nose as she pictured the results. "The wings will be pretty ugly."

"Right." Seth hastily looked down so Fifer wouldn't see his disappointment. But then he thought some more and looked up again. "But as long as they can fly, the dragons won't care, will they?" Seth turned to Ivis. "Will you?"

Ivis shook her head as much as the muzzle chains would allow. The dragons needed wings that worked in order to stay alive. They didn't care how ugly they were.

"Okay, well, I think we've got a plan, then," said Fifer, relieved. "And maybe if we're really lucky, the wings will work without me having to make them come alive."

Seth laughed. "Don't count on that. They'll just be extra deadweight, and they won't meld properly to the existing wings without magic. But we'll worry about that later. Let's get started." He tried not to grin too much, for there was still a lot at stake, and Thisbe to worry about, and besides that, no one knew if the plan would work. But it had been his idea, and he was pretty proud of that. He cleared his throat authoritatively. "We have twenty-two sapling branches that are all taller than me. So we can use two of them per wing to extend each by at least five feet, and we'll have two branches left over in case we need them. Do you think that'll be enough?"

Fifer sucked in a breath and let it out slowly, contemplating the impossible task. She shook her head, wishing hard for Thisbe's input. She'd know best what to do. But Fifer knew that Thisbe would be counting on her to pull this off, and then rescue her. There was nothing else they could do but try. They'd come this far, and they had to do it for the sake of the dragons—and themselves. "I sure hope it's enough," she said, resigned, and picked up two sticks. "It'll have to be."

A Stranger in the Dark

The soldiers dragged Thisbe, yelling and kicking, up to the grand entrance of the castle. They crossed to a wing on the opposite side, beyond the tigers, then went into a hallway. They pulled Thisbe down a long, uneven flight of stairs to a dungeon that felt even colder, darker, and more damp than the one the dragons were in. The floor was wet and the walls were slimy, and there were only a few torches here and there to light the way.

They weaved through narrow hallways, past other chained prisoners, who called out in anguish as the soldiers and Thisbe passed by. The soldiers shouted back at them to be quiet and threatened them with punishments. Thisbe held her breath, feeling more and more scared the deeper they went and the more turns they made.

Thisbe soon lost all sense of direction. She tried desperately to remember the turns they took, but there were so many that the journey became a blur, and she had no idea which way was out. Finally they came to a stop in front of a few small, open chambers that were unlit and seemingly empty. The soldiers pushed Thisbe inside and slapped iron cuffs around her wrists and ankles. Within moments they were gone, their footsteps just an echo in the stone hallways.

Thisbe soon discovered by feel and sound that the cuffs were attached to chains, and the chains were attached to the wall. She tugged at them, hard, but they didn't budge. "Release," she whispered, but she wasn't surprised when they didn't release her, since they hadn't been attached magically. It was strange—nobody seemed to do magic in Grimere.

She knew shouting for help would do no good but get her more punishments, so Thisbe sat down. The cold water seeped into her clothes. "Yuck," she muttered, feeling miserable and helpless. "This place is so disgusting." She choked back a sob, knowing that if she started crying now, she might not stop, and then she'd have a cry headache on top of it all.

She couldn't help but think of home and how it seemed more and more likely that they'd never make it back there again. Why had they come here? They'd been so foolish to attempt such a huge, dangerous task. Her brother was right. She deserved to be locked up, and now she was. "I'm so sorry, Alex," she whispered. "Please come and find us. Please. I'll never do anything like this again, I promise. Just . . . just please don't hate me. That would be the worst thing that could happen."

After a minute, the silence was broken by a new voice. It was thick and raspy and that of an old woman. "You must love Alex very much for that to be the worst thing."

Thisbe froze. She looked all around in the darkness but couldn't see anyone. "Who said that?" she asked. "Who are you?" She stretched out her hands and tried to put her feet up to help protect herself, but she couldn't lift them very far before the chain grew taut.

But the voice didn't come any closer. A chain rattled, and it wasn't one attached to Thisbe. "I am Maiven Taveer. And you?"

"Thisbe. Um, Thisbe Stowe."

"You speak the language of the dragons quite beautifully."

Thisbe didn't know what to think about that. "It's the only language I know besides Warbler sign language. Why do you call it the language of the dragons?"

"It has always been called so," said Maiven Taveer.

Thisbe thought about that. "But all the dragons I know can speak another secret language. I've heard Pan use it. I thought that was their language."

"I have not heard of Pan. Is he a dragon?"

"*She* is, yes. She's the ruler of the sea."

"The sea? There's no sea here, only a crater lake many miles away, beyond Dragonsmarche. What world does she rule?"

"The world of . . . Artimé, and the Island of Dragons and . . . well, five other islands. You don't need me to name them all. I guess people here call my world the Seven Islands."

"Ah," said Maiven Taveer. "I know of it, but have never been there."

"It's kind of hard to get there from here."

"So I've heard. Unless you're a pirate."

"A pirate?"

Maiven was quiet for a moment, and then said, "This is probably not accurate anymore. But once upon a time, pirates could travel between the worlds. They sold sea creatures in the marketplace. Quite rare here, as you can imagine. Since there's no sea, I mean."

"Oh." Thisbe didn't really feel like talking about pirates. The two chamber mates lapsed into silence, and Thisbe's thoughts turned to her miserable predicament and how uncomfortable she felt sitting in a quarter inch of cold running water. At least she hoped it was water. She shivered and hugged her knees, letting her forehead rest on them.

After a few minutes, Maiven Taveer spoke again. "Tell me about it."

Thisbe lifted her head and blinked in the darkness. "What?"

"The Seven Islands. Is it beautiful there?" Maiven's voice carried a strong melody of wistfulness that, for a moment, made Thisbe feel sorrier for her than she felt for herself.

"Most of it is beautiful. I live in the center island of the seven, on Quill and Artimé. Artimé is the magical side, you see. And Quill . . . well, the people there are not so bad now, but they used to call creative children Unwanteds and send them to their deaths." She laughed a little. "Now they just send them to us in Artimé and we take them in. We teach them how to use their creativity to do magic." She trailed off, thinking of Henry and Thatcher, and a spear of longing went through her. She missed them. She missed everything about home. "It's much better for the Unwanteds to be in Artimé."

"Hmm." The old woman was silent for a time, and then said, "Everything gets worse or better as time passes. It rarely stays the same."

Thisbe frowned. "What do you mean?"

"Lands, people, situations," Maiven said, passionately enough to send her into a coughing fit. When she could speak again, she continued. "Everything. It either gets better or it gets worse. Think about Quill—you said it was getting better. What about Artimé? Is it getting better there, or worse? Consider people you know—they are always changing one way or another. Think about *yourself*, Thisbe. Are you getting better? Or worse?"

The questions made Thisbe uncomfortable. She stayed quiet, pondering them. Thinking about her destructive magic and how she still couldn't stop it. And then she thought of what Hux had said about Dev, and about how he was exactly 50 percent good and 50 percent evil. And that time would tell which direction he moved in.

"I don't know," Thisbe said in a small voice.

Maiven paused. "I'm sorry—I've just realized you are a child, aren't you? You sounded much older before."

"I'm not a child," said Thisbe. "I'm twelve."

"I see," said Maiven solemnly. After a while she asked, "Will you tell me more about your world so I can see it in my mind forever? It will help me pass the days."

"How many days have you been in here?"

Maiven hesitated. "I don't want to tell you."

"Why not?"

There was a long moment of silence before Maiven broke it once more. "Because I don't want you to be afraid."

Thisbe Gets a Shock

While Seth and Fifer constructed the first set of wing extensions, using Seth's dwindling supply of scatterclips to wire them together and his remaining preserve components as glue to connect them to Arabis's existing wings, Thisbe told Maiven Taveer all about Artimé.

She described the lush lawn, the colorful trees and flowers, the fountains, the mansion, the magical creatures, and the jungle, which could be a dangerous place. She went on to describe Warbler's underground tunnels and outdoor shipyard, and Karkinos the crab island with a forest growing on his shell and sand around the edges, and his coral-reef claws, and the grandfathers' gardens on the Island of Shipwrecks. And before she knew it, hours had passed without her feeling especially terrible about having to be in the cold, damp dungeon of an ancient castle at the peak of the cliffs of Grimere, with no way to get home.

When they came to a natural lull in the conversation, Thisbe ventured to ask the old woman a few questions too. "Are you from Grimere or somewhere else? How did you come to be put in this dungeon? And do they bring any food and water around? I'm getting pretty hungry. We haven't eaten anything since the middle of the night."

But the old woman was silent, and soon Thisbe could hear a soft snoring sound coming from her direction. Thisbe realized she was weary too, but even though things were quiet in her area of the dungeon, she was too afraid to sleep. Instead she tipped her head back against the wall and stared into the darkness, thinking and worrying about . . . well, about everything.

After several minutes, Thisbe began to ponder her magic. And how being one of the most magical people in Artimé didn't mean much at all when she didn't know how to use it or control it. Her attempts at controlling it on this journey had failed miserably, but she'd tried—she'd tried very hard, in fact. Maybe Fifer was right, and the way to fix that problem was to go through Magical Warrior Training.

But of course Alex wouldn't allow it. Thisbe began to feel renewed anger building up inside as she thought about how Alex shielded her and Fifer from learning more, and how he'd forced everyone else to keep magic from them. He didn't demand that for any other children in Artimé. He barely ever let the twins see anything in action. For years he required them to stay in the mansion during the times Florence was leading Magical Warrior Training on the lawn. And then, when the girls had attempted to learn things by watching through their window, he'd moved the whole operation to Karkinos, out of sight.

And Alex had kept the components locked away. It was all very frustrating, because Fifer and Thisbe were really good at the magic they'd learned on the sly. If only Alex had taught them the right way to do things once they were old enough to understand the dangers, instead of hiding everything from them, she and Fifer might not be in this predicament right now. Maybe the good things that Thisbe could do with those kinds of spells would balance out all the bad things she did with her internal magic now.

Having so much time to stew about it only caused her anger to grow, until she was mad enough to rip the chains right out of the walls.

She frowned. And then she grabbed one of the ankle chains with both hands. She concentrated on what she wanted to happen and then tugged at the chain, trying to pull it apart. "Break!"

Nothing happened.

"Splinter!" she cried.

From a distance away, the sound of tinkling glass could be heard. "Not you, you lousy window," she muttered impatiently, but that was a spell she hadn't done before, so she took a mental note of it before trying something else. "Chains, rip apart! Uncouple! Fracture!" She yanked them, but they held fast. "Divide!" she tried. She was running out of synonyms, and wished she could look in the Giant Thesaurus that sat in the midst of a mess of books in the Museum of Large. Instead, she thought some more. "Snap! Crunch! Explode!"

It was no use. Either she didn't have the right verbal component, or she was doing something else wrong. She sat back, defeated. After a while her anger faded and turned to sadness. Finally her eyelids drooped.

As she began to drift off to sleep, she heard a ruckus in the dungeon and snapped awake, her stomach roiling in fear. Had they figured out that she'd broken the window? Were they coming to do something awful to her?

Or perhaps it was someone coming with food. But the commotion sounded a little too crazy for that to be the case.

The noises grew louder, and the dungeon walls echoed with shouts. The voices were familiar, almost. Was it Seth and Fifer? Or Dev? No, it wasn't any of them. She sat up a bit higher and strained her ears, trying to understand what the people were saying, but there was so much yelling and noise and echoing that Thisbe couldn't make out any of it.

Soon the noisy group approached the chamber that Thisbe and Maiven occupied. In the dim hallway light, Thisbe could tell there were two prisoners, completely immobilized and being carried by a ridiculous number of guards. They turned sharply into the open chamber next door, and Thisbe could hear the rattle of chains and the threats from the soldiers as they shackled the two.

Finally the guards exited the chamber. Some of them were swearing, others limping. But Thisbe soon forgot them because a voice rose above their noise. The voice was loud and clear and passionate, and it came from one of the new prisoners next door. "GIVE . . . ME . . . MY . . . SON!"

Hiding Something

Thisbe gasped, and the dungeon exploded into noise. Prisoners from the various chambers around them began hollering and bellowing, either mocking Carina or supporting her—Thisbe wasn't quite sure which. But the fact that Carina was here, just on the other side of the wall, made Thisbe's heart surge. "Carina!" she yelled, but she could hardly hear herself. She didn't expect Carina could hear her either.

She strained to listen, trying to figure out who the other prisoner might be, and her mind was filled with questions. How did Carina get here? How did she know where to find them?

She called out, "Carina! Carina!" but the words were lost in the din again.

"Wait a little," said Maiven. "Trust me!"

Thisbe didn't understand why, but she closed her mouth anyway. Soon the sound of jeers and yells faded, and the noise was overtaken by the sound of a squeaky, rattling cart coming down the hallway. The smell of rancid food filled Thisbe's nostrils, and she gagged and nearly threw up. After several minutes, the cart reached their chamber. The boy pushing it brought two trays inside, setting one by Maiven and the other by Thisbe. Thisbe could just barely make out his features. It was Dev.

Thisbe sat up and whispered harshly, "Dev, wait! Why am I down here? Can't you tell them I'm not a thief?"

The boy straightened quickly and took a step away. "I'm not Dev," he said in a fake voice. He fled, pushing the cart to the next chamber where Carina was, leaving Thisbe completely puzzled.

Then, from next door, Carina spoke sharply. "Freeze." Thisbe's eyes widened in the darkness. Did Carina have components? Or was that a noncomponent spell? She'd have to try it sometime.

"What did you do that for?" Carina's companion asked weakly. Thisbe's heart soared again as she recognized his voice. *Thatcher!*

"Because I'm mad."

"Well, that's a good enough reason. Though he's just a servant who didn't do anything to us. And now some of the prisoners won't get food."

Thisbe sucked in a breath. She was surprised how well she could hear them now that everyone had settled down, for they were talking normally.

"Fine," Carina muttered. "Release."

The clatter of the cart resumed as Dev served their trays. Soon the squeaks and rattles faded when Dev moved down the hallway.

"I can't believe we ended up in here," Carina muttered. "What is this disgusting crud?"

Thisbe nearly laughed aloud. Carina didn't talk like that whenever Seth and his siblings and the twins were around. She talked like a mom then. Now Thisbe wanted to be quiet so she could find out what else Carina might say.

"It's better than having nothing, like the past thirty hours," said Thatcher. He didn't sound at all like himself, and Thisbe wondered if he was ill or injured.

"I suppose."

Thisbe could hear their plates rattling, and Maiven's as well.

"Eat quickly or they'll take it away," whispered Maiven. "Talk to your friends later. Trust me," she said again. "I'll let you know when it's time."

"Okay." Thisbe attempted to eat her food. It was terrible, but Thisbe was hungry, so she ate almost all of it, and then drank the tall tumbler of water that accompanied it. It stopped her stomach from complaining—at least for a little while, until it realized what Thisbe had actually sent it.

While she waited for the signal, she wondered why Dev had pretended he was someone else. Thisbe knew it was him. She was certain. Why would he lie and avoid her? Something was definitely going on with him and his sneakiness, but she didn't know what it might be.

A while later, when Dev came back in and picked up the trays, Thisbe held out her hand toward the chamber opening and whispered, "Glass."

Dev moved to return to his cart and slammed into the glass

wall face-first. The trays went flying and clattered on the floor. Dev fell backward, crying out in pain.

"Release," whispered Thisbe, and the glass disappeared. As the boy got to his hands and knees, Thisbe said in a low voice, "Don't mess with me, Dev. I'm warning you." She'd never said such a thing to anyone before, and it felt terribly freeing.

Dev yelped and didn't reply. Instead he crawled to the doorway and began feeling around for the glass, which was no longer there. Once he realized the space was clear, he dove for the hallway and took off with the cart to Carina and Thatcher's chamber.

Thisbe lifted her chin and narrowed her eyes in satisfaction, and began to wonder if she was turning just a little bit bad.

A Familiar Voice

When all the food trays had been picked up and the dungeon had quieted, Thisbe waited for Maiven to give her some sort of signal that it was okay to talk to Carina. But it didn't come. Had the old woman fallen asleep again?

The evening stretched onward. Maiven remained silent until a sharp snoring sound came from somewhere in the hallway nearby.

"Ahh, there it is," said Maiven softly. "That is your cue, Miss Thisbe."

"Is that the guard?" Thisbe whispered.

Maiven went on. "There are guards stationed throughout the hallways at night. The one assigned between our chamber and your friend's is a loud snorer. Not so nice when you're trying to sleep, but perfect when you want to talk. You should be able to converse for several hours if you keep yourself low to the ground and speak softly."

"But how will my friend hear me?"

"Are you sitting in a stream of water?"

Thisbe frowned, confused. "Yes."

"Near the floor at your back is a small opening in the wall, the size of a brick, that leads to your friend's chamber. There is one in every wall. It's how they clean—by spraying water at one end and letting it wash through all the chambers. Not very sanitary if you ask me, but then again, no one ever does." Maiven paused, then continued. "Try to lower yourself as close as possible to that opening. Your voice will carry through. If the snoring stops, you stop talking."

"Thank you." Thisbe quickly slid her body to one side as far as the chains would allow, trying to feel for the opening. When she found it, she bent down and could hear the low rumble of Carina and Thatcher talking, though she couldn't make out the words. "Carina!" she whispered. "Thatcher!"

Their conversation paused, and Thisbe whispered again. "Carina! Thatcher! It's me, Thisbe. Down by the floor where the water goes through."

She could hear a scuffle as one of the two shifted to align with the hole in the wall. And then a glorious moment later, she heard a familiar voice.

"Thisbe?" It was Thatcher, sounding incredulous.

"Yeah." Thisbe started to cry. "Hi, Thatcher." She tried to sound upbeat, but the words came out sounding miserable.

"Are you all right?"

"I'm . . . cold and wet and a little scared." She hesitated. "But not much."

Thatcher laughed softly. "You're braver than me. How long have you been down here? Are Seth and Fifer there with you?"

"I'm alone." Thisbe explained everything, from the children's scary journey on Hux's back to their horrifying adventures in the first village to their trek up the mountain with Dev. "And the soldiers here don't like me because I'm demanding and I sent sparks flying at their faces, and they think I'm a thief because I have short hair, and now I'm stuck down here while

Fifer and Seth try to fix all the dragon wings. I wish they'd hurry up, but to be honest I don't know if they can do it without me."

As Thisbe talked, Thatcher relayed to Carina the parts of the story she couldn't hear. After she finished by telling Thatcher about Maiven's kindness, she asked Thatcher to tell his story.

Thatcher told her about their journey, from deciding who would chase after the children to stopping at Warbler to see Sky, to Thatcher's near drowning incident off the coast of the Island of Fire. "We lost all of our supplies except for what we had in our component vests," Thatcher said, "but we decided to continue the journey even though we didn't have food or water."

"No water? That's the worst part."

"Tell me about it. I got pretty sick, and I totally blacked out by the time we were crossing over to the land of the dragons, so I didn't even get to see what that big chasm or the cliffs looked like. But Carina said it was amazing."

"Well, I guess it was," said Thisbe. "We were just trying to hang on for dear life. And don't feel bad about blacking out.

Seth totally fainted when he was hanging by the vine over the chasm."

"I think I'd better not mention that part to Carina," said Thatcher with a soft laugh.

"What happened next? How did you get thrown in here? Didn't Simber protect you? Where *is* Simber?"

"When Simber landed, he took us straight into the forest to the river so we could get some freshwater. That helped a lot, but I was still really weak and needed food and to recover a bit. So Simber weaved farther into the forest to try to find something for us to eat while Carina built a fire and caught a fish from the river. We were having a nice time of it, actually, when a bunch of soldiers in green coats surrounded us."

"Those creeps are everywhere," muttered Thisbe.

"They sure are. Anyway, they thought we were thieves too—now we know why. Carina and I fought them off with the components we had in our vests, but it's really hard to fight in a forest. Even worse, I was weak. My aim was off and I hit more trees than humans, I think. I shackled one tree and made another do the fire step, and it totally uprooted itself and danced around for a few minutes there. Luckily, the roots took hold again when the spell wore off, or I'd have felt really bad."

The image of that made Thisbe smile. "Then what?" she demanded.

"Then we tried to fight them with our fists, but there were too many of them. They surrounded us and wrapped us up in ropes to keep us from doing any more magic. As they were dragging us off, Simber came back toward the camp, but being huge like he is, he couldn't weave through the trees or plow them down fast enough to get to us."

"Oh, poor Simber," said Thisbe.

"He knows where we are, though, and we heard the soldiers talking earlier about taking children as prisoners, and Hux's return. So Carina and I had a pretty good feeling you'd be around somewhere. I'm sure Simber's just sitting tight until we figure out how to get out of here."

"Do you really think we'll figure that out?" asked Thisbe.

"I'm sure of it," said Thatcher.

But somehow his reassurance only made Thisbe worry more.

Figuring Things Out

By now Fifer and Seth had completed construction on all the wing extensions and were doing their best with the few supplies they had to attach them to each existing wing. It was a tricky process handling the dragons, trying to get them to keep their wings still while the two of them balanced precariously on stable walls and the creatures' backs. And trying to find whatever they could that would help keep the extensions attached once they had them on.

They saved the hardest dragon for last. Drock the dark purple was the least helpful when it came to working with the children. He stomped his feet and banged against the sides of his stall, doing full-body shakes and making it difficult for Fifer and Seth to do much of anything with the tips of his wings.

With Fifer perched on Drock's back and pitching side to side, and with Seth climbing onto the top of the stall's wall and leaning in to grab the wing, the two tried to wrangle the dragon into obedience. But it was very late, and everyone was tired and hungry, and Drock wasn't having any part of it.

Finally Fifer sighed and gave up. She reached her arms around Drock's neck and hugged him. "I'm so sorry," she said, her voice like a song. "You must feel absolutely terrible stuck in here all the time. You can't even turn around."

Drock continued pitching from side to side, but less violently. Seth sat up straight on top of the wall, hanging on to the post with one hand and balancing the wing extension with the other, and rested for a moment while he watched Fifer.

Fifer ran her hand along the dragon's neck. "Your mother would think you are very brave," she said. "We saw her just a few days ago. She wanted us to give you her love, but with all this crazy work to do, I forgot. I'm sorry."

Drock shuddered and settled down a bit more. He seemed

to like being petted, and he certainly liked the kindness in Fifer's voice. Fifer began humming one of the many songs she'd made up over the years.

When Drock became fully calm, Fifer sat up and said very quietly to Seth, "I think there has to be a way to release these dragons from this awful prison once we have their wings working. We can do it, don't you think so? This is a terrible life for them."

Seth shrugged. He could see now why the dragons couldn't just torch whoever was trying to control them, even if they were 100 percent bad. And he could imagine that if this Revinir dude could threaten Arabis's life to get Hux to come back, he could certainly threaten the dragons daily with the same thing to keep them from trying to escape when they were out flying royalty around the various lands. "But how do we get them all out of here together at the same time?" asked Seth. "That's the problem."

Drock blinked rapidly and tried to nod.

"Good question. I'm not sure how we can do it without help. We can't get these stable doors open without a key. But once we have that, and once we figure out how to release the muzzles, couldn't all five of them storm up the ramp and just trample anybody in their way?"

Drock frowned.

Seth thought about that as a few of the dragons within ear-shot shook their heads. "No?" he guessed. "But why . . . ?" He scratched his head, and then guessed again. "Because not all of the soldiers are more evil than good. So they can't harm the good ones."

Now Hux and Drock nodded what little they could.

"That makes sense," said Fifer, motioning to Seth to help her with the wing extension now that Drock was calm. "Maybe they can use their tails to snatch up the good ones as we go along and set them aside. Though that seems like it would be pretty difficult."

"We need to create a distraction," Seth said. "One that would get everyone out of our way."

"And one that would get us the keys to open up these stables," Fifer reminded him.

"Right." Seth looked defeated. He had no idea how they'd manage that. "Plus," he said, crestfallen, "we have to find Thisbe and get her out of here too."

Just then, Dev came from the dungeon hallway with a cart of empty, dirty trays. The two Artiméans could hear some chanting happening in the human prisoner part of the dungeon.

"Hey! How did you get here?" Fifer demanded of him. "You didn't come down this way."

Dev's nose was swollen, and he had dried blood caked around his nostrils. He looked at them, seeming a bit rattled, and muttered, "I started on the other side and worked my way to here." He pushed on through the dragon area and went up the ramp past the guards.

Fifer and Seth exchanged a curious glance as if they'd just been given information inadvertently, though neither of them quite knew what good it would do them. Both of them sank into their own private thoughts as they used Seth's remaining scatterclips to hook the last extension onto Drock's second wing.

When they were finished, the two hopped down to appraise their work before attempting the harder, magical part of the job.

Fifer stood back so she could see the wings of all five

dragons. Seth joined her. Each beautiful, sparkling, colorful beast wore gray burlap sacks dotted with a few flower petals on the end of their wings, like giant, ugly socks. The extensions sagged precariously, since they were a bit too heavy for a few paper clips and glue to secure them properly. Fifer hoped the magic would fix that.

"They look atrocious," Seth remarked, trying out a new word he'd learned in Samheed's theater class.

"Thank you," said Fifer, who didn't know what it meant. "I think it's pretty good for someone like me. I've always been behind in Ms. Octavia's art class, but I think she'd be quite proud, don't you?"

"Mmm," said Seth with a little cough. To be kind he added, "I would think so."

Fifer smiled at the dragons, trying to look encouraging for their sake. Being stuck down here all day and evening had given her the slightest glimpse of what the dragons dealt with every day. "We're going to find a way to get you all out of here," she said to them just as Dev reappeared, without the cart this time. "I promise."

"Good luck with that," said Dev wearily. He held two trays

of food and set them roughly on the ground. "Late dinner, early breakfast, whatever you want to call it," he said sarcastically. "Sorry it took me so long. I only had five hundred others to get to first."

Fifer barely comprehended him. Instead she flashed Seth a wild look. She hadn't meant for anyone to hear her. She went over to Dev and laid a hand on his shoulder, giving him an earnest look. "Please don't say anything to anyone."

Her musical voice must have contained some amount of magic on its own, for Dev softened a bit. But he wouldn't commit to keeping her secret. "It's just not possible," he said quietly. "You'll never be able to do it." He dropped his gaze. "Especially with those black eyes. You'll be locked up or sold off soon enough. Just like I was."

He turned to go, but Fifer grabbed his arm. "Wait. What does that mean?"

Dev shook his head. "Haven't you figured it out yet? You and Thisbe are valuable slaves. I brought you here to get a reward because I'm a crummy person. It's not that complicated."

Fifer shook her head, numb. She didn't want to believe him,

but it was starting to make sense with the way he had acted. "Why would you do that to us?"

Dev sighed, his exasperation masking his feelings of guilt. "Because I do what I have to do, okay? And so will you one day. They might let *him* go," he said, pointing to Seth, "but neither you nor Thisbe will ever be free again. Just. Like. Me." He yanked his arm away from Fifer and muttered, "And soon *you'll* be crummy people too."

One Thing after Another

Leaving Fifer and Seth speechless, Dev slipped away, out of sight. Fifer wasn't quite sure how to feel. Dev had tricked them and profited from it. Could she trust that he was telling the truth about her and Thisbe? Could she trust him about anything after what he'd done? More confused than ever, and hungrier than ever, Fifer and Seth sat down next to the trays of food before attempting to make the dragon wings work.

"Do you think he's telling the truth?" Fifer asked. She sniffed at her plate and wrinkled her nose before bravely taking a bite. "I mean, he basically said he tricked us into having him guide us here so he could collect a reward. If that doesn't make him more evil than good, I don't know what does."

"I'm not sure, but I'm not leaving here without you," said Seth. "Even if they let me go free."

"It's not like you have anywhere to go," Fifer pointed out.

"Unless they let a dragon take me home, and then maybe I could get help."

"True. You'd have to leave us, then, though."

"Oh, yeah. I guess I would."

Fifer ate the prison food without really tasting it. She was hungry enough to eat sticks, so she didn't really notice how terrible it was. She broke off a hunk of stale bread and nibbled on it while trying not to freak out about their circumstances. But she could feel a familiar worry welling up inside her that had been all too common lately. She set the bread down. "So what are we going to do? Just pretend like we don't know they're going to keep Thisbe and me hostage?"

Seth shrugged.

Fifer stewed about it some more, and then she sat up, suddenly angry. "And who cares if our eyes are black! Why does that make us valuable slaves?"

"No idea. Probably just because it's so rare."

"Well, that's a really stupid reason."

"Shh," said Seth, looking over his shoulder. But the guards had remained a short distance up the ramp and weren't paying much attention to the two of them. It wasn't like they could escape.

They finished their meal. Both were exhausted, and they began fretting more and more about the situation. "We'll figure something out," said Seth, trying to be brave. "We have to. Once the dragons have the ability to fly again, we'll bust out of here—all of us." His voice pitched higher. "And we'll go back to Artimé, and everything will be normal like before."

Fifer felt a lump rise to her throat. She nodded, not trusting herself to speak. And she caught Hux's eye. Hux seemed to nod slightly too, as if he agreed with the plan.

"I wish you didn't have these stupid muzzles so could tell us how to get you out of here," Fifer muttered to the dragons. She pushed her tray away and pulled Seth aside. "I'm going to ask the guards a question so I can look for where they might keep their keys."

Seth raised an eyebrow. "Suit yourself. Though I really don't think we have any way of getting our hands on a set."

"At least I'm trying something." Fifer sniffed and went over to the guards. Seth climbed up the makeshift ladder next to Arabis's stall and looked carefully at the dragon's muzzle, trying to see if he could figure out how to take it off. "Does someone come to remove your muzzles so you can eat?" he asked her.

Arabis shook her head as much as she could, then jerked her snout toward the ceiling.

Seth looked up. There was a strange contraption he hadn't paid attention to before. It was a trapdoor with bits of hay sticking out, and a small clock attached to the door with wires. Arabis's clock was set for seven in the morning. Seth puzzled over it, then slid along the doors to Yarbeck's stall and checked the trapdoor above her. That clock was set for quarter past seven.

Seth frowned and continued awkwardly across the stables, checking each of the five clocks that were attached to the trapdoors. They were all set fifteen minutes apart.

Then he took a closer look at the muzzles. Those, too, had an unusual wire attachment that didn't seem necessary. Seth couldn't figure it out.

Soon Fifer returned carrying a pitcher of water, which she

apparently had asked for as her excuse to check out the soldiers. "I couldn't find where they keep their keys," she whispered. "I didn't see them, hear them—nothing. They must be inside their jackets."

Seth pointed to the trapdoors in the ceiling above the dragons' heads. "Check this out. I think the dragons are fed on a timer system. And somehow when their little timer goes off, it signals the muzzle to open far enough so the dragons can eat. They're timed so only one dragon's mouth is free at a time."

The two dragons in earshot nodded profusely, confirming Seth's guess.

"Wow," said Fifer. "Can you make it so the timers all go off at once?"

"That's exactly what I was planning to try. Do you think you'll have all the wing magic done by seven in the morning?"

Fifer felt a knot form in the pit of her stomach. "Sure, I guess." She glanced out the high window, trying to figure out what time it was. The sky was still black, but did she see a faint orange tinge? "Better make that eight, just to be safe. Then it'll be nice and light outside too."

"You got it," said Seth. He started to adjust all of the timers for eight o'clock, happy to be doing something useful. "Just remember that if the soldiers find out we've been messing with the timers, we'll end up in the dungeon like Thisbe."

Fifer grimaced, but her expression soon cleared. "Speaking of Thisbe, did you hear what Dev said? It sounds to me like even though they dragged Thisbe up the ramp, we can actually get to her part of the dungeon through that little doorway where Dev came out of. He said he started on the other side."

"Yeah, I caught that. I don't think he knew he gave anything away. I wonder how he got that bloody nose. I hope Thisbe punched him."

Fifer smiled. "I hope we'll be able to ask her soon. When I went to get the water, I peeked down that hallway again. It's lined with guards, one for every few prison chambers. I'm not sure they're going to be too keen on you and me just sauntering through there to find her."

Seth sighed. "This is so frustrating. It's like there are always five new problems for every solution we come up with."

"Yeah." Fifer took a deep breath, then started climbing into Arabis's stable. "Let's get to work solving this one first."

Stupid Magic

While Thisbe slept in the dungeon, Fifer wearily recounted to Seth everything she knew about what Alex had done with the dragon wings back in Artimé. And then she narrowed her eyes and studied the wings, feeling very unsure of herself and her ability to do the magic necessary to make the wings come alive. It had been Thisbe who'd brought the prison grid to life down in the village. It seemed like more of a Thisbe type of spell—beautiful, yet kind of tough and big in a theatrical way. Whereas the spells that appealed to Fifer were more musical and nature based. Fifer had barely been paying attention, what with keeping an eye on the ostrich statue and thinking she'd never have to be the one to perform it. "Do you want to try first?" she asked Seth.

"Me?" Seth looked horrified. "No stinking way. I'll just mess it up. I can barely handle scatterclips—the nonlethal kind. Besides, you're the naturally magical one here. You're the heir to the throne. Kind of."

"Throne of destruction, maybe." Fifer pursed her lips. She was trying to bolster her confidence and talk herself into being able to do it. She muttered something unintelligible under her breath, then guided one of Arabis's wings up into the air so she could reach the end of it, and stood up on her back. Seth helped Fifer hold the wing steady, and then she closed her eyes and laid her hand on the seam where the new part connected. She took an uneven breath, and then said, "Alive."

The word hung in the air, and Fifer opened one eye to see what had happened.

"Is that it?" asked Seth. "Isn't it supposed to look better now?"

Fifer gave him the side eye.

"Different, I mean," Seth said weakly.

"It didn't work." She stared stonily at what she now realized were hideous-looking wings, feeling like a failure. "I . . . I can't do it."

Seth's eyes widened. "But you have to." He thought for a moment. "In Samheed's plays, the hero never gets it right the first time."

"That has nothing to do with real life," said Fifer, who was more upset with her failure than she had been with anything in quite some time. "This is much harder."

"Well," said Seth, growing frustrated too, "at least try again."

"Why? It's obvious I can't do it."

Seth shook his head slowly. "I don't think that's how it works for most people."

"That's how it works for me." And it was true. Fifer and Thisbe hadn't experienced failure with learned spells. Granted, their internal magic generally came out by accident, and they often surprised themselves when something happened. But whenever they actually learned a spell by watching, they almost always got it right the first time. It was sneaking around to get the knowledge that had been the hard part. "I'm mad at myself for not paying more attention. I usually do, but I was distracted. Besides, Thiz was really into this one, and I knew she was watching closely. So I figured I didn't need to. That was stupid." Admitting that was almost as hard as failing.

"Look," said Seth, who was accustomed to frequent failure, "you're special and all that. Whatever. But normal people fail at magic all the time. You should see my class in Warrior Training. We all have to try a few times."

"I'm not like normal people."

Seth rolled his eyes. "I really can't stand you sometimes."

Fifer sat up and glared at him. "I can't stand you, either."

"I don't care! Just try the stupid spell again, will you?"

Fifer wanted to wring Seth's neck. Instead she expelled a hot breath and went through the motions just to get him off her back. She closed her eyes, waited a second, and then said, "Alive."

"Of course nothing's going to happen if you do it like that," said Seth.

"Then *you* do it if you know so much."

Seth was mad enough to take her up on it. "Fine. Don't talk to me."

"I'm not!"

"Shh!" Seth closed his eyes and took a few deep breaths, trying to calm himself down. His mom often told him that he and Fifer were a lot alike, though he personally didn't see it. But she said that was why he got along with Thisbe a little better. And even though he and Fifer got along fine most of the time, it was when things became intense that Seth usually backed down for the sake of survival. That left him stewing, which made their relationship start to unravel. This was definitely not a good time for that to happen.

He blew out a sharp breath and tried to stop thinking about that. Instead he filled his mind with thoughts about wings and flying. He pictured the new, hideously ugly wing tip turning beautiful like the rest of the wing as it became one with it. He imagined the dragon soaring through the air and gliding over the sea near Artimé, and thought about how cool it would be if he were the one to say, "I did that."

I can do this, Seth told himself. *I can do this*. He kept the calm dragon images in mind, and then took in a deep breath. "Alive," he whispered.

He opened his eyes. The wing looked exactly the same.

"I can't do this," Seth muttered, and turned his back on Fifer because he couldn't stand seeing the look on her face. "Are you sure that's the right word?"

"Oh, I see how it is. Now that you can't do it either, you think I got the word wrong." Fifer might have laughed if the situation weren't so dire. "Hard to admit you can't do it, isn't it."

"I just *did* admit it! Ugh!" Seth's face turned dark red as he tried to hold his frustration in check. But it was getting harder. He was exhausted and uncomfortable, and now he was expected to do a kind of spell even his mother had never tried—and she was amazing. He grabbed the stable post and slid down it, falling the last few feet onto his bottom on the cold, wet floor. "I'm taking a break."

Fifer watched him and let out a huff of annoyance. "There's nowhere to go for that," she said.

But Seth didn't care. He walked toward the ramp, at the very least wanting to get out of Fifer's sight for a few minutes.

The four soldiers nearest him were sitting propped up against the walls, asleep, though Seth could hear the murmur of voices around the first turn of the ramp. He crept up, sneaking past the sleeping ones, his hands automatically going for his vest pockets in case he needed to fight before he remembered they were completely empty. He slid along the wall as far as he dared, thinking if there were only two soldiers around the bend, maybe he could make a break for it and escape.

Part of him knew he couldn't do that to Fifer. But he was mad enough now to consider it. His nefarious plan was soon cast aside when he could make out at least four different voices.

"They're cartin' 'em to Dragonsmarche in the morning," said a woman. "Gonna sell 'em. They'll bring a fortune."

"Who, the Revinir?" said another.

"Nah. The king's not telling the Revinir we got 'em, else they'll be snatched away in a hot minute. Keeping it on the down low. It's the king who's offerin' them up. Word is spreading underground."

"I thought the king would want to keep them here," said a voice sounding suspiciously like Dev. He almost seemed disappointed.

"Nah. The pirates heard word of the auction, and they're willin' ta pay a shiny ton."

"There'll be a biddin' war for sure," said a man's voice.

"Mebbe they'll throw you in the mix, Dev. The lot of you are worth a fortune!" The man roared with laughter, startling the sleeping soldiers.

Seth jumped back, his heart in his throat, and ran past the waking soldiers toward Fifer before they could see how far he'd ventured out of the dungeon. But the head soldier was awake in a flash and caught Seth sneaking back. He stuck out his leg, tripping the boy. Seth went sprawling hands first and landed on his stomach. The head soldier grabbed him by the back of his vest and brought him to his feet, then pulled his dagger and held the point to Seth's neck. Seth's eyes widened. He couldn't breathe. Dev and the soldiers from higher up the ramp came running down to see what the ruckus was.

"Where've you been, boy?" asked the head soldier. His rancid breath was hot and moist in Seth's ear.

Seth, awash in fear, could feel himself slipping away.

Expelled

"Don't faint, don't faint," Seth whispered under his breath. He hated fainting, but he did it sometimes. He wasn't sure why, and basically he didn't care—he just hated that it happened. This time he was successful in willing it away, and slowly his vision returned.

"Let him go," said the woman who'd been talking earlier. "I was comin' down to take him out anyway."

Seth didn't dare turn his head to look for Fifer for fear of the dagger slicing his neck. The head soldier tightened his grip, and then he shoved the boy to the floor. Seth landed hard on his already bruised hands and knees, which made them sting horribly.

"Get up," said the woman. "You're comin' with me."

Seth pushed himself up to his feet, feeling like he was probably going to be killed any second. He started shaking. *Take him out*? That wasn't a comforting phrase. He fought off the blackness again and stumbled toward the soldier, who gripped his arm tighter than a shackle spell. She pulled him up the ramp past all the soldiers. Only Dev followed them.

"Why are you taking him out?" Dev asked.

"Princess ordered it. Said it wasn't humane to keep him locked up when he ain't got the black eyes, you see."

Dev was quiet. He saw, all right.

Seth chanced a look and saw Dev's head was down. He was still wearing the same rags as he'd worn on their journey. And his nose was still bloody. The inner corners of his eyes were puffy and turning black-and-blue. He'd been hit hard. Had Dev been up working all night too, like he and Fifer had been?

Dev glanced at Seth as they went into the entryway and past the spot where the bejeweled tigers were tied up. The two boys held each other's gaze for a moment. Seth was too scared to try to read Dev's look. He could only plead for help with his own.

Dev turned away.

The entry soldier stationed at the controls called for the portcullis to be raised and the drawbridge dropped.

"I'll see to it he finds the proper road," Dev said. "I've got to go out and get caught up on my chores anyway."

The woman laughed harshly. "No sleep for you again, I see."

"No. Got in a little trouble for sneaking away."

"Well, serves you right, letting Princess make you carry out all her whims."

"I suppose that's true," said Dev. He didn't regret it. Not much, anyway. They came to a stop as the drawbridge landed with a thud on the far side of the moat.

The woman shoved Seth. "Go on, then. You're free."

Seth froze. He told his feet to walk. And his feet wouldn't listen.

"Is he stupid?" the woman asked Dev.

"Only a little. Come on," Dev said. He pulled Seth by the arm and didn't let go until they were across the moat and on the path leading toward the forest.

When the drawbridge had gone back up, Dev stopped and

faced Seth as darts of pink and orange tinged the eastern sky. "You all right now?" he said, his voice much softer when he was away from the soldiers. "Have you got a way home?"

"N-no," Seth answered, still bewildered at the strange turn of events and feeling utterly lost and alone. "I—I—I . . . ," he stammered, and looked back at the castle. "What's Fifer going to think? That I just left her there?"

Dev's face grew hard. "It doesn't matter now."

"Tell her I'm sorry—we had a fight. Will you tell her? And that I didn't . . . I mean, I'll wait for her and Thisbe. They've got to escape." He slammed his mouth shut, feeling like he said too much to the enemy but hardly being able to help it in his current state. He dropped to his haunches and put his head in his hands, agonizing over what was just becoming real to him. He was out here, Fifer was trapped with the dragons and unable to fix their wings, and Thisbe was . . . where? "Where's Thisbe?" Seth demanded, standing up again and grabbing Dev's torn shirt. It tore a little more.

Dev narrowed his eyes. And then he shrugged as if it didn't make a difference anymore. "There's no way you'll get to her. She's deep in the dungeon. Compartment three thirty-three with Maiven. Not that Thisbe the thief will ever thank me for that, but she should. It was my suggestion they put her with the old hag. She's . . . really a decent person." His eyes flickered with pain, and he turned away, touching his bruised nose gingerly.

At the sound of a rooster crowing in the distance, Dev's stern demeanor returned. "Almost seven already," he muttered. "I've got to go." He pivoted and ran down the gravel road toward the forest.

Seth's heart pounded. "Don't leave me here alone!"

Dev ignored him and kept going.

"Tell Fifer what I said!" Seth squeaked, desperate.

Dev waved, and Seth took that as a sign that he'd tell her, which gave him a little bit of comfort. But then Seth realized what Dev had said. Almost seven o'clock. The dragon food alarms were set for eight. Would Fifer remember to change them back since the dragons still couldn't fly? Did she even know what the right times were for each dragon? Would the soldiers be suspicious when Arabis's trapdoor didn't release in a few minutes? Seth was certain they'd notice.

Helplessness and fear slammed into Seth's chest. The

feeling of being utterly, completely overwhelmed was overtaking every other feeling Seth had ever had. It started like a pebble in the bottom of his stomach, and it moved and rolled and grew, sending out waves of nausea in all directions. They were small waves at first, but those grew too, and soon his body was paralyzed by them. His throat closed up, and he couldn't catch his breath. His hands and feet went numb, and then his face, and he couldn't think straight. He sank to the dirt, a tiny being in this huge, strange world, gasping for breath as panic overtook him. His heart throbbed. Was he going to suffocate? At this point, he thought that anything would be better than feeling like this.

"One breath at a time," his mother would tell him. "It's always okay to feel scared." As Seth fell to his side, he tried with all his might to concentrate on taking one good breath. He closed his eyes as tears slid out and felt the waves of panic pounding him like they weren't going to let up. He took a quick breath, trying to slow the waves down, and let it out. And then he panted for a few seconds and tried another. He stared at the castle, at the row of dungeon windows, and began counting them very slowly out loud to help him get his breath back.

Finally, after a few agonizing minutes, Seth's heart stopped pounding so hard. His lungs thawed, and his breathing came easier. And the panic waves subsided. He remained on his side for several more minutes, all the strength sapped from him. But then he pushed himself heavily to a sitting position, knowing he had to pull his thoughts together to try to figure out what to do.

"The dungeon window," he muttered. That's how he'd talk to Fifer. He got to his feet and tried to figure out which of the low windows along the base of the castle might lead to her. And though he wouldn't be able to cross the moat and get close enough to whisper to her through it, at least he could shout something and she might hear him. He'd have to risk getting caught to do it, but he was willing to try.

Reimagining the route they'd taken inside the castle to the dungeon, Seth began to walk around the outside in the same direction, straining to see if there was any particular dungeon window that looked familiar. He had to find Fifer before it was too bright out, so he could still make a run for it if he got caught. And he had to do it before seven so that Fifer wouldn't get in trouble for messing with the timers. If she got sent to that maze of a dungeon like Thisbe did, he'd never find her.

At that moment Seth realized that, somewhat miraculously, he was developing a rescue plan all on his own, without Thisbe or Fifer. He wasn't sure if he'd ever actually done that before. It made him feel a little more grown-up than usual. He picked up his pace and strained his eyes in the dim light until he rounded the corner. One of the dungeon windows was lit up. It had to be the right one—the rest of the dungeon had been much darker than the dragon's area.

Seth positioned himself outside it, wishing he could somehow jump across the moat so he could talk directly through the window to Fifer. He'd even consider swimming, but he had no idea what was in that water, and he wasn't desperate enough to find out. Yet.

He tried to peer into the window to see if he could catch a glimpse of one of the dragons or even Fifer, but he could only see the dungeon wall and the flame from the torch that was attached to it. It was amazing the castle didn't burn down with all those torches everywhere. These people needed to figure out how to use magic to make light, Seth thought. The wooden stables that housed the dragons could go up in flames if a torch got too close.

Just as Seth leaned over the moat and put his hands by his mouth to guide his voice to Fifer, another voice from behind nearly made him face-plant into the moat.

"Now, therrre's a familiarrr face. I don't suppose you need a rrride to that window?"

Redoubled Efforts

By the time Fifer realized what was happening on the ramp, Seth was gone and she was alone. She didn't even have the heart to fight or argue with the soldiers, or to ask them what was happening. Instinctively she knew—they were letting Seth go free, like Dev had said would happen. She'd climbed up and stood on the top of Arabis's stable wall, leaning over to peer out the window, wondering if she could see him. But after a minute she couldn't hang on anymore, and she gave up. Now what was she going to do?

She climbed back down, then sat on the floor under the

window and put her face in her hands. She was so tired. They'd been awake for more than twenty-four hours. Her body was sore from all the climbing. And she was alone. What a rare thing that was. If she was ever without Thisbe, even for a few minutes, Seth was usually there for her to rely on. Now she had no one but herself. And if she was ever going to get out of there, she needed a plan.

She had to get the wings to work. It didn't matter how impossible it seemed—she was the only one left. She was out of options. Besides, the food timers were all set to go off in an hour, and that would release all of the dragons from their muzzles at the same time, which meant that Fifer needed to figure out how to free them from their stalls by then too, so they could escape. Fifer knew she didn't have much time. And the wings were the most important thing. She could only hope now that the soldiers didn't notice the trapdoors weren't opening on schedule . . . but she had a feeling they didn't care all that much to pay attention.

Wearily she got back up and climbed into Arabis's stall. She sat on the creature's back for a long moment, running her hand over the soft, silky skin and the smooth scales. "We're going to get out of here," she murmured to the dragons. "We have to. As soon as your food drops, be ready to do whatever it takes to bust out of here. Even if we have to break down your doors, we're going to escape, and we're going to get Thisbe, and then we're going to leave this place and never come back." She sounded more sure than she felt. But she wasn't going to cave in to fear now—she needed her twin and their best friend, and she wasn't going to put up with being without them any longer.

As she sat with Arabis, she went back in her mind to the day Alex had brought the wings to life. She tried to remember every detail. He'd put a hand on one wing at a time, and then he'd concentrated for a while, and then he whispered the spell. It was a single word. "Alive." Fifer was sure of it. She closed her eyes for a moment and rested her weary head against Arabis's neck. She just needed a second to gather her concentration. She melted against the dragon, her heavy lids unwilling to open, and sank hard and fast into sleep.

When Arabis shook her awake a few minutes later, Fifer sat up, dazed. She hadn't meant to drift off, but even those few moments of sleep had done her a world of good. She felt refreshed. Ready to tackle the spell.

“Okay, here we go,” she said to Arabis. “Bring your right wing up if you can.”

Arabis obliged, and Fifer stood on the dragon’s back so she could reach the spot she needed. She put her hand over the seam and closed her eyes. She imagined the wing the way she wanted it to be—sleek and strong. And all the same color wouldn’t hurt either, but she wasn’t going to be picky about that. She focused on the extended wing and the dragon being able to fly gloriously, to be able to go where she wanted to go. To live where and how she wanted to live.

Fifer’s eyes flew open. “Live,” she said. “Not ‘alive.’ It’s *live*!” Seth was right after all. She’d had the wrong word. And now he was going to tease her about it . . . if she ever decided to tell him. If she ever saw him again.

With renewed hope, Fifer closed her eyes and concentrated. She saw Arabis in her mind, swooping and soaring, wings outstretched and beautiful and having no problems holding the dragon in the air. A little shiver came over Fifer, and she knew she was ready. She took in a deliberate breath and let it out smoothly, then whispered, “Live.”

A moment later she opened her eyes. And there, at the tips

of her fingers, was a new, almost perfect extension of Arabis's wing. "Yes!" said Fifer, pumping her fist. It was ugly and gray, but it was securely attached and looked like a real part of the wing. Sort of. "Close enough," she said proudly. "Arabis, we did it. Let's get your other wing up here."

Arabis made an encouraging noise through her clenched jaw and quickly brought her other wing up for Fifer to fix. Fifer took her time once again, even though she knew she was battling against the clock. But rushing things wouldn't do any good, so she forced herself to do it properly.

Once Arabis's wings were done, Fifer jumped up onto the wall and climbed into the next stable to fix Yarbeck's wings. When she was in the middle of that, she heard a familiar sound. "Pssst!"

Fifer turned sharply, looking first toward the small hallway to the dungeon, but realized the sound wasn't coming from there. She looked all around and then finally up and to the outside wall where the little barred window was. Seth's face peered down at her. He waved.

Fifer's eyes widened as she saw another face push Seth's out of the way. "Simber!" she whispered. She felt like crying. "You came!"

"Don't worrry. We'rrre going to get you out of therrre," said Simber, and the sound of his voice took away every fear Fifer had been carrying for the past many days. But Simber continued with concern. "It's going to be verrry difficult, though. And we may have to leave the drrragons behind forrr now."

"But—no! I've figured it out," Fifer whispered. "I've got Arabis's wings done, and I'm about to start working on Yarbeck's. Their muzzles will be loose at eight, right, Seth?"

"Yes," said Seth. "Nobody's caught on yet that Arabis's food didn't drop at seven?"

Fifer shook her head. "They don't even come over here. I don't think they care about them at all." Her lip trembled, and she reached down to hug Yarbeck's neck. "But we care. And we can do this." She hesitated, and then looked at Simber again. "Did you come alone?"

Seth had been so overwhelmed to see the cheetah that he'd forgotten to ask the same question. The two children looked at him expectantly.

"No. Thatcherrr and Carrrina came with me."

Seth sucked in a breath. "My mom is here?" He'd never been more excited to see his mother. He didn't even care if she was mad at him. She would help take out the enemy—she was amazing. He looked around and toward the woods, in case they were hiding out. "Where are they?"

"Well," said Simber slowly, "that's one of the difficult parrrts of this rrrescue that I was telling you about. Because they'rrre capturrred too."

A Major Change of Plans

Simber explained what had happened with Carina and Thatcher as quickly as he could, but there was no time for details now. Then he and Seth told Fifer that the two of them were planning to storm into the castle right at eight, at the same time the dragons' muzzles unlatched. They'd help free the dragons, then go through the dungeon to find Thisbe, Carina, and Thatcher. Then all the dragons and Artiméans would meet outside on top of the castle to figure out how to secure the necessities like food and water for the long journey home together.

It sounded like a nice, easy plan—if you actually knew how

to get past all the soldiers to free the dragons and unshackle prisoners in a dungeon maze. And if Simber actually knew how to open the portcullis and the drawbridge. Fifer didn't ask too many questions.

They soon parted to begin putting the plan in place. Fifer continued magically fixing the dragon wings, finishing Yarbeck the purple and gold, Ivis the green, and her old friend Hux the ice blue.

With only a few minutes to spare, Fifer came to Drock the dark purple at the end of the line. He remained the most temperamental of the bunch, and she really needed him to cooperate. "Okay, Drock, we need to hurry a little," she said, which wasn't the best suggestion to make to a dragon like Drock. "Lift your wing up here, nice and high."

Drock, who was anxiously anticipating his one measly meal of the day, didn't want to do anything of the sort. The girl had been climbing all over him and the others for hours, and he was getting tired of it. Plus, he didn't like the sock things they'd stuck on his wings, and he tried to scrape them off. One of them was barely hanging on by a couple of scatterclips.

"What have you done?" Fifer asked, dismayed. She was

growing desperate. "Please, Drock, I need your help. I can't lift your wing by myself. This magic will make you fly again. And we're going to get you out of here—we're all going to escape. Okay? Can you lift your wing for me? Please?"

Drock wouldn't do it. Hux made a loud noise from the next stall over, trying to cajole his brother into doing it, but that didn't work either.

The clock was ticking. Simber and Seth would be storming through here any second. If she didn't do her part of the job, it could end in disaster. Fifer reached down and tried yanking the wing up. She struggled and tugged again. Drock squealed and bucked her off his back. She went sailing out of the stall and landed on the floor, the breath knocked out of her.

Just then, the woman soldier who'd escorted Seth out of the castle came into the dragon area with the head soldier. They picked up Fifer by the armpits and started dragging her away. "Time for you to go to market," said the woman with a laugh. "Dragonsmarche, here we come."

Fifer barely had any struggle left in her, but she reached down deep. She kicked and wriggled and shouted, but she was no match for the adults.

A second after Fifer was dragged away, all five of the trapdoors over the dragons' heads dropped down. A huge pile of food fell into each stall. The distinct clicks of five muzzles being released could be heard . . . but only the dragons were there to hear it. They looked at one another in stunned silence. Theoretically, four of the five of them could fly again. Their muzzles were loose for fifteen minutes, all at the same time. They knew the plan. But with Drock stuck with his old wings and Fifer carried off, they had no idea what they were supposed to do now.

To the Rescue

At the same time Fifer was struggling and trying to catch her breath so she could yell for help, two different soldiers deep inside the dungeon grabbed Thisbe, who was sound asleep. They unshackled her and dragged her off. "Thatcher!" she yelled. "Carina! Maiven! Help!"

Her voice woke her friends, but there was nothing they could do. "We'll find you!" Carina shouted. "Stay strong!" She cursed under her breath.

"Maybe Simber will see what happens to her," said Thatcher.

"I hope so." Carina yanked at her chains, but it did her no good.

Thisbe punched and kicked and yelled the whole way through the dungeon maze, whenever she could get a limb free. As the soldiers pulled her up the staircase on one side of the castle, Fifer's soldiers were dragging her up the ramp on the other. Someone ordered the portcullis to be raised and the drawbridge lowered. The two parties reached the vast entryway at nearly the same time, but the girls were too busy trying to fight to do much more than acknowledge the presence of one another. They went past the glorious tigers and the lines of soldiers that started to multiply, and turned toward the castle entrance.

The portcullis was up by now, but they had to wait for the drawbridge to descend. As it began to drop, a monstrous noise erupted in the entryway. Splinters of wood went flying everywhere. People scattered. Both Thisbe and Fifer stopped struggling for a moment to see what was going on. Then they caught sight of their beloved Simber, who had crashed through the drawbridge with Seth safely protected inside his mouth. The beast was flying high above their heads.

The soldiers shoved the girls to the walls to contain them and keep them away from the strange flying creature. But Fifer still had a chance to shout, "Seth! Fix Drock's wings! The word is 'live'! Hurry!"

Seth stared down at the growing mayhem, looking all around, but he couldn't find Fifer in the chaotic sea of green coats. "Okay!" he shouted back, but he knew there was no way he could do such a remarkable thing. He wasn't capable.

Now that they were through the drawbridge, Seth climbed out of Simber's mouth and pulled himself up onto the cheetah's head, then slid down his neck and hung on.

"Do you see them?" Simber demanded, now that he could speak. "Wherrre arrre they?"

But the girls had soldiers hovering over them, keeping them hidden from view as they moved toward the exit. When Simber continued flying farther inside the ornate castle entrance, the soldiers began herding the girls across the splintered drawbridge, avoiding the huge hole.

Simber flew onward, with Seth directing the mission. "We don't have time to search for the girls right now," he said anxiously. "We need to keep going to the dungeon while we still can." Seth was nearly as eager to rescue his mother as he was his two best friends, but he had other matters to attend to first. "The dragons' muzzles are only loose for fifteen minutes, and now I've got to figure out how to fix a pair of wings, too. Go that way," he said, pointing to the right. "Down the ramp!"

The walls of the ramp were wide enough for Simber, but the turns were too sharp for him to fly down it. So he landed and began running and skidding around the corners. Seth hung on to the cheetah's neck, his backside bouncing around on Simber's back. They mowed down the first wave of guards, then the head guard and his three fellow soldiers. Finally they skidded to a halt in the dragons' dungeon area.

The dragons, except for Hux, reared up in surprise, for it had been quite a long time since they'd seen anything like Simber.

"That was easy enough," said Simber, who had no problem trampling anyone who got in his way. He stood guard while Seth slid off his back to the floor.

"There are a lot more soldiers in the dungeon," Seth warned. His legs felt wobbly from the bumpy ride, but he didn't have time to dwell on that. He quickly climbed up the stable wall near Drock and assessed the situation.

The muzzles were loose. The timers said it was ten minutes past eight. They had five minutes before the muzzles would snap tight around the dragons' mouths again. And from the looks of everything, only Drock needed magic to make his wings work.

Seth knew what he had to do. But he also knew what Simber had to do.

"Simber," said Seth, sounding quite authoritative in spite of how timid he felt, "I need you to get these stall doors open right now. We only have a few minutes before the muzzles click tight again."

"Why don't you take the muzzles off them?" asked Simber. "Now that they'rrre loose, isn't therrre a way to do that?"

Seth stared at Simber, remembering when they'd returned with Hux and how the soldiers had put the muzzle back on him. "Why didn't I think of that?" He scooted over to the stall door and perched on it, then took Arabis's head in his hands. "I'm sorry if I hurt you. Please don't burn me up. I'm going to get this thing off you."

"There's a lever on the right side of my mouth," said Arabis carefully, who could talk a little now that the muzzle was loose.

"It has two catches." She snaked her ropelike tail up to her face and pointed them out. Her tail was too thick to wrap around the muzzle and yank it off herself.

"I see them," said Seth. He messed around with it, trying this way and that to make the muzzle unhitch. Finally he got the first catch loose, and the second one gave way shortly after. The muzzle fell open. Seth removed it and let it fall.

"Whew," he said under his breath. He moved to the next dragon, sweat pouring from him now. Three minutes left. Meanwhile Simber started slamming his head like a battering ram into Arabis's stable door, splintering it. Then he reared up on his haunches and began ripping pieces off so Arabis could get loose. In between, he roared and chased soldiers who came running to see what was happening. None of them was curious enough to stick around.

Luckily for Seth, having learned from the first muzzle, Yarbeck's came off a little faster. And Ivis's a little faster than that. Seth teetered off balance and nearly fell as he went from Yarbeck's stall to Hux's. Hux, who'd been watching what Seth was doing, had been able to use the very tip of his tail like a finger and nearly had the first latch of his muzzle undone already.

Seth's fingers shook as he unhooked the second latch and pulled the restraint off, and now Hux's head was free. With less than a minute left, Seth dove for Drock's stable. The dragon startled and reared back, even though he knew Seth was coming his way. Seth lost his balance and fell to the ground on top of the feed. With a groan, he rolled over and climbed up the stable wall once more. He tried to control the temperamental one's head so he could unlatch the muzzle.

"Come on, Drock!" Seth said, growing desperate. "If we don't get this muzzle off, you'll be stuck here. Look—Arabis is free!"

But the combination of Seth yelling in his face and Simber slamming his head against Yarbeck's door was too much stimulation for the young dragon. Drock wiggled and snorted, nearly yanking Seth off balance again. Arabis stuck her head in Drock's stable and spoke to him in what Seth remembered as the real dragon language, the language Pan had used with Hux when they had reunited.

"Thirty seconds left," Seth muttered. Sweat flooded his eyes, blinding him. He wiped them with his sleeve.

Drock was settling down. Quickly Arabis nodded at Seth

and kept her head close by. Seth moved in once more and swiftly unhooked the first latch. And then, at last, he released the second. As he ripped the contraption off Drock's head, he could hear the distinct sound of the five muzzles slamming together tightly, all at once.

Seth nearly collapsed from the stress of it all and the racket Simber was making. But the rescue was far from over.

Yarbeck and Ivis were free from their stables now too, and suddenly there was no room outside the stables for Simber to tear down the last two doors. "Keep moving," Seth said to the three free ones. He climbed down the outside of Drock's stable to give some instructions. "Go up the ramp and torch the crud out of any soldier who comes this way."

"You know we can't do that," Arabis reminded Seth.

Seth blew out a breath and waited for Simber to stop pounding. He'd forgotten about the dragon code, of course. "Well, torch the bad ones and just pretend like you're going to torch the good ones—they'll run away."

Arabis seemed amenable to that.

"Okay, great. I'll holler when the other two are free, and I want all five of you to stick together and get out of here. Take for the skies above the castle. We'll meet you there, and we'll all fly home together. You hear me? Drock, do you understand?"

"Yes," said Drock. Now that his muzzle was off, he seemed a bit calmer.

The three females all moved up the ramp and out of the way. Then Simber started slamming his head into Hux's stable door.

Hux was very smart and a fast learner, so once Simber had used his stone noggin to split the wood, Hux put the weight of his shoulder into pressing against it, helping Simber to tear off giant planks of it.

"Try to hurry," Seth muttered. He stood aside, and now and then he could hear a lot of yelling coming from inside the dungeon. And then he jolted back to reality. In all the intensity of getting the muzzles off, he'd forgotten about Drock's wings. "Oh crud," he said. How was he supposed to do that? The pit of fear and panic began inside him and started to grow again.

He pushed it back. And for the millionth time that day, he began climbing into the stable. Feeling defeated before he even began, and knowing he wasn't capable of this kind of magic, he settled on the wall and looked at Drock. They'd had a rough time of it so far, these two. But Seth was bound and determined to get these dragons out of there. It almost felt like a test. Was he good enough to be here? To be doing this? Or was he really only good for doing the grunt work, like Thisbe and Fifer had told Pan? He frowned and tried to push the doubts away so he could concentrate.

"Drock, listen," he said softly, even though the noise around him was ferocious. Drock's ears twitched, and Seth continued. "If we don't fix your wings, you won't be able to escape with the others. You'll be stuck here. And that might ruin everything, because I have a feeling that the reason all of you haven't escaped in the past is because you'd always have to leave someone behind. You're loyal, and that's really admirable. I like that a lot."

Drock faced forward but stayed still, and Seth could tell he was listening. He went on, trying to keep his voice calm like Arabis had done, but knowing he had to be firm. Kind of like his mom. He could definitely channel his mom here.

Feeling a little more confident, he rested his hand on Drock's neck. The dragon arched but settled again, and Seth spoke. "If you want to get out of here, and if you don't want to ruin your brother and sisters' chance at freedom, I'm going to need you to bring your wings up here one at a time. I'll be checking to make sure the new pieces are still attached, because they're looking a little rough. And then, once everything is in order, I'm going to rest my hand on the seam of the new part. And . . . and I'm going to concentrate, and whisper a spell, and it might take a few minutes. And it might take a few tries. But, Drock, I promise you, once we're done . . . you're going to fly again. And we're all going to get out of here. Together."

Drock didn't buck or kick or rear back. He didn't do a full-body shudder or slam against the stable wall trying to knock Seth off. He stood, breathing hard, trembling a little.

Seth watched him. And then suddenly it dawned on him that what Drock was going through was a bit like what Seth had gone through earlier. The dragon was overwhelmed and panicking. And Seth understood completely. "It's going to be all right," he soothed. "Just take one breath at a time. It's okay to feel scared."

Drock blinked a few times and, despite Simber slamming his head against his stable door, kept the flinching to a minimum. After a moment he lifted the wing closest to Seth and held it in the air.

"Great job." Seth moved his hand off Drock's neck and gently slid along the top of the stable wall to reach for the wing. The new piece was barely hanging on. Seth did his best to stay calm and repair it as Simber battered Drock's door into submission.

From up the ramp, they could hear the sound of marching feet—apparently the soldiers had organized and were preparing to fight Arabis. Seth knew he didn't have much time.

"I'm going to climb on your back now, Drock," said Seth. "Is that okay?"

Drock nodded, still trembling. Seth moved carefully onto the dragon's back, draped the first wing over the side of the stable, then moved to repair the second wing. It, too, was falling apart, but Seth adjusted the wiry scatterclips the best he could. As Simber ripped the last of the door away, Seth sat motionless on Drock's back, almost going into a trancelike state of concentration.

"Stay still now," said Seth, rising up to his feet and balancing. Drock shook a little and breathed hard, but even though his stable door was gone and his head was free from the muzzle, he remained as motionless as he could.

Seth reached up for the first wing, remembering what Fifer had shouted to him. He pressed one hand gently on the seam. Then he closed his eyes, putting his full trust in the dragon and trying to ignore the chaos that was going on outside the room. He pictured the dark purple dragon flying free, his wings sleek and strong. He thought about the care and love he and Fifer had put into the wings, and how, because of that, they were beautiful.

He breathed deeply, feeling a strange calmness come over him like he'd never felt before. The noise around him was drowned out by the peacefulness inside him.

When he was ready, he whispered, "Live."

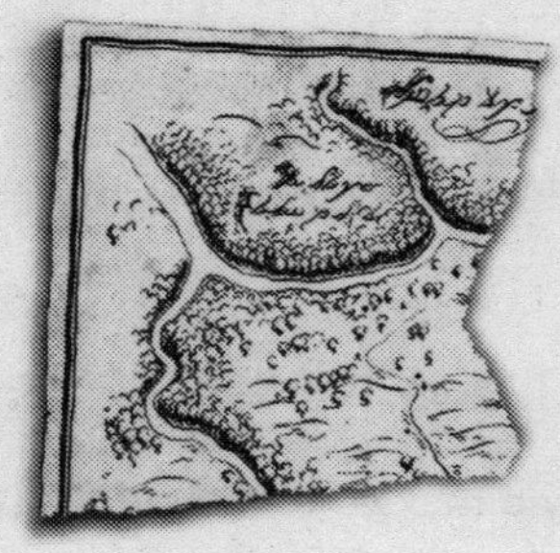

Taking Flight

Simber tried not to distract Seth. He understood the difficulty of bringing a nonliving thing to life. After all, he'd had his own traumatic experiences with that. But while Seth was seemingly taking a nap on Drock's back, the surprise attack was quickly becoming a non-surprise. The soldiers had organized and were threatening the dragons. And Simber still had to rescue Carina and Thatcher, but he needed Seth to tell him how to find them—besides, he couldn't leave Seth here alone. They had to stick together or risk the boy getting captured.

So Simber paced in the open area outside the stables, wishing for Seth to hurry up.

When Seth opened his eyes, he was silent for a long moment. He examined the wing, and then looked closer. The new piece had melded to the old, and it looked like an actual dragon wing instead of burlap and flower petals. Seth's heart surged. "I did it," he whispered. He whirled around. "I did it!" he shouted to Simber. Drock started and almost bucked Seth off.

"Good," said Simber. "Hurrry up with the otherrr one orrr we'll neverrr get out of herrre."

"Oh, right!" said Seth, softer. He turned quickly but carefully, letting Drock know at every move what he was doing. He reached for the second wing and concentrated, imagining Drock flying, until he felt the same sense of calmness he'd felt before. And then, as if he'd done it a hundred times, said, "Live."

The second wing extension came alive, just like the first one had.

"Well done, Drock!" Seth said, throwing himself at the dragon's neck. "It's over. You did it! Now go join your siblings and don't get caught."

The dragon needed no urging. He burst out of the stall, knocking Seth to the floor one last time.

Seth scrambled to his feet. "Dragons, go!" he shouted. "Tell them, Simber."

Simber let out a bellow that rose above the din, commanding the dragons to take flight and escape from the castle by any means necessary. And within a moment, Drock had made his way up the ramp behind the others, bits of fiery breath filling the air around his mouth. He was ready to fight for freedom.

Seth, exhausted, limped to Simber's side. The cheetah helped him up on his back. "Let's find yourrr motherrr," said Simber. "Wherrre do we go?"

"Down that hallway," said Seth. "Watch out. There are guards all along it."

Simber approached the passageway and eyed the narrow space. "I can't fit thrrrough therrre," he said. "Is therrre anotherrr way?"

"I think so, but I have no idea where it is, or if it's any wider than this." Seth's heart sank. "We have to get to them. Please don't make me go alone. Please, Simber. I . . . I can't do it. I'm so tired. There are hundreds of soldiers, and they'll kill me for sure."

"Therrre," said Simber, a rare hint of sympathy for the exhausted boy coming through in his voice. "Of courrrse I wouldn't send you in alone. We'll go togetherrr. Make yourrr-self as small as you can on my back, and coverrr yourrr face and head. We'rrre going in. Just stay on my back, keep yourrr arrrms and legs close to my body, and don't worrry about fighting."

Seth had no idea what Simber was planning, but he didn't question the cat. He leaned forward against Simber's neck and covered his head with one arm while hanging on tightly with the other. "I'm ready," he said.

Simber needed no urging. He stepped back to create the longest runway he could make, and then sprang forward and ran at the too-narrow doorway, wings folded, muscles rippling under his sandstone skin. "Hold on!" he growled, and slammed through the hallway, his broad shoulders hitting on either side. He burrowed a new, larger hallway as he plowed along. Sparks flew as stone scraped stone, Simber's magical body, fortified by preserve spells, winning out on almost all counts.

Seth wasn't an eyewitness to any of it. He kept his head down and hoped not to die now, after all he'd accomplished. It was a rough ride. Thousands of tiny stones pelted his back and neck and buried themselves in his hair. Soon his body was covered in a film of dust. Occasionally soldiers went flying up and over Simber's wing as he took them out along the way.

Seth surfaced for a moment. "I don't know which cell they'll be in!" he shouted, his voice jiggling. "But Dev told me that Thisbe was in three thirty-three, so there are hundreds of them. She was really deep inside, nearer to the other exit, I think." He didn't know if it would help them find his mother and Thatcher, but it couldn't hurt.

"Don't worrry," said Simber. "I'll be able to find them."

Seth sank down in relief. It was amazing to have Simber here. And it was wonderful not to be in charge of anything once again. He liked it this way far better.

While Simber and Seth were forging a new, larger hallway in the dungeon, the five dragon siblings, with Arabis leading, reached the top of the ramp. They headed for the exit, dodging the soldiers' projectile weapons the best they could. The first four dragons stayed diligent to their code of only harming those who were more than 50 percent evil. But Drock wasn't much of a rule follower, and he torched anyone who got in his way.

As soon as the ceiling opened up in the grand entryway, the dragons took flight, a bit cautiously at first. But the new wings worked moderately well from the first flap, even if they weren't much to look at. Arabis continued to lead the way, soaring up and toward the drawbridge. And then she faltered in the air and swooped around, making a circle at the ceiling. Because there was just one problem.

The portcullis was back down and the drawbridge was up. And though the drawbridge had an ample hole in it the size of Simber, which the dragons could probably squeeze through, the iron bars of the portcullis stood between them. There was no way out unless someone opened the portcullis for them. All they could do was circle in the vast castle entry, dodging spears and arrows and whatever else the soldiers and guards were throwing or shooting at them, and hope that the barriers would open. But there was little chance of that. Only a member of the royal family or the entry guard himself could command it to be done. The dragons were trapped.

As they flew around, they knew eventually they'd have to come back down and face the wrath of the king, and perhaps even the Revinir. Things were looking terribly grim.

» » « «

Near the area where the tigers were chained, Dev pushed through the crowd, dropping the load of firewood he'd just gathered. He searched the entry, knowing he had only one job when chaos came into the castle—to find and protect the princess. He scanned the area, trying not to get trampled by the king's soldiers, and ran toward the tigers, where he thought Shanti might be.

"Shanti," he called, forgetting formality under the circumstances. "Shanti!" Not finding her, he ran through the entryway, glancing in awe at the loose dragons above his head and wondering how Fifer and Seth had managed to free them, before refocusing. "Shanti!" He dashed through the legion of soldiers, ducking when necessary to avoid getting clobbered, and headed toward the perimeter of the room where the crowd was thinner.

"I'm here!" cried Princess Shanti from the west wing of the entrance. She gripped the wall and flung her garment train up over one shoulder to keep from tripping, and headed toward the tigers.

Dev breathed a sigh of relief. If something happened to Shanti, he'd be responsible. He weaved toward her, getting shoved and slammed into along the way. Finally he reached her.

Shanti was more than a princess to Dev—more than someone to boss him around. She was his only friend. "There you are," he said with relief. "What happened? I went outside to get firewood for your dressing room, and came back to this mess."

Shanti gave him a sly grin as she pushed her way to the tigers, who were yanking against their chains in angst. Dev followed. "Finally some excitement in the castle," she said lightly. "It's about time. It's been ghastly boring around here." She looked up at the dragons. "I see the magicians got the job done before being dragged off to market. Nice work bringing them here. Did you find your reward?"

"Yes." Dev looked at the dragons and pressed his lips into a thin line. The gold had been on his cot as promised. That small nugget was worth more than all his possessions put together. More money than he'd ever had in his life, which admittedly wasn't much. "So . . . the magicians are gone, then?"

"I would imagine so, by now," said Shanti. "Dragonsmarche opens early, and they expect quite a lot of bidding for the black-eyed ones." She said it callously, then added, "I told the soldiers to let the boy go, though. Father won't care—he's not worth anything."

"Yes, so I heard." Dev frowned and pointed to the dragons. "How did they get loose?"

"Not my problem," said Shanti. "But I'm glad they're out, at least for a little while. I couldn't stand seeing them muzzled like they were. It's not humane." She petted the chained-up tiger nearest her.

"I guess not." Dev agreed wholeheartedly with her. He also thought it was terrible that she kept her pet tigers chained up all the time, with all those glitzy cloaks and jewels layered on them, but he wasn't supposed to have an opinion. "I ought to get you out of here, you know," he said. "Before you get hurt."

"I won't get hurt," she scoffed. "Besides, it's such fun watching."

"True." Dev stifled a yawn. He'd been up all night doing punishment chores except for a few short naps when no one was looking, and all he really wanted was to go to bed. But he knew the princess well, and he knew she wasn't about to be whisked into hiding just to give him a chance to sleep. So he summoned up renewed vigor and tried to appear as eager as possible to entertain her. In a low voice, he said, "I suppose there's a way we could cause a bit more of a ruckus before it's over, if Your Highness is interested."

Shanti looked sideways at Dev, and a smile played at her lips. "Is there?"

Dev nodded solemnly. "This dangerous situation may require me to take *you* out of here on the tigers' backs. If you call for the drawbridge to be let down for our escape, well, who knows what else could happen?" He glanced up at the dragons, and then he looked at Shanti. A tremor of fear flitted through him. Had he read her wishes right? Or had he gone too far?

Thankfully, Shanti was a rebellious princess, and she seemed to appreciate the way Dev was always coming up with ways to amuse her. Sometimes she even treated him like a friend instead of her servant. Dev lived for those moments.

Before she could answer, a skirmish among the soldiers broke out not far away. The two of them ducked as fists and weapons began to fly. "We'd better get out of here," Shanti said, trying to hide her delight. She turned and addressed the guard who controlled the portcullis and drawbridge. "Open the gates," she commanded.

The entry guard seemed startled, but he complied. As the portcullis went up and the drawbridge was lowered, Princess Shanti and Dev untethered the tigers and climbed on. A moment later, they were off, racing through the entryway that was now littered with weapons and injured soldiers. "I'm going to be in so much trouble," said the princess with glee.

"And I'll be in even more," said Dev grimly, who would take the physical punishment for both of them. But perhaps giving the dragons a chance to escape would help atone for the guilt he felt in tricking the twins. The gold sat like a painful lump in his pocket.

As they reached the drawbridge, Dev whistled sharply to get the dragons' attention and pointed out the opening escape hatch. The dragons roared and dove for the exit, dodging spears and swords, spewing fire from their mouths with reckless abandon, caring only about their freedom now—they would have it no matter the cost, no matter the code. Soon the five dragons were soaring outside over the moat, free for the first time in many years.

Back in the dungeon, things weren't going quite so well.

Seth Rides Again

Simber and Seth continued plowing their way through the catacomb-like dungeon full of prisoners. But it didn't take long before the constant vibration from Simber's shoulders and wings digging trenches in the walls began to affect Seth. First his hands and legs grew numb from it. Then the rest of his body.

"I—I—I ca-a-a-n't fe-e-e-l my finger-r-r-s!" he said, keeping his head down as more and more bits of rock poured on him. "O-r-r-r my ar-r-rms!" He couldn't tell if he was holding on tightly to Simber's neck or if he was even gripping the beast at all.

“Hold on the best you can!” Simber told him.

The stone cheetah wasn't worried about getting tired, for that almost never happened with Artimé's living statues—except for Kitten, of course, who could sleep through an entire war. Simber didn't need to rest. However, he was starting to get worried about chipping or falling apart. He wasn't sure if his shoulder joints or wing tips were holding up or wearing away. It wouldn't be good at all if they were disintegrating. And his wings had never been so important as they were now, stuck in a different world where flight was the only way to get home. But there was no other option except for him to continue.

A valiant soldier stood fast in front of Simber, holding a spear pointed at the cheetah's eye. Simber ducked and plowed into him. The soldier and his spear flew up in the air and landed hard in the path of dust and rubble Simber left behind him. One by one Simber clobbered all the men and women who stood in his way. They didn't have a chance.

But Simber was worried about Seth. He knew the boy must have been through a lot already, and this trek wasn't easy. But there was no way to make it better for him. They had to stay together to get to Carina and Thatcher, then escape the castle and find the twin girls. Nothing would stand in Simber's way. Alex was counting on him, and he would never let the head mage of Artimé down. He couldn't manage a glance behind him, but he could tell by instinct that at least some of the guards he'd knocked down were back up again and following him. He moved faster.

Seth hung on as well as he could until Simber took a sharp turn. The boy's numb fingers could hold on no longer, and before he knew it, he was sliding off Simber's back and landing facedown on the dungeon floor. A flurry of dust and dirt flew into his face and down his throat, so he could barely choke out, "Simber!"

The winged creature realized a moment later that he'd lost his rider, but of course in the narrow hallway he couldn't turn around. He stopped momentarily, then started backing up awkwardly—something he'd never quite mastered the art of.

Quickly Seth sat up, coughing and choking. From the dust behind them, soldiers' shadowy figures grew larger. Seth reached for his vest pockets, remembered how empty they were, and found them still empty. He scrambled to his feet and tried to run, but he slipped on the gravel. On one knee, with soldiers fast approaching and Simber still several yards in front of him, Seth tried a new spell for the second time that day.

"Glass!" he shouted, barely getting the word out in a fit of coughing. He pointed in the direction of the soldiers. Nothing happened, and soon they were coming out of the dust and reaching for him. "Glass!" Seth repeated as he tried to run again.

This time a sheet of glass appeared between him and the soldiers, cutting them off. They slammed into it. The last thing Seth saw was four faces pressing against it before he turned and vaulted onto Simber's back once more.

"Feel frrree to do that spell a few morrre times," Simber remarked as they were on their way again. He sniffed, trying to find the familiar scents of Thatcher and Carina.

"I didn't know I could do that," said Seth with newfound energy despite his growing list of aches and pains.

Simber burrowed through more hallways, with Seth hanging on and occasionally throwing more glass spells. Sometimes they worked, sometimes they didn't. But if there was one thing Seth had learned that day, it was not to give up when something didn't work.

Finally Simber slowed and turned down a hallway. He sampled the air. Then, with a loud roar, he charged forward. Familiar voices rose up in response, guiding Simber down the right path until they came to the correct cell. Simber screeched to a halt. Seth vaulted up and over Simber's head into the chamber where Carina and Thatcher were imprisoned. He landed awkwardly, then righted himself and ran straight to his mother. He wrapped his arms around her neck. "Mom!"

Tears flowed down Carina's cheeks, and she struggled against the chains, trying and failing to hug her son.

"I'm really sorry," Seth said.

She was shaking. It made him feel even worse.

Carina closed her eyes against the tears and couldn't respond. Meanwhile Simber pressed his shoulders into the walls on either side of the opening, breaking through those too so he could fit inside the chamber. Once through, he reached Thatcher and wasted no time chomping on the chains that were attached to his wrists and ankles, leaving the cuffs attached for now—they'd worry about those later.

"Was Thisbe in herrre with you?" asked Simber. "Herrr scent lingerrrs."

"She was next door," said Thatcher. He eased his sore body to a standing position, then gently guided Seth aside so Simber could chomp off Carina's chains. "Come on, Seth—let's stop these soldiers from reaching us. We don't have time to waste on them now. Where are the girls?"

Seth explained what they knew as he and Thatcher climbed over Simber into the hallway. Carefully they looked this way and that, throwing glass spells down the hallways around them so that they could reorganize without any soldiers attacking.

Seth climbed onto Simber's back so he'd be ready to go once Carina was freed. As Simber finished destroying the chains and got himself turned around in the tight space, Thatcher poked his head into Thisbe's old cell. He knew whoever had been in there with her had helped her.

"Thank you," said Thatcher, peering into the darkness.

"You're welcome." Maiven's old voice trembled. "Tell Miss Thisbe I enjoyed her company. I won't forget her."

Thatcher wrung his hands. Should they try to rescue the woman, too? If they did, would she even survive trying to exit as Simber barreled through the hallways? Could she move quickly? Did she have a place to go? And if she took a spot on

Simber's back, would there be enough room for the twins?

The old woman settled his mind for him. "Go now. Quickly. That precious girl's life is in your hands."

Thatcher ran in, gave the old woman a hug and a kiss on her wrinkled cheek. "We won't forget you, either," he whispered. He ran back out and hopped onto Simber's back behind Seth and Carina.

Leaving Maiven Taveer behind, they were off.

Making Their Escape

"Stay low!" shouted Simber. "Keep your heads down!" The stone cheetah crashed through the first of the many glass barriers Seth and Thatcher had put up. He decided the best way to get out of the maze of the dungeon was to go back the way they came, since the tunneled walls were a sure sign they were heading in the right direction, and it would mean less wear on his shoulders and wings.

Carina bent low to protect her son, though he certainly had proven that he could protect himself pretty well without her. Simber made a few turns, then sped up through a straightaway.

"Do you have any components?" asked Seth when he had a moment to breathe. "I'm completely out."

"Nothing much left," Carina said. "A couple blinding highlighters. Preserve spells. We used up everything else."

"Mom!" Seth said. "I was counting on you to have more."

"Well, I was counting on you to not run away from home." They crashed through another barrier. Most of the shards of glass flew forward, but some rained down on them, and they all became preoccupied with getting them off.

Carina had a few more retorts for her son, but she held her tongue. She didn't want to have an argument here. Besides, she had mixed feelings about what Seth and the twins had done. It really wasn't much different from what Alex and Lani and Meghan and Samheed had done when they were thirteen . . . only they hadn't had parents around to tell them not to. It was definitely a deeper issue that Carina wanted to figure out inside herself before she slapped down any new rules or punishments. Besides, she was proud of her son. He'd stepped up in a way she'd never seen from him before.

Carina squeezed Seth a little harder as Simber called out a warning for another glass barrier, and then she suddenly realized they didn't need to be jumping through them at all. "I've got this one!" she called out to Simber.

She leveled her hand toward it. "Release," she muttered. The glass melted to the floor and Simber passed through.

"I can only put them up," said Seth. "My release spell isn't really working so great yet."

"It all takes time," said Carina. "You'll get there."

"But I made one of the dragons fly."

Carina tilted her head, not sure if she heard him right. "You . . . what?"

"I made Drock's wings come to life. Fifer got taken away before she could finish, so I had to do it."

"And . . . it worked? That's a difficult one!"

"I really had to concentrate hard. I didn't think I could do it, but I knew I had to or everything would fall apart. So I did it." He flashed a sheepish glance over his shoulder. "Are you proud?"

Carina's eyes pooled, and she was silent for a long moment. Then she said quietly, "I am amazed by you."

Finally Simber made it back to the empty dragon dungeon. The soldiers who saw him coming fled for their lives, so Simber took a moment near the stables to let everybody shake out their clothes and assess the damage. Despite all the magical protection and preserve spells that had been used on Simber to keep him virtually indestructible, the act of scraping a wider tunnel through rock had scratched him up a bit. He had a spot on each shoulder that had worn down, and the tips of his wings were marred. But the injuries appeared to be superficial, and, after licking them a bit, he was soon ready to proceed into the madness.

They could hear it—the sounds of complete chaos coming from the top of the ramp. Had the dragons made it out? When Thatcher, Seth, and Carina were ready to go, they climbed on Simber's back once more. Then Seth spied Thisbe's rucksack near one of the dragon stalls. He ran over and snatched it up, strapped it to his back, and returned to his spot.

The cheetah had a few gruff instructions for them. "One," he began, "don't fall off me. Two, if you'rrre about to fall off, don't. Arrre we clearrr?"

"Yes, Simber," they all said. Seth vowed to hang on to the cheetah's neck and never let go.

"All rrright. Let's get out of herrre." The great cat looked over his shoulder to make sure his human cargo was secure, then crouched and sprang for the ramp, tearing up it at full speed, taking the corners as though they didn't exist. Seth squeezed his eyes shut and held tightly as they swayed.

Soldiers charged, but Simber batted at them with his wings or butted them with his head and didn't slow down. Before long he was trampling the ones who wouldn't get out of the way. As soon as the Artiméans came to the entryway, Simber spread his wings wide, knocking more soldiers down, and began flapping. They rose up out of reach and sailed toward the exit.

"The dragons made it out!" exclaimed Seth.

"It appearrrs so," said Simber, pleased.

"Close the drawbridge!" someone royal bellowed to the entry soldier. "Bring down the portcullis!"

"Uh-oh," muttered Thatcher.

A second later, the pointy iron stakes of the portcullis began to descend.

"Oooh boy," muttered Seth. "Hurry, Simber!"

Simber flapped harder. The portcullis kept dropping.

"Hurry!" shouted Carina.

"Flatten yourrrselves!" cried Simber. "We'rrre not stopping now!"

The three passengers did as they were told, all of them imagining what it might feel like to be stabbed into the ground. Seth could feel the familiar panic well up inside him. He couldn't control any of this. Desperately he pushed the feelings back and told himself he could panic later if he still needed to. But not now. The feelings didn't listen, and his chest tightened even more.

As they raced toward the lowering gate, Simber dove. "Hang on!" he roared. The people below ran for cover. When Simber reached the portcullis, he stretched his wings wide. Just in time he ducked his head and glided under, his stomach scraping the ground.

The stakes missed Seth and Carina. But one caught the collar of Thatcher's shirt. Thatcher was violently yanked off Simber's back and thrown to the ground under the portcullis. He looked up. The sharp iron points were about to run him through. He screamed and rolled away, his shirt ripping down the back. The portcullis clanged shut ominously, with Thatcher just barely safe on the outside.

“Whoa,” Thatcher said under his breath. He felt paralyzed for a moment, but the outdoor soldiers charged toward him and he sprang to life.

“We’rrre coming back arrround!” Simber roared. He rose up in the air and circled, then dove back down and snatched Thatcher as gently as possible in his claws. Lifting him up, he flew over the moat to safety.

Thatcher barely comprehended what had happened to him, and now his life continued flashing before his eyes as he dangled from a dizzying height. How many times had he nearly died on this rescue trip so far? It was becoming too many to count. He had more and more admiration for Henry and Lani and Alex and the others all the time. He glanced back at the soldiers. “Good riddance,” he muttered.

“Call out to the drrragons,” Simber ordered as they flew toward the tree line. “Seth, you do it. They know you best.”

“Drock!” shouted Seth, sitting up and looking behind them. “Arabis!” When he caught sight of the breathtaking castle and the grounds from this height, and the sun hitting the waterfall that plunged off the cliff to nowhere, he nearly sighed at its beauty. His panic subsided. One day, he thought, he’d write a play like Samheed was always doing. And it would be set in a castle just like this, with a reluctant princess and a servant boy and magic and twins . . . He blinked and came back. The twins were still missing.

As he called out to all the dragons, he spotted them perched on the castle ramparts near the cliff. "They're sitting on top of that wall!" he told Simber, and pointed them out.

Simber glided around and headed toward them. And as he did so, Seth spotted two more familiar figures being dragged across the grounds toward the drawbridge by a large man in a black cloak. The tigers were being led behind them. Dev and Princess Shanti were arguing with the man, but it looked to Seth like the two of them were in big trouble.

"At least they got caught doing something," Seth muttered to himself, feeling a smug sense of satisfaction.

Little did Seth know just how rebellious the princess and her servant were. They weren't about to let this setback stand in their way. There were more ways out of the castle than on the backs of gilded tigers.

Together Again

Thisbe and Fifer found themselves jiggling in the back of a fast-moving buggy, sitting trapped among sacks and boxes of unknown items. Their wrists were tied down. Everything familiar to them in this strange world was quickly disappearing, and they could do nothing about it.

"Come on, Simber," Fifer pleaded. She worked her wrists in the restraints.

Thisbe looked out the back, contemplating jumping if they could find a way to untie themselves. But they were moving downhill quickly, away from the castle.

Seeing her, and knowing instinctively what Thisbe was thinking, Fifer shook her head. "We're going too fast. Besides, I twisted my knee when they dragged me out. I won't make it far if we try to run, way out here in the middle of nowhere."

"But how will Simber find us?" asked Thisbe. She rested her cheek against the cool back window and stared out behind them, wishing desperately for Simber to appear. But she could barely see the castle now. It was the size of a toy on the horizon, with the fortress wall stretching out behind it. The sinking feeling in her chest became a chasm of worry.

"He'll find us," said Fifer, sounding more sure than she felt. She tugged at the ropes again, but they only got tighter. "At least you and I are together now. What happened to you?"

Thisbe told Fifer about her experience in the dungeon and about her cellmate, and Thatcher and Carina. Then Fifer told Thisbe about everything that had happened with her and Seth and the dragons, expressing her worries about poor Drock not getting his wings finished. "I hope Seth understood what I yelled at him." She shook her head, imagining the disaster that would follow if Drock couldn't fly. "I don't know if he can do it."

"I just hope they find us, before . . ." Thisbe trailed off and turned, looking forward to where the cart was headed. She didn't have a clue what they were about to face. "Those are horses, right?" She pointed at the creatures pulling the cart. None of the seven islands had horses, so the girls only knew of them from pictures in the books in Artimé's library, many of which had been washed ashore or brought to the island by previous generations of people whose ships had been sucked into the Dragon's Triangle.

"I think so."

"They're bigger than I thought they'd be."

"Yes. Pretty, though." It was hard to get a good look at them from the back of the buggy. Every now and then, as they journeyed farther and farther inland, they could catch a glimpse of a huge city in the valley below.

As they lapsed into silence, a thunderous booming sound filled the air.

"What was that?" asked Fifer, alarmed. She whirled around and saw a trail of black smoke rising to the sky far in front of them.

Thisbe turned too. "I don't know." She was quiet for

a moment, but the sound didn't happen again. "The driver doesn't seem worried about it."

The smoke made a cloud, and it floated slowly with the wind. The girls watched it for a while, then turned back and forgot about it. They couldn't see the castle at all anymore behind them. And they had plenty of other things to worry about.

Finally Thisbe said what both girls had been thinking. "I can't believe Dev sold us out like that. Why would he do this to us?"

"Yeah." Fifer looked down. "That was pretty mean."

Thisbe felt worse about it than she wanted to admit. She was stupid for trusting Dev and being fooled. People didn't behave like that in Artimé. In Quill they might. But the twins hadn't experienced something like this before. It made Thisbe feel sick inside that Dev was the kind of person who would care so little about another person that he would lead them around for days just to get a reward. And now what? Would they ever see their brothers again? She couldn't believe Dev wasn't more bad than good. Maybe this would put him over the edge as far as the dragons were concerned. It was a shame because

Thisbe had almost thought a couple of times that they could be friends. But it didn't matter now. They'd probably never see him again either.

The city grew larger, and the traffic on the road became busier. There were other horse-drawn carts like the one the girls were in and some vehicles that moved on their own like the Quillitary vehicles back home.

As Thisbe's stomach knotted tighter and tighter, she worked the restraints that held her down but couldn't figure out how to untie or even loosen them. Abandoning all hope now of proving anything to Alex, Thisbe tried to get mad enough that her eyes sparked again—she'd been intrigued when she'd done it accidentally before. But she couldn't get that to happen either. After a moment, Thisbe closed her eyes and sank back in defeat.

Fifer scanned the horizon behind them. "Where is Simber?" she fretted.

"I don't know."

They kept their fears to themselves, but both girls were growing more and more anxious about what would happen at Dragonsmarche. Why did people think it was okay to sell other people? What made black-eyed people so valuable?

The girls had no idea. Perhaps they'd never know.

By the time the buggy slowed, they were immersed in a busy city with vehicles and carts going every which way. The sounds around them were loud and unsettling—it was definitely not something the girls were used to. Perhaps under different circumstances, Thisbe might have found the big city at least a little bit exciting. But at the moment she would have greatly preferred to have been anywhere else but there.

Fifer didn't like it. Even if she hadn't been restrained, she was too scared of getting run over by a passing vehicle to consider jumping out and making a break for it. Neither of them had the first idea where they'd go. And there was something about being so terribly unsure about what was happening that froze their decision-making abilities.

The cart eased down narrow cobblestoned alleyways, sometimes bumping against the buildings that lined the roads. Soon they entered a city square where there were no buildings. It was similar to the market square in Glen Freer, only much bigger. People buzzed about in growing crowds as vendors in the marketplace set up their booths and unloaded their goods. Some vendors had fresh produce; others had bread and baked goods. Still others offered clothing, dried goods, or strange animals the girls had never seen before. There was a huge aquarium in one section of the square with sea monsters inside.

Thisbe pointed out the aquarium to Fifer. "Maiven told me about that," she said. But then their view was obstructed and their cart came to rest.

They found themselves next to an enormous carved-stone fountain, which had a basin that was embedded deep into the ground. There was a large platform stage nearby. Immediately ten or fifteen people surrounded the cart, pushing and shouting. Fifer and Thisbe shrank back.

"I want to see them!" said one.

"I don't believe it," muttered another.

"I thought they were extinct," said a third, opening the hatch and reaching in.

"Don't touch me!" Thisbe kicked at the woman's hand, and she pulled away. The twins exchanged a fearful look and cowered as far as they could from the opening. Finally the green-uniformed soldier who'd driven them appeared at the back of the buggy. "Back off," he said to the crowds that were forming. "We need room to move, or you'll never have a chance to inspect them."

Fifer dug her fingernails into Thisbe's hand. "What's happening?" she whispered.

Thisbe shook her head, mystified as more people came crowding around them.

"What time is the auction?" asked a stranger.

"Noon," said a different soldier. "Now move out of the way."

The people shrank back as the soldiers reached in. They untethered the girls and grabbed them, holding their arms and legs down so they couldn't move.

Fifer struggled, twisting and bending, but the men and women only held her tighter. Thisbe fought to free her hands, but the soldiers held her fast. It was no use. "Fifer," whispered Thisbe. "Do something! Call the birds!"

"What good will that do?" Fifer gave one more attempt at freeing herself, but the captors were too strong. Finally, as the soldiers were delivering them to the display area, she let out a little scream.

A flock of birds came flying to her and fluttered about uselessly, more annoying than terrifying. The soldiers waved them off and shackled the girls to two wooden posts.

Thisbe's face grew hot as more onlookers gathered to stare at them.

"Open your eyes wide!" barked a soldier at her. "Or I'll force them open with sticks."

Thisbe reared back as much as she could with her limited movements. What a horrible thing to say! She could feel her anger rising up, and briefly she considered the boom spell, but the thought of killing any human still turned her stomach. She couldn't do it. It didn't matter whether she was able to or not. Plus, they were surrounded. It wouldn't help anything.

The streets grew busier, and the square filled up with vendors and goods and shoppers. The smell of baking bread was soured by the odor of fuel and exhaust from the passing vehicles. As the hour of noon approached, the crowd around Thisbe and Fifer's platform grew larger, so much that people were pushing and shoving to have a chance to see what was going on.

Fifer and Thisbe stood tied to the posts, their shoulders

turned in, heads down, trying to shrink away. Their hope of Simber finding them was fading fast. They'd gone away too quickly and too far, it seemed. Even the enormous cheetah couldn't do everything perfectly. Besides, he had the others to rescue.

"He's not coming, is he," said Fifer, a lump stuck fast in her throat.

"He doesn't seem to be," said Thisbe. "Can you think of anything we can do to stop this?" Angrily she wrenched her arms, but the action only hurt her.

"You could start sending out boom spells," Fifer said, like she actually wished Thisbe would do it.

"I . . . I just can't."

"I know." Fifer quickly became empathetic. "I'm sorry I said it. I wouldn't be able to either."

"I can put glass spells up to protect us."

"Yes," said Fifer. "That'll help for a while. At least until they beat their way through them to get at us."

"Still, it might buy us a little time. In case . . ." Thisbe trailed off. In case Simber was still coming. She didn't want to say it for fear of jinxing it.

“Do it,” said Fifer. “If you can manage without being able to move your wrists.”

Thisbe tugged against her wrist wraps, trying to see if she could rotate her hands enough to fling a glass spell. She gave it a try. “Glass,” she whispered, and flicked her fingers. A sheet of glass planted itself inches away from Fifer’s face.

“Yikes,” said Thisbe. “Sorry.”

“It’s fine. You missed me.”

Murmurs rippled through the crowd at the sight of magic. “Price just went up,” one onlooker said. The audience tittered.

Thisbe threw a few more wild glass spells, trying to at least partially encase her and Fifer so people would be forced to keep their distance, but she didn’t have enough movement in her hands to do it properly. She managed three panes, shielding the front of them from the crowd, but didn’t dare risk any more for fear of planting one too close to Fifer or herself. These would have to do.

Their fears began to worsen the higher the sun rose in the sky. Noon was fast approaching, and Simber still hadn’t shown up. Men and women with stern faces and commanding presences walked up to the girls and moved around the glass to examine them. They spoke quietly to one another as if the twins couldn't hear them, talking about money and how much they thought the black-eyed girls would be worth. Thisbe wondered if they might be pirates. She narrowed her eyes.

None of the money numbers meant anything to the twins, for they didn't use currency at all in Artimé—they had no need for it and didn't really understand it. But hearing the word "thousands" in relationship to anything seemed like an awful lot.

Finally the green-coated soldiers came up and stood at the corners of the platform. A slick-looking man in an ill-fitting suit approached and looked at the girls like they were a selection of cheeses, or a rack of garments. He bumped into one of the sheets of glass and stepped back, startled, then realized where the other ones were as well.

"All right," he said to the girls with a sneer in his voice. "We're about to get started. Look your best now, so that the kingdom of Grimere gets a fine price for you."

Dragons Away

Simber reached the dragons on the top of the wall. He set Thatcher down safely and landed, then called them together. Carina hopped off Simber's back to inspect the dragons' wings and make sure they were all secure.

"Do you know wherrre they've taken the twins?" the cheetah asked Arabis.

"Yes, where?" asked Seth. He was getting extremely worried.

"There is only one place," Arabis replied solemnly. "It is not a place we dragons can go, or surely we'll be shot down and captured. It's called Dragonsmarche—it's the Dragon Market, where dragons and other creatures and goods are bought and sold."

"Isn't this world called the land of the dragons?" said Thatcher. "How is it possible that you are so oppressed?"

Arabis lowered her head. "Many years ago the dragons lived free. That is what our mother believed to be true when she sent us here. She thought she was saving us from the pirates. In the centuries after the great split, which left our world separated from the seven islands, humans spread out to the cliffs of our land and began to capture dragons and use them as slaves."

"That's terrible," said Carina.

Arabis went on. "Only the two families of black-eyed rulers fought against the others to try to keep the dragons free. But the black-eyed rulers were shunned for their actions. They too became hunted." Her words turned bitter. "Now they are a prize. A status symbol. As are the dragons."

"Wait," said Seth. "The people with black eyes are . . . were . . . rulers?"

"They ruled in tandem and harmony with the dragons," said Arabis. "But that ended. We knew nothing of these drastic changes when we arrived here. Things only got worse when the Revinir took control of the kingdom around the time we arrived. We were young and innocent, and we were immediately captured. We've been slaves ever since. And now . . . now you and the twins have freed us. Unfortunately, the soldiers have the girls. You must go quickly to rescue them before it's too late. It's some distance into the valley to get to the city." She pointed in the direction of the market.

Simber growled in frustration. "And you must go back to the seven islands, forrr the pirrrates have been eliminated frrrom therrre. You'll be safe." He wished the dragons could stay and help, but he knew it was too risky for them. "Yourrr motherrr will be glad to see you all . . . even if you'rrre a little worrrse forrr wearrr." He nodded at their makeshift wings. "Carrrina, will they make it home safely?"

"I'm surprised, really," murmured Carina, now that she had looked at each wing carefully. "The kids did a very good job considering the circumstances and the supplies they had to work with. But I think the dragons should head home directly and have Alex redo their wings to make sure they will hold up for the long term. They're a little ragged and loose, and the extensions could rip off eventually. But they're safe to cross the chasm."

"We did the best we could," said Seth.

Carina smiled at her son. "I'm so proud. Alex will be very impressed. You got them out of the dungeon—you freed them. And gave them functional wings. You and Thisbe and Fifer did some excellent magic here today. That's more than any of us can say."

Simber looked at Carina. "I think you and Seth should go with the drrragons. It'll be easierrr for me to carrry only Thatcherrr and the girrrls on the rrride home."

"Oh," said Carina, growing concerned, "but I promised Alex I'd find the girls."

"We know wherrre they arrre," said Simber. "Besides, the soonerrr you get worrrd back to Alex that we've found them, the less he'll worrry. And he worrries too much these days."

Carina looked doubtful. "If you're sure," she said.

"I'm surrre the drrragons need to leave as soon as possible, forrr theirrr own safety, and I'm also surrre the long rrride back will be morrre comforrrtable if the rrriderrrs split up. Therrre won't be rrroom forrr any food or water on my back if I'm carrrying the five of you." The giant cat startled as a clatter of weapons and voices rose from within the castle's courtyard. "They've spotted us up herrre, no doubt," he said. "You must hurrry!"

Seth looked both disappointed and relieved at the prospect of leaving now. He glanced at his mother. "We don't have any components. I won't be of any use if we stay."

Carina gave Simber a final doubtful look, then gave in. "All right. Come on, Seth," she said. "Arabis, your wings look the strongest. Can you take us to Artimé?"

"It would be my honor," said the orange dragon. "We'll stop at the waterfall to catch some fish and collect water for the ride."

The noise from the soldiers grew louder, and Simber nodded to Arabis, handing over any further instructions to be given by her.

"Take flight now," Arabis ordered her brothers and sisters. "Watch out for the projectile weapons. Go straight toward the waterfall and stay out of range. We're free at last! We mustn't tempt fate."

One by one, Drock the dark purple, Hux the ice blue, Ivis the green, and Yarbeck the purple and gold leaped off the wall and soared high into the air, a stunning, shimmering sight against the bright blue sky. Carina and Seth climbed onto Arabis's back, and soon the mother and son were waving back at Simber and Thatcher. "We'll see you soon in Artimé!" Thatcher called after them.

Simber rose too. The soldiers came charging up the stairwell and out of the turrets onto the fortress wall just a moment too late. They were left gasping for air, with little to aim their weapons at.

As Arabis maneuvered over the waterfall, the other dragons swooped down and dangled their tails in the water to catch fish. Seth and Carina leaned over to drink and fill Thisbe's canteens before the long ride home. Simber and Thatcher headed inland at great speed. They followed the road that Arabis had pointed out, heading to Dragonsmarche. And making another appearance on the grounds below, amid the chaos, the princess and her servant slipped away unnoticed, this time galloping down the mountain on horseback.

On the Auction Block

The bidding began, and the crowd continued to grow around Thisbe and Fifer. Most people of the city didn't have the wealth to place a bid, but they came to witness the rarity of not one but two black-eyed children up for sale. Twins, no less. It was a phenomenon. Surely no one in all the land could afford both children, though it seemed a shame to split them up—they were like finely matched horses. Well, except for the obvious thief. But her hair would grow back again in time, and she'd most certainly be taught many lessons about never stealing again.

The pirates and aristocrats filled the area closest to the

girls. Thisbe and Fifer tried not to let their fear show. They were stuck here for this moment, Fifer kept telling herself, but Simber would come for them. Soon. She had to believe it, or she'd start freaking out and never stop.

"I wonder if this is what happened to Dev," Thisbe whispered to Fifer. "If he got auctioned off too." She imagined him standing up here and having the king and princess staring coldly at him before deciding to offer up the winning bid.

Fifer swallowed hard. "If it did, well . . . I guess I feel pretty bad for him."

"Especially if he had to do it alone."

"Yeah. At least we have each other."

Both of them added silently, *If we get to stay together*. That was the scariest part. Neither girl could imagine what it would be like to be servants, forced to entertain spoiled royal children, or worse—pirates! Much less having to do it without the other.

Murmurs rippled through the crowd as the bidding soared for the black-eyed pair. The auctioneer kept the crowd heated while the girls grew silent and withdrawn, finding it more and more difficult to process what was happening to them, and bewildered by the frenzied way the crowd was reacting. Every now and then they turned their gazes to the sky, searching for any sign of Simber. But they couldn't see much past the frame of the stage they stood upon. Hope was all they had left.

Fifer, who'd barely slept since Hux had startled them awake two nights before, began trembling and couldn't stop. Her limbs felt like rubber, and she sank against the pole, her body giving up. Uncontrollable tears started trickling down her cheeks. Thisbe, watching her, strained harder at her ropes, tearing the skin on her wrists but making no progress. "Hang on, Fife," she whispered, feeling hopeless. A lump rose to her throat.

Just then a group of soldiers wearing blue uniforms swarmed in and began forcing people back. The castle soldiers, in green, drew their weapons, but they were clearly outnumbered, so they held back from attacking and instead demanded to know what the other soldiers were doing.

The soldiers in blue didn't respond. Instead they cleared an area of the square in front of the platform, rudely and unapologetically shoving people back. At once the ground started trembling. A circular section of the cobblestones separated from the rest of them and began to rise up in the air.

The crowd gasped. The auctioneer paused in the bidding process as whispers began. A few people started moving hurriedly away.

"What's happening?" cried Thisbe. Fifer only stared.

"The catacombs lie beneath this square," whispered a bidder near the stage. "Could it be . . . ?"

"The catacombs!" repeated others, and soon the words were rippling through the crowd. "A secret entrance?"

The circle of ground rose steadily upward as many more in the crowd turned and began fleeing, knocking onlookers down in the process. Still others pointed up into the sky and began screaming. They tripped and trampled the townspeople in their hurry to get out.

Fifer, reviving a little, strained weakly at her shackles and tried to figure out what the people were pointing at. But she still couldn't see anything much beyond the overhang of the structure she was tied to. And all Thisbe could do was stare at the cylinder slowly rising from the ground. It was like . . . like a tube. An actual tube. From Artimé. Could it be Alex? Did one of the secret buttons lead to *here*, of all places? But no . . . it couldn't be.

As bits of earth and stone and dust flew off the cylinder, more and more visitors and merchants around the market square became aware of the strange happenings. The panic pitched higher when an enormous shadow swept over Dragonsmarche. Screams filled the air.

"Was that Simber?" asked Fifer, frantic. "Thisbe! Is Simber here?"

Thisbe couldn't take her eyes off the rising tube. Almost instinctively, before the crowd began to whisper, her heart clutched, and she knew who would step out from it. It most definitely wouldn't be Alex. As if in a trance, she stared, unable to care at all about Simber's approach. She could only watch as the dusty tube inched higher and wait as its opening rotated toward her. When the opening finally came around, there was only one surprise. It didn't reveal a man, as Thisbe expected to see, but a woman.

Despite that, Thisbe's guess was confirmed when the few people remaining in the square whispered the name. "It's the Revinir."

All went silent for a moment. And then the silence was broken by the roar of the stone cheetah. At top speed, Simber swooped in to grab the girls. But the strange sight of the Revinir caught his attention. His eyes left the girls for briefest of moments, and he didn't see the glass until it was too late. Before anyone could warn him, Simber smashed right through the invisible glass barrier that Thisbe had cast in front of Fifer. The girls screamed. Shards of glass flew everywhere. At the unanticipated impact, Thatcher went sailing off Simber's back, landing hard on the stage. Fifer's face, at first joyous at seeing Simber coming toward them, turned to shock at the impact, and then horror afterward as she glanced down at her body. Bright red bloodstains spread over her clothing. And then, without a word, she slumped unconscious, only her shackles keeping her from falling face-first to the stage.

"Fifer!" yelled Thisbe.

From the tube, the Revinir watched, unfazed. "Hmph. What a pity." She turned up her nose at the blood and looked away. "Guards!" she cried. "Free the thief!"

Blue-uniformed soldiers rushed to the stage. With a few simple swipes of their swords, Thisbe was freed from her restraints. She tried to run to Fifer, but the Revinir reached out and grabbed Thisbe around the middle. She yanked the girl into the tube with her.

"Save Fifer!" Thisbe screamed to Simber. The cat had circled by now, ready to snatch up Thisbe, but her cries were cut ominously short as the tube shot down into the earth. The Revinir's long, curling fingernails entwined around the girl, securing the priceless black-eyed goods.

To Safety

Near the platform, Simber landed hard on the cobblestones where the cylinder had been. Thisbe was gone. He growled in rage. Then he turned quickly to ward off anyone else who would attempt the same with Fifer, but people shrank away from the bloody heap. Thatcher, still somewhat stunned from being thrown so violently from Simber's back, got up and stumbled over to Fifer. He began trying every magical spell he could think of to release or cut through her shackles. At the same time, Simber began biting and tearing at the shackles at Fifer's feet, and that proved more efficient.

Once she was free, Thatcher hoisted her up onto Simber's back, trying to be careful of her wounds, many of which still had glass sticking out of them. "Go!" he cried when they were ready. Simber galloped across the stage, paying no heed to anyone in his way, and leaped into the air. He took flight, once again startling those who remained in the marketplace.

"What about Thisbe?" shouted Thatcher. "Did you see that woman? The Revinir? Did you see who it really was?"

"Yes," said Simber, a strong note of disgust in his voice. "I saw herrr. She was about the last perrrson I could have everrr expected. How Queen Eagala surrrvived herrr trrrip down the volcano is beyond all comprrrehension." He looked over his shoulder as he flew across the square. "How is Fiferrr?"

"Still unconscious and losing blood quickly. We have to do something."

Fifer's eyes fluttered and opened. She found herself looking down on the marketplace, which was a strange sight. Nearly empty of merchants and villagers by now, only the goods remained, with a few brave and desperate souls looting what they could.

Her gaze focused on the corner of the square where the

giant aquarium stood—the one that Thisbe had pointed out. As Simber flew past it, she could see the strange-looking sea creatures more closely. Fifer's eyes blurred as a spotted sea monster came into view. It looked familiar, somehow. In fact, it reminded her of Issie, their sea monster friend who lived on the Island of Legends. But Fifer's mind was fuzzy. She closed her eyes briefly, feeling faint again, then opened them and turned her head. "Thatcher," she said, noticing him for the first time. "What happened?"

Thatcher looked down at her. "You've been hurt," he said. "We're finding help."

"Oh." Fifer didn't feel hurt. She didn't feel anything. She wanted to ask where Thisbe was, but her tongue wouldn't form the words. Soon her sight went black again.

Thatcher put his hand on Simber's neck. "She was awake for a moment. Should I take the glass out or leave it stuck in her? I don't know what to do." He tried desperately to think like Henry or Carina, who were healers, but the uncertainty of everything overcame his sense of good judgment. "We don't have any medicine."

"Just wait," said Simber. "That'll only make it bleed morrre,

I think. We need to find something that will stop the bleeding." *Beforrre she dies*, he added to himself. He wore a defeated expression, taking full blame for what had happened.

They reached the outskirts of the city. Simber flew low to the ground between the road and the forest, looking at the foliage and wondering if anything there would help them.

"I'm afrrraid this is all my fault," muttered Simber.

Thatcher held on to Fifer, feeling helpless. "You couldn't have known about the glass spells. I didn't see them either."

"I should have!" growled Simber. "I also should know about the healing naturrre of plants. But as a statue, I've neverrr needed them. It was stupid of me to send Carrrina home. We need herrr now morrre than everrr."

Thatcher didn't know what to say. He'd never seen Simber so vulnerable and hard on himself. As they flew along, they saw two horseback riders coming toward them. When they grew close, Thatcher recognized one of them. "That boy—Dev. He's the servant from the castle who fed us. And I'll bet that's the princess Thisbe was telling me about. Perhaps one of them knows a little about medicine as well."

Simber was desperate enough to stop and ask them for help.

He landed a short distance off so as not to frighten the horses. The princess and Dev slowed their horses and looked warily at the strange flying statue before them. Thatcher laid Fifer out on Simber's back and climbed down.

"Hi," he said. He approached cautiously, ready for Simber to snatch him up if these two tried to capture him. He held up his hands to show he was coming in peace.

Dev spoke quickly and quietly to the girl next to him, all the while trying to see what was going on. Then he stared at Simber's back for a long moment. He got off his horse and came running toward the cheetah, realizing something was terribly wrong.

"What have you done to her?" he demanded.

"Dev!" said the princess. "Be careful!"

Dev ignored her and ran closer. He gasped when he saw Fifer covered in blood.

"Please," said Thatcher earnestly. "Do you know what will stop the bleeding? We need your help to save her."

Dev stared at Fifer in horror. "What happened?" Then he quickly turned to his companion, who had approached on her horse, pulling Dev's along. "Princess—they need help. May I . . . ?"

She lifted her chin. "Is that one of our black-eyed girls? What about the auction?"

Dev tried to hide his sudden disgust for his only friend. How could she be so horrible? "Shanti," he said quietly. "Please. Look at her. She needs help."

The princess frowned at his use of her name in front of others, but Dev didn't flinch. Finally she nodded primly.

Dev turned back to Thatcher. "That creature won't hurt the princess?" He pointed to Simber.

"You have my word. He'll protect her if anything."

"Come with me." Dev took off toward the forest with Thatcher right behind. He zigzagged around trees, looking for the right plant, and finally he found a grouping of them. "Yarrow," he said, pulling one up. "What did you do to her?"

"We didn't— It's broken glass. It . . . shattered right in front of her."

"More glass? Like what Thisbe did to me, I suppose." He touched his sore nose gingerly, then pulled up another plant.

"I'm sure she's sorry about that."

"I deserved it. So . . . ," he said, glancing back at Simber. "Where is the thief?"

"The . . . what?"

"Thisbe, I mean." He pulled on another plant and tried to pretend not to care very much. But a wave of fear washed through him as he wondered what might have happened to her.

Thatcher remembered what Thisbe had said about their short hair. He hesitated but saw no reason to lie. "Unfortunately, she's been captured. The Revinir rose up from the ground in the square and snatched her."

Dev stopped and stared at him. His expression betrayed him. "The Revinir?" he whispered.

"Yes. She rose up from inside the earth."

"The catacombs," said Dev, as if he were piecing the story together. The knot in his stomach tightened. "Thisbe's lost for good, then." His face wrinkled up, and he fought to pull his feelings together. He was used to losing everything, and he knew how to handle it. But this . . . this news rocked him in a way he didn't understand. Quickly he blocked her face from his mind. After a moment he forged ahead, picking more plants. "You'll never see her again."

"Don't say that. We'll find her. We have to."

"How? You can't. You need to get Fifer home. She won't survive out here. And I hope you know better than to ask for help from anyone else. Her black eyes . . . She's not safe anywhere in our world." He stood and started back toward the road.

Thatcher grabbed his leaves and followed. He wasn't sure if he should believe the boy after all Thisbe had recounted. He decided to test him, to see if he'd lie. "How do you know so much about the twins?"

"I spent a couple days leading them to the castle," said Dev. "Thisbe . . ." He thought about how she'd saved him by destroying the snake, and he felt his throat tighten. And then he shook his head. "Never mind."

It was truthful enough. They reached Simber's side. Dev showed Thatcher how to pull the glass out of Fifer's body and administer the plant to stop the bleeding. "I'm glad you freed the dragons," he said in a low voice. "You mustn't ever let them return here. And you'd better get out of here too, before Princess Shanti's father learns what happened, or hordes of soldiers will be on the move to find you. You won't make it to the gorge alive." He looked at Simber. "Not even him."

Thatcher looked at the boy. "But we can't leave Thisbe here."

Dev dropped his gaze. "I'm not exaggerating. You may as well forget her. The Revinir won't ever give her back—not in a million years."

Grave Peril

Thatcher stared at Dev, trying to comprehend the finality of his words.

"Servant!" said the princess impatiently from her horse. "Enough already. We need to go."

Dev looked at the princess as if he'd been struck. "I was just helping . . ."

"Quickly," she said. She glanced back toward the castle and gave Dev a hard look.

Dev bowed his head. "Coming." After a second he looked at Thatcher. "Take her home," he warned, "or you might end up losing them both."

Thatcher nodded. "Thank you for your help."

Dev let his eyes rest on Fifer's ashen face and handed the remaining plants to Thatcher. Then he quickly ran to his horse, pulled a sack of food and a canteen from his pack, and ran back to Thatcher. He shoved it at him. "Here," he said. "I . . . I owe it to them."

"Dev!" said the princess, making the boy cringe.

Thatcher raised his eyebrow at Shanti and took the sack. "Thank you, Dev."

Dev nodded and ran back to his horse. He mounted it, dug his heels into its flank, and clicked his tongue. Soon he and the princess were off, heading down the road toward Dragonsmarche. He forced himself not to look back.

Thatcher worked quickly to clean Fifer's wounds, then went to fill the canteen with water from the river. He held Fifer's head up and tried to get her to drink a little, but she was still out cold.

"Do you agree with Dev?" Thatcher asked Simber.

"It's prrrobably forrr the betterrr," said Simber. "And we should go now." His ears twitched and turned. "Soldierrrs arrre alrrready coming this way."

"So we're really going back to Artimé? Without Thisbe?"

Simber was quiet for a long moment. He stared at Fifer. "Unforrrtunately, I don't think we have a choice if we want to save herrr."

Thatcher sighed deeply but climbed on Simber's back and tried to make Fifer as comfortable as possible. "I can hardly stand the thought of this," he said under his breath. Leaving Thisbe a world away? But he could come up with no alternative. They had to save the one they could save.

Soon they were soaring over the forest, then the hills, then the castle of Grimere, out of range of the soldiers' spears and arrows. As they crossed the divide between the worlds on their way back to the seven islands, Thatcher barely looked at the stunning landscape. He could only think of their failures. And of how Thisbe must be feeling right now—totally and completely abandoned.

"We'll be back for you," Thatcher whispered.

Simber, who heard and saw nearly everything, didn't acknowledge the young man's words out loud. But inside, his stone heart was breaking in two.

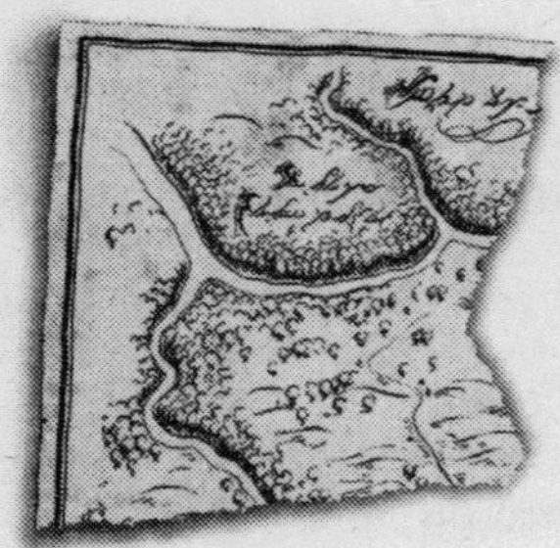

The Catacombs

Too shocked to struggle, Thisbe hung numbly in the Revinir's arms as they plunged into darkness inside the tube. She wanted to scream but couldn't find her voice. She wanted to demand answers but couldn't form the questions. She could only stare in front of her, trying to make sense of what was happening.

The tube looked very much like the ones in Artimé except for the fact that it was moving—they weren't traveling anywhere magically. And the control panel was completely different. None of the buttons looked familiar. After several seconds the tube came to a stop. Through the dusty glass, Thisbe could see small wall torches providing a dim view down a long hallway. Every few feet there were ancient stone-and-iron doors set into the walls.

The Revinir forced Thisbe out of the tube and started down the hallway.

Stumbling along, Thisbe found her voice. "Where are you taking me?" She tried to yank her arms away, but the old woman's long fingernails entwined around Thisbe's arm. Thisbe recoiled at the sight of them. She'd never seen anything like it. She remembered stories about someone with fingernails like that before—someone who had permanently maimed her dear brother—but that person was dead . . . wasn't she?

The Revinir didn't answer her. Surprisingly strong for such an old woman, she dragged Thisbe down another hallway that also had crypts along both sides. Eventually she stopped at one doorway that had cobwebs hanging from both upper corners.

Thisbe shuddered. "What are you doing to me?"

Using one of her fingernails, which had been sharpened and shaped like a key, the Revinir unlocked the door. It creaked open, revealing its contents.

The room was full of bones.

Thisbe gasped. The Revinir shoved the girl into the crypt and slammed the door shut. Then she locked it again and smiled to herself as she walked away.

By the time Thisbe finally stopped screaming for help, many hours had passed. She kicked all the bones into one corner and collapsed to the floor as far away from them as she could, and stared up at the ceiling. A single torch made shadows on it. Thisbe knew she was stuck here. Nobody was coming to rescue her—they'd have been here by now. Fifer was badly hurt. Maybe even dead. And Thisbe was all alone with hundreds of gross bones and all of her fears and regrets. Her skin pricked, feeling her identical twin's pain in all the same places.

How she wished she'd been allowed to learn more magic, for what she knew was woefully inadequate to have done anything against such powerful people. How she wished she wasn't filled with such destructive natural power—her attempts at controlling it, at doing good with it, had failed miserably, over and over again. She was stuck with the few spells she'd learned and whatever else happened naturally, and none of those could be changed.

There was only one thing Thisbe could focus on now. And that was figuring out—all on her own—how to get out of here, and get back to Artimé, and find out if her sister was still alive. To do it, she would have to fight against the most powerful person in this world. Perhaps it was time to embrace the destructive magic that brewed inside her.

Thisbe curled up and faced the wall, feeling terribly alone. Escaping the Revinir seemed more overwhelming than anything she had ever faced. And she had no idea if she'd be able to do it.

As it turned out, she would have many days to think about it.

A Final Blow

Far away, Simber, Thatcher, and unconscious Fifer flew through the day and night and day again, until Warbler was in sight. Simber pushed for the island as fast as his wings would take him. They could make an emergency stop there to stock up on food, water, and medicine on their way back home.

When they approached the sandy beach, they were greeted by the frantic waves and shouts of Copper and Scarlet. Sky was nowhere in sight. Simber landed nearby.

"What's happened?" asked Thatcher, alarmed. He couldn't imagine something else could have possibly gone wrong. Yet a wisp of fear grew inside him—he knew well enough by now that there was no end to the bad luck that had befallen them on this mission.

"It's Sky," cried Scarlet. Copper could only stare numbly as tears flowed down her face.

"What happened?" demanded Simber.

"Where is she?" asked Thatcher, looking all around. The wisp became a knot and rose to his throat. Surely she was fine. She had to be. But a cold, horrible feeling came over him. Something must've gone terribly wrong for Sky's mother to have that look on her face. "Scarlet, please—tell us what happened."

Scarlet's face was anguished. "She was working on stabilizing the volcano's core temperature, trying to stop it from sinking so often."

Thatcher nodded. "Yes, she told us. Is she all right?"

Scarlet forged onward. "Her work caused the warning tremors to slowly dissipate. Eventually she had to guess when the volcano would plunge underwater, but she thought she had the timing figured out. Even so, she made me stay a safe distance away in my skiff." Scarlet swallowed hard, and fresh tears flowed. "She was being very cautious, but then today, without any warning at all . . . the volcano went down."

Thatcher and Simber stared. "IS SHE OKAY?" shouted Thatcher, growing desperate to hear the answer. But he knew she couldn't be.

Scarlet shook her head. "She made it to the white boat, but couldn't get it going in time. She went down with it."

Copper let a heartbreaking sob escape. Scarlet reached around the woman's trembling shoulders, trying to support her in her grief.

Simber and Thatcher stared in stunned silence, tried to comprehend it. Their beloved friend Sky, Alex's strength, his light, the love of his life, had been caught in the suction of the plunging volcano. She was gone.

Fifer lay motionless. Thisbe, held captive by the Revinir in a foreign world. Sky had been sucked down the enormous maw of the watery volcano. And Simber and Thatcher had to deliver all of this wrenching news to Alex.

The time of peacefulness was over. Chaos, fear, and grief had returned to the land of Artimé and its people. The disastrous repercussions of all that had gone wrong would no doubt spread far and wide across the world of the seven islands, and beyond.

There was no way to tell what threats, trials, and quests lay ahead. But they were sure to be more dangerous than the people of Artimé had ever known.

Fifer's and Thisbe's stories continue in

THE UNWANTEDS QUESTS

BOOK TWO

Dragon Bones

Turn the page for a peek. . . .

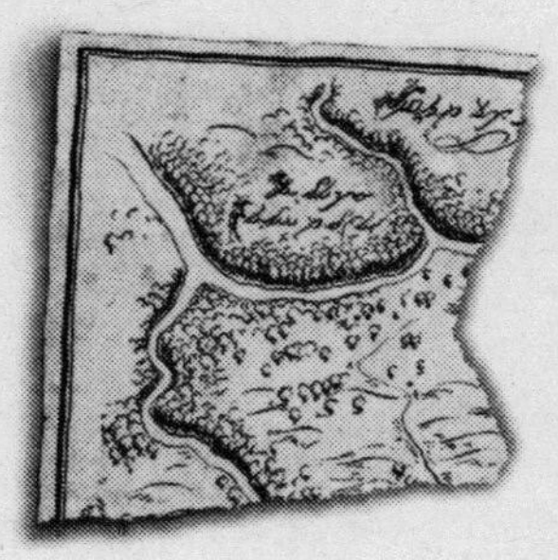

Breaking the News

There was a rare thunderstorm over Artimé when Simber returned, carrying Thatcher and an unconscious Fifer Stowe on his back. All was quiet in the mansion, for it was not quite dawn, and the dark skies kept most of the mages in their beds with the covers pulled up around them, listening to the rumbling in their dreams.

A three-headed tiki statue stood guard in Simber's place to the left of the door, and Jim the winged tortoise, with his brightly colored mosaic shell, floated lazily in the air on the right, his white feather wings flapping just enough to keep him rising and falling without hitting the ceiling or the pedestal below him. They hadn't sensed Simber coming until he burst through the door.

"Get Alex and Henry!" Thatcher shouted. "Bring them to the hospital ward right away!" His voice was harsh and gravelly, for he'd barely slept in the days it had taken them to return home from the land of the dragons. With Fifer limp in his arms, he slid off Simber's back and stumbled to his knees, his legs numb and body aching from the journey. He got up and hobbled toward the hospital ward as the two statues figured out what was happening. Simber followed Thatcher.

Jim flew upstairs with the tiki statue behind him, mysteriously able to glide up the steps on his flat, legless bottom. At the balcony Jim headed for the family hallway to locate Henry Haluki, Artimé's chief healer and Thatcher's partner in all things, while the tiki statue slid to the farthest hallway on the left. Many of Artimé's mages couldn't see that magical hallway—they saw a mirror on the wall instead—but the tiki statue had no problem finding it. He charged toward Alex's apartment and pounded his top head against the door.

In the hospital ward, Thatcher gently lay Fifer on a bed and looked around, feeling helpless and a bit guilty that he knew so little about the medicines Henry had so lovingly created. He went to get a cup of water and a sponge to soak and press against the young twin's parched lips, in hopes that drops of water would seep inside her mouth and trickle down her throat without choking her.

While Thatcher lifted Fifer's head and administered the sponge, he swept his troubled gaze over the girl. Her clothing was full of rips and stained dark with blood after Simber, the enormous winged-cheetah statue, had unintentionally smashed through the glass barriers in Dragonsmarche, sending shards like a thousand daggers into Fifer's body. An instant later Fifer's twin, Thisbe, had been snatched up by the Revinir—someone Thatcher and Simber had recognized as the former Queen Eagala from Warbler Island, who should've been dead—and taken underground to her lair among the catacombs.

They'd had to leave Thisbe behind. In order to save Fifer's life, they'd flown nonstop for days, all the way to Warbler, where they'd learned of even more heartrending news: Sky had been swept underwater into the mouth of the plunging volcanic Island of Fire and was gone.

Thatcher heard a commotion on the stairs and looked up, feeling his heart in his throat. He and Simber had a lot of explaining to do, and there was no easy way to go about it. Delivering this news to Alex was the hardest thing Thatcher had ever faced, including everything he'd just been through.

"Thank goodness," Thatcher murmured when he saw Henry racing toward him, one arm slid inside the sleeve of his healer's coat, the rest of it flying behind. The two quickly embraced; then Henry slipped his other arm into the jacket and reached for his medical supplies. "Tell me everything," he demanded.

Before Thatcher or Simber could begin to tell him, Alex arrived inside the ward. At the sight of his sister on the bed he paled, and his mouth slacked in shock. "What happened? Is she okay? How did this come about?" He looked around frantically. "Where's Thisbe? Carina said—Carina told me— You were all supposed to be coming right behind them!"

Simber looked to Thatcher to fill in everyone as Henry began assessing Fifer's condition, then working on her wounds, cleaning them and applying the magical plant-based concoctions he'd developed over the years. Thatcher spoke hastily about what had transpired after Carina and Seth had left the castle Grimere with the five young dragons. Things had not gone as planned.

Alex listened, stunned. He could hardly take in the information about Thisbe or how the Revinir had snatched her up and disappeared. Or who the old woman really was. "Queen Eagala is the Revinir?" he whispered. "How can that be? She's been dead for over ten years!"

"We don't know," said Simber. "But I'm cerrrtain it was herrr."

"We have to go after Thisbe," Alex said, growing frantic. "She must be absolutely sick with fear! But Fifer—is she . . . ?"

"We'll go after Thisbe," said Thatcher, trying to calm Alex down. "Shortly we'll start to organize and figure out a plan for that. But . . ." He gave Simber a pleading look.

"Rrright," said Simber in a grave voice. "Alex, therrre's . . . something else."

Alex looked at Simber. His hand shook, and he reached for a bedpost. "Something else?" he said weakly. "What more could there possibly be?"

Simber's body sagged, and he closed his eyes as if he couldn't bear to see Alex hurt even more. After an agonizing moment, he opened them and looked squarely at the mage. "It's Sky," he said quietly. "She was worrrking on the Island of Firrre, and it plunged below the waterrr without warrrning. She was swept in." He paused for a moment as he watched Alex, dazed, sink heavily to the bed next to Fifer's. And then Simber growled, "She's gone."

When Everything Shatters

Henry turned sharply away from treating Fifer to look at Simber. "*What?* Good gods! You can't be serious."

"Sky?" Alex stared in disbelief. "No," he said, faltering. Then: "No!"

Thatcher, his expression wretched, went over to Alex and sat beside him. "I'm so sorry. I'm afraid it's all true." He put a gentle hand around the head mage's shoulders.

Simber bowed his head. "I'm sorry. I can't begin to imagine yourrr pain. The shock of all of this must be overrrwhelming."

Alex was numb inside, and his skin turned cold and aching.

He'd heard the words and understood their meaning, but he couldn't absorb the wrenching truth of everything he'd experienced in the past few moments: Fifer lying bloody and unconscious, Thisbe kidnapped by Queen Eagala, and now his beloved Sky, gone? The scope of the news was beyond his ability to comprehend. He was completely struck down. He couldn't catch his breath. He couldn't see—everything wavered in front of him. He felt like his soul had left him and risen above his body to escape the words. Like he was a spectator looking down on this horrible scene. He doubled over, the world spinning, and put his hand over his face. This couldn't be real. It had to be a nightmare. "Tell me what happened," he cried. "Tell me everything." Then he slid off the edge of the bed to the floor and crumpled there, sobbing.

"Go get Aarrron rrright away," Simber ordered Thatcher. "And Crrrow. Hurrry!"

Thatcher nodded and dashed out of the hospital ward without a word. Simber watched Alex shuddering on the floor, then closed his eyes and sighed heavily. He knelt next to the mage to let him know he was there and quickly filled him in. He could do nothing else for him right now. It was the worst moment in Simber's memory.

After a time Alex quieted. He lifted his head and looked through red-rimmed eyes at Simber. When their eyes connected, more tears started pouring down the head mage's cheeks, and he moaned in pure agony, feeling physically sick, the losses hitting him in waves until he wished he could slip into unconsciousness to escape it.

He began to cry harder. And when he could finally catch his breath and speak a few words, he turned to Henry. "Is Fifer . . . ? Is she . . . ?" He couldn't finish.

"She's hurt very badly, but she's going to live," said Henry, determined and working steadily. His face didn't betray the range of emotions he felt. He had one job, and that was to see Fifer through. He couldn't bear the thought of Alex losing all three of them, especially after having lost so much in his life already. "She's waking up now, Alex. I need your help—can you come and stand by the head of her bed? Let her know you're here?"

The grief surged again. Alex didn't know if he could get up, much less walk over to Fifer's side. But he reached his right arm around Simber's neck and pulled himself up off the floor. The stone cheetah helped him walk. Alex quickly tried to dry his tears on his shirt so Fifer wouldn't be scared. "What do I tell her?" he said to Simber, in agony. "Does she know about . . . this? About Thisbe or any of it?"

Simber's expression was filled with sorrow. He shook his head. "I don't think so," he said. "She's been unconscious. Just tell herrr that you'rrre herrre. Tell herrr that you'rrre with herrr and she's safe. Just like you'd have done forrr any of us back in the old days."

Alex stared at Simber, a look of bewilderment on his face. His role as chief comforter in times like these had all but disappeared since the final battle. And he'd focused his care inward since that time, so much so that it felt strange to remember he wasn't the only one who needed a guiding hand in this moment. With a start he realized that no matter how much he was hurting, he *was* the guiding hand . . . like he used to be. Like after Mr. Today, the original head mage, had died and all the magic in Artimé had disappeared. How would Fifer feel once she heard the news? And Crow? And Aaron? "It hurts," he whispered, and choked back a sob. "Worse than any pain I've ever known."

"I know," said Simber, standing by him. There was nothing

else to say that could possibly help. He could only stand by.

Alex's mind awhirl, he reached Fifer's side and stood near her head. He gripped the bedpost as a new wave of pain went through him and stifled a moan, then tried to smile as his sister's eyes fluttered. "Hey there, Fife," he said softly. "It's me, Alex. You're home. You're safe."

Fifer opened her eyes and focused on her brother's face. She was confused. Her lids closed for a moment, then squeezed shut, then blinked open again. Her eyes filled with tears. A jumble of horrifying memories bounced around in her head. "I'm so sorry, Alex," she choked out. She began to cry inconsolably.

Alex lost it again and cried with her. He smoothed her hair from her face and kissed her cheek, his tears raining down on her. "It doesn't matter," he said. "It doesn't matter. I'm just so glad you're okay. You're . . . alive." As he said the words, he couldn't stop the next wave of pain that came with the thoughts about Thisbe and Sky, and everything inside him shattered once more. He was in turns frozen, overwhelmed, and on the verge of blacking out from the pain stabbing through him. Yet here was Fifer. Alive. He clung to her life like a raft in the sea.

A tiny piece of his shattered heart found another tiny piece, and they melded back together. Fifer was here. Awake. Alive. He hadn't lost them all.

In that moment he loved her ferociously, more than he'd loved any other human being or creature in his life, and he swore in his heart to protect her from anything like this ever happening again. "Never again," he whispered.

Alex had lost one sister, but Fifer had lost her twin. Alex had known that feeling once and the physical pain that went with it. She would need him to be strong for her now.

In the midst of Alex's grief, something inside him, a remnant of his old self, fluttered awake after a long sleep. He planted his feet and then took Fifer's hand in his. He looked her in the eye with a lifetime's worth of compassion and, as gently as he could, told Fifer what had happened to Thisbe.

She didn't have the strength to comprehend or react and soon slipped into unconsciousness, the words twisting around her mind like a nightmare.

Alex's survival mode switched onto autopilot, and he began running things as usual, pushing the pain and distracting thoughts back so he could govern properly. He ordered Thatcher to dispatch Spike Furious, the intuitive magical whale, to go in search of Sky. Then he stoically delivered all the terrible news to Aaron and Crow.

Their reactions were about what Alex had expected, and the pain remained raw. But Alex soldiered on, with support from Simber and Thatcher.

"How is my mother handling this?" Crow asked. He ripped his hand through his long dark hair, feeling completely frantic to be a full day's journey across the sea from her with not only the news of the girls, but of his sister, Sky. "And Scarlet? Is she okay?"

"Copper and Scarlet are together on Warbler," said Thatcher. "They have each other for comfort until you can get there. Simber will take you once you're ready."

Aaron appeared stunned at the news and handled it with little outward reaction at first. He reverted back to turning off his emotions, which was reminiscent of how he'd grown up in Quill. Moving abruptly away from the others, he went to stand near Fifer, who was asleep, and tried to make sense of it all.

After a while he reached for Fifer's hand and held it. He

studied it, watching how her long thin fingers curled naturally in his. He felt like he was drowning and kept trying to surface long enough to let some of his emotions out, but he could barely breathe. And his mind kept going back to his youth, to when he'd said good-bye to Alex for what he'd thought was the last time, at the Purge. It sparked something still raw in him, and his grief was bitter.

"They've been forced to grow up like we did, Al," he said, looking over his shoulder to where Alex sat. "All in one day. Separated and everything." Then he shook his head, and the tears began. "This is *their* Purge." He was quiet for a moment, thinking back to when the governors of Quill had taken Alex away while he stood there watching and thinking his life would be the better of the two. How wrong he'd been. "But which of them is me," he added softly, turning to Alex, "and which is you?"

"*Keeper of the Lost Cities* is a little bit *Alice's Adventures in Wonderland*, a little bit *Lord of the Rings*, and a little bit *Harry Potter*. And it's all fun!"

—MICHAEL BUCKLEY,
New York Times bestselling author of the Sisters Grimm and NERDS series

***NEW YORK TIMES* AND *USA TODAY* BESTSELLING SERIES**

"A delightful and dangerous adventure with complex characters and relationships you'll root for to the end of time."

—LISA McMANN,
New York Times bestselling author of *The Unwanteds*, on *Keeper of the Lost Cities*

EBOOK EDITIONS ALSO AVAILABLE

ALADDIN

SIMONANDSCHUSTER.COM/KIDS

Samantha's intercom buzzer sounded. On shaky legs, she padded to the kitchen and pressed the button to hear who was there.

"Ms. Reid, this is Officer Johnson of the Plymouth Police Department. Your intruder says he has a right to be here. Would you mind coming down?"

A few seconds later, Samantha cautiously unlocked her door and peered out into the night. A pair of officers held a man between them—someone she recognized. She glanced up into the stone face of Ryan Davidson, the same man she'd seen in a photo earlier that day.

Their gazes locked, and raw emotion flickered in his blue eyes. The power of his bewildered pain snagged her breath. In recent times, she'd seen that look in another pair of eyes.

Her own.

JILL ELIZABETH NELSON

writes what she likes to read—faith-based tales of adventure seasoned with romance. By day she operates as a housing manager for a seniors' apartment complex. By night she turns into a wild and crazy writer who can hardly wait to jot down all the exciting things her characters are telling her, so she can share them with her readers. More about Jill and her books can be found at www.jillelizabethnelson.com. She and her husband live in rural Minnesota, surrounded by the woods and prairie and their four grown children who have settled nearby.

EVIDENCE *of* MURDER

JILL ELIZABETH NELSON

Published by Steeple Hill Books™

STEEPLE HILL BOOKS

Recycling programs for this product may not exist in your area.

ISBN-13: 978-0-373-44327-7
ISBN-10: 0-373-44327-7

EVIDENCE OF MURDER

This edition published by arrangement with Steeple Hill Books.

www.SteepleHill.com

Printed in U.S.A.

Who shall separate us from the love of Christ?
Shall trouble, or hardship, or persecution, or
famine, or nakedness, or danger or sword?...No,
in all these things we are more than conquerors
through Him who loved us.

—*Romans* 8:35, 37

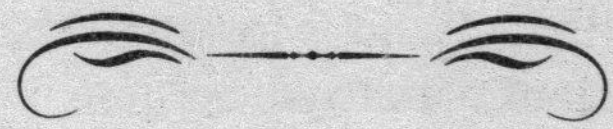

To the victims and their families affected by violent crime. May they find peace and comfort in the Lord who loves them.

Acknowledgments

Heartfelt thanks goes out to numerous people who contributed to this book in priceless ways.

First of all, many hugs to my husband, Doug, who is so patient with my busyness and distraction, particularly when deadlines loom. I'm also particularly grateful to my cousin, Neil Wicks, who willingly answered endless questions about the Boundary Waters canoe area based on his personal experience. Also, many thanks go to Ira Casperson and the staff at Monte Cleaners in Montevideo, MN, who provided a tour of their fine facility. Waving from shore to Mike Fries of Great River Houseboats for filling me in on the operation of a houseboat business. Many kudos to my fine editor at Steeple Hill, Emily Rodmell. She applied the necessary sandpaper and polish to this story. Finally, to my agent, Beth Jusino—you're the bomb!

ONE

One more nasty surprise in this old building might send her screaming for the funny farm. Samantha Reid glared at the door in front of her. Another unexplored room to tackle. What mysterious trial lay beyond? They'd disturbed a mouse nest in one of the dryers, and herds of spiders scurried for cover every time they moved something. Did spiders run in herds? They sure seemed to around here, especially down below in the basement—mice and spiders. Sam shuddered.

Good thing nothing was down there except museum-quality dry-cleaning equipment that must have dated back to the early days of the industry. That stuff could stay put until she found a place interested in carting the heavy pieces away. But up here on the main floor, she didn't have the luxury of delaying the project.

Squaring her shoulders, Sam turned the knob and eased open the door to the storeroom. She groped along the wall and flipped the light switch. A pair of fluorescent tubes flickered to life as smells of dust and chemicals nipped her nose. Her gaze scanned the twelve-foot-square room, and she puffed out a long breath that didn't stir the sweaty bangs plastered to her forehead.

How had a lifelong bachelor like Abel Morris accumulated so much junk? She stared at a maze of stacked boxes and metal shelves stuffed with dust-coated paint cans and half-empty jugs of cleaning solvent.

"Great!" Sam rubbed the small of her aching back. Her best friends, Jenna and Hallie, were going to be delighted at this discovery of a fresh room full of junkyard treasures. They'd been sorting and throwing things away for hours and had barely made a dent.

Fur brushed Sam's bare calf. She stiffened then relaxed at the familiar rumble that accompanied the touch. An Abyssinian cat wound around her sneaker-clad feet. Chuckling, she bent and scooped up the long, lean feline. The cat's motor revved up a notch as he rubbed his head against Sam's chin.

She stroked the soft, blue-gray fur. "So, Bastian, was I nuts to buy this neighborhood dry cleaners and expect to make a go of it?"

Her breath hitched, as it had many times since she signed on the dotted line. She'd paid out a big chunk of the inheritance money from her grandmother in order to become an independent businesswoman in Apple Valley, Minnesota—a healthy distance from her loving but smothering hometown. Twenty-six ought to be old enough to strike out on her own, shouldn't it? Nine years had passed since that one horrible night. Sam shook herself and deposited the cat on the cement floor. She had to stop going to that place in her mind.

The throaty tones of Hallie Berglund's television-personality voice came from the front room, followed by Jenna Newmann's bright laugh. Sam's shoulders relaxed. With the help of her friends and God, she could make a success of this business. She would.

Sam studied the room again. Her gaze caught on a toaster-size cardboard box high on a set of freestanding metal shelves in the middle of the room. The side of the box was labeled in red marker: *Lost, but alas, not found*. She laughed. God rest his soul, Abel Morris had been no ordinary hoarder; he was a poetic packrat. Now that was one box she had to open.

She stepped to the shelves. Her five-foot-five-inch height put the box level with the top of her head. Grasping the sides, she pulled it toward her. It was a little heavier than she liked. She put one foot back to brace herself. Something soft squished beneath the heel of her sneaker.

Mrrrow!

Bastian! Sam jerked her foot up. The box tilted toward her, threatening to land on her head. She ducked, still on one foot, teetered, and grabbed for the shelf. Off balance, she fell forward, toppling the set of shelving onto a stack of boxes, which thumped to the floor every which way, scattering contents.

Umph! Sam found herself spread-eagled and facedown atop the set of shelves that now rested on upended boxes. Acrid fumes from broken solvent bottles stung her throat and eyes. Throbbing from various body parts let her know she'd have a fine set of bruises in the morning.

"What happened?"

Hallie's alarmed voice brought Sam's head around. The tall, slender woman stood in the doorway, dark eyes wide, long-fingered hand clamped over her mouth. A short, generous figure shoved past her into the room.

"Phew!" Jenna coughed. "Are you all right?"

"Yes, just help me up so we can get out of here." Sam struggled to push away from the set of shelves and find the floor with her feet. Two pairs of hands grasped her arms and hauled her upright. She pulled her friends with her out the door and slammed it shut.

Choking, they headed for the side exit and fresh air. The route took them between antiquated clothing presses, puffers and a pillow-cleaning machine—nothing like the state-of-the-art equipment due to arrive in a few weeks.

Mere steps behind her friends, Sam barreled into the side alleyway and hauled in a breath of outdoor oxygen.

Next to her, Hallie shook her head like a dog shedding water. "Whoa! Whatever was in those bottles is potent."

Jenna pinched her nose. "Stink and a half!"

"I know." Sam slumped against the brick wall of her building. "Perchloroethylene. Perc for short. It's petroleum-based and so toxic and flammable it's all but banned in the industry. That's why I have to pay an arm and a leg to have a hazardous-material company haul it out of here. We're not to touch it…well, except to clean up the mess I just made."

In the late afternoon, the two-story dry cleaners cast shade across the space between it and the print shop next door. The coolness was welcome on this late summer day. Sam's nose and eyes cleared, but a weight still pressed her lungs. How could she possibly finish this gargantuan cleanup task in time to—

Stop it! Breathe in, breathe out. All would be well. This was a minor setback. She— "Bastian!"

Sam tore open the door and raced back inside the building. The smell wasn't too bad from this distance, but what if she'd shut her cat in the storeroom?

A plaintive meow brought her up short. She changed direction, charged through a doorway and skidded to a halt in a small vestibule facing a closed and locked exit to the rear alleyway. She turned and gazed up the wooden stairs that skirted the wall and led to her second-floor apartment. The Abyssinian perched regally on the top landing, slim body encircled by his long tail. The jerky tip-twitch matched the glare from those copper eyes.

A muted giggle slipped past Sam's lips. "Your humble servant begs your pardon. I have mightily offended your highness. Allow me to admit you to your chambers." She trod up the stairs and let him into the apartment, then headed down to find her friends. As she reached the bottom, they came toward her from the direction of the odorous storeroom.

"I'll take that." Hallie reached for something Jenna held in her fist.

The shorter woman danced away, tucking the item behind her back. Both of them laughed, but Hallie crossed her arms over her long-tailed shirt. The two friends were a study in contrasts, like a dusky-skinned Amazon queen matched with a jovial munchkin.

But they were identical in their attention to personal grooming—except for today.

Not on her life was Sam going to tell the elegant Channel Six news reporter that tufts of her black hair stuck out like she was Einstein's photonegative image. Nor would she inform the fastidious head chef and part owner of The Meridian "fine dining experience" that she looked like she'd been dipped in wheat flour. Thank the Lord for friends who would give up a Saturday and risk their manicured nails to help with a dirty project like hers.

Sam grinned. "What's up with you two?" She looked from one to the other.

Jenna held out her arm and opened her fist. A roll of 35 mm film rested on her palm. "I thought I kicked something when I ran out of there. I found it under one of the presses."

"Strange. Maybe the film was in that box of unclaimed property I was trying to get at when I took my tumble."

"Could be, but I want to develop it," Hallie said.

"Why? It's probably just shots of some stranger's boring vacation from sometime in the last century." Jenna surrendered the roll.

Hallie flipped the canister in the air, caught it, and stuffed it into her jeans pocket. "Call it journalistic curiosity. Besides, I don't often get a chance to process film the old-fashioned way."

Sam shook her head. "Go upstairs and order a pizza, ladies. I'll crack a few windows and open that storeroom door so things can air out awhile before I lock up for the night."

Jenna snorted. "Why not leave the windows ajar? Maybe some idiot thief will sneak in and take a few of these priceless treasures off our hands."

Thief? Sam's stomach rolled. Sensory impressions clamored for attention in her head. A door crashing inward. A dirty face with crazed eyes. The sear of burning flesh.

Sam blinked and shook off the flashback as she walked away without a word.

"Nice going, Jen." Hallie's fierce whisper carried to Sam's ears.

On the other side of the building, Sam shoved a window sash upward. Why was she still so touchy about the subject of break-ins? The incident happened when she was seventeen. She was a grown woman now. It was past time to get over it. But the pep talk didn't wash the sawdust from her mouth.

Two hours later, alone with her cat, Sam started running a bath. As the water splashed into the tub and steam rose, she opened a bottle of scented oil and poured a healthy dollop into the rising pool. The exotic floral aroma enveloped her. Wonderful!

She pulled the padded band out of her ponytail, and her thick, honey-brown hair fell loose to brush her shoulder blades. As soon as the water filled two-thirds of the tub, she eased in. Bubbles tickled her neck, and the knot in the small of her back loosened. The phone jangled, and she sat up, then shook her head and lay back again. Whoever it was could leave a message. She was going to enjoy a good, long soak.

By the time she climbed out, her muscles were relaxed and supple. Sam glanced across her shoulder into the wide mirror as she dried her back. The towel ran with little sensation across pale splotches of faded scars and puckers of skin-graft seams. She took a long-handled sponge, dipped it into an open jar of emollient, and rubbed every inch of the damaged skin until the lotion was absorbed. She rinsed the sponge, then donned pajamas before slipping into the smooth robe of real Chinese silk Jenna had brought back from a mission trip to the Far East.

On slipper-clad feet, she wandered to the kitchen for a glass of milk. Bastian, recovered from his sulk, twined around her legs and purred. Milk in hand, she surveyed her domain. Once the business was up and running, she'd have to remodel this apartment. Fifties retro was back in style, but all this burnt orange wasn't trendy décor; it was the real deal.

A blinking light on the phone caught her attention. She crossed the room and pushed the button. Static hiss came through, then a shaky sigh, followed by, "I'm coming over. We've got a big problem."

Sam frowned. That husky growl sounded like Hallie. Couldn't be. Nothing ever got the queen of poise that ruffled.

A buzz sounded near Sam's ear, and she let out a squawk. Someone was downstairs at the private entrance. The buzz sounded again, loud and long, like the person was leaning on the button. The noise let up. Gingerly, she pressed Talk. "Hello?"

Heavy breathing answered. The hair on Sam's arms stood at attention.

"It's me." A familiar voice spoke—familiar but off. "Let me in. I have to see you. Now!"

"I'll be right down, Hallie. Are you okay?"

"In! Now!"

Sam bounded down the stairs and opened the door. Hallie barged past her. She'd changed clothes into embroidered white capris and a fitted button-down shirt. Her long legs devoured the steps to the apartment two at a time. Sam trotted behind.

"What's the matter?"

Hallie didn't look at her. Lips pressed together, she was laying out photos in a long line on the kitchen table.

Sam crept forward and gazed down at the pictures. Chills cascaded down her spine. Bloody bodies. A woman's head lolled back on a couch, bright spatters on her slack face. A young girl stared from a separate frame, crimson-chested, eyes wide and lifeless. Another showed someone—maybe a man—with the barrel of a shotgun tucked under his chin and a good portion of his head missing. Samantha let out a shriek and leaped backward, hand to her throat.

TWO

"What are we going to do about those?" Sam stabbed a finger at the photos on the table.

"Burn them, shred them or report them. Take your pick. It's probably someone's idea of a sick joke—a staged Halloween prank or something."

Sam shook her head. "The people look too real. And the blood."

"Lots can be done with makeup and cameras. I should know."

"But you raced over here with them. You think they're genuine. We have to turn the pictures over to the police."

Hallie blew out a long breath. "I thought you should see them first. Shall I make the call?" She pulled a cell phone from her purse.

"No! We'll take them to the station ourselves." Keeping her eyes averted from the gruesome evidence, Sam swept the photos into a stack. "I'm not having a police cruiser pull up outside and cops knocking on my door. This is an upscale neighborhood. If anyone sees, they'll wonder what hinky things are going on with the new owner." She handed the pictures to Hallie. "Put these in something. I'll get dressed."

Half an hour later, they stood facing the night duty sergeant on the other side of a thick window—bulletproof, no doubt. The man stared at them with pale eyes set in a square face above a pair of Brahma bull shoulders. Intimidation on the hoof.

Sam swallowed. Hard.

"I'm Sergeant Garner. You wish to report a crime?" The officer's voice was surprisingly gentle coming from that massive package. Graying hair and a lined face put him in his upper forties.

"I'm Hallie Berglund, reporter for Channel Six news, and this is my friend—"

"Samantha Reid." Sam raised her hand like she was in grade school. Her face heated, and she offered a weak smile as she tucked her arm to her side.

Hallie placed the bag containing the film casing into the dip in the counter that allowed objects to pass under the barrier. "This was found at my friend's place of business. I developed it tonight and came up with these." She set another baggie with the prints into the tray. "They appear to be photos of a multiple murder."

Garner eyed the material without touching it, and then assessed both of them with his gaze. "You haven't actually seen any bodies?"

Sam and Hallie shook their heads as one.

"Just pictures, and no idea where and when the crime may have occurred."

They nodded in tandem.

The sergeant pursed his lips. "Can you show me some ID? We'll take your names and contact information. If we need to talk to you after we see what you've got, we'll be in touch."

On Wednesday afternoon, Sam lugged another sack of junk out to the rented Dumpster in the back of the building. She hefted the bag and slung it over the edge. A *crunch-thump* announced a safe landing. She dusted her hands together and headed back inside, humming.

She hadn't heard a peep about the pictures. That must mean they weren't really crime scene pics. Good thing, too. She was neck-deep in renovations. Of course, she'd had to break down and hire a cleaning crew—an expense not in the budget, but worth every penny if she could open her business on schedule.

She waved at a couple of the workers as she threaded between machines to her cracker-box office beside the customer service area at the front of the building. Seated behind her desk, she pulled out the ledger and checkbook and started working on the stack of bills. Honestly, how did that inheritance money evaporate faster than snow in July? Her business plan showed start-up capital available for at least a year…but only if she didn't have any setbacks.

Sharp raps sounded at the front door. Who would be at the customer entrance when they were clearly not open for business? The knock came again, and she hurried to answer, then stopped dead in her tracks.

The wide front window showed a police cruiser parked at the curb. At the door stood a lean man in a suit and two uniformed officers, one male, one female. The suited man flipped open a black case and displayed the PD insignia. The guy looked around the age of the duty sergeant from the other night, but he had thinning, silver-sprinkled hair and was angular-bodied where the sergeant had been bulky.

Maybe the visit had nothing to do with the photos. And maybe water flowed uphill.

Sam unlocked the door and eased it open.

"I'm Detective Connell," the man said. "Are you Samantha Reid?"

"Yes."

"May we come in and speak with you?"

"Certainly." Sam held the door wide. "Is this about—"

"It is." The detective and the uniforms stepped inside. Voices and clatter from the work area drew Connell's hawkish gaze. "Who's here with you?"

"Just my cleaning crew. I'm getting ready to open, and this place was a mess."

"Could you tell your people to stop work?"

"Now?" Sam blinked at the detective.

"Right now. We have a warrant to search." He handed her a folded sheet of paper.

What had she just been thinking about setbacks? "You'd better come to my office and explain what's going on."

Connell jerked a nod to the uniforms and followed her alone.

Sam faced the detective from behind her desk. "Those photos were for real?"

He nodded, dark eyes flat. "A family named Davidson. Ten years ago, they were shot to death in their home a few blocks from here. The incident was ruled murder/suicide. But those photos prove there had to be at least one more person at the scene. Maybe someone who set it up to look like the dad shot his wife and daughter and then himself. The case has been bumped up to straight murder, and now we're looking for a killer a decade after the deaths." He jaded tone said he didn't hold out much hope of solving the crime.

Sam sank into her chair. Here she'd told her mother this was a safe neighborhood. "What do you want with me? I was a clueless teenager ten years ago, zits and giggles and all. And I lived in Eau Claire, Wisconsin."

"You're not a suspect, Ms. Reid, but we need to search this building."

"What else could you possibly expect to find after all this time?"

"We have to be thorough. The film was here. Something else could be."

"Fine, but you'll have to assign someone to Dumpster diving." She marched out into the work area. Her cleaners were gone, and the two uniformed cops were already digging into things.

The detective stepped up beside her. "Could you show me where the film was discovered?"

"Just the room where it was found. Except for some perc cleaning solvent awaiting pickup by the hazmat people, the box it was in and everything else has already been cleaned out. Good luck sorting through the garbage."

Connell frowned. "Did you save anything from the box?"

Sam headed back toward her office. "Odds and ends. They're in here."

She handed him the paperweight from her desk. It was a smoky crystal rendering of a trout mounted on a hefty slab of black obsidian. "That was in the box. And this." From the front of the filing cabinet, she plucked a ceramic magnet that featured a picture of a baby sitting in a high chair, bawling. The inscription said, *No Whining!* "Seemed like a good daily reminder." She gave it to the detective.

"There were any number of hotel key cards accumulated from customer pockets, but I threw them out. I did keep these, however." She opened the top drawer of the cabinet and pulled out a small bucket. The contents clattered as she plunked it onto the desk. "Lots of regular keys, but no way to know what they open or who owned them."

"I can have this stuff tested for blood and prints, but if nothing pops up, you'll likely get them back." He shook the contents of the bucket. "I'm surprised you haven't tossed these."

Sam smiled. "There's a crafter in my hometown who makes wind chimes out of old keys. I was saving them for her."

"What else was in the box?"

"I'm not sure. I knocked a shelf over, and the contents spilled out when I was getting it down." She crossed her arms. "We found assorted manicure items, a few eyeglass cases, combs, pillboxes, that sort of thing scattered on the floor. But they're—"

"In the Dumpster."

"Right."

The detective's gaze traveled around the room. "Did you bring in the furnishings for this room, or were these things here when you bought the place?"

"Mr. Morris used this room as a storage area, not an office. Everything in here came from outside."

"What about the contents of the closet?" He jerked his chin toward the closed door at the side of the room.

"Same thing. I emptied this whole area."

"More Dumpster work." One side of his mouth curved downward.

"No. Sorry. This was one of the first places I cleaned out. That Dumpster-load has already been collected by the city. How do your officers feel about combing the landfill?"

Connell shook his head. "I'll tell the uniforms to leave this room out of their search."

"I'd appreciate it."

The detective reached inside his jacket and pulled out a five-by-eight photo. Sam took a step backward.

"Don't worry, Ms. Reid. This one isn't of a dead body. Have you ever seen this man?"

Sam took the picture and studied a man a little older than herself, wearing faded jeans and a Nike T-shirt. He stood on a dock with a sparkling river in the background. The Mississippi? Close-cut blond hair framed a bold-featured face—straight nose, square chin, wide lips pressed into a thin line. Nothing extraordinary, except for the eyes. Blue as a mountain lake and twice as chilly. Her pulse rate jumped up a notch. "I don't know him, and I'm glad. Is he a suspect?"

"Our job would be a lot easier if he was. Relatives usually top the list." Connell took the picture back. "Ryan Davidson. He came home from college and found his family like your photos showed. At least that's what he's always claimed, and we have reason to believe he's telling the truth."

Sam pressed her palms together. "How awful for him. He still lives around here?"

"A houseboat near Hastings, about thirty-odd miles from here, right where the Mississippi and St. Croix Rivers converge. He owns a rental houseboat company that caters to tourists."

"Really! What does he do in the winter?"

"He's got no ties. Just takes the whole shebang south to Missouri." He shook his head with a tight smile.

Either the detective envied Davidson's footloose life or thought he was nuts. Personally, she'd go with the latter. What was life about except settling in to become a vital part of a community? "How long will your people be out there?" She gestured toward the workroom.

"At least twenty-four hours. We'll finish as quickly as we can. Since this isn't a crime scene and you're not suspected of anything, feel free to come and go, but don't remove anything further from the building. Have a good day, Ms. Reid." The detective walked out.

Sam wilted into her chair. By the end of tomorrow, the rumor mill could have her reputation as trashed as the garbage out back. With that cruiser parked in front and uniformed officers searching, what were the neighbors already thinking in their fine houses up the street? A cloud of suspicion could doom her business before she even opened the doors.

A muted clatter outside her bedroom window jerked Sam awake. Save for the glow from her bedside clock, her room lay wrapped in darkness. She lifted her head from the pillow and looked at the time. The digital numbers read 1:32 a.m. A sharp bang resounded below.

Outside or inside? Her heart *kabumped* and every nerve ending buzzed. Maybe it was just some critter digging in the garbage. Not likely. She'd closed that lid.

Bastian mewled and leaped up on the captain's bench in front of the window, his lean form a shadowy outline. The direction of his stare was fixed as if he could see through the curtains and make out something—or someone—in the alley. A rattle carried to Sam's ears. That sounded like an attempt at the private entrance door.

Muscles rigid, Sam lay motionless. Her pulse throbbed.

Bastian growled, deep and low.

She couldn't just lie here until whoever it was found her and did whatever he came to do. How many books had she read where the stupid character did that? Or, dumber still, snuck around with some lame weapon like a bat to try and nab the burglar herself? She'd always wanted to yell, "What do you think nine-one-one is for, dummy?"

As suddenly as the paralysis had gripped her, it lifted. Sam sprang upright and grabbed the cordless phone from her nightstand. A few punches and she was talking to a no-nonsense woman who took her information and promised to get a car there immediately.

With the line still open to the dispatcher, Sam scooped Bastian up and perched on the edge of the bed, staring into the darkness. Her hand ran the length of her cat's back. Again. Again. Bastian's fur crackled and stood on end. He hopped off her lap, growling a protest. The operator kept assuring her help was on the way, but where were they? Sam gripped the edges of the mattress, ears perked. Sure, the police hung around here all day, and now when she needed them—

Sirens blared outside and lights flashed. Voices yelled, followed by clatters, then quiet. The cruiser lights continued to strobe.

Her intercom buzzer sounded. On jelly legs, Sam padded to her kitchen and answered.

"Ms. Reid, this is Officer Johnson of the Apple Valley Police Department. Your intruder says he has a right to be here. Would you mind coming down?"

Why did the police always ask questions like a person really had the option to say no? "Let me get my robe."

A few seconds later, Sam unlocked her private entrance and peered out into the night. Under the entrance light, a pair of officers she'd never seen held a man between them—someone she did recognize. She glared up into the stone face of Ryan Davidson.

Their gazes locked, and raw emotion flickered in those intense blue eyes. The power of his bewildered pain snagged her breath. In times not long enough past, she'd seen that look of a stunned victim in another pair of eyes…whenever she looked in the mirror.

Why was this woman staring right through him, all white face and big green eyes? Was he a ghost or something?

Ryan studied her. One arm hugged her trim waist. The opposite hand clutched her robe at the neck. She was kind of cute with that heart-shaped face and tousled hair, but it looked like he'd scared her something fierce. Not his intention. So what had he meant to accomplish by his impulsive visit to the old neighborhood? Insomnia wasn't much of an excuse.

His shoulders slumped, but the officers retained their grips like manacles around his biceps. He was lucky he wasn't in handcuffs. Yet. "I'm sorry, ah…Miss Reid, isn't it? I didn't mean any harm."

She frowned. "Why are you skulking around my property?"

"I wasn't skulking exactly. Not even looking for physical clues. I was searching my memory of that night. Did you know I cruised by here right before I went home to find—" His voice cracked. "Anyway, I ended up pacing back and forth in this alley. Kicked the Dumpster in frustration, and I've got the throbbing toe to prove it." He lifted a tennis-shoed foot. "I suppose that's what woke you."

"Do you want us to run this guy in for trespassing, Ms. Reid?" asked the officer who'd identified himself as Johnson.

Ryan held his breath. She wouldn't. Would she?

Her gaze darted away, and the tips of white teeth nibbled at her bottom lip. "I don't know. I doubt Mr. Davidson poses a danger, but—"

"You know him?"

"You know me?"

Ryan's words tangled with Johnson's.

"From a photo." A flush spread across her cheekbones.

Yes, definitely attractive, but where had she seen a picture of him? "I wasn't in those photos you turned in. The detective laid out the whole roll for me to see." What shadowed her eyes? Pity? Ryan's jaw clenched.

She met his stare. "I assume it was the same detective who showed me a print of you down by the river."

Ryan snorted. "Sure, updating their file with a sneak shot after they get me all riled up. Bet I looked like a lunatic."

Static crackled from the nearby police cruiser, followed by a garbled voice. The officers released Ryan and backed away. "If you're not going to press charges, Miss," Johnson said, "we need to answer that call."

"You should go, too, Mr. Davidson." Samantha Reid narrowed the door opening so he could only see half of her body. "There's nothing for you to find here. The police haven't uncovered anything new, and I doubt they will."

She moved to close the door, but before she could, a small creature darted from the doorway into the alley.

"Bastian, come back here!" the woman called. "Oh, no, I must not have shut the door tight above."

"I'll find him. Little animals have certain ways of moving in the dark. Hang tight. I'll bring him to you."

"But—"

"It's the least I can do for getting you up in the middle of the night. Besides, you're not dressed for a walk."

Her brows scrunched together. "Bastian won't come to you."

"We'll see." He headed in the direction the cat had disappeared, a mental *Here, kitty, kitty* going in his head. Not that he'd ever talk out loud that way to such a dignified animal.

"Of all the arrogant guys!" Samantha fumed as she threw on jeans and a T-shirt. He'd better be gone by the time she got downstairs again, or she'd clobber him with her flashlight. Bastian was particular about who he allowed to touch him. She was the only one who could get close, and who knew how long that would take? Her night's rest was officially over.

She stormed down the stairs and flung open the outside door.

"Hi." Ryan Davidson grinned down at her, the purring Abyssinian cradled in his arms. "He was just investigating your alley and didn't go far."

She gaped up at him.

"Here." He handed her the cat.

A mewl mixed with his purr. The cat's head swiveled toward Davidson.

"Nice Aby. Good ticking in his coat." He scratched behind Bastian's ear, and the cat nosed the man's hand. "Well, g'night, then. Hope you can still catch some z's." He gave her a lopsided grin and turned away.

"Th-thank you." Sam watched his broad-shouldered figure stride into the night. She hugged her cat close. "Traitor," she murmured into his perked ear. Her heart was a traitor, too. It had done a distinct pitty-pat when Ryan Davidson smiled.

THREE

Muted dock lighting played over Ryan's bedroom ceiling in rhythm with the slight sway of the water beneath the boat. He lay on his back with his arms under his head. The murmur of the river teased his ears. The soothing sights and sounds usually had him out in seconds, but his carefully constructed world had blown apart again with the discovery of those pictures.

How had the roll of film ended up at Old Man Morris's dry cleaners?

He'd hoped a walk through the area might jar his recollection of something suspicious he'd seen that night. But then, who was to say he'd encountered a single thing connected to his family's deaths? Would he even have noticed if he had? Arriving in Apple Valley following the end of his sophomore year at the University of Wisconsin, he'd zigged and zagged aimlessly through the neighborhood, dreading going home, his father's angry words from their phone call echoing in his head.

His gut soured. He heaved himself into a sitting position on the edge of the bed and rubbed his forehead.

Dad, would you ever have understood my decision not to follow in your footsteps as an investment banker? His family's deaths had robbed him of the opportunity to find out. What if he'd headed straight home? Could he have saved them? Or would he have joined them stone-cold in the grave?

At least his dad hadn't killed himself or mom and Cassie. A breath trembled in his lungs. How did he feel about that? Relieved. Yeah, beyond belief. But guilty, too. Why had he ever believed the cops' conclusion about that night?

But if his dad didn't do it, then someone else murdered them all. Ryan shot to his feet. He paced, fists clenched, bare feet smacking the hardwood floor.

Who would do such a thing? A psycho? Then why hadn't the nutcase been caught committing similar atrocities? That kind seldom stopped killing voluntarily.

But if the murders were done in cold blood for a reason, then finding the cause would reveal the killer. Sure, the police were back on the case, but why should he trust them? They'd treated the tragedy like a slam-dunk murder/suicide and closed the book. Now, ten years after the fact, the authorities were sniffing up a cold trail with dozens of hotter cases piled on their docket.

No, he was the only one with a strong enough motive to dig and not give up until he found something.

Dad, I promise I'll find out who killed our ladies and you.

Too bad he couldn't have a chat with Abel Morris and ask where the guy found the film. Miss Reid sure got stuck with a mess not of her own making, but maybe she knew something from scouring through the building that she didn't realize was important. It might be in his best interests to be friendly with her. He'd shot himself in the foot tonight with his prowler act, but maybe finding the cat had helped his cause.

Tomorrow, he'd do what he could to cement a better impression. Besides, even if nothing further panned out in the investigation, a guy would be certifiable to pass up the opportunity to get acquainted with a smart, fine-looking woman who showed rare character by turning in those photos. Not many people would step forward these days to get involved in someone else's troubles. He knew lots of people who would have just shredded the nasty pictures and gone on with their lives without a second thought.

Ryan stretched out on the bed and willed his limbs to relax. What would it take to make Miss Reid smile?

At 9:00 a.m., someone knocked on the front door of the cleaners. Not the police. They were already here. She answered the summons to find a grinning teenage boy bearing a gift.

Flowers? Who would they be from?

Sam took the enormous glass vase from the delivery person's hand, tipped him, and then carried the vase of white calla lilies to her office desk. She worked the small envelope from its holder and opened it.

Humble apologies. Your Midnight Marauder.

Sam laughed. Who would ever have thought she'd find anything funny about an apparent break-in attempt? Her eyes narrowed. Oooh, this Davidson guy was slick. He'd better not have some notion of getting on her good side so she'd let him hang around. She had a business to get started and enough distractions without adding one more to the list, even if Bastian had given his stamp of approval to the big, blond outdoorsman.

A crisp thank-you note accepting his apology ought to be the end of it. A quick search on the Internet yielded the address for Davidson Houseboats. Sam dashed off her thanks and took the note with her as she headed out the door to meet Hallie for lunch at Jenna's restaurant. Then she had a truckload of errands to run. She might as well make herself scarce until the police finished combing the building later today. Hopefully.

A fifteen-minute drive through busy suburban streets brought her to the white stucco and half-timbered restaurant in Lakeville. Sam stepped into the welcome of savory and delicate aromas. Her gaze searched the wood-beamed dining room for Hallie. She spotted her, sleekly groomed in a tailored green pantsuit, waiting at a cloth-covered table. Sam waved and Hallie answered with a wide grin. Sam settled opposite her friend, and they ordered their favorites—seafood fetuccini alfredo for Hallie and a chicken salad pita with a garlic dill pickle for herself.

"You look frazzled." Hallie spread her napkin on her lap. "You need to ease up and take time to smell the roses."

Sam wrinkled her nose. "How about the calla lilies?"

Hallie's eyebrows climbed. "Spill your guts, girl."

By the time Sam finished telling about the police intrusion yesterday, the Davidson disturbance last night, and the flowers on her desk this morning, her friend was leaning halfway across the table, jaw slack.

"Oh, hon." She settled back. "And I thought a reporter's life was adventurous."

Sam sniffed. "This feels more like a trial."

"The Perils of Samantha Reid." Jenna's words and chuckle brought Sam's head around.

"How long have you been standing there?"

"Long enough to get the whole scoop, as Hal might say." Jenna winked a hazel eye. "That Ryan fellow sounds like a dish. Better keep him."

"I second the motion." Hallie lifted a hand and waggled slim fingers.

Sam scowled from one to the other. "Romance has no place in my life right now, and certainly not in his. He's got a murder investigation swirling around him." She groaned at the conspiratorial look her friends exchanged. Thank goodness, the food came just then, and Jenna glided back to her kitchen while she and Hallie dug in.

A half hour later, Sam paid her bill and exited into the warm sunlight outside the restaurant.

"Just a minute!"

Hallie's urgent tone stopped Sam halfway across the parking lot. She turned to find her friend striding toward her, unsmiling.

Sam's brows drew together. "What's up?"

Hallie stopped in front of her. "I didn't want to mention it over lunch. Spoil anyone's appetite, you know. But now that something's happened with those pictures, I have to come clean with my station about what we found." Her gaze darted away and then returned to meet Sam's. "I have to do my job, or I'll lose it. There will be media attention, most of it directed toward Ryan, but—"

"I get it. Someone besides the police will be asking me questions. Will they assign you to the story?"

"If the main crime reporter is too busy, I might get a taste of the action." A smile crossed her lips then morphed into a frown. "I just wish you weren't involved."

"Don't worry about it. Maybe some good can come of this mess, and you'll get another step closer to that anchor spot."

Hallie's gaze warmed. "Spoken like a true friend, thinking about the other person first. You can always say, 'No comment,' and let us get our answers from the police and Davidson."

Sam shrugged. "It might be kind of nice to speak my piece. At least people will know that all the police attention isn't because I'm running drugs out of the dry cleaners or some other nefarious activity at my shop." She smiled, but the edges of her mouth quivered. How *would* she handle a camera in her face? She barely managed standing up front in the church choir.

Hallie put a hand on her arm. "I know you hate the spotlight. Too bad you've got a reporter for a friend."

"Finding that film wasn't your fault, and we both turned it in."

"Like we had a choice?"

"Right. But none of this involves us directly. It'll blow over. You'll see." It better, or her family would start camping out on her doorstep. *Aaagh!*

"Speaking from experience," Hallie said, "with the next homicide, this cold case will go in the deep freeze again, and you'll open your business on time."

"Sure, but Ryan will be stuck not knowing who killed his family."

"Ryan, is it? I knew you liked him." Hallie strolled away, laughing.

Scowl plastered on her face, Sam hustled to her car. She gripped her car key, tip pointing through her fingers, a defensive preparation that had become second nature. "Just because I feel for the guy's situation doesn't mean I'm the least interested in any other way," she grumbled under her breath. "I've got too much on my plate to take on old mysteries." She slid into the driver's seat and picked up the thank-you note from the center console. After she mailed this, there would be no reason for further contact with Ryan Davidson.

At the end of the afternoon, Sam returned to the dry cleaners to find the police gone, but a mess left. Evidently, their job description only required tearing things apart but excluded returning anything to proper order. She spent over an hour in the back alley chucking things back into the Dumpster. The disarray inside the building could wait. It would have to, because her energy fuel gauge was running on empty.

She called the cleaning crew to resume in the morning then handled a few bookkeeping chores before shutting the office door and checking the locks on all of the outside doors and windows. Hallie was right. She was exhausted and needed to unwind. A movie and popcorn sounded like a great evening.

When she opened her apartment door, Bastian darted out. The feline streaked down the stairs and into the main building.

Sam shook her head. "Okay, so you're annoyed at being cooped up all afternoon. Enjoy playing watchcat tonight." Stifling a yawn, she stepped into her kitchen. He'd be all right. He had a litter box, a bed and food and water in a corner near the storage room.

A few hours later, Sam crawled between the sheets and slept so deeply a tornado could have blown her out of bed and she might not have noticed. The next day, feeling rested, she went out for her morning run in the nearby park. When she returned, sweaty and breathing hard, she headed for her office. A truck would be here in a few days to cart the old machines away, and with a little extra hustle the building should be ready on time to receive the new stuff. The plan was back on track.

She opened her office door, stepped over the threshold, and halted on a gasp. Her beautiful vase lay shattered on the floor, flowers strewn everywhere. "Bastian, what did you do?"

No, the cat couldn't have been in here. The door was closed.

The desk phone shrilled and Sam jumped. It rang again, and she tiptoed between glass shards to answer it.

"Hello, I'm Vince Graham from Channel Six news." A male voice rumbled. "We'd like to speak to you about—"

"Sorry. No comment." Sam smacked the phone into the receiver. Who cared about news stories right now? Somebody had been in her building!

Heart pounding, she scurried from window to door, testing all the locks. At last she came to the window above Bastian's empty bed. A breeze caressed her face like a subtle taunt. The sash gaped open wide, and the antiquated window had been missing its screen since the day she bought the place. She'd meant to have one installed, but it hadn't happened yet, and now—Sam hugged herself, the scars on her back tingling. She'd had an intruder for real, and she slept through it. And where was the Abyssinian? In all her racing around, she hadn't seen hide nor hair of him.

Her spine stiffened. Only one person had shown an unnatural interest in this building besides the police. And he'd mesmerized her cat. Maybe Bastian went with him when he snuck out after rummaging through her office. So much for apologies. The louse!

She should call the police immediately. She— Oh, no, not that again.

Her business didn't need any more attention from the authorities. With the police search and a middle-of-the-night visit from a squad car, neighborhood confidence in her business was probably in the tank. She could confront Davidson herself. Sure, she could. What was he going to do to her? It was broad daylight, and if she went right now, she'd catch him at his business. Let him take some negative publicity this time, the sneak. Someone needed to tell him he'd gone over the line—and he'd better have her cat all safe and sound.

Sam whirled on her heel. If Davidson thought his life was insane right now with the police investigation and reporters sniffing a story, he was about to get a visit from one mad woman.

FOUR

Standing on the dock, Ryan shook his customer's hand and gave him the keys to the four-passenger houseboat that swayed on the river's current. "Take it nice and easy navigating the locks and dams, Mr. Timmons. When you stop, make sure to set your anchor like I showed you, and keep your outside lights on during the night so other craft won't run into you. Printed instructions are in the wheelhouse, if you need to refresh yourself on anything. But most of all," Ryan stretched his lips into a smile, "enjoy yourselves."

"Sounds good." The pudgy man beamed. Behind him, a pair of grade school–age girls chased each other, giggling, on the upper deck. The man's stocky wife, clad in shorts and a tank top, lolled on a lounge chair in the bow of the boat.

Ryan waved as Timmons joined his family on board. "You folks have a great time on the Old Miss." He untied the boat from the dock and watched them go on their way. Heat from the morning sun bathed his neck. Too bad the sun couldn't warm anything beneath his skin or make his smile for real.

"Mr. Davidson." The clack of feet on the dock accompanied the voice.

Ryan turned to see a tall woman with a caramel complexion picking her way toward him across the boards. Why did females torture themselves with high heels? If one of those silly spikes wedged in a board, she'd topple over, and he'd be fishing her out of the drink. The woman's face looked vaguely familiar. Behind her clomped a shaggy-haired guy toting a video camera on his shoulder. Ryan looked beyond the mismatched pair, and his stomach clenched. A van with the Channel Six logo painted on the side sat on the asphalt in front of his log-cabin-style office building.

Uh-oh! How had the news media gotten wind so quickly?

The smiling woman reached him and held out a slender hand. "Hi, I'm Hallie Berglund, a friend of Samantha Reid's."

Ryan narrowed his eyes at his visitor. So that was how. Ms. Reid couldn't wait to garner attention for her business by letting her reporter pal in on the action. He'd misjudged her as a woman of integrity when she was really out for number one like anybody else.

The reporter-woman's smile faded. "I'm sorry. I know this must be a difficult time for you, dredging up bad memories. Looking at those pictures was bad enough for me, but—"

"You saw the photos?" Ryan's spine stiffened. "Did the police show you? Not hardly! Or was it the lady dry cleaner angling for a little free publicity?"

Color bloomed in Hallie's cheeks. "I developed those photos." She squared her shoulders. "And Samantha's other friend, Jenna, found the film at Sam's place. We're all in this happy little conspiracy together. Sam and I turned them in to the police, so maybe now you and your family will have an opportunity for a killer to be caught. All I want is to chat with you so we can air a segment that maybe, just maybe, will flush a rat out of hiding…or, at the least, entice someone to come forward with helpful information."

Ryan's mouth opened, but he was fresh out of things to say. How could a guy speak with a mouth full of crow anyway? A wry chuckle gusted from his chest. "Come on in." He waved toward his office. "I guess I could share some more of my foul mood, if it'll help your ratings and my family's chance for justice."

"Now you're talking." The smile returned to the reporter's face.

They stepped up the dock toward the sidewalk that would take them up to the building, the cameraman backpedaling ahead of them. Ryan shook his head. The guy'd been filming the whole time. How much of himself shooting blanks from the hip would come out on the TV news? Ouch! He hadn't been firing harmless blanks; he'd been filling his own foot with lead—again—where the attractive Samantha Reid was concerned.

"Don't worry." The woman next to him spoke under her breath. "Your quantum leap to Planet Wrong Conclusion will end up on the editing floor. You have a lot to learn about Sam, and I'd like you to still have that chance."

Ryan stared down at her. Was the woman a mind reader? And what was that knowing smirk all about? Her gaze turned toward the parking lot, and his followed. A midsized car jerked to a halt on the tarmac, and a woman dressed in jeans, a T-shirt and a practical pair of running shoes lunged out of the vehicle. She charged toward them, small purse slung over her shoulder, glossy ponytail swinging.

Sam? Er, Miss Reid? She looked steamed enough to blow a gasket. No way could she have heard his conversation with her friend.

"Where's Bastian?" She halted in front of them, hands on hips. Little gold flecks in her green eyes glinted up at him.

"Ba— Oh, your cat. Last time I saw him, he was purring in your arms."

"Don't try to tell me you didn't sneak into the dry cleaners last night to finish your snooping expedition. My vase is broken, my flowers are wilted, a window is open and my cat is gone!"

"Someone broke into your building?" The reporter gripped her friend's arm. "Oh, how awful! Are you all right?"

Ryan looked from one woman to the other. Hallie's mouth had drawn up into a tight line, and Sam deflated and that full lower lip quivered.

"I'm f-fine." She sure didn't look it. "I slept through the whole thing."

The women's stares at each other conveyed volumes of information Ryan couldn't read.

"Honest, Miss Reid—"

"Sam." She met his gaze.

Good. Now he had official permission. "Sam, I was nowhere near your neighborhood last night. You have my word on it."

Her gaze searched his face. "Then who…" The words trailed away.

"Maybe the same person we're all looking for."

"Please don't tell me that. As furious as I was with you, I wanted you—no, *needed* you to be the one. Then I wouldn't have to imagine other possibilities."

If only he was guilty. Maybe that would take the haunted look from her eyes. He knew the feeling all too well. What was her story, anyway?

"It seems like none of us is going to have any peace of mind until we get to the bottom of this." Hallie's voice drew their attention. "Maybe finishing the interview will be a step in the right direction."

Ryan nodded in unison with Sam.

The reporter grinned. "You two make quite a pair of intergalactic travelers. You arrived at the same planet on the same morning!"

Clearing his throat, Ryan led the way toward his office building. The cameraman brought up the rear, not filming for the moment.

"What did Hallie mean by that?" Sam asked as she fell in step beside him. The girl had long legs and a runner's stride. Another thing to like about her.

Ryan shrugged. "Oh, some remark she made earlier about a quantum leap to a conclusion."

"Huh?"

"Never mind."

As they climbed onto the porch, Old Jake heaved himself to his feet and ambled over.

Sam scratched the animal's head. "Labrador, right?"

Jake groaned his ecstasy and leaned into Sam's leg.

Ryan laughed. "We figure he's mostly Chocolate Lab with a little Springer Spaniel thrown in."

"Is that why he's got a few splotches of white in his coat and around his muzzle?"

"The gray face is his age showing."

"You must've had him for a long time then."

"This summer. He's mostly deaf, as well as old and a little arthritic. Whoever owned him decided he was no good for hunting and dumped him off in the country to fend for himself."

Her eyes flashed. "That's awful!"

"No argument from me. He wandered up here this spring, skin and bones."

"He's well fed now." She ran her hands down his sides.

A throat cleared behind him. "Oops, sorry!" Ryan turned and motioned to the reporter and the cameraman.

Then he led the way into the cool office lobby. A faint scent of cedar greeted them from the genuine wood that lined the walls and floor.

Larry, one of the staff, looked up from behind the long reception counter and froze with his hand poised over calculator keys. "Did I space out some business interview we were supposed to do today?"

Ryan waved at him. "Personal. About…you know."

Larry jerked a nod then went back to pecking at the machine. Ryan led his guests into his office, which looked out the side of the building nearest the guest parking lot.

"Not much for frills, are you?" Sam stood gazing around the room. "And I thought *my* office was bare."

Ryan took fresh stock of his surroundings. An old metal desk, a bit scuffed and dented but serviceable, took up much of the floor space. A lone filing cabinet stood nearby, and a state-of-the-art computer center filled one corner. No artwork hung on the pale walls, just a plaque indicating membership in the local chamber of commerce. No photos or other personal memorabilia sat on the desk.

The nicest piece in the room was a rather crude oak gun case that he'd cobbled together in high school. It worked fine to hold his several shotguns and rifles, though. The only other item of interest was the view from the French doors behind his desk, and that showed only a small deck, the paved guest parking lot and a wall of trees beyond that.

Yeah, his world had gotten pretty stark. The fault of one devious killer, and Ryan meant to find out who that was.

"Let's do the interview out there." Hallie pointed toward the deck. "That will give us the outdoorsy feel without standing under the hot sun."

"I'm game." The deck offered a clear view of his boats and docks, as well as the access road to his property. He did as much of his paperwork as possible out there, listening to the wind ruffle through the pines that crowded his place.

Ryan opened the French doors, and soon he and the reporter stood on the end of the deck closest to the river. The camera would be able to take in the water and boats behind them. Sam perched on a bench built into the deck rail, out of range of the electronic eye. Ryan wiped his palms on his jeans and glanced at the reporter. "What would you like to know?"

She looked toward the camera. "You rolling, Stan?"

"Still getting the angle and focus," he answered, fiddling with his lens.

"Could we have a quick practice run?" Ryan cleared his throat. "I'd kind of like to know what you're going to ask." And maybe take the edge off his gut reactions before the real deal.

"That's fair." Hallie nodded. "I'll probably start out with something like this— It's been ten years since you found your family shot dead in your home. In all this time, did you never suspect that they had all been murdered?"

"No, I didn't." He shook his head. "My dad was under unusual stress at work and not acting like himself. Besides, I was too busy blaming myself to take a closer look."

"How could their deaths have been your fault?" Sam's cry broke in. "You weren't there."

Her gaze riveted with Ryan's. His face went hot and tense. "We had a major fight on the telephone that evening, my dad and I. I figured I broke his heart, and that was why I lost my family." What was it about this woman? That was more than he'd ever told anybody.

Her lips molded into a soft O. "What a terrible way for things to end between you." If he didn't know better, he would have said she was seeing straight into his soul, just like the other night.

"It doesn't matter now." Ryan's voice came out rough. "Whoever killed my mom, and my sister and my dad had better hide under the biggest rock he can find, because I won't rest until I find out what happened. And why?"

Hallie's shoulder moved between him and Sam. "What do you hope the discovery of the photos will accomplish?"

He returned his attention to the reporter. "New evidence means a fresh investigation that is bound to uncover facts that were never looked at before."

"Anything specific you can share with us?"

"Let's just say I've given the police access to—"

Brakes squealed and tires screeched. Ryan turned. The next client wasn't due for twenty minutes…but this was no client. *Yikes!* None of those vehicles held clients. A *Minneapolis Star Tribune* newspaper van roared up the drive, followed by a Channel 11 TV truck, flanked by a *St. Paul Pioneer Press* car, jockeying for position. The whole world chased a scoop.

Hallie whirled toward Sam, who sat with mouth agape. "So do you want to wait around and be mobbed or get out of here?"

"But what about your interview?"

"If I know Stan the Man, he got it the first time."

"Too right." Grinning, the camera guy lowered his equipment from his shoulder.

Ryan glared from reporter to cameraman. All that personal stuff that popped out of his mouth had been caught on film? Wasn't the cameraman supposed to wait for some kind of cue from the reporter?

Sam rose. "My car sits between the ones for the *Press* and the *Trib.* We'll never make a getaway."

"There's a pickup in the back." Hallie nodded toward Ryan. "Yours, right?"

"Wait a minute—"

"If you wait ten seconds, you'll have a feeding frenzy, not an interview." She pinned him beneath a pointed stare. "Go. Leave us. We'll stay and thumb our noses at the competition."

People were piling out of the vehicles in his public parking lot. It was hard enough to talk to one reporter about his family's murder. If a mob of them got in his face, he'd probably slug somebody.

He met Sam's beseeching gaze. "We're outta here!"

Her teeth flashed as she grinned and headed for the French doors. "I'm with you."

Ryan grabbed her hand, and they dashed inside through his office and out into the hallway behind the reception desk. "Circle the wagons!" he called to Larry, who gazed at them wide-eyed. "Don't let them take you alive."

A throaty laugh came from the woman next to him. Her warm hand in his, Ryan tugged her up the hall and out the back door, leaving his employee gaping after them. They piled into his gray Silverado, and he peeled out of the staff lot toward the gravel road that provided a second egress to the property.

"Where are we headed?" Sam turned toward him, flushed face alight.

He smiled. "Your place. I feel like huntin' me a cat. And while we're at it, we may as well catch a burglar."

By the wary glint that entered her eyes, he knew he'd better not add *killer.* He hated to tell her, but whoever sneaked into her place and snooped through her office might be connected to the murders. She was up to her dainty nose in this investigation whether she wanted to be or not.

FIVE

Sam studied the profile of the man behind the wheel of the pickup. Nice strong chin, a little on the square side, but not jutting, and definitely not weak. Just right. And his hand holding hers had been just right, too, wrapping her palm and fingers in a big grip, but not squeezing.

All well and good, but why was she alone in a pickup with a guy she'd just met? She'd wanted to escape the deluge of reporters as much as Ryan, but why did she feel perfectly at home sitting here? And safe? The police maintained he wasn't a suspect in the murder case. However, those words hadn't meant a lot to her inner security barometer. Less than an hour ago she'd believed him capable of breaking and entering. What had changed?

The dog. Despite his tough exterior, the man had a core of kindness. Even her moody cat knew it and trusted him. And Sam trusted animals. They had a sense about people that human beings often didn't.

Ryan shot her a glance with his intense blue eyes, and the corners of his mouth tilted up.

What was the matter with her? She'd better quit staring, or the guy would get the wrong idea.

She looked out the window where the tree-lined bluffs of this picturesque area flashed past. Ryan's place of business was roughly a half hour from her dry cleaners. Funny that they both lived where they worked and owned their own businesses. Did that mean they were the same sort of people?

Not really, because that was where the similarities ended. He lived in a secluded woodland area, she in a business district. His house traveled with him whenever he wanted to pick up and leave, while hers stayed planted where she intended to put down roots. No, when a person looked at it logically, they weren't much alike at all. If they could get this awful investigation behind them, they would have no basis to develop an ongoing relationship. She'd just have to disappoint Jenna and Hallie in the matchmaking department. So why did that thought make her heart sink?

Shake it off, girl. Stick with the program. "Why do the police say you couldn't have been the one who—er, you know? They generally look at family first. Excuse me for asking. My gut says you're okay, but my head's not quite there yet."

Ryan let out a short laugh. "I'm familiar with that internal tug-of-war, and I don't blame you for asking. They *did* suspect me at first. Who wouldn't? But they ran into a brick wall when they considered timing and gunshot residue."

"I don't follow what you're saying."

"A stray pellet stopped the clock on the wall behind my dad's desk, pinpointing when the shootings took place. When the crime scene techs tested me from top to bottom for gunshot residue, they didn't find a speck. No way could I have taken a shower, changed clothes, dried my hair, and dispose of my tainted outfit between the time the murders were committed and the time the first squad car arrived on the scene. They were pretty much forced to acknowledge that my part in events was exactly as I said. That's when they decided the whole thing was murder/suicide, and my dad was the bad guy." He snorted.

"Precisely what whoever did it wanted people to believe."

Ryan met her gaze, grim-faced, then turned his attention back to the road. "And I was no better than the cops in my thinking."

"Why should you have been?"

"Because he was my dad, that's why! A son should know better!"

Sam lifted her hands, palms out. "I get the point."

His shoulders sagged. "Sorry. I'm still riled about all this."

"I don't blame you. When you and Hallie were talking, what were you about to say you gave the police?"

"The code for a storage unit. They said they'd check it out today. I rented a unit near the old neighborhood, and that's where I stuck all the family stuff I didn't get rid of after the funerals. I was pretty shook up and didn't sort through anything after selling the house and the furniture. Just boxed it and stuffed it into a rental garage. I pay the rent bill every month, but to tell you the truth, I haven't been back since."

Sam frowned. "I can understand why you were in no shape to look at things at the time, but ten years is quite a while to leave your family memories locked away in a storeroom."

His knuckles whitened around the steering wheel. "Not if you think your bid for independence as good as pulled the trigger."

"Do I ever understand that 'bid for independence' thing! I'm still fighting for mine."

"What do you mean? You own a business, and I don't see you living with parents."

"A month ago you would have seen exactly that." Sam rolled her eyes. "And no business, either."

"No kidding!"

She bobbed her head. "Not even a teensy exaggeration. After finishing high school half a year behind the rest of my class, it took me another six to finish college because I needed to work so much to help pay old medical bills. Happily, my job was in a dry cleaners, where I learned a trade hands-on. So when my maternal grandmother left her only granddaughter a sizable chunk in her will, I suddenly found myself free of financial obligation and able to pursue a career that combined my experience with my business degree." Sam stretched out her legs in the roomy interior and tucked a stray strand of hair behind her ear.

"The only hitch was finding a dry-cleaning establishment to purchase that would get me out from under my family's watchful eye and yet not be so far away that they would have instant heart failure when I told them I was moving."

Ryan chuckled. "Where are you from?"

"Eau Claire, Wisconsin. Hallie's from there, too, as well as another friend I'm close with, Jenna. She's part owner and full-time chef at The Meridian."

Ryan whistled under his breath. "I've heard that restaurant is the hottest taste sensation since buttered toast."

Sam laughed. "I take it you haven't paid a visit."

He waved a hand over his polo shirt and jeans. "Suits and ties and power lunches were my dad's thing, not mine."

"Jenna's restaurant welcomes tennis shoes seated next to designer leather loafers. We'll have to go sometime." Sam halted on an intake of breath. Did she just ask this guy out?

"Sounds great!"

By the size of Ryan's smile, that's exactly what she'd done, and there was no taking it back now. At least not totally. "You know, to apologize for accusing you of taking my cat. You did flowers—I guess I can do lunch." She forced a big smile. Could he see her pulse racing? Well, he probably couldn't miss the flush that heated her face.

"You know," Ryan said, "Bastian likely just slipped out to explore the neighborhood. He seems to possess a normal case of curiosity, considering his species."

"You're probably right. If you can find him as easily today as you did the other night, I'll owe you big-time."

"Like dinner *and* a movie?"

Sam sank in the seat, face blazing. This guy was milking her mistake for all it was worth. Why? With all that was on his mind right now, romancing the woman who found those brutal photos couldn't be high on his priority list.

"Did you call the police about the break-in?"

What did he say? She shook her head free of confusion fumes. "Oh, the break-in? No, I thought it was you."

"So, it's okay if *I* break into your place, but no one else?"

"Davidson, if you're trying to push my buttons, you're doing a stellar job. I'll call the police right now." She snatched her purse from the floor where she'd tossed it and yanked out her cell phone. She almost dropped it when she heard a shrill ring. But it wasn't her tune. She looked over at Ryan.

He pulled a cell from a belt holder. "Davidson here." Long pause. "What? How did anyone get there before you? The case hasn't even broken on the news yet." Another pause. "Oh, I see. Yes, I'll be right there."

Ryan snapped the phone shut and turned toward Sam, gaze bleak. "That was the police. They opened my storage unit, but someone beat them to it…years ago."

"I don't understand."

"Someone made a stew of my family's stuff, but it wasn't a recent job. Everything's covered with dust. They want me to get over there pronto and tell them if something's missing. The trouble is I'm not sure if I'll know. I was in such a fog when I put everything in storage."

The rasp in his tone jerked a knot in Sam's heartstrings. "If they need you now, let's do it."

"You'd go with me?" Furrows smoothed from Ryan's brow, and his ice-blue gaze heated.

Sam's heart-knot melted. "Well, I'm not too keen on being left on the side of the road. Besides, I can report my break-in to the authorities there."

Ryan smiled. "Smart lady."

Ryan stared at the carnage in the Gopher Storage garage. Boxes had been upended and the contents rooted through—loose papers tossed everywhere, his mom's novels jumbled amidst his dad's textbooks. Broken items were strewn across what little floor space remained among the crammed-in personal belongings. He spotted his mother's favorite white blouse, torn and dusty and yellowed, tossed carelessly on top of a collection of his sister's high school tennis trophies.

Memories sucked him under like quicksand.

He tore himself away and staggered the few feet to his pickup. Gripping the edge of the truck box, he hung his head, hauling in deep breaths. A warm hand fell on his shoulder. He glanced down into solemn green eyes.

"Give yourself a minute," she murmured. "You'll be okay."

"Yeah." He exhaled loud and long. "Seeing that stuff hit me hard."

"Mr. Davidson," a terse voice spoke from behind them, "did you notice anything missing?"

Ryan turned to face the officer who had introduced himself as Detective Connell. The lean man stood with a pen and small notebook in hand. Ryan shook his head. "Nothing obvious, but I'll have to go through things in order to be able to give a better answer."

"Fair enough." The detective stuffed the pen and notebook in his suit jacket pocket. "Our guys will be through dusting for prints soon, and then we can turn you loose on the place."

"Thanks."

"Detective Connell," Sam spoke up, "my business was broken into last night."

The officer stiffened.

"I found evidence of the intrusion this morning," Sam continued, "and my cat is gone. At first, I thought it was Ryan paying me a return visit, but he says not, and I believe him."

Connell cocked a brow at Ryan. "Yes, I heard you were prowling the old neighborhood the other night."

"I didn't break into the dry cleaners."

Seconds ticked past as their stares dueled. Ryan's jaw clenched. What did the guy expect to see—a guilty sign flashing behind his eyeballs?

Abruptly, Connell shifted his attention to Sam. "We'll look into this as soon as we're done here." He crossed the pavement toward the garage where a pair of technicians worked.

"Let's get in the truck and turn on the AC while they finish," Ryan said to Sam.

They climbed in, and Ryan started the vehicle. He ran his palms up and down the steering wheel, his gaze fixed on the white police van that sat nose to nose with the Silverado. "It'll be tough to go through that stuff, but it's probably needed to be done for a long time."

Sam didn't say anything, just nodded. Silence fell, not uncomfortable, just…heavy, as if patiently awaiting something significant.

Ryan cleared his throat, swallowing the lump that kept creeping up his windpipe. "The last time I spoke to any of my family wasn't much fun."

"Tell me."

Ryan closed his eyes and tumbled back in time.

He whizzed up the Interstate, tunes from a mellow country radio station keeping him company. His cell phone rang, and he checked the caller ID then turned down the radio. "Hi, Dad."

"Where are you?"

No "Are you all right, son? We've been worried." Ryan squelched the sarcasm before it reached his lips. Michael T. Davidson didn't have warm fuzzies in his vocabulary. Why should his offspring expect any? "I'm almost to St. Paul."

"Good. You'll be home in less than an hour. Your mom and sister have nose prints all over the front window."

"Yeah, I got a late start. Loose ends to tie up."

"I'm on the Internet right now studying the business offerings for junior year, and I've got a plan mapped out that will shoot you straight into Stanford for your postgraduate work."

Ryan squeezed his eyes shut then popped them open. Dad's

voice droned on about "the plan" that would have Davidson and Son printed on the stationery of his investment firm. A sour taste settled on Ryan's tongue.

"I'm not going to major in business. I've decided to take forestry." Wow! Did that pop out of his mouth right here on the phone? Silence roared from the opposite end of the connection. "Sure, I get good grades in the number-cruncher classes," Ryan continued, "but I'm bored stiff. I love the outdoors—working with nature. Remember those Boundary Waters canoe trips I went on with my youth group? And all those weekends on our Mississippi houseboat? When you let me tag along hunting with your business clients, you said I had a knack—"

"I'm not in the mood for this joke, young man." Dad's tone was a brick wall. "You know my position. Hunting and fishing are relaxing hobbies, but there's no money in it. My son is not making a career out of such wasted effort."

"Too late, Dad. Before I left school, I declared forestry my major."

"Are you on drugs, nature boy?" The words sliced like razors.

"Huh?"

"We're not about to toss away everything you've planned and worked for all these years on a whim."

Heat seared Ryan's veins. "Wrong! All the things you've planned for me and made me slave for all these years. I'm not a kid anymore. I'm twenty—"

"You are a child, Ryan. An unstable little boy. I won't have your mother and sister upset by your antics. Don't you even mention—"

"Mom and Cassie won't care what major I take, as long as I'm happy. You're the one who goes ballistic if anyone tries to wiggle out from under your thumb." Ryan winced. Had he just shouted at his father?

A foul word entered Ryan's ear. He blinked. His controlled dad never cursed. But more followed—worse than dock lingo—mixed with orders about what an ungrateful son could do with his trees, and his wildlife, and his canoe and his pigeons. Pigeons?

His mom's voice, high-pitched, entered the background. Dad's thunder dialed up in volume, and Ryan pulled the phone away from his ear, words still pummeling him.

"Ryan?"

Mom. She must've snatched the phone.

"I'm here." His words rasped through a tight throat.

"Come home, okay? Whatever's going on, we'll work it out."

The noises faded and disappeared. Mom must have left Dad's office.

"Cassie and I can't wait to see you. This'll be a great summer." Her voice quavered, and she cleared her throat. "Don't worry about your dad. He's had a tough time at the office lately. We have to give him a little space to work it out."

Good old Mom, the enabler. He'd learned that bit of shrink-speak in his general psychology elective. "See you soon. Tell Cass she'd better have her tennis game polished up, because I'm going to wipe the court with her."

Mom let out a thin chuckle. "Sure, honey. Bye."

Ryan opened his eyes, back in his pickup, staring at the police technicians' van, his family dead and gone. "That was the last time I heard my parents' voices, and I never got to speak a word to Cassie, not then, not ever again."

A slender hand covered his, resting on the seat. "I'm honored you shared that with me. You've kept everything bottled up for too long. Talking it out is one of God's ways of bringing healing."

"God? If He exists, He's the One who let all this happen." Ryan pulled his hand away. "Mom trusted Him. Cass, too. And I did once upon a time in a fairy tale."

Sam's gaze darkened, but she met his glare strong and steady. "Happily ever after doesn't come without trials in this world. But if I didn't know it was there for us with a loving God, I would've given up and died years ago—mentally and emotionally for sure. Maybe it's time for Ryan Davidson to join the living again, too."

He snorted. "Yeah, well, you can keep your 'loving God' theory. And just where do you get off lecturing me about life, Ms. Sheltered Homebody?"

The color drained from Sam's face at the same rate as the anger seeped from Ryan's heart. Would it help if he bit his unruly tongue off? He had no right to expect another ounce of grace from her, any more than he expected any from the God who let his family die.

SIX

Sam groped for the door handle. "I'll see if Detective Connell is ready to investigate my break-in." She hopped out. "He'll probably give me a ride home so you can get busy here."

"Wait. I'm sor—"

She shut the door and hurried, stiff-legged, toward where the detective was consulting with one of the lab techs. The humid breath of summer wafted across her skin, but a chill fist gripped her heart.

She'd been right when she first saw Ryan Davidson's photograph. He was a cold and bitter man, and by his own admission, not a believer or, for sure, had seriously backslidden. Obviously, he needed the help and healing only God could give, but she was no counselor. At least she could count herself officially beyond temptation to think of him in any romantic light. Not that she had been, of course, but now she had an unanswerable comeback for her conniving friends.

"Detective Connell," she called. "Whenever you're ready to leave, I'd like to ride with you to my place."

The detective looked up, but his gaze traveled to a point beyond her shoulder. Sam turned and almost bounced off Ryan's broad chest. The guy was sneaky quiet. She hadn't even heard him get out of the truck.

"You left your car at my place," he said.

"I'll get Hallie or Jenna to bring me over to get it later."

"No need. This project will have to wait a little longer." He jerked his head toward the garage. "I have to get back to work now because we have three families coming for boats this afternoon, and Larry can't handle all that alone. But as soon as we close up shop, we'll bring the car to you if you'll trust me with the keys."

His open gaze and gentle smile sent tingles to Sam's toes. She rifled through her purse. Honestly, this guy was confusing, a prodded badger one minute and faithful collie the next. She separated the key for her car from the rest of her ring and handed it to him.

His smile broadened. "See you soon."

She watched him stride away. As he opened his truck door, he met her gaze. "If Bastian hasn't turned up by then, I'll help you hunt for him, and we can talk about our date at The Meridian."

"It's not a date," she blurted, but he climbed in and shut the door on her words.

Behind her, she caught a soft chuckle from Detective Connell. She whirled on her heel and marched toward the detective's unmarked sedan. Conversation was light on the way to her neighborhood. Sam sat in the front passenger seat and watched increasingly familiar landmarks pass by. The lab vehicle followed them. As they pulled up behind her empty carport in the alley between her business and the one next door, she spotted the green van belonging to the professional cleaners parked out front.

Sam groaned. "Oh, no! I got so upset over the break-in, I forgot they were coming this morning. When I left, I locked everything up tight, so they've been waiting there, accomplishing nothing all this time." A vision of the bill for the unproductive hours flowed past her mind's eye.

"Doesn't look like anyone's in the vehicle," Connell said. "Maybe they went for coffee."

"Maybe." Sam stepped out of the car, pulling her building keys from her purse. "I'll open up."

The detective trailed her to the side door that led into the main work area. She aimed the key toward the lock then halted. "Do you hear that?" She stared up at Connell. A scrape and thud came from inside the dry cleaners.

Connell frowned. "Are you sure you locked this door?"

"Absolutely positive. Securing doors and windows is like a reflex with me."

"All right." Connell and motioned her back.

Sam stood between the pair of lab technicians who'd come up behind them. With the thumb and forefinger of his left hand, the detective gripped the edge of the doorknob. Skin prickling, Sam watched the knob turn.

Face set in stony lines, Detective Connell slid his gun from his shoulder holster and lunged through the door. "Police! Freeze!"

From inside, a curse in Spanish fell on top of an exclamation in English. The tightness in Sam's chest eased. She knew those voices. "Oh, no, it *is* the cleaning crew." She rushed through the doorway.

Connell stood with his firearm trained on four men, their mouths agape and hands raised.

Sam groaned. "I'm so sorry, everybody. I thought someone had broken into my place again."

The detective shot her a grimace and holstered his gun.

Ramon, the crew leader, stepped toward her. "Did you not say to come to work this morning?"

"Yes, but I had an intruder overnight and left in something of a hurry this morning. But I know I locked the door after me. How did you get in?"

The crew leader glanced at Connell then back at Sam. "The door was open. We thought you left it that way for us."

"I always lock doors. I—"

The detective raised a hand. "Just show us the break-in evidence, Ms. Reid."

Sam swallowed a bitter taste on her tongue. The police didn't believe her about the door and neither did her cleaning crew. They cast her dark glances as they returned to work. Stiffening her spine, Sam stalked toward the other side of the building. They'd have to start believing her when she showed them the open window by the storage room and the shattered vase in her office.

She stopped, mouth open, in front of the closed window, its lock hasp now in place. "Ramon, did you or your men shut this window?" A chorus of denials met her question. She turned toward the detective. "Then someone sneaked in here again after I left and before the cleaning crew arrived. They left that side door open and shut this window in order to make me look like an idiot."

Connell's left eyebrow raised a miniscule degree, but he said nothing as she led him toward her office. Her stomach burned. Her intruder might as well have slapped a *hysterical female* sticker on her forehead with this monkey business. Good thing everyone would change their minds in a minute.

"Here now. See?" She thrust the office door open then stopped and stared. Her glass vase brimming with calla lilies sat unscathed on her desk. Impossible!

Detective Connell brushed past her into the room. "You say your vase had been knocked to the floor?" His gaze scanned the linoleum then moved toward the desk.

"I'm not making this up, Detective. I know what I found when I came downstairs this morning. Scared the daylights out of me."

The detective let out a noncommittal grunt, bent and ran a finger across the flooring. Then he stood and leaned over the vase, hands clasped behind his back.

At least the officer was taking a close look.

"At first, I thought my cat knocked the flowers over," she said, "but the door was shut so he couldn't have been in the office. It wasn't until a little later that I realized Bastian was missing altogether, and the thief must have taken him or let him out."

Meowww!

The feline complaint came from the direction of the closet on the other side of Sam's desk.

"Bastian?" Sam hurried forward, but Connell stepped in front of her.

He pulled a white hanky from his pants pocket and used it to cover his fingers as he worked the knob.

Fingerprints. Of course. Sam gave herself a mental smack.

The detective eased the door open. Tail straight up, Bastian scuttled out. He circled Sam's feet, then stopped and mewled up at her. She scooped him into her arms. "Bastian, I was so worried about you! Where have you been?"

"Right here, apparently." The comment came from a smirking technician.

Sam glared at him. "My cat was in my apartment upstairs all day and didn't come down until after I closed the office last night and secured the doors and windows. You can think I'm crazy, but I know I had an intruder, and that he returned with a fresh bouquet and my cat this morning in order to cover his tracks."

"We'll dust the vase, the stick that holds the gift card, the windowsill, and the doorknob for prints." Connell nodded toward the techs. "And get Ms. Reid's here for elimination."

The pair shook their heads, but started unloading their kit.

"Thank you, Detective." Sam watched as she stroked Bastian, who'd settled in to purr. She scratched him under his chin, and her fingertips encountered something crusty. A closer look revealed a dark streak of gunk in the hair beneath his jaw. Sam touched it. A bit sticky and her finger came away streaked with a ruddy substance.

"Bastian's been into something," she told Connell. "At the risk of appearing foolish again, I'd say it looks like blood, and it's not the cat's. He doesn't have a scratch on him."

The detective performed his own examination then nodded toward one of the lab men. "Let's test this, Gabe."

The one called Gabe chuckled and shook his head. “If you say so.”

Sam held her cat’s head still, turning Bastian’s purrs to growls, while the tech swabbed the area. He sprayed a chemical onto the cotton tip of the swab, and the dark substance turned a vile purple.

Eyes wide, the tech met Connell’s gaze. “It’s positive for blood.”

SEVEN

Around 7:30 p.m., Ryan pressed the buzzer by the entrance that led to Sam's apartment. The twilight of the back alley enfolded him, though the sun wouldn't go down for another two hours. The shade brought the temperature of the ninety-plus degree day into the more comfortable eighties range.

Behind him, a vehicle door slammed. That would be Larry getting out of the pickup. They'd made quite a caravan coming up the road—he in Sam's car, Larry in Ryan's pickup, and Larry's son Derek in Larry's SUV. Ryan pressed the buzzer again.

"Davidson!" Larry called, and Ryan swiveled toward his friend's voice. "Catch." Larry grinned as he sent Ryan's pickup keys arching through the air.

Ryan snagged them and waved as his friend hopped into the SUV beside his mirror-image son. The vehicle drifted past him on the way out of the alley, and Larry stuck his head out the window. "Catch that good-lookin' woman while you're at it."

Ryan sent him a mock scowl. "Get lost, Lar."

The man chuckled as the SUV pulled away.

The door behind him rattled, and Ryan turned toward the sound. Sam's unsmiling face peeked up at him.

"I'm so glad it's you." She flung the door wide. "You'd better come in."

"I like the welcome." He grinned down at her and stepped across the threshold.

"You might change your mind in a minute." She poked her head outside. "Where's your employee? Larry, was it?"

"His son arrived home for the weekend from summer term at college just as we were closing up shop. We left Derek's car at the office. He'll get it tomorrow when he and Larry go in to work. The kid's going to help Lar while I take an unheard-of summer Saturday off to start going through that garage." If he didn't know better, by the quiver in his chest, he'd say he was almost eager for the task.

"Okay, then, it's just you and me. That's probably good because I need to talk to you." She brushed past him, grim-faced, and led the way across a cavernous workroom that smelled vaguely like chlorine.

"Uh-oh!" Ryan trailed behind her, glancing around. The place was spotless and bare, except for large pieces of equipment that seemed to sprout out of the concrete floor like stalagmites in a cave. By the white marks in the yellowed paint, even the shelving had been removed from the walls. "What did I do? Or more to the point, what do you *think* I did now?"

She glanced over her shoulder, a spark of amusement in her green gaze, and poked her tongue out at him.

Ryan laughed. Every time he was with this woman, he liked her better. So why did he always get testy and start acting like Bigfoot on steroids around her? He wouldn't have been too surprised if she'd snatched her car keys just now and shut the door in his face after the way he snarled at her outside the storage garage. Either he was more charming than he thought, or she was one forgiving woman. Most likely the latter. Another reason to like her more than he should. He needed to remember that acquaintances were fine, but attachments were the plague.

Gutteral feline yammering sounded from across the room, and he stopped and looked around. Sam's Abyssinian bounded toward him. The cat practically climbed up his pant leg, but lack of claws hindered the effort, so Ryan scooped him up. “Hi there, Bastian. So you came home on your own after all.” The cat purred. Ryan grinned and winked at Sam. “This is terrible, you know. It means *I’ll* have to pay for the movie.”

Sam shook her head, a slight frown on her lips. “That is so unfair. Bastian never likes anybody, even me sometimes.” She wagged a finger in his direction. “And I didn’t say I’d go to a movie with you, Davidson.”

“Well, then, we’ll have to find something fun we could do together. Rock climbing? Ballooning? Skydiving?” He wasn’t getting a smile out of her. Maybe she was mad at him after all.

“Would you be serious? You’re wrong about the Aby returning on his own. He was brought back and planted where my mystery intruder wanted me to find him.”

Ryan’s grin faded. “I’m officially serious. You’d better tell me what happened.”

“Come in here and I’ll show you.”

She went through a doorway framed by some nice old woodwork. Ryan followed and found himself in the glass-fronted customer section of the building. Without a pause, Sam skirted a big mark in the floor that indicated a large counter had stood there. She disappeared inside an adjacent room. Ryan stepped behind her into an office containing furniture almost as bland as his, except bright paintings and photographs graced the walls. A small television sat on top of the filing cabinet and a large glass vase stuffed with white flowers perched on her desk.

“See?” She pointed to the floral arrangement.

“I thought you said the bouquet I sent was on the floor this morning and the vase smashed.”

“This isn’t your bouquet. Oh, it looks a lot like it. In fact, the container is identical, but it’s a style common to most floral shops. I know. I made a few phone calls.”

“Shouldn’t that have been Detective Connell’s job?”

Sam shrugged a shoulder. "I suppose he's made the same calls by now, but I had to know for myself and couldn't wait."

"Curiosity, eh? A trait you share with your pet." He set the cat down and peered at the vase of flowers. "Did you ask the shop workers if anyone came by this morning and bought a bouquet of calla lilies?"

"Of course, but the results were negative. Whoever pulled the switcheroo was too smart to buy the flowers in the area."

Sam bent beside him over the bouquet, and a soft floral scent drifted to his nostrils, not from the lilies. *Nice.*

"See here?" She pointed to the gift card. "The handwriting on the greeting looks similar to the original—basic calligraphy. However, I didn't notice until after the police left, but I'd swear that the ink on the original was black. This is dark blue."

She straightened. Ryan stood tall and looked down into her face.

"Maybe your gift card got wet and the ink faded so your intruder couldn't be sure if the color on the original was black or blue when he tried to have it duplicated."

"You believe me about the break-in?"

"Why shouldn't I?"

"The police didn't. Well, not at first anyway. Then I found the blood."

Ryan's heart jerked. "The what?"

"The intruder stuck Bastian in the closet. The cat heard our voices and started meowing up a storm. When we let him out, we found blood under his chin."

"He was hurt?"

"Not a mark on him. Wherever Bastian was, someone was bleeding."

Ryan sank back onto the edge of the desk, throat tight, as if ghostly fingers pinched his windpipe. Images of his family flashed before his mind's eye. His nose recalled the scent of their lifeblood and the acrid remnants of shotgun powder saturating the air.

"Ryan, are you all right?"

"Yeah." He leaped up and paced the length of the office. "Memories. They get to me at the oddest times."

"I know what you mean."

He halted and met her gaze. Would this woman ever stop piercing his soul with her compassion? She did know. How?

"You need to get out of here." He strode forward and gripped her arms. "If someone can slip in and out, apparently at will, it's not safe for you to stay."

Those green eyes turned to stone, and she pulled away from him. "I appreciate your concern, but I will not be driven from my home again. I. Will. Not."

Again? Ryan studied her with a narrow gaze.

That stubborn chin came up. "If my clandestine visitor had wanted to harm me, he would have done so already. I think he was more concerned about throwing dust in the authorities' eyes about whether he was even here. Chances are this is the end of it."

He crossed his arms. "Don't tell me you're going to sleep well at night."

Her gaze fell. "In time I will. Besides, I had all the manual locks changed this afternoon, and a state-of-the-art key code and alarm system goes in on Monday, about the same time as the antiquated dry-cleaning equipment goes out."

Ryan snorted a chuckle. "You are a most independent woman, but no one could accuse you of being slow in the head."

One side of her mouth lifted. "Thank you. I think. I know you don't quite get why my independence is so priceless to me, but—"

"Then help me understand."

She tilted her head as if contemplating a deep subject. "I may do that sometime."

"Rain check, then." Ryan went to the closet door and opened it. He measured the thickness between his fingers and opened and shut it twice, rattling the latch each time. Then he did the same for the office door. "They're both real sturdy. Solid wood. And they fit snug in the frame. They don't make doors like this anymore unless they cost an arm and a leg. No way your cat brushed up against either of these and popped the latches loose like you can with some of the flimsy doors these days."

"I agree. Without an intruder, there's no logical explanation for how Bastian got into the closet, much less into the office." She flopped her arms against her sides. "But there's nothing more to be done about it right now. Let's watch Hallie's interview with you on TV."

Ryan looked at his watch. "The news isn't on yet."

Sam gave him a long-suffering look. "We were on at five o'clock. I recorded it."

"We?"

"You'll see." She grimaced and picked up the remote control from beside the set.

He perched on the desktop again, while she took the chair.

Soon Hallie Berglund's face appeared on the screen. In the background, sunlight sparkled on the rippling river, and several of Ryan's houseboats bobbed on the surface. Both his and the reporter's faces filled the screen, but only briefly. The camera wide-angled, and Sam's lithe figure joined them in the picture. There he went spilling his guts to her and the whole world about the reason he blamed himself for his family's death, followed by his hotheaded threat to the killer. Of course, he hadn't realized he was already being taped at the time. Sizzling footage for a news interview, but man, oh, man, what had he been thinking?

"What was I thinking?" Sam moaned.

Ryan turned toward her at the echo of his thought. Her face was pasty pale. She punched the remote, and the television fell silent.

Her eyes were fathomless pools. "If my family catches wind of this murder-investigation thing, they'll camp on my doorstep. And now I've been on television." She moaned and dropped her head onto her arms atop the desk.

"I'm about ready to camp on your doorstep. I may have poked a hornet's nest with my big mouth, and if the killer was watching, there's no way he's going to believe you're a disinterested party."

Sam's head rose slowly until she met his gaze with eyes like green steel. "Then I guess we're in this together until a murderer is caught."

EIGHT

Around nine o'clock the next morning, Sam pulled up outside Ryan's storage unit. His Silverado was backed up to the raised door, tailgate down, but there was no sign of the man's blond head. She sat still, gnawing on her lower lip. Should she go in? She hadn't exactly been invited, but she couldn't seem to stop herself. After her morning run, driving over to check on Ryan seemed like the natural thing to do.

After all, she had a legitimate interest in seeing solutions found. But her presence in no way meant she had anything more than a sympathetic interest in Ryan's situation. Temporary allies were all they could be. If he'd even let her stick around today. And if she had the guts to go inside.

Well, for pity's sake, she was here, wasn't she? The worst he could do was toss her out.

Inhaling a deep breath, Sam climbed out of the car and stepped into the relative dimness of the garage. A thump from deeper in the garage drew Sam down a narrow aisle between stacked boxes, scattered debris and small pieces of furniture.

Ryan was manhandling a box from the top of a stack as Sam rounded a corner and caught sight of him. He must have heard her approach because he turned toward her.

His face lit. "You're here!" The smile dimmed, and he shifted from one foot to another. "I mean, just because I mentioned I was doing this today, I didn't expect—"

A knot dissolved in the pit of Sam's stomach. He wanted her to be here. "No worries, Davidson. I had nothing better to do this Saturday than to see if we can get a few clues. Besides, it was a good way to avoid calls from reporters. I don't need any more of that kind of publicity." There. That should let him know her presence was strictly business.

Ryan grimaced. "I think we've had plenty of limelight." He set the box on top of a chest of drawers. "Did your parents give you any grief over the news broadcast?"

Sam echoed Ryan's grimace. "I don't think they've heard about it. We talked on the phone last night. They didn't mention it, and I didn't bring it up."

"Brave girl."

"Believe me, in this case, silence is the better part of valor."

Ryan grinned and pulled the tabs free on the box. "Want to see what's in here?"

Sam laughed and pointed.

"What?"

"You've got a cobweb hanging from your ear."

Ryan swatted at the side of his face then wiped his hand on his jeans, leaving a white streak behind. "Glad I could be your entertainment this morning. Now let's get down to business."

"Aye, aye, Cap'n!" Sam saluted, still grinning. "What's the plan?"

"It's going to take more than a day to get through all this, and I don't want to handle anything more than once so I've mentally divided the garage into quadrants. This is the left rear quadrant. We'll look at things piece by piece and carry them out to the truck bed when we're done. Next we'll do the left front quadrant and stack the stuff in the left rear as we finish with them. Then we can put the things from the truck back into the garage before we start on the other half of the unit. Make sense?"

"Mr. Organized."

"You got it." He flashed a smile.

"Are you going to keep everything?"

Ryan shrugged. "Probably not. The pickup will come in handy to haul out what I'm going to junk or donate to the Salvation Army."

"Gotcha. So open that box already."

Ryan pulled the flaps up and reached inside. He came out with a square, fuzzy-topped bed pillow in a vivid shade of pink. "My sister's. These are her things." He reached in again and emerged holding an eight-by-ten framed photo. "This is her senior picture. She was within a week of graduating." His face went flat.

Sam's heart wrung at the bleakness in his voice. "The best thing we can do for her now is find out why she never go to wear her cap and gown."

Ryan met her gaze, a muscle twitching in the side of his jaw. "I'd just as soon slam the door on this garage and walk away again. The best thing you can do for *me* today is keep me on task."

"May I see the photo?" She held out her hand. Ryan gave the picture to her, and Sam studied the young woman. Cassie. The name suited her.

Glossy brown hair framed a pixie face with a glowing complexion. The brown eyes contained a spark of mischief mixed with anticipation, as if she could scarcely wait to find out what life held for her next. What an outrage that someone dared to snuff out that bright promise! A price needed to be paid for such a vicious act. That was justice. She knew a thing or two about the subject. Sam's jaw ached, and she suddenly realized she was grinding her teeth together.

"You look ready to bite the toenails off a bear," Ryan said.

Forcing her jaw to relax, Sam handed the picture back. "She was beautiful. Let's get to work."

"Okay. Do you want to finish going through this box? I'll move on to something else."

"What should I be looking for?"

"Anything inconsistent with a teenage girl that might point to a potential killer."

"But I won't know if something of hers is missing."

Ryan shook his head. "I wouldn't, either. I may have packed the boxes, but I did it in a hurry. When I was growing up, the contents of Cass's room were a deep, dark mystery to me, so it doesn't matter which of us looks through her things. In fact," he fished out a lacy bra between thumb and forefinger then dropped it back into the box, "you're probably the better candidate. I'll assign you Mom's things, too. How about that?"

"Sounds like I'll be doing most of the work." She sent him a mock pout.

He laughed. "Then you have no clue how much stuff my father had in his study. It was practically a library. And then there are the rest of the household goods. You should feel sorry for me, lugging around heavy cases."

"In your dreams, buddy." Sam brushed past Ryan and reached into the container for the next item.

Chuckling, Ryan moved into another part of the garage. "Thanks," he said from the other side of a wall of furniture and boxes.

"You're welcome. After dealing with that dry-cleaning building, I'm an old hand at sorting through things."

"I don't mean just for helping out with the grunt work. You've already made this day less of a nightmare for me. That's priceless."

Oh, why did he have to say something so sweet? The backs of Sam's eyelids prickled, but she pinched the bridge of her nose and kept the moisture in. She took a few deep breaths. "I'm glad," she finally managed.

Ryan hefted another box of books that used to belong to his father. The dry texts had no interest for him, but might for the library. He carried the container out to the truck and shoved it onto the bed with about a dozen others containing different things. He'd thought today would wring the heart out of his chest, but most of what he'd handled was fairly impersonal property. Maybe he'd get through this with his cool intact.

He swiped at his sweaty forehead with the back of his arm. Well, maybe not his cool. That garage was turning into a cooker. His watch showed nearly eleven o'clock. Time for a break, and then they'd better come back with some fans or else hang it up for the afternoon. Mornings and evenings might be the only workable times for this activity.

"Sam, you ready for a break?"

No response came from the shadowed interior of the garage. Ryan wandered back inside. "Sam?"

"Hmmm?"

"Are you all right?"

"What? Oh, sure. I was just engrossed."

Ryan stepped around a pile of boxes and found his helper perched on a crate near a shaft of sunlight. A pile of rumpled notebooks sat by her side, and one with a red cover lay open in her hands.

She smiled up at him. "My family complains that I have a gift for tuning out the world when I'm concentrating on something."

"What are those?" He gestured toward the notebooks.

"Your sister was an amazing writer."

"Oh, you found her school assignments. She always got As in English courses."

"No, these are private journals." Her eyes widened, and she leaped to her feet. "I'm so sorry! I shouldn't be reading her personal thoughts. I should have given them to you right away and let you look, but I didn't know what they were at first, and then I just got carried away. I—"

"Whoa! I invited you to go through Cassie's things."

"But—"

"No problem, and that's the end of it. Did you find anything?"

She shook her head. "I discovered a tender heart and a fresh and witty mind. The world is the poorer without Cassandra Davidson. But no discernable clues about murder. Of course, I haven't reached the end of this one. It's dated the most recent to her death."

"Bring it with you." He turned away and motioned her to follow. "Let's go get something to eat."

"And drink."

"You got it. I'm about ready to spit whole cotton balls. And while we're on the road, we might as well drop this stuff off at the library and the Salvation Army." He held the passenger door of his pickup open for Sam.

She glanced at her car, parked at an angle in front of the storage unit. "Will the Malibu be okay there?"

"Should be. We won't be gone long."

Nodding, she climbed in, and Ryan shut the door. Then he locked the garage and hopped in behind the wheel. Sam looked natural sitting beside him in tan capris and a baggy T-shirt knotted at the waist. At home in a truck. No fancy airs about her. She was as damp and dusty as he felt, but utterly appealing with that smudge of dirt on the tip of her nose. The cute snoot was already buried in the journal.

He chuckled and started the pickup.

"What?" She blinked at him.

"Not a thing." He turned up the air-conditioning. "I think we'd better save The Meridian for another time."

She laughed. "Yes, they might draw the line at early American sweatshop attire. It's a fast-food kind of day."

"You're talkin' my language, li'l lady." He headed the truck out of the lot and, a few turns later, merged with traffic on I-35. "Salvation Army first? It's on the way."

"Mmm-hmm."

Ryan shook his head. Better not plan on much conversation. What was in his sister's journals, anyway? Could he read them without freaking out? Maybe he needed to take the chance.

Half an hour later, they'd dropped off the clothing and household items at the Salvation Army and sat across from each other at the burger place.

Sam laid the notebook on the table beside her lunch tray and tapped her fingertips on it. "Your sister had a lot of perceptive thoughts about her friends, school, your parents and you, too."

Ryan groaned. "What did she say about me?"

"Mostly that she saw how unhappy you were with the choices that were being forced on you, and that she hoped one day you'd break loose."

He sat back in the booth hard enough to jerk the legs up. "Wow. I didn't think anyone else noticed."

"Cassie picked up on many things. You'll have to take the whole stack of notebooks home with you when we're finished for the day."

Ryan chomped a bite of his burger and chewed, his gaze fixed on the blazing red cover of the last journal his sister ever wrote. Would he feel like a voyeur, invading her innermost thoughts? He wouldn't know until he tried. Besides, he'd post the contents of those journals on a mile-long billboard if he thought it would net him a killer.

He swallowed his bite. "Any word from the police about that blood on the cat?"

Sam stuffed a French fry into her mouth and shook her head. "Too soon. Police labs are notoriously swamped. And a cold case isn't a top priority for them."

Ryan wrinkled his nose, but changed the subject. "Bastian. That's a unique name for a cat—well, anything, for that matter. How did you come up with it?"

She smiled, still working on her pile of fries. "I've watched a lot of movies and read a lot of books, more than most people in my little lifetime. I love stories and their power to help you see the world with fresh eyes…to carry you away to places you've never been and may never go…to set your mind on a quest for answers you may not have sought before. Stories were Jesus's favorite teaching method, because they pierce the soul like little else, except perhaps music."

"I read more magazines than books, but a good country tune can haunt me for weeks." Ryan crumpled his burger wrapper. "And this leads to Bastian how?"

"*The Neverending Story*. It's a movie about a boy named Bastian who finds a mysterious book in an old bookseller's shop. As he reads it, he gradually realizes that he is literally part of the story. Unless he—the boy from the real world—can find a way to convince people to believe in stories once again, the beautiful land of Fantasia will be consumed by the Nothing, and his world—our world—will become a place of despair dominated by reason without heart." She shuddered. "So I named my cat Bastian to remind myself that the world I experience with the physical senses wouldn't even exist unless it was sustained by the unseen realm where God dwells."

"Whew!" Ryan laughed. "You got all that out of a movie?"

Sam frowned and stared down at the remnants of her meal. "I guess I can put together some odd analogies. It came from having a lot of lounge-around time. Don't you believe in God?" Her head came up, and that green gaze zinged straight through him.

Ryan shifted in his seat. "At one time, I thought I did."

"Not good enough, Davidson." Her eyes narrowed. "Did you decide to shove God away because of what happened to your family?"

"That just sealed the deal. I remember walking into the house that night hoping Mom wouldn't ask me if I was keeping up with church attendance in college. Hah! I figured she'd be the one to chuck me out on my ear, not Dad, if she found out I was sleeping in on Sundays. But what was the point of keeping on with a religion I questioned?"

"Questions, eh?" A grin stretched Sam's lips that matched the gleam in her steady gaze.

"What's that supposed to mean?"

"God's not afraid of questions, but I think you're too chicken to ask them. Want to come to church with me tomorrow? I've started attending Community Bible Church near my business. Right in your old neighborhood."

"Now you really are talking nuts. That's where my family used to go to church. I don't need to be gawked at and accosted by long-lost buddies of my parents." Ryan got up and stuffed his garbage into the container.

Sam followed suit, still with that smirk on her face. Well, Miss Know-It-All could take her chicken theories to the dump. He got his final answer about how much God cared for him when his family died.

They got back into the pickup and headed out again on the freeway. Some tailgater did the same. Ryan moved over to the center lane. The tailgater moved over, too—a couple of guys in a Ford SUV.

"If you're in such a hurry," Ryan spoke to the rearview mirror, "why don't you grab the fast lane, buddy?"

"Huh?" Sam looked up from the notebook that had reclaimed her interest.

"I wasn't talking to you, just some pinhead who can't keep his distance."

Sam laughed. "Not that unusual in this city, I've learned." She returned to the journal.

Ryan studied the traffic. He'd get back over into the right lane after he passed this convoy of semis. He checked the rearview. Finally! The SUV was moving into the far left lane. Ryan accelerated to overtake the semis. Pinhead accelerated faster and came alongside the pickup. Ryan glanced over, and his heart did a somersault.

He gaped into the barrel of a pistol pointed out the window by the SUV's passenger, who aimed at one of Ryan's tires.

The muzzle flashed. Two bangs sounded one on top of the

other. The pickup fishtailed. Ryan fought the wheel, but it was a losing battle on only three tires. At 75 mph they hurtled into the midst of that convoy of semis.

Air horns blasted and a scream stalled behind the giant goose egg lodged in Ryan's throat.

NINE

A shriek burst from Sam's throat. The notebook flew as she dug her fingers into the edges of the seat. Air horns wailed, brakes squealed, road stripes blurred, a semitrailer loomed then slid past. The pickup bucked and slid sideways onto gravel at the edge of the road.

Impact struck from behind. Metal crunched on metal, and the Silverado lurched, jarring Sam's spine to from neck to tailbone. Tilted up on the two wheels of the driver's side, the pickup dove into the ditch.

Sam's scream climbed another octave.

The truck whumped down onto all fours as it plunged nose-first toward the grassy embankment at the bottom of the ditch. Sam's seat belt brought her up short, and pain shot through her shoulder and stomach. A pop sounded from the dash with a flash of light and a stink like a firecracker exploding in her nose. Her scream ended in a faceful of smelly air bag as the Silverado slammed to a halt in a screech of tortured steel.

The air bag shriveled away, and Sam hauled in a shuddering breath. A taste like ashes filled her mouth as fine gray dust settled in the cab. Long seconds ticked past, marked by tooting horns from traffic on the road above and the labored grind of the pickup engine.

"Ryan?" The question came out a croak. A groan answered her. Gingerly, she turned her head. Well, her neck wasn't broken, anyway, but her chest hurt like she'd been pummeled by a steel balloon.

A pruned air bag lay in Ryan's lap. He sat slumped, eyes closed, but his heart beat so hard the pulse showed through his T-shirt.

"Ryan?"

Head wobbling like a drunk, he turned and looked at her. "They shot at us."

Even with a brain stuffed with gunpowder-smelling wool, that statement made no sense. "No, I think…" She concentrated. "We blew a tire and almost got run over by a herd of semis."

Ryan's arm lifted and a shaky hand reached for the key in the ignition. He clicked the switch off, and the hiccuping engine died. "The tire…" Ryan halted, coughed, and slumped back against the seat. "That guy in the SUV blasted it with a pistol. We're supposed to be dead." His head came up, and he grabbed her hand. "Are you all right?"

"'Not dead' is pretty all right at the moment."

A smile quavered across Ryan's lips. "You are the most amaz—"

Whatever he said was drowned in sirens and shouts from the roadside above.

Sam unbuckled her seat belt. "Shall we make our grand entrance?" She put her hand on the door latch, but Ryan's fingers closed around her other arm.

"Let me get out and make sure the gunman didn't come back to confirm his kill."

"He'd be an idiot if he did with all these witnesses around." She checked the side-view mirror. Vehicles and people stood at the edge of the ditch, and a squad car was coasting to a stop among them, bubbles whirling. "It looks like a three-ring circus out there."

"Nice to be the center of attention again."

"So let's get this over with." Their gazes met, and Ryan dipped a slight nod.

She pushed open the door and jumped out onto the grass.

Oops! Jumping was a mistake. The world spun, and she hit her knees. She could count every bone in her body. Her muscles, too.

"Just stay still, Miss."

Sam looked up.

Deep brown eyes squinted down at her from the dark face of a young man in a police uniform. The name pin on his shirt pocket said Edwards. "An ambulance is on the way."

"Ambulance?" The word came out as a squeak. "No! No ambulance. I'm fine. Just shaken up. See?" She pressed a hand against the side of the pickup and hauled herself to her feet.

"Miss, really, you should stay still until the paramedics look at you."

"Fine. They can look, but no ambulance and no hospital." Sam stepped forward and pain speared up her left calf. Oh, goody, she'd pulled a muscle, but she would eat dirt before she let on.

"You allergic to hospitals, Hopalong?"

"Who?" Sam blinked at Ryan, who'd rounded the rear of the truck and now stood a few feet from her.

He shot her a half grin, half grimace. "You've never heard of Hopalong Cassidy?"

She shook her head. Her ignorance might be showing, but this was a way better topic than ambulances and hospitals.

"I guess you're not a fan of old Westerns. I'll have to educate you. But first—"

"Is this your pickup, sir?" Officer Edwards interrupted.

"It is."

"The front driver's-side tire is blown," a new voice said.

Sam turned. On the other side of the truck stood another man in uniform, studying the pickup and the gouge in the earth that led from the lip of the road to the crash site.

"It was a drive-by shooting," Ryan said.

Both officers stared at Ryan. Sam's stomach quivered. Someone had shot at them! The reality sank in. She gripped the edges of the truck box.

"Someone in another vehicle fired at you, missed, and hit the tire?" Edwards pulled a small wire-bound notebook and a pen from his shirt pocket.

"No, they aimed for the tire. I saw the weapon. It was a pistol, maybe a .45. They could hardly miss."

Edwards's pen skimmed across the paper, while the other officer moved around the pickup, studying the vehicle from every angle. Edwards looked up and narrowed his gaze at Ryan. "Description of the vehicle and the shooter?"

Ryan frowned. "The whole thing didn't take more than a few seconds, but I noticed this brown Ford Explorer practically riding our bumper earlier on. Minnesota plates." He scratched the back of his neck and blew out through his nose. "Didn't notice much else, except when the SUV pulled alongside us, I saw a patch of rust about the size of a silver dollar on the passenger's-side door. Then the gun grabbed my attention, so I didn't zero in much on the guy holding it. Dark brown hair, and he wore glasses. The sun glinted off them. Could have been Hispanic or maybe Caucasian with a deep tan. That's about it." He shrugged.

Edwards made no comment, just wrote.

The other officer joined his partner. "I spotted no bullet holes in the vehicle, but the remaining tires show wear."

The pen stopped, and Edwards's gaze fell on Ryan.

Sam stepped away from the pickup. "We were shot at. I heard two bangs, one right on top of the other."

Ryan looked from one officer to the next. "I had an appointment for a tire change next week. I know they're ready to be replaced, but they weren't ready to blow."

Edwards scribbled in the notebook. "Did you see the gun, too, miss?"

"No, I was reading." Sam stopped on a gasp. "The journal! I almost left it."

She turned and hobbled back to the passenger door, flung it open, and spotted the edge of the red book on the floor, peeking from beneath the deflated air bag. She snatched it up and grabbed her purse that had also upended on the floor. Good thing the zipper had been closed or items would have been strewn all over the cab.

A siren let out a pair of *bleeps* from the road above. Sam looked up as an ambulance cruised to a halt. Her stomach lurched. She swallowed and looked beyond the medical vehicle. Wow! She hadn't notice before but a semi was jackknifed on the freeway about a hundred feet up the road, blocking two of the three lanes. No wonder vehicles were still inching around the site. Traffic would be bottlenecked for miles.

Ryan stepped up to her side. "I figure we're about as popular with the commuting masses as a pair of squirrels at a blue jay convention."

Sam laughed. "You have this knack for picking up on what I'm thinking. Only you put it more colorfully."

"I've thought the same thing about you." He grinned down at her.

Sam's heart did that odd little pitty-pat she'd come to associate with the effect Ryan had on her. Foolish woman! She dropped her gaze.

A rumble neared from skyward, and they both looked up.

"Unless I'm mistaken," Ryan said, "and I rarely am, that would be a news chopper. Let's take cover."

His arm went around her waist, and that pitty-pat morphed into a gallop. She let him guide her up the embankment toward the paramedics heading down toward them. The medical personnel closed in around them, firing questions about their condition. The good news was they were distracting her, but the bad news was that the whole troupe was drifting toward the waiting medical van. She'd have to smell those antiseptic scents, see that equipment, remember…

"You'll be fine," Ryan murmured, and his arm tightened around her waist.

How did he know what she was feeling? She hadn't told him why…yet. But he was right. Everything would be okay. These people wouldn't take her anywhere she didn't want to go. They were just trying to help.

A few seconds later, she and Ryan were perched on the fender of the ambulance, being examined by the paramedics—pulses and blood pressures taken, pupils examined for evidence of concussion, more endless questions asked.

"You have a nasty scrape here, sir," a female medic said to Ryan. "We'll have to dress this."

Sam looked down. The woman cradled Ryan's left arm in her hands, checking out a three-inch rounded area that showed purplish flesh dotted with blood spots.

"How did that happen?"

The medic glanced at her with a slight smile. "Probably the flying cap from the airbag in the steering wheel. It's not an uncommon injury after an accident. I've seen worse."

"Well, it hurts worse than it looks," Ryan huffed.

Sam's laugh joined the paramedic's, and fresh air inflated her lungs. She hadn't realized she'd been taking shallow breaths. This wasn't so bad. Not bad at all. So much for irrational fears. She beamed at Ryan, who scowled then winked and shook his head.

Warmth spread through Sam's insides. This would be one of those rare perfect moments in life if she wasn't sitting on the edge of an ambulance after being shot at. Or maybe the surrounding circumstances were what made this a perfect moment. Or maybe she was simply nuts to indulge any feelings whatsoever for Ryan Davidson. He was not a candidate to win her heart. If only she didn't have to keep reminding herself of that fact.

TEN

"They don't believe me about the shooting," Ryan said, as he watched the squad car pull out of the storage lot, where he and Sam had just been dropped off. "They think I'm trying to make an excuse for the accident."

"Join the club." Sam touched his arm. "When the evidence technicians left my office yesterday, I got the impression they were still snickering at me behind my back."

Ryan sighed and gazed down into her soft green eyes. "With my tire shredded all over the freeway, they might not find any evidence of my claim."

"You should still make sure Detective Connell is made aware of what happened."

"I'm pretty tired of talking to police officers."

"Can't say that I blame you." Sam headed toward her car. "Let me take you home."

Ryan fell in beside her. "You should stay with one of your friends for a while. I don't like you being alone, and you probably shouldn't hang out with me anymore. I'm a trouble magnet."

Sam stopped, turned and poked a finger into his chest. "Look, Davidson, I didn't ask to be thrown into this mess, but here I am. And whether our stories are believed by the authorities or not, someone is trying to stop us from discovering anything more about what happened to your family. That makes me angry."

Ryan folded her hand between both of his. "Be wise. Protect yourself. Maybe you should go back to Eau Claire for a while."

She pulled away, gaze hardening. "If I run and hide now, I'll lose everything I was trying to gain by moving here. Don't misunderstand me—I'll take precautions, but ultimately I'm not my own protector. Somebody bigger than both of us saw us through today."

His heart felt like a rock in his chest as he strode toward the passenger's side of the vehicle. "I can't handle being responsible for your life. I've got my hands full with my own."

He slid into the car and slammed the door.

Sam plopped in behind the wheel and glared at him. "Don't get a hero complex, Davidson." Her door slam trumped his. "I'll be just as glad as you will when this gets resolved, and we can go our separate ways."

Ryan deflated against the seat. "I didn't mean…" His words trailed away. What had he meant? Was he so used to taking care of only himself that there was no consideration to spare for anyone else? If that was true, his world had grown pitifully small.

Sam set Cassie's journal on the seat between them and started the car. The trip passed in silence. All too soon for Ryan, they crossed over the Mississippi River at the bridge in Hastings. Sam turned onto Highway 10, and they entered wooded lands. The big river loomed on their left. A few minutes later, the sedan nosed into a parking spot outside the log cabin that housed the boat business and came to a stop.

Ryan heaved out a long breath and made no move to exit. "Larry's out on the dock with the clients, so he must have left Derek inside to jockey the reception desk."

"I'm sure that's a favorite chore for a teenager on a beautiful summer day."

Suppressing a smirk, Ryan glanced at the woman beside him. Her gaze no longer held anger, just a gentle sadness. He curled his fingers against the impulse to tuck a stray lock of honey-brown hair behind her ear. "How are you doing?"

"Sore."

"Me, too. If you even suspect a problem you should see a doctor. Don't hesitate. If you don't have insurance, mine will cover."

"You got it."

"All right then." He opened the door and stepped out.

"Ryan!"

He stuck his head back into the car.

She held out the red notebook. "Don't forget this."

"Thanks." Their gazes held. Did she get that he was thanking her for a lot more than handing him the journal? No one had stood by him like this for years. Never, really.

Her chin bobbed in a small nod.

He smiled and clutched the notebook to his chest as he watched her drive away. His battered muscles protested the simple walk into his office building. By the time he'd offered explanations to his employees, made light of their alarm, and the last patron had been dealt with for the day, Ryan had never been so glad to climb aboard his houseboat and relax at the galley table with a glass of iced tea. Old Jake slept on the floor next to him. The journal beckoned him from the center of the table.

At last he picked it up and flipped through it. His sister's flowery scrawl filled only about a third of the pages. He settled back and started at the beginning. Pretty soon he was smiling. He'd forgotten about the spring musical she starred in a month before she died. He could practically hear the enthusiasm in her voice. Cass never did do anything halfway, and she was always up for a challenge. Maybe that was why Sam reminded him of his sister from time to time.

Ryan read on and found Cassie's thoughts about him and how she wished he'd take control of his future. The entries turned darker. His parents had started arguing a lot. Or rather, Dad was ranting, and Mom was placating and crying. Cass was worried about them. If Ryan had been home, he would have been worried, too. He turned the page and came to the last entry, dated the very day before the murders.

Dad was at it again tonight. Mom forgot to pick up a couple shirts at the cleaners today, and Dad went ballistic. I went to the top of the stairs and listened. I know I shouldn't do that, but I can't help it. This isn't about shirts or being fifteen minutes late meeting Dad for lunch like yesterday. This is more, and I have this terrible feeling that something awful is going to happen if I don't figure it out. I wish Ryan was here. He'd know what to do.

Ryan's throat tightened. She'd had so much faith in him, but she was wrong. He wouldn't have had a clue…any more than he did now.

I wonder if Mom and Dad are thinking about getting a divorce. I hope they can work it out. Maybe there's a chance. Before Dad stomped off to his study, he said something about seeing a counselor. Hah! I'd love to be a mouse in the corner if he does. Dad taking advice from a shrink? Get real! Even though sometimes I think we'd all be better off in therapy.

I mean, we look like this model family. All upright and prosperous and churchgoing. But behind closed doors, we're pretty messed up.

Now I'm depressing myself. I'd better try to get some sleep. I have a test in trigonometry tomorrow. Ewww!

Ryan closed the notebook and set it on the table. Sam had been right. Cassie saw a lot that nobody would ever have guessed with her social-butterfly personality. The giggles must have been her mask to fit in with the Davidson public persona.

So Dad was going to see a counselor. Ryan took a sip of his tea. He believed that about as much as Cassie had. Did Dad say that just to appease Mom? Doubtful. Michael T. Davidson never backed down from confrontation, nor did he compromise. Ryan was his father's son, all right. Just look at how he defied his family's killer on television. And he meant every word.

If the shooter thought he'd scared Ryan out of finishing his investigation of the storage garage, he was wrong. Maybe it was time to start asking questions of his father's old business associates. It only made sense to assume the murders were connected to something his father was into. Dad was the one who suddenly started acting out, and anyone who thought his mom or sister could possibly be involved in something deadly had a screw loose. Besides, he'd noticed a pattern in the debris in the storage shed. Everything that had been his father's had been rifled through and not as much of his mom's or sister's.

The mob? They did hits, didn't they? Had his dad been a closet gambler? Ryan shook his head. The family finances he'd inherited showed no sign of fiscal mismanagement. Then what?

The answer had to be big, and bad and worth killing a whole family over. Now he and Sam were targets of someone who would do anything not to be found out—someone who got wind about the case reopening before it was even broadcast on the news. Someone who had people to do his bidding. A chill crawled across Ryan's skin.

How could a couple of ordinary citizens stand against a murderer with resources inside the system? But what were the alternatives—give up or get killed? Sam wasn't buying that, and neither was he. She'd better be praying hard and have some pull with the man upstairs, because Ryan sure didn't have His ear.

ELEVEN

Every joint protested her movements as Sam dragged herself up the front steps of the church the next morning. How heavenly if someone would carry her. A pair of strong arms attached to a blue-eyed outdoorsman appeared in her mind, but she cast the image into the oblivion it deserved. No good could come of such fantasies.

She spotted Jenna as soon as she stepped into the narthex. Her friend was chatting with Mrs. Stevens, a quick-witted octogenarian that Sam had liked from the first day she attended this church. But right now her gaze was glued to the woman's walker. How much would the old gal take for that thing?

"Hey!" Hallie breezed past, grinning. "Get a move on." She threw the words over her shoulder. "The choir is due on stage in five minutes."

"Move, shmoove," Sam mumbled. "A shuffle is top speed today." Despite her words, Sam increased her pace and hobbled into the choir room a few feet behind her friend.

"Why are you limping?" Hallie handed Sam a midnight-blue robe.

"I'll fill you and Jenna in after the service. And I'm going to pick a bone with you about that news broadcast at Ryan's place with me front and center."

Hallie grimaced. "They didn't edit you out of the clip like I recommended. You and Ryan were just too good together.

Speaking of tall, blond and striking, where did you and he go after you skipped out on the rest of the news services? Boy, were they spitting mad!" She laughed. "If I was a chicken, I would've been fried for sure."

"You're living in ancient history. Enough water has flowed under the bridge since then to float the thing clean away."

Both of Hallie's eyebrows flew into arches beneath artfully tousled bangs.

Sam grimaced. "Didn't you know? Ryan and I made the news again last night."

Hallie flapped her arms against her sides. "I was out on assignment. Didn't even turn a television on."

The call came for the choir to move onto the stage.

Sam touched Hallie's shoulder. "I'll tell you later." Then she fell into line with the sopranos, while her friend filed in with the altos. Prelude music swelled from the baby grand piano and electric guitars, with a snappy drumbeat keeping time.

Sam gazed out on the gathered worshippers. The five-hundred-seat sanctuary was largely full. Most of the congregants were middle-aged or senior citizens. Families with young children were scattered among them. The demographic fit the area, which housed primarily the prosperous and established in life. They were not the sort that wanted their security threatened by such things as a messy murder investigation, and she was the neighborhood newbie. No wonder so many eyes had fastened on her. Dark disapproval shouted from compressed lips. Or was her paranoid imagination playing tricks on her?

The cue sounded, the director lifted her arms and the choir burst into song. At least her throat didn't hurt, and as the glorious melody of praise went on, inhaling against bruised ribs became less of a challenge. Her surroundings faded.

Sam's eyes filled with moisture. God was so good. She and Ryan had lived through what might easily have been a gruesome accident. The news had reported last night that the truck driver who rear-ended them was fine, too. Excellent reasons to praise God. If only Ryan could return to the joy and peace of faith.

Aches and pains faded to a minor annoyance as the service progressed. Pastor Myles gave a rousing sermon on Psalm 91 that confirmed Sam's conviction that divine protection had staved off disaster yesterday. Too bad that stubborn Davidson man wasn't present to hear it.

Sam returned to the choir room after the service, basking in the glow of grace rediscovered. She squeezed her way between boisterous knots of choir members, intent on hanging up her robe.

"Say, Samantha." A hand closed around her arm. "I've been dying to ask."

She looked into the plump face of Martha Stahl, a fellow soprano with sprinkles of gray in her brown hair and the restless gaze of a wary animal. In the space of three seconds, the woman's eyes focused somewhere over Sam's shoulder, above her head and to one side, but never straight at her.

"Ask what?" Sam said.

"However are you coming along with your business renovations?" Martha twittered a laugh. "I mean, with the police and reporters around all the time." She leaned in close enough for Sam to smell the woman's spearmint gum. "It was so spooky, you finding those old murder photos." A shudder flowed through the ample frame. "Do you suppose Abel Morris had something to do—"

"No, I don't think so, and the police don't, either."

"Well, that's good." Martha's smile didn't climb above her nose. "Eldon and I took our clothing there for years. We'd hate to think we were dealing with a…well, you know—a crazed killer." The last words came out a stage whisper.

Heat crept up Sam's neck as she realized talk was subsiding around them and heads were turning their way. She reached for a hanger, threw her robe around it, and thrust it back into the closet. "Some people are waiting out front for me. Nice talking to you, Martha." *And may God's mercy cover me for that bit of polite prevarication.*

Sam headed out of the choir room, hunting for a glimpse of Hallie, but she must already have gone to the narthex.

"My husband and I were good friends with the Davidsons, you know." Martha's voice sounded right on Sam's heels. "Eldon did business with Michael's investment firm. Hasn't found one he's been satisfied with since."

Sam paused in the narthex. Lots of people loitered around the large, vaulted foyer, chatting, but where, oh, where were Hallie and Jenna to rescue her from present company?

Martha hovered alongside her. "Say, whatever happened to the young man who survived the tragedy? What was his name? Ooh, he was on the news with you, too." She snapped her fingers. "I can see his face but— Ryan Davidson!"

"Yes, that's it." Sam's gaze swiveled another direction.

"No, that's him!" Martha pointed.

Sam turned to look, and her eyes widened. She'd found Hallie and Jenna, all right. They were part of a group gathered around a fair-haired man.

Ryan?

He came to church! She hurried forward, ignoring twinges from her sore leg and leaving Martha in the dust. Ryan broke free from the circle and beelined toward her, brow furrowed, chin down, as if bucking a strong wind. This was a man on a mission, not a penitent seeking God.

Sam stopped and let him finish crossing the distance between them. "What are you doing here?"

"You invited me, remember?"

"You laughed at the idea. So what epiphany brought you here?"

"No epiphany. Insight. I realized last night that lots of my dad's old business contacts attend here."

Of course. It had been expecting too much for Ryan to suddenly leap into the waiting arms of God when he'd spent so many years putting distance between them, but this motive reeked like dead fish. The great outdoorsman had come hunting a killer in church!

What happened to the welcome? Ryan studied Sam's face. A minute ago she'd glowed like one of those scented candle thingies with a bulb inside them. At least she smelled good. Her floral perfume drifted to his nostrils. Her swishy calf-length skirt, lacy blouse and the unbound hair flowing around her shoulders made her feminine as a china teacup, except he'd seen firsthand how tough she could be.

She folded her arms. "Find anything out?"

"Got a few business cards so I can look people up later." He displayed the cards in his palm. "As I expected, everyone's falling all over themselves to talk to the long-lost—"

"Ryan Davidson, you look just like your father when he was a young man." The voice boomed from a stocky giant of a man with a hefty woman attached to his arm like a limpet.

They looked familiar. Ryan's brow puckered.

The woman beamed. "Eldon and Martha Stahl. Remember us?"

"You were in Dad's golf league." Ryan held out his hand to the balding man and found it swallowed in a meaty paw.

"We golfed together, shot skeet together, made money together. Why, I even gave him legal advice on occasion."

"Oh, yes, you're the lawyer." Ryan retrieved his hand a little the worse for wear.

Martha bobbed her head. "Your mother and I collaborated on more fund-raisers than I care to count. I still miss her." The woman's full lower lip quivered.

Ignoring the pang in his own heart, Ryan forced a smile. "Good to see you again. Would it be all right if I contact you another day? I'm talking to a few people who knew my folks well. Now that new evidence has come to light I've got way more questions than answers."

The lines around Eldon's eyes and heavy jowls deepened. "Martha and I were vacationing in the Bahamas when the tragedy happened. I don't know what help we can be to you, son, other than to sympathize."

"And maybe that's all he's looking for." Martha nodded. "Sometimes it's good to reminisce about the departed. You come anytime. I make a mean coffee cake." She winked.

Ryan's taste buds suddenly remembered sampling some of that cake when he was a kid at a church social. She was right. It was mean.

Eldon cleared his throat and began moving away, but his wife resisted, leaning toward Ryan. "I never believed that your father did…well, what they said he did. I simply wouldn't listen to the talk."

The woman's husband won the tug-of-war, and they headed up the hall. Eldon dipped his head toward his wife and spoke out of the side of his mouth. "You soaked up every gory detail, Martha."

Ryan barely caught the words, but they left him cold to the marrow. His family had been the whisper of the neighborhood ten years ago, and now they were gossip fodder again. Only this time Ryan was going to encourage every word until someone spilled what they knew. Was he mistaken in thinking that Eldon Stahl would prefer to avoid further conversation? Not hardly. His dad's former legal advisor just went to the head of the interview list, even if that meant he had to eat Martha's coffee cake.

Speaking of eating…Ryan's stomach growled. What happened to Sam? He looked around. Maybe now would be a good time to try The Meridian. He spotted her heading out the front door, flanked by Hallie Berglund and a short woman who must be her other friend, the chef, Jenna Newmann.

Ryan's shoulders slumped. He'd wanted to ask her how she was feeling today. Personally, if his quest for truth hadn't spurred him out of bed this morning, he'd have taken a couple of aspirin and slept in till the crack of noon. If Sam hurt half as much as he did, she had to be a true believer to attend service, much less get up and sing in the choir.

He wandered toward the door. How would it feel to have something to believe in again?

He snorted as he stepped into the hot, humid sunlight of full summer in Minnesota. Faith had to be whole hog or nothing. He could see that much by watching Samantha. She'd been through something really tough, but she still hadn't told him what, and she'd come through it with her faith intact. No, if anything, her trust in God had grown deeper. Unshakeable. Why hadn't his survived the test?

She might avoid him for the moment. For some reason she was angry with him. But he'd track her down later, because he had some gut-aching questions for Samantha Reid that had nothing to do with catching a murderer.

TWELVE

Sam sat back in the easy chair she occupied in the living room of Jenna's town house. Her stomach was full of yummy eggplant parmesan prepared as Sunday dinner by the master chef herself. Sam had withheld her update on the Davidson saga until after the meal. Now that she'd spilled her load, Jenna and Hallie stared at her like pups at a new dish, as her dad would say.

"You walked away in one piece from an accident like that?" Hallie faded against the plushy white couch as if wilted by a blast of heat.

"I'm amazed, too. The pastor's sermon on Psalm 91 was so appropriate."

"How are you today?" Jenna laid a hand on Sam's knee.

Sam chuckled then clutched sore ribs. "When I was drying myself after my shower this morning it was easier to count the places I *wasn't* bruised. Other than that, I'm fine."

Hallie sat up straight as a board. "You were shot at, girl. Consider me overthinking that you and that cute guy should get to know each other better. The further you stay away from this investigation the better. Let the police do their jobs."

"You mean I've done my civic duty, and now I should mind my own business?"

"Exactly." Hallie gave a sharp nod. "Here's your next project. Keep away from Davidson at all costs."

"I think that issue has taken care of itself. Yesterday, Ryan instructed me to keep my distance for my own safety. Then he showed up at church this morning, not for spiritual enlightenment, but to look for a murderer in our midst. I'm afraid that didn't impress me much. The man is obsessed, and not with the right things."

"He's not a believer?" Jenna shook her head. "That's sad. He's trying to deal with a horrible loss in his own strength. I can hardly imagine the pain."

Sam sighed. "I think sympathy for him has prompted bad decisions on my part." What else could have caused her to lose her focus on getting ready to open her business? Infatuation? She'd better not be that wimpy where her heart was concerned.

"Mmm-hmm." Hallie bobbed her head. "Like running over to that storage garage to help him sort through his old life."

"He's a fun guy if you don't push the wrong buttons, and faith is one of them."

"Fun guy or not, right now he's poison for you. And I can't believe you didn't come over and spend the night with one of us after what happened."

Jenna dipped her chin. "You've got more guts than me to stay alone in your apartment."

"You know my reasons, ladies." Sam gripped the arms of her chair. She would not, could not, give in to fear.

Hallie sniffed. "By the dark circles under your eyes, you spent a sleepless night."

"Okay, so what?" She lifted her hands in mock surrender. "A security company is coming tomorrow to install an alarm system. I'll sleep better after that."

Jenna and Hallie looked at each other. "Slumber party!" they said in unison.

Hallie grinned at Sam. "It'll be girls' night in at your place tonight."

"Oh, I couldn't let you—"

"You can't stop us." Jenna rose from her end of the couch. "I'll get packed. This is going to be fun."

Sam shook her head. "You haven't tried my guest bed yet." She showed a scowl to the obstinate pair, but her insides danced. How did she ever get blessed with such great friends? Too bad Ryan didn't have a few buds like these. And why couldn't she keep her pesky thoughts off that man?

Curled up in her pajamas on the love seat in her apartment, Sam sipped her steaming lemon tea then choked and wiped a trickle from the corner of her lips. "You two are insane!"

Her friends' laughter brought a giggle from Sam. Hallie threw another piece of popcorn, and Jenna made like a snapping turtle, snatching it in midair with her mouth. She crunched the kernel with smacks and grins. Sam and Hallie hooted.

"I'm so glad I thought of this," Sam said when she could catch her breath.

"Yeah, right." Hallie licked the tips of her fingers. "You and your ideas."

Smiling, Sam settled back in her cushy seat, eyelids weighted, limbs loose as taffy. Bastian snuggled beside her, occasionally kneading his clawless paws against her leg. How refreshing to laugh and relax. It had been many days since she'd felt safe. She hadn't realized how uptight she'd become.

Her phone jangled. Sam set Bastian on the floor, heaved herself out of the chair and grabbed the wireless unit on the side table. "Hello, Reid residence."

A familiar deep chuckle answered her. "For a second there, I thought maybe I'd called my own house, and your mother answered."

"Oh, hi, Dad." Sam perched on the arm of the couch.

"What's this crazy stuff we hear about you finding evidence in some old murder case?"

Sam gulped and took a deep breath. "Not one to beat around the bush, are you?"

"So there's something to the rumor?" All lightness had left her father's tone.

Sam shot a grimace at her friends, who gazed back sober-faced. The moment of truth had arrived, but just how much of it did she need to tell? Too many unnecessary details would net her a pair of houseguests determined to haul her back to Eau Claire.

"Some old 35 mm film, Dad. The photos were rather awful, but Hallie and I turned them over the police. They came and searched my building for more evidence, but didn't find anything. I don't expect more to come of it from my end."

"Hmmm. Well, your mother and I want to know if anything develops…and I don't mean that as a pun." Increased volume underscored his seriousness. "We're not used to you being this far away from home."

Sam forced a laugh. "Dad, you're not used to me being away from home, period."

Long, heavy sigh. "I know, baby girl. We're doing the best we can to let go, but it isn't easy. The old house seems pretty empty without you. Your mom and I just rattle around here at loose ends."

Sam stifled a groan. Way to lay on the guilt trip. "I couldn't bunk at home forever, Dad. It was about time for me to get a life, don't you think?"

Should she tell them about Ryan? What was the point? She had good reason to back off from that association, and keeping a low profile would probably remove her from some unknown villain's radar. Maybe. Hopefully. Evidently, her parents hadn't caught wind of her accident and might never. So why should she worry them? "Dad, I'm the soul of caution. You should know that by now."

Across the room, Jenna shook her head, and Hallie rolled her eyes. Sam stuck her tongue out at them.

Her dad snorted. "You forget I *do* know you. You're all guts and heart. That's how you got through…well, everything. You also have the work ethic of a whole colony of ants, so make sure you get out and have some fun once in a while."

"Actually, I'm having fun tonight. Jenna and Hallie are here, and we're laughing till our ribs ache." She rubbed her side. Her ribs ached without the giggles, but who was telling? *Shut up, conscience!*

"In that case, I'll let you go."

"Love to Mom."

"Sure thing, honey."

They said goodbye, and Sam cradled the handset.

She stifled a yawn behind her hand. "I don't know about you two, but I'm going to have to get some shut-eye. The truck's coming bright and early in the morning to cart away the old equipment, and then the painters will show up and the security people."

"We're working girls, too." Jenna stood up and stretched. "Ready to turn in, Hallie?"

Hallie stuck out her lower lip. "Am I the only night owl?"

Sam waved at her on the way toward the bedroom. "Knock yourself out with my DVD collection until you're ready to hit the sack." She stopped and turned at the bedroom door. "Bastian will keep you company."

"Thanks a lot." Hallie wrinkled her nose at the cat, who ignored her and went on grooming himself on the love seat.

Chuckling, Sam closed her bedroom door and crawled between the covers. In the room next to hers, she heard Jenna settling onto the guest bed. She yawned and rolled onto her side. How good to feel safe.

Ryan hunkered down in the driver's seat of the Ford Ranger he'd rented until he found a new full-sized pickup. Ten p.m. and summer night had settled around the dry-cleaners building across the street, as well as the other businesses in this small pocket of commerce. Street corner lights illuminated large areas, but Ryan had selected a shadowed section of curb to park beside. The streets were deserted on this edge of a business district that offered no night spots.

Ryan rolled down his window. A distant crowd roar let him know that somewhere in a nearby park a softball game was winding down. The balmy evening breeze carried the scent of summer cookouts. He gazed down the road into the residential neighborhood surrounding the businesses. If he started the Ranger and drove five blocks ahead and another half a dozen south, he'd pass his old house. Something he'd never done in ten years—until just last week, when the new evidence was discovered. Now he'd driven past nearly every day, struggling to recall anything he might have noticed back then that would lend another clue.

Just went to show how self-absorbed he'd been that night. No memories other than his own misery had surfaced yet.

Shaking his head, Ryan blew on his supersized convenience store coffee. The rising steam carried the bitter bite of the jet-black brew. He studied the brick dry-cleaners building. All the lights had gone off in the apartment above. By the hint of blue flickering in one window, someone was watching television. He'd put his money on the reporter lady.

When he pulled up to the curb outside the business earlier this evening and saw those three women going inside together, he'd scrapped the notion of letting Sam know he'd stick close tonight. Her two watchdogs might start needling him with questions again like they'd done at the church.

Does Sam know you're here?

Say, there's a bandage on your arm. What have you been up to?

Did you enjoy the sermon?

Hah! Psalm 91 and all that divine protection business must be for someone else, not him or his family.

It was time people close to him stopped getting hurt, and it looked like prevention was his responsibility. Sam had gotten involved in his problems through no fault of her own. After all the unexpected support she'd given him, he could spare a little guard duty until she got that new security system installed. He should have thought about doing this last night, since mulling over his sister's journal kept him awake until the wee hours anyway.

Ryan yawned then sipped his coffee. He'd had a few hours' shut-eye before he got here, and he'd head home as soon as it got light for a couple hours' nap before his workday started. Sure, he was tired, but it was a good tired. At last he was doing something for somebody else. Something that would have made his mom and sister proud. Maybe even his dad.

Nobody was going to touch Samantha Reid. Not on his watch.

THIRTEEN

"Police. Step out of the vehicle!"

The sharp voice and a metallic rap on the side of the pickup jerked Ryan awake. He sat straight, wincing at the protest from his bruised muscles, and stared into a granite-jawed face. Then the beam of a flashlight blinded him, and he put up a hand to shield his eyes.

"Let's see the other one, too," the voice commanded. "Nice and easy."

Heart hammering, Ryan lifted both hands. Was this guy really a cop? The glint of light off a gun inclined him not to ask.

"Out! Real slow."

Ryan eased the door open and stepped one foot onto the pavement. Bubble lights came on atop a patrol car parked nose to nose with his SUV. Police for sure.

"Keep the hands high." A second voice came from the far side of the patrol car.

They had him in a crossfire. Ryan lifted his arms and dragged his other foot out of the vehicle. Ooph! His leg had started to go to sleep. "I'm not—" His knee buckled under him, and he toppled to the sidewalk, barely catching himself on his palms. The sting chased the last vestige of sleep from his brain.

A curse sounded above him. Rough hands hauled him to his

feet and shoved him facedown across the hood of his truck. A second pair of hands frisked him.

"He's clean."

A snort. "He's either drunk or high."

"I'm not. I can explain. I'm here to keep an eye on Samantha Reid."

"Who?"

"The woman who owns the dry cleaners and lives in the apartment above." Still flattened over the vehicle hood, Ryan looked over his shoulder at one of the officers.

"A stalker then." The man's sneer rivaled Clint Eastwood's. "Or maybe the mystery prowler that's got us doing double drive-throughs in this neighborhood."

"You don't understand. I—"

"Save it. They'll want to hear everything down at the station."

His hands were dragged behind his back, and cuffs clicked shut, ringing his wrists in cold steel. But not as cold as the iron band that squeezed his heart.

He'd fallen asleep on the job. Maybe they *should* just haul him down to the jail and lock him up for all the good he ever did for people he cared about. And he *did* care about Sam, whether he wanted to or not.

A ringing noise tugged at the edges of Sam's consciousness. Her eyelids flickered. What? Not the alarm yet. Her room was still too dark for morning to be here. The ringing stopped. Sam drifted toward sleep. The ring tone came again. Her eyes popped open. The telephone!

She glanced at her bedside clock. Four-thirty a.m. Who could be calling at this hour?

Sam rolled onto her elbow and grabbed the handset from her nightstand. "Hello?" Her voice sounded like she'd been chewing sand.

"Ms. Reid, this is Detective Connell. Sorry to call so early, but we were hoping you could come down to the station as soon as possible."

"We?"

"Ryan Davidson and I."

"Ryan's at the police station? What's he doing there?" All thought of sleep fled.

"He was arrested for parking after hours in a business district and on suspicion of stalking."

"Oh, my! Who did he appear to be stalking?"

"You."

Was that laughter Sam heard in the detective's tone? "I'm sorry. You're going to have to explain that to me."

"Evidently he's been parked outside your building, determined to protect you from whoever he thinks has been perpetrating attacks against the both of you."

"You mean to catch whoever it is so he can find his killer." A slow burn started in her middle.

"No, he says that consideration was secondary."

"Really?" Sam's tummy did a little flutter, and the burn turned to mellow warmth.

"Can you join us at the station?"

"I think I'd better." Sam threw the covers off her legs.

"Excellent. I have something to share that may set you both at ease." The man said goodbye and hung up.

Curiosity running full blast, Sam threw on jeans and a blouse then padded into the living room. She stopped by the couch and shook her head at the long, lean figure stretched out on the cushions, an afghan thrown over her, and the cat curled in a nest near her feet.

Hallie stirred and lifted her head. "Where are you going? The sun's not even up yet."

"You spent the night on the couch? The spare bedroom is only a few feet away."

Hallie chuckled. "You warned me about that bed, remember?

Besides, I fell asleep watching TV, then woke up about 2:00 a.m. to shut it off and couldn't get my lazy self to leave the couch. It's comfy!" She hauled herself into a sitting position and ran a hand through her hair. Bastian protested the disturbance with a mewl then repositioned himself and went back to sleep.

"Don't get up on my account. I'm going down to the police station."

"You're going where? Now?" Hallie's brown gaze bored into her.

"Ryan's there. He was arrested for stalking me."

"Get outta here! He's a perv on top of being an obsessive killer hunter?"

Sam laughed. "Killer hunter? I'm going to have to share that original phrase with him. He might put it on a T-shirt. No, he was standing guard outside the building last night—until he got arrested for sitting out there."

"And you're just going to run because he called."

"That was Detective Connell on the phone. He says he has something to tell both of us."

"I'll bet he does!" Hallie flopped back. "Something like 'butt out of police business.' You could have said no. I thought you'd decided to swear off Davidson for good."

"Get some more sleep, Ms. Groucho. But don't you try to tell me you'd ignore any man who'd get himself arrested trying to protect you."

Her friend chuckled. "Excellent point. Go ride to the rescue of your knight in shining armor. I'm willing to bet he'll need a lift from the police station."

"You're right. I hadn't thought of that."

"Oh, and if Detective Connell tells you anything that's an actual news scoop, let me know so I can be the first reporter to call and ask what's up with the case."

"Will do, newshound."

Smiling, Sam went down to her car, which was parked under

the port between her building and the print shop. The sky had begun to lighten, but no streaks of dawn yet showed on the horizon. She sobered as she drove toward the police station, not a place she wanted to see the inside of again, but here she went because of Ryan. Hallie was right. She needed to guard her heart. God was doing something in Ryan's life, and the last thing either of them needed were some misguided romantic notions getting in the way of what was eternally important. If only her pulse didn't do the salsa whenever he turned that lazy grin her way.

"God, give me strength to keep my priorities straight where Ryan is concerned." She spoke her prayer aloud as she pulled up near the station.

Inside, the dispatcher buzzed her through the vestibule. Then a night duty sergeant—not the intimidating hulk of her earlier visit—escorted her to a bare little cubicle where a scarred table sat surrounded by three dingy white walls and a dull mirror. Ryan slouched at the table, sporting the shadow of a beard and a brooding gaze. His head came up when she walked in, but he didn't smile, just nodded, looked back down and picked at a gouge in the tabletop.

Sam pulled out a chair and sat. "If it makes you feel better, I don't plan to press charges."

One side of his mouth lifted, and his vivid eyes glinted under thick lashes. *Brad Pitt, eat your heart out*. Sam looked away and cleared her throat. "Detective Connell says he has some kind of big announcement. Any idea what it is?"

"Wish I did. Then I could prepare myself for whatever new humiliation lies in wait."

Sam bit her lip to hold in a snicker. The guy was seriously miserable.

Ryan folded his hands in front of him and met her gaze. "I've been sitting here for an hour and a half, mostly alone, but Connell dropped in about twenty minutes ago to say you were coming to get me. He seemed too full of himself to suit me. He actually cracked a smile and bounced on his heels."

"That's major excitement for the stone-faced detective."

"You said it." Ryan scratched at his temple then smoothed his hair. "I'm really sorry for getting you dragged out of bed this way. Creating another problem for you was not my intention."

"Apology accepted, and if the police have anything that leads to a resolution of more serious issues, I'm all for being called in to hear it."

The door opened, and Detective Connell strode through. His hawklike gaze took them both in as he settled into the remaining chair. He laid a file on the table and placed one lean hand on either side of it. "Several individuals' fingerprints were lifted from the film casing that contained the photographs of your family's deaths." He nodded toward Ryan. "We eliminated Hallie Berglund's and Jenna Newmann's prints. A couple others matched Abel Morris's military records. We were left with one more partial thumbprint."

Sam leaned forward, heart thumping. "Did you get an identification?"

"We have found the individual."

Ryan leaped up, chair legs scraping on the scuffed tile. "You have him in custody?"

Connell lifted a silver brow. "Kindly be seated, Mr. Davidson."

Ryan opened his mouth, snapped it shut, and plunked into his chair. "I'm seated and in control of myself."

The fist that lay on the table near Sam said otherwise. She laid her palm across it and squeezed.

Color returned to Ryan's face, and the rigid set of his shoulders relaxed a millimeter. "Okay, now I'm as calm as I'm going to get. Please tell me you've got this joker behind bars, and you can give me a name."

"We know where he is, but not who, and he will never occupy a jail cell."

"What?" Sam's spine stiffened. "How can that be?"

Ryan rocked back as if struck.

Connell held up a hand. "The man who presumably took those photos is a John Doe who occupies a grave in the county cemetery. He was killed in a hit-and-run near the Morris Dry Cleaners on the night of the murders and was never identified. Nothing was found to connect him to the Davidson homicide, so the cases were treated as unrelated events."

Ryan snorted. "Awfully coincidental that the murders and the fatal accident took place in the same neighborhood on the same night."

"Agreed. But police must follow a chain of evidence. Now we have the link that connects the two cases. It's a fair assumption that our John Doe is also the murderer. Whether he acted on his own or had an accomplice remains unknown."

"Pretty suspicious that Mr. Doe was run over blocks from the crime scene." Sam rubbed a spot between her eyebrows where a headache had begun to form. Even a giant step forward still left them in the dark. "Abel Morris must have found the film somewhere on his property and tucked it into his lost-and-found box, not realizing what was on it."

"Yeah." Ryan nodded. "The film could have flown out of the killer's hand when he was struck. Old Man Morris maybe didn't even find it until some time after the accident. If it *was* an accident."

"Valid speculations." Connell's gaze moved from Ryan to Sam and back again. "We have reopened the file on the hit-and-run. A camera was indeed found near the body, but since it contained a blank roll of film, no wider search was made for missing film. You may rest assured that any other possible leads will be followed, but that is all I can tell you at this time."

A memory teased the corners of Sam's consciousness. What had she noticed recently that might fit with this scenario? Oh, yes!

"Hold on one red-hot millisecond." The men's heads swiveled toward her. "When I bought the dry cleaners, I did a meticulous inventory of Abel Morris's records to see what had been done to the building in the last couple of decades." Both men sat forward, elbows on the table, gazes intent. Sam gave them a grim smile. "I remember thinking it odd to find a notation of a single basement window replaced in the fall ten years ago, and no other renovations at that time."

Ryan made a sound like a press releasing steam. "The hit-and-run took place in the spring. If he didn't notice the broken window until fall, Morris probably didn't connect the dots."

"Hold on." The detective lifted a hand. "A case of film is unlikely to shatter glass."

"Which means something heavy was with the film," Ryan said.

"Maybe." Connell nodded slowly. "Or the break might be unrelated to the hit-and-run. I'm certain the investigators at the scene would have noticed a breached window in the building next to where the incident took place."

"Not necessarily," Sam spoke up. "Bushes lined the front facade on either side of the entrance. I've had them torn out now in order to plant something more attractive. But back then a heavy object could have arched behind them and gone through a window, no one the wiser until Mr. Morris checked his furnace in preparation for winter."

"Which means," Ryan's voice came out brisk, "that there likely is something else to be found at Sam's place of business."

She shook her head. "Unfortunately, it's probably in the city landfill by now."

Ryan slumped back in his chair.

The detective pursed his lips, brows knitted together. "I will note this information in the file. Please go home now and let us do our job."

Ryan stood and leaned toward Connell, the pads of his fingers pressed against the table, knuckles white. "I have no problem with the police doing their job, but I do have a problem with being shot at on the freeway. And an even bigger issue when an innocent party is my passenger at the time."

The officer rose and tapped the edge of his file folder on the tabletop. "I've read the report of the incident."

Ryan straightened, crossing his arms over his chest. "I suppose you're going to tell me I was seeing things when that guy poked a pistol in our direction."

"I have no reason to disbelieve your story, but you've made the assumption that the incident is connected to your family's murder case. Perhaps it was exactly what you called it—a drive-by shooting. The vehicle you described is similar to one involved in a gang altercation last month. We're following up. You can trust us on that, as well."

Sam waved a hand like a student asking to speak. She seemed to have that habit in this police station. "What about my break-in, my vase, the blood on my cat?"

Connell smiled down at her like an indulgent instructor. "The results aren't back yet from the lab, but I'm certain we'll find a logical explanation for everything."

Resisting the urge to smack the detective, Sam got to her feet and grimaced at Ryan. "Let's blow this joint."

"Get outta Dodge, you mean?"

"Whatever, Mr. Cowpoke."

"Hey, I'm just a city boy with a country heart."

A smile tilted the edges of Sam's lips as she led the way out of the station. Ryan Davidson could charm a poodle out of its bow. Way bad for her peace of mind. But he was so much fun to be around, even in the midst of a murder investigation.

The charmer sat silent on the drive back to the dry cleaners in the early morning light. A dozen questions tangled themselves in Sam's mind, but she couldn't bring herself to ask any of them. Ryan needed a chance to process what he'd heard. She pulled up behind his vehicle and stopped, but left the engine running.

He turned toward her. "So they've found the shooter. I thought I'd feel some sort of relief when that happened, particularly since he's as dead as my family, but mostly I'm just confused. Too much still doesn't make sense."

"I'm with you on that."

Ryan sighed and shook his head. "Let's leave it for now. I've got some thinking to do. But in the meantime, would you let me treat you to supper next Saturday?"

"Aren't I the one who owes you a meal at The Meridian?"

"I'm talking about letting me cook for you at my houseboat. I grill a juicy steak."

Sam gripped the steering wheel. "I don't know, Ryan. I do like you, but we need to be careful about…I mean, this is an emotionally charged situation as it is without—"

"Don't worry." He looked away. "I didn't mean the invitation as a date, more like a thank-you for all you've done. I'll invite Larry and his family, too. Besides, can you really turn down a cruise on the beautiful Mississippi?" He shot her a lopsided grin.

Her heart did its usual boogie. "Well, when you put it that way…"

His grin went full-blown. "I'll pick you up at six."

"I'll drive myself. No point in you making two round trips." Did she sound as breathless as she felt?

"Stubborn woman."

"I prefer to consider myself sensible. What can I bring to contribute to the meal?"

"Just yourself. This is all on me." He stepped out of the car, turned and sent her a wink then shut the door.

She watched him go to his vehicle and snatch something from the front window. He strode back toward her car, and she powered down her window.

"At least they didn't tow it." He waved a parking ticket. "See you later, Miss Sensible."

Chuckling, Sam headed her car for the port. When she got out, Ryan's vehicle was gone. She glanced at her watch. Going on 7:00 a.m. Too late to grab a few more z's. It was time for her morning run, anyway. Then she'd treat her overnight guests to scrambled eggs and toast before the equipment movers arrived.

A flutter overhead drew her attention. She spotted a little bird, a sparrow maybe, peeking over the edge of a vent hood in the side of her building. There must be a nest up there. Funny she'd never noticed the vent until now. It couldn't be more than eight inches wide, and it wasn't in the right spot to connect to any of the old equipment that was about to go down the road. But Abel's records showed this wasn't the first time the building had been renovated.

She stepped closer and looked up into the hood a foot or so above her. A tuft of blue-gray fur waved from the crack between the brick and the metal. How had Bastian gotten up there?

FOURTEEN

"At least we know how Bastian got into the closet." Sam stared at the jumble of items on the floor of her office—everything from the closet, including the shelving. After emptying the storage area, she'd found the interior end of the vent way in the back, the tin cover hanging by a single screw. The duct led to the outside and was open at both ends. She'd felt the breeze.

"It's a good thing you discovered this before winter hit," Jenna said. "Abel Morris must have been paying through the nose for heat with a hole in the wall like that."

Hallie snickered. "I've got this picture of him at his desk huddled in a sweater, wondering where the draft was coming from."

"I hate to bust your bubble," Sam said, "but Mr. Morris never used this area as an office, even though that's what it was supposed to be. Maybe the lack of a window bothered him. Not that a window would have been much to look through when your only view would be the alley and the wall of the building next door. Anyway, the door to this room was closed and locked, and it was chock-full of junk just like the rest of the place. I cleaned it out for myself before I even roped you two into helping me."

"That's why he didn't know there was a problem." Jenna nodded. "Now you can fix it."

"Sure, I can cover the holes for now, and I'll put filling in the ductwork on my list for fall work, but I'm still left with a huge puzzle. For starters, how did my cat climb seven feet straight up to get into the hole? He doesn't even have claws. Even if he did, as marvelous as cats are in their mysterious ways, they don't climb brick walls. That means someone pretty tall stuffed him into the vent."

Jenna humphed and nudged a box with her foot. "Maybe Bastian bit the guy who did it, and that's how the cat got blood on its chin."

"Oooh, smart thinking, girl!" Hallie held up a hand and collected a high five from Jenna.

"Okay, another conundrum answered. Maybe." Sam picked up a shelf board and leaned it against the wall. "I'm sure Detective Connell will let us know results on the lab test soon."

"Speaking of the police," Jenna said, "shouldn't you tell them about this?"

Sam groaned and rubbed a hand across her forehead. That headache had never quite gone away. Probably a product of too little sleep and too much excitement. Her bruises from the accident ached from all the activity of emptying the closet, and she hadn't even gone for her run.

"You know what?" She planted her hands on her hips. "I'm going to wait until Connell drops by or calls. The way things have gone in this investigation, he'll no doubt figure I let the cat outside by accident, and some passing vagrant stuffed him into the vent as a joke. Unless, of course, my substitute vase or my window casing yields the prints of some desperate felon. Then they might take me seriously, but I'm not holding my breath."

"What?" Hallie said. "For the prints or to be taken seriously?"

"Both."

A knock sounded at the front door.

Sam headed that way. "Either the movers or the security people are here." She stepped into the front room. A man with the moving company logo on his jumpsuit stood outside. She waved to him then turned toward her friends. "My day is off to a rousing start. Just pray that it settles down from here and everything goes smoothly. I've got to get my mind off all this weirdness and concentrate on preparing to open my business."

"You got it." Hallie hugged her, and Jenna joined them.

They broke apart, and Sam took in a fortifying long breath. "Thanks, ladies, that felt good. I'll remind myself all day long that your prayers are with me."

"You just do what you need to do." Jenna touched Sam's arm. "We'll let ourselves out the back. I've got to scoot. I'm cooking for the lunch crowd, and I like to arrive at the restaurant plenty early to get everything lined up." She leaned in toward the others. "Veal scallopini or pilaf-stuffed eggplant with mango sauce, if either of you are hungry later on."

Sam's stomach growled. "Oh, man, I forgot to eat breakfast or feed you two, either."

"Fuggedaboudit," Hallie said. "That fresh scoop on the Davidson case was all the breakfast I needed. Once again, Channel Six got it first." She and Jenna moved off in the direction of the apartment stairs.

"Thanks for everything!" Sam called after them.

The man outside pounded on the door again. Sam pasted a smile on her face and went to answer. *Please, God, could the rest of this day be normal?* But then, with all she had on her plate, not counting murder mysteries, she probably wouldn't know what normal looked like.

An average, boring day, that's all he wanted. Was it too much to ask?

Ryan bent and picked up more trash with a gloved hand and stuffed it into a plastic garbage sack. The whole boat had looked like one giant party pad when this group brought it back this morning, and they'd done a number on the transmission from mishandling. They hadn't been happy when he'd refused to return their damage deposit. Tough! You play, you pay.

So far the only good thing about today was no more customers on the schedule. Mondays were typically slow, so that was no surprise. After he finished cleaning this boat, he'd start canvassing the people he'd met at church who said they'd speak to him about his family. Maybe by the time Sam came for their cookout and cruise on Saturday he'd have progress to report. Ryan smiled and attacked his job with renewed vigor.

By 2:00 p.m. he had locked up shop and was on the road toward his old neighborhood. His pickup seemed to naturally take a route that brought him past Sam's business. A security company van sat in the alley between the cleaners and the print shop.

Good. They could both rest easy tonight.

Five blocks farther on, he made a right turn. As he straightened the wheel, a picture flashed through his head.

It had been so dark that night. No stars. No moon. Streetlights, sure, but no houselights because it was late and people were in bed, which left lots of dark patches. The streets were deserted—all except this muscle-bound jogger in a gray sweatsuit who raced up the sidewalk toward him. The man clutched a paper sack, face shadowed under a raised hood.

Heart pounding, Ryan pulled the Ranger over to the sidewalk and put it in Park. His hands shook. He pulled them away from the steering wheel and pressed them together between his knees. That was no jogger. More like a runner. Somebody tearing pell-mell from the scene of a crime. And a sound had carried to him, faint and jumbled amidst the turmoil in his head.

Laughter.

The glee had seemed then like a cruel god mocking his private pain, but it had really been a killer chuckling over a family left dead in their own blood.

Ryan struggled to breathe against the fist that squeezed his insides. A black film coated his vision. Blind rage. He'd heard of it but never been in it—until now. And the rage was against himself! How could he have driven right past his family's murderer and not known?

He slammed the heels of his hands against the steering wheel. Stupid anger. Foolish thing to blame himself for, but his head and his gut didn't see it the same way.

The guy had been carrying something away from the crime scene. Something bigger than just a camera and a roll of used film. Did whoever ran the man down take the sack he carried? The break-in at his storage garage said maybe not. Had they found what they wanted in the storage unit? Not if they were still nervous about what might be discovered at the dry cleaners.

A wolf smile grew on Ryan's face. Somebody was running scared. Yeah, he'd kind of guessed that much. But whoever it was didn't have everything in his possession that he considered vital to his safety. That meant he and Sam might still run across something. Or rather, he might find it. Sam had been through enough trouble over his family's tragic history. He needed to keep her out of any further investigating. Later this evening, after he made his rounds in the old neighborhood, he would go through that storage garage like a whirlwind, even if he had to stay up all night and work by flashlight to finish.

Ryan started the pickup and drove up the street, a strange buoyancy in his belly. What was it? Hope? Now there was a scary thought. He'd lived without that luxury for so long it was hard to know whether to trust such a feeling. What if all his efforts led to nothing? What if the police investigation came up empty? What if— *Cut it out, Davidson. Keep your eyes on the prize.*

He stopped in front of his childhood home and turned off the truck. Only the general shape of the house remained the same as he remembered. The structure had new siding and new windows. The picture window was now a bay window. The maple tree in the front yard was bigger, but the elm tree that had been on the opposite end of the yard was gone, no doubt victim to rampant Dutch elm disease.

A black Lexus coupe sat in the driveway in front of the leftmost stall of the triple garage. Someone was home. He probably should have called first, but he wanted to catch people unprepared.

Sucking in a breath, Ryan got out of his vehicle. On stiff legs, he went up the sidewalk and the front stairs. These had been redone, too, and the door was a deep maroon, not the brown he remembered. The doorbell was in the same spot, though. He pressed it. New ring tone.

Maybe he could stop being so nervous about possibly being asked inside. Chances were it would look like a stranger's home to him—which it was. The door opened, and a citrus scent carried out to him on machine-cooled air. A gray-haired woman in a sequined blue T-shirt and designer jeans peered up at him through thick-lensed glasses. Over her shoulder, Ryan looked into a vestibule done in bold reds and golds. Not at all similar to his mother's understated taste.

"May I help you?" The woman's voice came out as delicate as her slim frame.

"Excuse me. My name is Ryan Davidson. My family used to live in this house. I was wondering—"

"Oh, *those* Davidsons. Young man, I cannot possibly imagine what you've been through." Her tone said she had no intention of trying to imagine. "But I'm tired of all this hounding. I've already told the others—"

"What others?"

"Why, the police—some Detective Connell, I think—any number of reporters, and that private investigator fellow who came by Saturday morning. Now he was at least charming and gracious."

"Private investigator?" Ryan stiffened. "Did he say who hired him?"

The woman glared up at him. "My goodness, young man, can't you keep track of your employees? He said he was working for you."

"Me!" Ryan rocked back on his heels. "I have never hired a P.I."

"How very odd." She pursed her lips. "He showed me his license and a piece of paper with your signature on it. Well, it said Ryan Davidson anyway."

"What did he look like?" He held his breath for the answer. *Let this be a solid lead at last!*

"Dark hair. Glasses almost as thick as mine. Not quite as tall as you, but stocky and somewhat older. He smiled a lot, but I wasn't sure the teeth were real. They were so white in that tanned face."

"Possibly Hispanic?" Like the guy who shot at his pickup.

The woman shrugged. "Could have been, but I'm not sure." She opened the door wider. "Come in, and I'll give you as much of the conversation as I remember."

"Great! Thanks." Ryan stepped over the threshold. From the entry hall, the living room opened up before him. The new owners hadn't changed the dimensions of the room, but nothing else was the same—carpet, drapes, furniture, wall hangings, all different.

"I'm Anna Parkins." His hostess led the way into the living area.

Ryan took a hesitant step into the room. On the far side lay the kitchen. The new owners had opened up part of a wall and installed a peninsula that gave the whole area a more spacious feel and offered a clear view from room to room. Not the case that night a decade ago.

Then, he'd entered the house through the garage into the kitchen. Right off, he'd caught the faint reek of gunpowder. Not believing his nose, he'd proceeded toward the living room, calling, "Mom, I'm home." No answer but a burst of canned laughter from a television sitcom turned up unnaturally loud. He'd rounded the corner and caught sight of a pair of dark heads sticking above the back of the couch.

"Hey, you two, I'm home. Where's the welcome wagon?"

No reaction.

He stepped farther into the room. Tripping over his own feet, he staggered to a halt. Now he identified another smell that had been nagging for his attention.

Blood.

Like the red that coated the fronts of his mother's and sister's shirts and splashed the off-white fabric of the couch.

"Young man, are you all right?"

Ryan jerked at the woman's voice. "Um, yes." He cleared his throat. "I'll be fine." He shook his head and focused on the here and now.

The woman perched on the edge of an overstuffed couch situated in a different position than the arrangement he remembered.

Ryan took a seat in an armchair. "This supposed private eye have a name?"

"Sam Diamond. I asked him if he was as good a P.I. as Sam Spade, and he thought that was pretty funny." She laughed, and then stopped and pursed her lips. "Considering that you say he wasn't a real private detective, I'll bet he chose the name Sam Diamond as a play on the book character."

"Unfortunately, you're likely right. I don't imagine he left a business card, fake as it might be."

"He didn't, and that should have tipped me off." The woman sighed. "I feel like an idiot. The real deal would have left one so I could contact him if I thought of anything."

"Don't beat yourself up, Mrs. Parkins. You didn't do anything wrong. So what did this faker ask you?"

The woman crossed her arms and sat back. "He asked some of the same things as that police detective. Had anyone been around snooping into the old murder case? When we remodeled, did we find anything suspicious—keys, hidden safes, lockboxes, that sort of thing? Have there been any rumors going around the neighborhood about the suspicious deaths?"

"What were your answers?"

"No to everything. Nobody snooping, except the police and him, and we'd never heard a peep from our neighbors about the murders. It was like they went out of their way *not* to talk about it." The woman grimaced and shook her head. "As the home owners, we didn't need to be reminded about it everywhere we turned, anyway."

"I can understand that." Ryan leaned forward with his elbows on his knees. "When did you buy this place from the people I sold it to—Eckert, I believe was their name?"

"Oh, about nine years ago. They only stayed here for a few months. I think they got creeped out by… Well, anyway, we got the place and changed things to suit us."

"And, as you told Detective Connell and this fake P.I., you never ran across anything unusual?"

"Not unless you call a hornet's nest in the eaves unusual." She slapped her knee and giggled. "That was quite a surprise on old Herb. I've never seen him run so fast in all his life."

"What about my dad's study? Did you do anything different with that room?"

"Sure did. It's a guest bedroom now. Do you want to see?"

"No, that won't be necessary." Ryan stood, heart thudding in his throat. Walking into that room might just about undo him. "I've taken up enough of your time."

The woman narrowed her eyes in his direction. "Son, I think it would do you good to take a look. Come on."

On stone feet Ryan followed his hostess up a hallway. Not the hallway of his memory—all different in color and style and the wood floor, bare of carpet, beneath his feet. Still, his pulse ran riot, and he tasted bile in the back of his throat. Maybe he should turn around.

Mrs. Parkins threw open the door. "Go in."

Stomach quivering, Ryan stepped over the threshold and halted, gaping.

His hostess chuckled. "Herb let me do my worst in here. Over the top, isn't it?"

"That's one way to put it." Hard to say if this sudden prickling behind his eyes was relief that this room contained no vestige of old tragedy or heartfelt thanksgiving that he would never have to sleep here.

The place looked like the Attack of the Man-Eating Sunflowers. A gargantuan specimen was painted on the ceiling, and every available surface sported some size or shape of sunflower. The dimensions of the room were different than he remembered, too, changed in order to accommodate the attached bathroom to his right. From what he could see, sunflowers lurked in there, as well.

He turned toward Mrs. Parkins. "What did you do with my father's built-in bookshelves? They were primo mahogany. He always went on about it."

"Eldon Stahl from up the street bought the shelving. Insisted on removing the wood himself. Paid a good price, too. Never knew what he did with the boards. I assume he made shelves in his own study. I have to say, though," she said as she stepped into the room, "he was mighty funny about the project. I'd come in here and catch him tapping on the walls."

Ryan's teeth ground together. Stahl again. If his dad's bosom golfing buddy had anything to do with— He aborted his thought with a shake of the head. There were too many questions unanswered to go leaping to conclusions. A guy didn't hire a killer in order to get some bookshelves.

But what kinds of deadly secrets might be shared around the ninth hole, or more like in the clubhouse after throwing down a few? He'd gobble a whole pan of Martha Stahl's coffee cake to find out.

FIFTEEN

Ryan walked up the sidewalk toward the Stahl's brick colonial home, shaking his head over a couple of interviews he'd done while waiting for someone to be home here at the lawyer's house. People from the neighborhood had been very talkative to the bereaved son. Who would have guessed that his mom had been known as the sharpest bridge player in the neighborhood, or that his dad saved old coins and gave them to a friend next door who collected them? Calculation in his mother and thoughtfulness in his father were unexpected traits.

He rang the Stahls' doorbell, and a dog yapped while footsteps sounded on top of the barking. The door swung open, and a fluffy white animal lunged at his tennis shoes. Ryan bent and picked up the Pekingese, which anointed his chin with its tongue.

"You're right at home already." Martha Stahl's laugh warbled. "Chauncy likes you."

"Most critters do." He turned his head away from more licking and took in the stout woman's casual attire, a flowered muumuu. Her gaze dodged his and went to the dog, then to the door frame. "Have I stopped by at a bad time?"

"Only if you wanted some coffee cake. I'm fresh out today, but come on in."

Ryan set the dog down and followed her up a high-ceilinged hallway. The heels of her strapless mules clacked on the tile floor. So far, so terrific. He was inside, and he didn't have to eat any cake. He glanced into a room they passed on the left, but it was a formal dining room and not a study. He'd give his right arm to see what Eldon Stahl had done with those bookshelves.

Mrs. Stahl led him down a couple of steps into a sunken living room covered in plush carpet from wall to wall. An enormous flat-screen TV hung above a fireplace that dominated one wall, and surround-sound speakers blended into elaborate corner pieces of the vaulted ceiling. Judging by the richness of the classical music filling the air, the system was integrated with a top-notch stereo, as well. A pair of enormous mullioned windows took up most of another wall and let in a flood of sunlight, though the air conditioner kept the room comfortably cool.

Most of the backyard, featuring a cement patio surrounded by a manicured lawn, was visible from here. The yard was enclosed by a tall privacy fence, which somewhat defeated the purpose of the great big windows. At the far end of the yard, several small enclosures sat on legs that lifted them a couple of feet off the ground. Rabbit hutches? No. He caught the flutter of gray wings. A dove cote? Some sort of birds lived in there, anyway.

He turned and his hostess twinkled at him like Mrs. Santa gone Hawaiian, only her gaze went somewhere over his shoulder. "Make yourself at home. I baked some monster cookies yesterday—the ones with everything but the kitchen sink in them—so I'll get some."

Ryan gulped. "Don't go to any trouble."

"Oh, it's no bother, dear. None at all. You know us Norwegians." She chuckled. "We can't have company without feeding them." With an airy wave, she left the room, Chauncy on her heels. The dog's toenails *click-clicked* on the hard flooring of the hallway.

Ryan wandered over to the wall to the right of the fireplace, where framed photos dominated most of the space. He recognized Mr. and Mr. Stahl in some of them, posing with younger adults who resembled them. The Stahls' children, he assumed, but couldn't say for sure, as they were too old to have been in high school at the same time Ryan was. Other photos held an even younger generation. Grandkids, most likely.

He paused at an eight-by-ten enlargement of Eldon Stahl with a rifle cradled in his arm. A wide, toothy grin announced his glee at winning the shooting trophy in his other hand. Behind him, Ryan recognized the skeet range where the elder Davidson used to take his son from time to time. So Mr. Stahl was handy with a gun. Ryan grunted. Maybe so, but Stahl was not the man Ryan had seen running that night. That guy had been muscular, not portly, and a good bit shorter than Eldon Stahl's jumbo dimensions. Besides, the unknown runner now occupied a spot in the graveyard.

Shaking his head, Ryan moved on down the line then stopped again. This photo looked out of place. It was half the size of the others and hung in a spot that disturbed the symmetrical proportions of the rest of the grouping. He wasn't much of an interior decorator, but he could tell that much.

Ryan studied the photo. Five men crowded near a pair of golf carts, wide grins on their faces—big boys out to play. Behind them the fairway stretched lush and green, beckoning their next shots. All of their faces were familiar, though Ryan could put names only to Eldon Stahl: Rick Granger, the now-deceased husband of the neighbor who'd told him about his mom's bridge prowess; and his dad.

Ryan's pulse rate quickened. The photo must have been taken the summer of the murders. The senior Davidson was wearing the monogrammed polo shirt Ryan and Cassie had given him the previous Christmas. Too bad he was clueless as to the identity of the other two guys. Another example of how kids paid scant attention to their parents' world as people with lives and friends of their own.

His dad's face looked genuinely happy in the picture, like his life was as cloudless as the pale blue sky above the little group.

Whatever took him into agitation and depression must have happened soon after this.

"Here we are, young man," Mrs. Stahl singsonged behind him.

Ryan turned, then hurried forward and took the metal tray with a clear pitcher of yellow liquid, two glasses, and a plate of megasize cookies on it.

"Set it on the coffee table. Thank you so much." The woman's muumuu rustled as she went to an armchair and eased into it. "Be a dear and pour me a glass of that lemonade."

"Happy to." Ryan gave her a glass and took one for himself. What could she have done wrong with a container of lemonade? The powdered stuff was pretty much mix and stir these days. He took a sip, and his throat puckered. Cold all right and as tart as—

"Fresh lemons." Mrs. Stahl held up her glass. "I always squeeze them. Takes time, but the flavor is worth it, don't you think?"

Ryan put off the need to answer by taking another tiny sip. No sugar or unnatural additives, that was for sure. He set his glass down.

"Try a cookie." The woman grabbed one for herself and took a generous bite, attention fixed on the unlit fireplace.

He picked one up between thumb and forefinger. "Who are all those guys with my father?" He pointed the cookie at the mismatched photo.

"Your father?" She halted her cookie half way to her mouth. "Where?"

"The little picture at the far end."

Mrs. Stahl stepped over to the photo and studied it as if she were trying to make sense of a Picasso. "How did that one get into the collection? I took it down years ago. I— Eldon!"

Ryan stood up. "Your husband? Where is he, by the way?"

"What? Oh." She blinked at him. "The dear man's out of town on a case. He'll be back on Wednesday, and then we leave the next day for a convention in Los Angeles. I can hardly wait to dive into those shops on Rodeo Drive." She tittered.

Ryan frowned. More delays in visiting with Mr. Stahl. "When will you be back in town?"

"Next Monday…unless we decide to stay a little longer and see the sights." She returned her attention to the pictures. "I wonder why he put this old momento back up?"

"You're saying it's a recent change?" Ryan joined her by the photo.

"My, yes." The hand not holding a cookie fluttered near her throat. "Maybe after he saw you the other day, he got sentimental."

Or felt guilty and did it to punish himself. Guilt was a strange motivator. Ryan frowned.

"I know the other guys, but who are these two?" Ryan pointed to a short, slender man, almost frail-looking, who stood next to his father, and a stocky man of average height who stood with a golf club over his shoulder.

"Don't let the size of the small one fool you." His hostess chomped at her cookie. From the snap of her teeth, it had been a hard bite. "Randolph Hanes is a shark. He was senior partner at Eldon's firm until he became Hennepin County district attorney. Now he's a candidate for state attorney general in this fall's election. And the other one." The hand did its flutter again. "Warren Seiler's outstripped them all. State Supreme Court judge now. A nicer fellow you would never want to meet and fair as the day is long. A very good choice for our state."

"So my dad was out golfing with your husband's entire firm?"

"Why not?" Mrs. Stahl glanced up at him then away. "He invested money for all of them."

"I didn't know that." His gaze followed her back to her seat, but he remained by the photo. "They must have respected him."

"Yes, and liked him, too. He had this dry wit about him, you know."

Ryan shook his head. No, he didn't know, and liking his dad was a foreign concept. Maybe if the two of them had shared some of the mutual respect the senior Davidson had reserved for his business associates things might have been different. Maybe if they'd had more time to— Save the speculation! He'd never know now, and finding out who robbed him of that opportunity was Priority One.

"I suppose now that Mr. Hanes and Mr. Seiler have moved on, your husband is senior partner."

"Oh, no. Eldon deferred that to someone else. He's semiretired. Has been for years. I'm surprised he took on this out-of-town case and then committed to go to that conference. You haven't tried your cookie." She waved her half-eaten one.

Ryan gave her a smile—if he was lucky, it didn't too much resemble a grimace—and took a bite. He chewed, then looked at it and then at her. "These are pretty good." She'd managed to put together an array of ingredients like oatmeal, M&M's and chocolate chips into a tasty treat. Maybe it was just simple stuff like cake and lemonade she had trouble with.

He sat down across from her. "The woman who lives in my old house now tells me your husband got my dad's mahogany bookshelves from his office."

Her pudgy face screwed in on itself. "Really? That can't be possible. Eldon's had the same oak décor in his office for fifteen years."

"You don't know anything about my dad's bookshelves?"

Mutely, she shook her head, at last meeting his gaze straight on.

Ryan looked away. It was either that or let her see the suspicion in his eyes. He pulled a business card from his wallet. "I've been leaving these with everyone I've talked to today. My cell phone number is written on the back. Please tell your husband that I'd like to speak with him at his soonest convenience." He held out the card to his hostess.

She snatched it with a smile tighter than a rubber band and tucked it into a pocket of her muumuu. "Well, I suppose you need to get on with your evening now."

So he was being given the boot. "Thank you for your time…and the cookies and lemonade."

"You're most welcome, young man." She led the way into the foyer. "Sorry I couldn't help you with any information."

But you did. More than you know. He stopped beside her at the front door. "Did you by any chance have a visit from a guy a little shorter and stockier than me, wearing glasses and a big smile in a tanned face? He might have been pretending to be Sam Diamond, a private detective in my employ."

Mrs. Stahl peered at him like he'd asked her if the moon was made of cheese. "Whyever would someone like that drop by to see me?"

"No reason." Ryan shrugged and bid her goodbye. He climbed into his pickup and headed for home, thoughts churning.

If the purchase of the bookshelves in his old house hadn't been an excuse to check out the office area, he'd guzzle a whole pitcher of Mrs. Stahl's lemonade without taking a breath. And who else needed to search that area than a man desperate for something still missing? But bookshelves and mutual business associates didn't add up to motive or proof, and without a reason for the murders, proof might be impossible to come by.

Maybe the proof and the motive were all wrapped around the item others so desperately sought. He *had* to find it before they did.

SIXTEEN

On Thursday afternoon, Sam ran her hand across the smooth faux marble surface of the newly installed customer service counter in her front room and smiled. Finally, tangible progress. She inhaled and filled her nostrils with the scent of fresh paint. This area was almost ready to receive the public. Too bad the work space still had a long way to go. At least, passersby could look in the big picture window and see a pleasing appearance. Hopefully, that would whet their appetites to use her services when she was ready to throw open the door.

Time to get back to the task at hand. She grabbed the handle of the cart containing her paint supplies and wheeled it into the rear workroom. The space yawned like a massive cavern. The dingy walls sure resembled the sides of a cave, and they were all hers to tackle. Paying a cleaning crew had taken any money she might have used to have the painting done.

Steeling her jaw, she broke out a clean paint roller and installed it on the end of the handle. A crew was scheduled to arrive next Tuesday to lay the new floor cover, when the hazmat folks would cart away the old chemicals. That day would creep up all too soon. There was no time to waste. She would not be daunted.

A shrill ring came from the direction of Sam's office. Who could that be? Jenna and Hallie would be tied up at work, and the next edition of the phone book hadn't come out yet for other people to have access to her business number. Maybe it was Mom or Dad. With no new harrowing events in recent experience, she could handle that. She leaned the stick of the paint roller against the cart, went into her office and picked up the phone on the fourth jingle.

"Hello. Reid Cleaners."

A low whistle met her ears. "Very professional, Sam. I almost wish I was calling about the status of my suit."

Sam laughed and relaxed with a hip on the edge of the desk. "You own a suit, Davidson?"

"I'm crushed." Ryan's laugh answered hers. "I'll have you know I'm a very classy dude."

"So how'd you get this number, Mr. Bowtie and Tuxedo?"

"Now you've stepped over the line, woman. I don't do tails, and this country boy wears a string tie to go with his high-gloss leather cowboy boots under the suit pants."

"I stand corrected, and I'd like to see you in that getup sometime."

"Don't hold your breath. I'm not sure where I put my suit after the funeral. But to answer your question, I called directory assistance. I wasn't positive you'd have a listing yet, but I should have known you'd be on top of that detail."

Sam settled in the chair behind her desk. "What's up?"

"How do you know something's going on?"

"With all the crazy stuff that's happened, I thought—"

"Maybe I just wanted to hear your voice before Saturday." His tone was intimately serious. Heat crept up Sam's neck, and she squirmed in her chair. Getting together for a cookout might be a bad idea if Ryan thought there could be something going on between them.

"No worries, Miss Skittish," Ryan went on. "You know I'm big on keeping things casual. Happens I am calling for a purpose. But first, any more suspicious activity at your end?"

"Not so much as a bump in the night. I'm on the fast track toward Grand Opening."

"That's great. You should be relieved to know that I finished going through the storage garage."

"Wow! Weren't you nervous someone would try to stop you?"

"I brought my dog along. He wouldn't bite a postman and couldn't hear a Mack truck, but he'd bark if he smelled anyone sneaking around. And I do happen to know how to use the shotgun I kept within arm's reach, but Old Jakester snoozed the whole time."

Sam humphed. "Pitiful that a person has to go around armed to take care of their personal business. But that's a big job done, and you did it all by yourself."

"You got it. Me, myself and I. In my grandiose dreams I thought I could finish in one marathon night. However, it's taken me the last three evenings and almost no shut-eye, but I know exactly what's missing."

Sam sat forward and put her elbows on the desk. "Ooh! Tell me."

"The box of items from my dad's desk. Not a trace of it. I'm not clear on exactly what was in there. I swept everything into a container and taped it up. But the fact that the whole thing is gone indicates pretty clearly that someone was after something that was in my father's possession, but I don't think they've found it yet."

"With all the weird happenings, I suspect you're right." Sam rose and paced to her filing cabinet and back. "Office stuff, huh? Did your father have a computer? Is that missing, too?"

"Nope. I kept that and used it for a while after downloading everything business-related and making sure his clients got what pertained to them. Then the machine got obsolete, and I junked it for a newer model. If anybody had wanted something from that computer, they never made an effort to get it."

"Strange." She stopped pacing and leaned a shoulder against the doorjamb.

"This whole mess is beyond bizarre, but how do you mean that?"

"These days most folks hide confidential things on their computers."

Ryan snorted. "That would not have been my dad's modus operandi. This was tén years ago, and he was in his upper forties then. Computers were necessary evils to him. He knew how to operate one to conduct his business, but still used pen and paper whenever possible."

"Have you called Detective Connell about your missing box?"

"Done. In fact, I had a bunch more to tell him that I found out from visiting with a few people in my old neighborhood. It's too much to go into on the phone, but I thought you might like to know this tidbit since you helped with the project."

"Thanks. I did want to know, and you've got me curious for more."

Ryan's chuckle warmed her ear. "See you on Saturday then."

"I'm salivating for that steak. Medium rare."

"Yes, ma'am. You just made my job easy. That's the way I like mine, too."

They hung up, laughing. Sam sobered, staring at the phone. Had Davidson meant the remark as a sign of compatibility? Uh-oh! He might claim he wanted to keep things casual, but did he mean it? And what about Larry and his family? Ryan said he was inviting them. Were they still coming, or was the evening going to be just the two of them?

She should call back and make some excuse. Her hand closed around the receiver, then she released it as if scalded. Ryan would see through her in a heartbeat and make some remark that would disarm her defenses. No, when she called to bow out of their nondate that kept sounding like a date, she needed a real reason, and she knew exactly the creative pair of friends to help her come up with one.

Sorry, Ryan. She headed back to her painting project. *I can't let galloping attraction derail the work of God in your life or get me sucked into a relationship that's not right for me. Besides, I've got a business to get up and running. There's a ton at stake for both of us.*

Several hours later, bespeckled with dried paint, Sam leaned back in her office chair on the phone with Jenna. "It would be so much easier to keep my distance if I didn't like Ryan on so many different levels. When I'm away from him, I can think sensibly, but when I'm talking to him, I feel like I've known him since diapers, and he makes me laugh. Sometimes we say out loud exactly what the other one is thinking. It's almost spooky! And he's protective without stifling my independence. You know how much that means to me."

Jenna laughed. "I don't suppose it helps any that he's cuter than a bug's ear, like my grandma would say."

Sam snickered. "My grandmother used that saying too. I never could figure out what would be so good-looking about a bug's ear…if a person could see one. But I will admit that if a bug's ear resembled Ryan it would be pretty cute."

She and Jenna shared a chuckle.

"Seriously, though," Sam resumed, "I've got to keep my head on straight, and I need your help. Think up some personal crisis that requires me coming to your rescue so I can get out of going to his place on Saturday. A hangnail, anything!"

Jenna clicked her tongue. "Sorry, girlfriend. I'm at a culinary trade show this weekend in Atlanta."

"Can you stick me in your luggage?"

"I'd love to, but I think you'd better just deal with this issue head-on."

"You mean, tell him I cannot—will not see him anymore?"

"If you think that's what the Lord is leading you to do."

"You sound skeptical." Sam put her tired feet up on the desktop. "Do you honestly think I should encourage a relationship with a guy who's not walking with God? At least not yet, anyway."

"You think he's headed that direction?"

"I'm convinced he's on a collision course with a pivotal

decision, and I don't think the Almighty's going to take no for an answer."

Silence echoed over the line for several breaths. "I can't say I'm crazy about the physical danger that could be a part of your association with Ryan, though the recent quiet could indicate that maybe, just maybe, that road incident was unrelated to the murder case, as the police have implied."

Sam let out a loud, long raspberry.

"Okay, you don't buy that," Jenna went on. "I have my doubts, too, but let's take a peek at this hot/cold thing you've got going in your head about him. Now please understand that I don't recommend you fall for a guy who's not on the same page with you spiritually, but there's a question that begs to be asked. Have you ever considered that your contact with him is not a hindrance, but a vital part of what's drawing him toward renewing his faith?"

Sam plunked her feet to the floor and groaned. "If I accept what you're saying, then I have to keep risking *my* heart."

"The job bites, doesn't it?"

"Thanks for noticing, Jenna."

"That's what friends are for." She laughed. "But if you're supposed to hold the communication lines open with Ryan, then you can rest assured that the Lord's plan will be good for you, too. There's nothing wrong with friendship, if that's all it can ever be."

"I'm going to call Hallie and see if she'll go with me to his place."

"Now you're thinking constructively."

They ended the conversation, and Sam immediately punched in Hallie's number. Ten minutes later, she hung up the phone and slumped in her chair. She'd forgotten that Hallie was scheduled to cover a special event at Valley Fair on Saturday night, and then she was headed out bright and early the next day for a Berglund family reunion in Branson, Missouri.

"Now what am I going to do?" Sam asked out loud.

A meow answered her. She looked down to find Bastian

perched at her feet, staring up at her. A slow smile crept over her face. "You'll go with me, right? Keeping you and Old Jake away from each other should be sufficient distraction for both Ryan and I. If you can't handle a deaf, arthritic dog, I'll demand you turn in your feline license." She scratched the cat between its ears. "And if Larry and his family happen to make it to the party, so much the better."

She rose and headed for her apartment, Bastian at her heels. Sound decisions ought to make a person feel at peace. Then how come her insides were jumping around like popcorn? If only she could tell whether the unsettled feeling was dread or anticipation.

The next afternoon, loud rapping at the front door carried to Sam's ears over the contemporary Christian music playing on the radio. "What now?" She balanced her trimming brush on the edge of a paint can and wiped her hands on a rag. Stepping into the front room, she spotted Detective Connell peering in at her, a sack in his hands. She hurried forward and opened the door.

The detective stepped inside with a nod in her direction. "I'm returning the things that came from the box where you found the film. Nothing unusual came up with any of it." He handed her the sack. "Usually we call people to come get the items, but I was driving past."

"Thanks, that was good of you. As you can see," she gestured to her paint-spattered clothing, "I'm a little busy. Any results on the vase and the blood?"

Connell scratched behind an ear. "That's another reason I came by. We're at an impasse."

"And that means?" Sam clutched the sack to her chest.

"Among some inconclusive smudges, no clear fingerprint, but yours was found."

"Fingerprint? Singular?"

A teensy smile turned the edges of Connell's lips upward. "Your intelligence makes it difficult to dismiss your claim of a break-in, but if I may speak frankly, your history may make you more susceptible to exaggerated fears in that regard."

Sam took a step backward. "What do you know about my past?"

"The information isn't that hard to come by for a police officer. A phone call to the department in Eau Claire, Wisconsin, answered a lot of questions."

"All right. So you know about the attack. That still doesn't answer why only one fingerprint was found on all those objects."

"The only clear print was on the vase." Sam opened her mouth, but the detective held up a hand. "The smudges could also belong to you and no one else."

Sam lifted her chin. "Follow me." She led him into her office and flung open the closet door. In terse sentences, she explained about her discovery of the vent. "Even if, as you imply, I accidentally left the workroom window open so my cat could get out, and I hallucinated the broken vase from a hysterical preoccupation with intruders, there is no way Bastian climbed seven feet up a brick wall to get into the ductwork and end up in my closet. And how do you explain the blood on his chin?" She plunked the sack of keys and other items onto her desk and faced the detective, arms crossed.

Connell returned her stare with a bland face. "I don't know how your cat reached the vent, but the blood was not human."

"Not?"

"It came from a bird."

Sam gaped.

"A pigeon, to be exact," the detective continued. "Cats do catch birds, don't they?"

She snapped her jaw closed. "Not cats without claws."

Connell shrugged. "Perhaps he came across a fresh carcass. Birds get run over from time to time." He headed for the outside door.

Sam glared after him, stomach churning, nails digging into her palms. Was the detective's insinuation true? Had the stress of moving away from home, starting a new business, and discovering grizzly murder photos shoved her over the deep end into paranoid delusions?

SEVENTEEN

Ryan flipped the steaks in the marinade pan that sat on the counter of the galley in his houseboat. Then he opened the refrigerator door and checked to see that he hadn't imagined putting the seven-layer salad together or buying the Boston cream pie from the grocery deli. Everything was there...just like the last time he looked.

Man, he was wired tighter than an electric guitar. Why did he want so badly to impress this woman? Because he liked her way too much, that's why. He smacked the fridge door shut.

Get a grip, Davidson. Just because Samantha Reid was exactly the kind of girl his mother would have loved to see him bring home didn't mean he had to fall for her. In fact, he'd better not, for her sake as much as his. Then why had he invited her here tonight? Gratitude? He snorted aloud. At least he could pretend that was the reason—to everyone, including himself.

Ryan climbed the stairs onto the deck and took a look at the coals in the grill. They were just beginning to turn white around the edges. Not yet time to tuck the foil-wrapped potatoes into them. Gas grilling was okay if a guy was in a hurry, but charcoal gave a much better flavor.

He glanced at his watch. Sam could be here any minute. He stepped off the boat and strode up the dock, boards echoing a hollow tattoo beneath his feet. Old Jake barked from the water's edge, and a flock of gulls squawked and flapped into the air. Ryan reached the bank, laughing. The dog trotted over to him, tail wagging, and teeth bared in a doggy grin.

Ryan scratched the old boy behind the ears. "We picked a good night for a cookout, didn't we?" The frequent Minnesota wind had given it a rest today, and the temperature hovered in the low eighties under a sunlit sky dotted with wispy white clouds. Even the humidity had dropped off, leaving the air fresh, but not close. He inhaled and savored the tang of pine.

The hum of a motor brought his head up. The dog stiffened and faced the road. "Here she comes, boy. Ready or not, eh?"

Sam's Malibu wheeled into the driveway then stopped in a parking slot next to the office. She stepped out dressed in a T-shirt, jean shorts and sandals, her glossy hair up in its usual ponytail. Glancing his way, she smiled and waved. Ryan's pulse did a little dance. She opened the back door of her car and leaned inside. He strode toward her, battling to keep a Lake Superior–size grin down to no more than Lake Minnetonka-sized, but not having much success.

What was the matter with him? Sam was cute and smart and funny, but so were lots of other girls he'd dated. Yeah, but none of those others saw into him like he was a window without shades. And none walked hand in glove with the Almighty, either. His step slowed. Maybe if he kept reminding himself of that daunting fact it wouldn't be sheer torture to steer his boats south in the fall. Of course, if he didn't solve the mystery of his family's deaths, he wouldn't be going anywhere. Not even on his annual solo trek into the Boundary Waters wilderness area this fall. Usually he— *Oh, no! She didn't!*

Sam turned, face flushed, cradling her cat in her arms.

Haroo! Behind him, Old Jake's howl sounded much like the bay of a bloodhound and prickled the hairs on the back of Ryan's neck. The cat yowled and squirmed. Sam struggled to hang on to her pet but lost the battle. Bastian hit the ground on all fours and streaked toward Ryan. Was the animal so crazy for him that the dog didn't deter it? Jake lunged ahead, and Ryan grabbed for his collar and missed. The animals met on the lawn between Ryan and Sam. They both rushed toward the scene of what could soon become carnage. Then Ryan put on the brakes, and so did Sam. They gaped at the animals, then at each other and burst into laughter.

"What's up with this?" Sam planted her hands on her hips.

"Goofiest thing I've ever seen." Ryan scratched his head.

The cat and the dog stood nose to nose, sniffing at one another. Jake's tail wagged fit to pop right off its rump, and Bastian purred like a motorboat. The cat stopped sniffing and twined around Jake's front legs, rubbing and arching its back. The dog swiped his new friend's head with its tongue.

"They like each other." Ryan laughed.

"Instant BFFs." Sam giggled.

"Maybe we should get them matching collar tags—Best Friends Forever."

"How about BFFF—Best Furry Friends Forever?"

Their gazes met then darted away. The pets ambled off, side by side, toward the porch of the building.

"Hey, you two." Larry's voice came from behind Sam. "We're here with our appetites." Vehicle doors slammed.

Ryan shook himself and waved at the threesome walking toward them. He'd been so out of it he hadn't heard them drive up. The trio stopped a few feet away. Larry needed to stow that smirk in a hurry. Ryan shot him a scowl. Lar just grinned bigger.

Ryan turned toward Sam. "You've met Larry, but the linebacker beside him is his son, Derek, and the gorgeous female riding herd on both of them is Larry's wife, Nancy."

Nancy gave a mellow laugh and clasped one of Sam's hands between both of hers. "Larry's told me about you. I'm tickled pink to meet any woman who makes Ryan Davidson blush at the mention of her name."

Sam stared toward him, eyes wide, while heat crept up Ryan's cheeks. "One thing you'll learn about Larry's family—they all have an outrageous sense of humor."

She quavered a smile and returned her attention to Nancy. "I can't tell you how relieved—er, glad I am that you were able to join us."

"Let's go see what we can accomplish in the galley." Nancy hustled toward the boat, Sam in her wake.

Ryan stared after them. Relieved?

Sam settled back in the chaise lounge chair on the afterdeck of Ryan's houseboat and patted her full stomach. That was some dinner her host put on. Ryan and her dad could get some heavy rivalry going in the grilling department.

Her misgivings about this evening had been all wrong. Great food and great company—who could ask for more?

Charming woman, that Nancy, and quite pretty with a rich crown of close-cut chestnut hair, barely touched with silver, and a sprinkle of light freckles across her pixie face. Larry looked like a lumberjack compared to her, but he was a card and a half.

Sam's tummy muscles ached from all the laughter—and the inch-thick steaks, too. Derek took after his father in appearance and seemed a good-natured kid, soft-spoken and witty in an understated way. But Chef Ryan had been downright subdued. Even while they sat around a table inside a screened-in portion of the foredeck, gobbling Ryan's delicious food and joking, he'd laughed at the right times but said little. After the meal, she'd been shooed away from the galley by Nancy and Derek, who took over the cleanup.

Now, comfortably enthroned in the chair, Sam watched Ryan stow the last of the grilling gear in a small chest. He glanced at her, and she tried a smile on him. His mouth curved upward then he turned and disappeared down the hatch that led into the living quarters.

This was an amazing boat. Larry, who'd conducted the tour while Ryan cooked, said the *River King* was a top-of-the-line custom-designed floating house. The main deck circled the central living quarters, which were accessed from the foredeck and the afterdeck via a short set of stairs that left the top half of each room with a view of the outside through large windows. The interior contained a complete kitchen—er, galley, a spacious living/dining room, a pair of bedrooms and a bathroom a lot of nice hotels would envy. Above the living quarters was a canopied top deck with an enclosed wheelhouse for the driver overlooking the foredeck.

"So what do you think of the *River King?*" Nancy settled on a chaise next to Sam.

"You read my mind. I was just thinking about how impressive it is. I'm surprised at the amount of space in such a compact package. It's almost as roomy as my apartment. I can see why people would enjoy renting one these things for a weekend or a week."

"But you wouldn't want to live in one?"

Sam blinked at the petite woman. "I'd never thought about it."

"Ah. Well, this one is a cut above the rentals anyway. The helm on one of those is on the main level cutting back some of the living space." She gazed out over the water. "We'll cast off soon and cruise down toward lock and dam number three, then turn around and come back. By that time the full moon should be out. It'll be a gorgeous night."

A soft meow sounded near Sam's feet. Bastian hopped up on the lounge chair and proceeded to march up Sam's body and settle on her chest. Jake sidled between the lounge chairs and rested his muzzle on Sam's arm, big eyes fixed on the cat.

Nancy chuckled. "You're almost as popular with the critters as Ryan is."

Sam shook her head. "I'm Bastian's humble servant. He deigns to allow me to feed and house him and maybe pet him once in a while. It's each other these animals are crazy for." Purring, Bastian stretched out a paw and patted Jake's nose. The dog heaved a sigh. "See what I mean?"

Ryan's laugh joined theirs. Sam looked up to find him watching them from the upper deck next to the wheelhouse.

He leaned his elbows on the railing. "You know what? I don't think it was me Bastian took to—I think he smelled Jake on my clothes."

"Have you ever heard of a cat and a dog making instant friends?"

"Sure, but it's not the usual thing."

"I'll say not. I wonder if Bastian will let me take him home."

Ryan grinned. "We'll cross that bridge when we come to it. Time to head out. The best view will be on the foredeck." He saluted and withdrew into the wheelhouse.

"I guess we've been told." Nancy rose and stretched.

Sam set Bastian on the deck and got up. She followed the woman toward the front of the boat. Glancing back, she shook her head. The cat and the dog had taken over the lounge she'd vacated. Jake lay stretched across the cushion on his side with Bastian curled between his legs.

She went on and found Nancy standing by the front rail. A motor rumbled to a start below while Larry and Derek charged around tossing information back and forth about lines cast off. A minute later, the boat eased away from the dock and entered the current.

Sam looked down into the dark water parting before their craft. The wake whooshed away from the blunt nose of the houseboat, and a not-unpleasant briny smell wafted on the breeze. Her gaze was drawn to the wooded bluffs above the banks sliding past.

"Look." Nancy nudged her side.

Sam gazed in the direction the woman pointed. A trio of brown ducks paddled and flapped along the water's edge.

For the next hour she moved around the boat, chatting with

members of Larry's family and enjoying the sights, but a void took up an ever-larger residence in the pit of her stomach. Where was Ryan? She glanced toward the wheelhouse. Well, technically she knew where he was, but why didn't he get Larry or Derek to spell him so he could come down and join the fun?

She leaned against the rail on the port side and frowned into the gathering darkness. Why wasn't she happy they were keeping their distance? Wasn't that what she wanted? Not really. She'd be comfortable with friendship, all right, but that wasn't going to work when every time she looked into his eyes, she wished he would wrap his arms around her. Still, they were caught up together in a situation that needed to find resolution. Hadn't he said there was more to tell about his interviews with neighbors this week?

Maybe she should break down and visit the captain at his station. She could just pop in there, and if he wanted to talk he would. If not, she'd find an excuse to return to the deck.

Sam turned and—*oof!* She bounced off a solid chest.

"Sorry about that." Ryan chuckled.

Sam gazed up into his dusk-shaded face. "That's the second time you've done that to me. You move quieter than Bastian."

"I didn't mean to sneak up on you, but you looked lost in thought, and I didn't want to interrupt."

"Derek or Larry took over for you at the wheel?"

"Nope. Nancy. But she brought her enforcers with her. The guys threatened to toss me overboard if I didn't get down here and take advantage of the full moon." He gestured toward the golden orb hovering above the midnight-blue horizon. "In case you haven't noticed, my crew members are up to their meddling necks in a matchmaking conspiracy."

Sam laughed. "They're not too subtle, no. My friends were playing the same game until they got nervous about somebody making targets of us. Or you, anyway, and me getting too close to the action."

"Yeah, I'm probably an idiot for asking you out here. It was an impulse, but I didn't want to take it back."

She prodded him in the ribs with her fingers. "It was my choice to accept the invitation." No reason to tell him she'd wanted out, or why, when her biggest misgivings had little to do with physical danger.

The boat began a sharp turn, and Sam staggered. Ryan caught her and held her steady. His warm arm around her felt even better than she'd feared. With her nose in his shoulder, his leathery, slightly spicy, cologne pleased her nostrils.

"Knock it off, you jokers!" Ryan hollered toward the upper deck. "Sam and I don't need all this help."

Chuckles answered from somewhere in the dimness above, but the angle and speed of the turn eased off. Ryan released Sam, and she stepped away from him, struggling to calm her pulse. She was in deep trouble and loving every second of it.

"Let's go forward." Ryan offered his arm.

"Hey, you two." Larry's voice carried to them. "Don't worry about the animals. They're fine in the wheelhouse with Nancy."

"Busybodies," Ryan muttered under his breath.

With a giggle, Sam twined her hand around his elbow and walked beside him to the bow. The running lights on the ends of the rail made halos on the water, and an owl hooted nearby.

"This is fun and relaxing. I'm glad I took the chance and came, but I suppose we can't avoid unpleasant topics forever. I had a visit from Detective Connell." She faced Ryan, who gazed into her eyes, brows drawn together. She told him about the inconclusive fingerprints and the detective's noncommittal reaction to the mystery of how her cat ended up in the closet.

Ryan frowned. "I don't get this guy. At first, I thought he was pretty on top of things, but now he seems determined to ignore every anomaly."

"I know what you mean, but there are a couple of factors that contributed to his nonchalance. First off, he checked my background and found out why I have a phobia about intruders. Secondly, he got the lab results from the blood on Bastian's chin. It was pigeon."

"Pigeons! Of course! That's what they were." Ryan paced across the foredeck.

"What are you talking about? You look like you're about to jump out of your skin."

He closed the distance between them, shoulders rigid. "My dad mentioned pigeons in that phone conversation the night he was killed. I had no idea what he meant. Then I saw something when I visited on Monday with Martha Stahl—"

"The woman from church?"

"That's her. They have cages full of birds in their backyard. I was too far away to see what kind they were, but they were big and gray."

"Like pigeons. What in the world would pigeons have to do with your family's deaths?"

"I haven't a clue. Not yet. But I do remember my father wise-cracking sometimes about this group of guys around the city who were into training and flying carrier pigeons." He gripped the rail of the boat. "I have to find out who was in that club. Eldon Stahl knows. I think he knows a lot. He and Martha were in the Bahamas when my family was killed, but that doesn't mean he couldn't have hired it done."

"Not Eldon and Martha!" He could have slapped her and not surprised her more. "Sure, they're a little different, but why—"

"I know. I know." Ryan lifted his hands. "Until I have a motive, I'm just shooting my mouth off. This is good progress, though." He gusted a long breath. "So what about you then? Isn't it about time you told me—"

"Ouch!" Sam smacked at her forearm. "My mosquito repellent must be wearing off."

"Come on. We can sit at the table inside the screen room and frustrate those bloodsucking Minnesota state birds."

Sam laughed and let him usher her to the back of the boat and into the screened-in area. A small light from inside the living quarters shed a faint glow around the area. "Maybe Larry's family wants to join us." She took a seat.

"Nah. They're probably hanging out in the wheelhouse. I doubt we'll catch a glimpse of them, what with their nefarious objectives."

Grinning, Sam shook her head.

Ryan's gaze turned sober. "I'm going to be honest here. If it weren't for my absolute commitment to see justice done for my family, you'd be the first woman in the last decade to tempt me to get acquainted beyond a few laughs and then *sayonara.*"

Sam's throat thickened. "To tell you the truth, you've thrown me off balance, too. I almost chickened out of tonight. I have to confess I brought Bastian because I thought trying to keep the animals apart would distract us from each other. A relationship isn't in my calculations while I'm so caught up trying to start my business and—" She stopped and swallowed.

"And?"

She looked him straight in the eye. "Honesty, right?"

Ryan nodded.

"Any man I look at seriously needs to share my faith."

"Oh."

He was taking this pretty coolly. Why? "All you have to say is *oh?*"

Ryan ran a fingertip across a seam on the clear plastic tabletop. "I'd already figured that out. My mom preached the same message to me before I went off to college. 'Don't get hooked up with someone who doesn't believe like you, or you're asking for heartache.' She meant well, but she didn't realize I was already having my doubts."

"At least you're not offended that I spoke my mind."

He sat back so his face was hidden in the darkness. "Do you trust me enough to let me in on whatever happened to you and how your faith survived?"

EIGHTEEN

Sam's heart rate quickened. He was asking for a story she hadn't told anyone in years. Even with her parents, she rarely revisited the specifics. Yet, she'd known this moment would come with Ryan. Could she get it out in a way that might make an eternal difference to this man?

She drew in a quavery breath. "I was seventeen years old, barely into my senior year in high school. My mom and I have always been close. We like to do hobbies together. One of them used to be candle making."

"Used to be?"

Sam held up a hand. "Don't interrupt. This is going to be tough enough."

"I'm all ears and no mouth. Go ahead."

She wiped sweat from her forehead that had little to do with the warm summer night. "One fall evening my mom and I were home by ourselves melting wax in the kitchen when the back door crashed open. I whirled toward the sound, and my mom whirled, too, with the pot of hot wax in her hand. The whole thing splashed across my back. I remember searing pain and screaming fit to burst my throat.

"This big, grungy guy with whacked-out eyes rushed toward us. He had a knife in one hand and a stick in the other. That stick whipping toward my head is the last thing I knew until I woke up with the paramedics loading me into the ambulance."

A deep groan answered her from across the table. Sam closed her eyes and sat back in her chair, hands squeezed together in her lap.

"The intruder was high on meth and needed money for his next fix. He demanded my mom give him her purse, and when she tried to help me instead, he cut her on the arm and the face. She healed quickly, but she still bears the scars…on the inside, as well as the outside. Finally, he got the purse, then grabbed a DVD player and disappeared into the night.

"The entire horrible thing took only minutes, but I spent ten months going from one skin-graft surgery to the next, and battling infection in between. Somewhere in there, we moved out of the house I grew up in. We couldn't stand to live there anymore. And I didn't get to graduate with my class. It took me until the winter of the following year to earn enough credits for my diploma."

Sam opened her eyes and found Ryan leaning toward her, gaze fixed on her face.

"I can only imagine the courage it took for you to recover."

"Courage? Not hardly." A stiff laugh escaped her lips. "If it had been up to me, I would've given up and died from one of those infections. Pure grace carried me. I lived in the Psalms during most of that period. There was something in that book of the Bible for every mood and trial I experienced. Want to know the verse that got me through the darkest times?"

Ryan's nod was barely perceptible.

"Psalm 27:13. 'I am still confident of this; I will see the goodness of the Lord in the land of the living.'" Sam moved toward him until their faces were mere inches apart. "I have seen that goodness. I see it every day, and it trumps the meanness of people every time."

Ryan eased away from her into the dim perimeter around the table. "Did they catch the guy?"

She shook her head and settled back into her chair. "They tried. One police lieutenant was particularly diligent about the case. He had a daughter around my age. My mom and I would get called in now and then to ID a potential suspect. Or mostly my mom did. I wasn't up and around much during that time."

She shrugged. "Maybe seeing the man brought to justice might have given me some sort of closure, but I figure it this way. It's almost impossible for anyone so enslaved by a chemical to get free without divine help. And unless he takes that help, he lives in his own hell that will eventually kill him…and then hell really begins. What do I need with retribution?"

Ryan's chair legs scraped against the planks as he stood. "You think I should give up my hunt for a killer?"

Sam placed her elbows on the chair arms and studied her fingers steepled in front of her. Did she? "No. Not really. I admire your commitment."

"I hear the *but* in your voice."

"Doing it on your own isn't going to give you the satisfaction you expect."

"So I should leave it to the police?"

"You should leave it to God." She gazed up into Ryan's drawn face. "Let Him guide your steps. Have you ever stopped to realize that He knows who arranged what happened to your family?"

With something like a growl, Ryan turned his back to her. "Then why hasn't He done anything about it?"

Sam barely heard the words. Good question. An indifferent God, that's what Ryan must see. *Lord, please give me wisdom here.* "Certain divine laws are in place in this universe. They work every time, but not always in our *timing.* Of course, in this case, you'll notice the shooter was dead minutes after the crime, probably victim to whoever hired him. Evil devours evil—one of those divine laws. At the moment, it appears like whoever ordered the deed has gotten away with murder. That's a lie. He never will."

She rose and touched Ryan's shoulder and found the muscles tense and hard beneath her fingertips. "I have the strongest impression that the answers you want are on the way, but if your heart isn't right when they come, you will lose way more than you gain."

He whirled away from her touch and plopped into his chair, staring into the darkness. "What more could I lose?"

"Your future. The life your family would have wanted you to have."

A muscle flexed in his jaw. "What about *their* lives? Oh, sure, if my mom and sis were right about what they believed, they're okay. Better than okay. But my dad—" He exhaled with the sound of a teakettle under pressure.

"So that's what's got you hung up." Sam slipped into a chair beside him and held out her hand. He gripped it. "You're not sure where your father is, and you can't stand the thought of accepting the mercy of God that he may have missed."

"I loved him."

The tortured words raked through Sam's insides. "I know." Her statement came out as hoarse as his.

Ryan bowed his head, and a drop of wetness *plink*ed to the tabletop.

"That woman did it again," Ryan grumbled under his breath, and threw himself over onto his other side in bed. She dragged his guts out for the world to see—well, just her and him, but sitting there letting his emotions leak out felt like running naked through the streets.

He sat up and propped his elbows on his knees, pressing the sides of his head with his palms. Since he was just a kid, had he told his dad that he loved him? How could he, when he hadn't thought about his father in those terms beyond early grade school? Had his dad ever said those words to him? Not that he remembered. How pitiful was that for both of them?

Ryan looked at the bedside clock. One in the morning and he hadn't slept a wink. He crawled out of bed. Without turning on a light, he padded in his bare feet and pajama bottoms to the kitchen. He filled a glass with cold water from the fridge door, then settled onto a stool at the peninsula counter. Moonlight spread shadows around the living/dining room. A dark lump on the carpet moved and whuffled in its sleep.

Was Old Jake dreaming of Bastian? It was a good thing the cat was completely sacked out when Sam brought his carrier up to the wheelhouse and put him in it. He'd woken up then and yowled all the way to the car with Jake barking up a storm from the boat where Ryan held him by his collar. The old dog had given him the most disgusted look when Sam drove off, and then he spent the rest of the evening moping around—much like his master.

What was that last thing Sam whispered in his ear before she walked off into the night? *God's not like your dad. You don't have to win His approval to have His love.*

Ryan let a sip of cool water glide down his throat. Did that mean God loved him right now in all his anger and confusion? Had He loved him when he doubted anything to do with faith in his high school and college years?

Did God love him the night his family died?

"That's a tough one to get my head around, Lord." Ryan shook his head. Now he was talking out loud to Someone he didn't know if he believed in. No, that was wasn't quite right. He might as well admit he believed God existed. Ryan just wasn't sure He could be trusted.

From up the hall, a tune started playing. Leaving his glass, Ryan went back to his bedroom, picked up his cell phone from the nightstand, and checked the caller ID window. An international call? Who did he know that was out of the country? Ryan flipped open the phone and settled onto the edge of his bed.

"Davidson here."

"If you had the sense of a gnat, you'd be long gone from Minnesota."

Ryan's heart thumped. "Who is this?"

"You know."

"Eldon Stahl? I thought you were at a convention in Los Angeles."

"Apparently, I'm smarter than an insect. You have no idea who you're threatening."

"And you do." Ryan made it a statement rather than a question.

"I have…suspicions. Nothing I can go to the authorities with even if I wanted to."

Ryan lunged to his feet, stranglehold on the phone. "You were in on it!"

"Never!" The word blared in his ear. "But I've got to protect…" The man didn't finish his sentence.

"Protect what? Who?"

No answer.

"Tell me who killed my family."

Deep sigh. "Just get out of there. Go into hiding and stay gone. I won't call again."

"Don't hang up! Who's in the carrier pigeon club?"

Click.

"Hello? Hello? Argh!" Ryan punched his mattress. Then he froze, eyes narrowed, nostrils flared.

So he hadn't imagined the danger he was in, like the police hinted. Someone was out there, stalking, biding his time for the kill.

"Okay, God. Sam told me to let You guide my steps. I'm open to ideas right now on how I can keep from being killed and nab a killer at the same time."

Slowly, a picture unfolded in Ryan's mind of himself standing on the bank of a Boundary Waters river, fly-fishing. He cast the bait out and reeled it in, something struck, and his rod bent nearly double. He'd hooked a monster!

Ryan shook himself. What a foolish fantasy when he was trying to figure out how to catch a— Wait a minute!

He rose, went to his closet and dug out his trekking backpack. When a guy needed to hook a monster, he should choose his spot to best advantage and use the perfect bait. Ryan knew just the place—the wilderness; and the irresistible morsel—himself.

NINETEEN

Roll up. Roll down. Up. Down. Dip the roller in the paint another time. These walls were endless! At least, she'd had no distractions this afternoon after church, and the clock was already edging up on 4:00 p.m.

Bastian was still pouting from being taken away from Jake and hadn't tried to jump on her cart, play with the brushes, or pounce on the roller while she was attempting to get more paint on the wall than on herself or her cat. Those two animals made quite the unique pair. Sam smiled and hummed along with the worship CD on the player.

How was Jake doing today? For that matter, how was Ryan? When she left last night, he'd looked pretty shell-shocked. Not her doing—well, maybe a little, but mostly God's in a good way. Evidently, Ryan wasn't quite ready to come back to church, but hopefully he would deal with his baggage and get on a healthy track with his life, whether that included her or not.

A sudden pinch in Sam's chest halted her roller. Yeah, right. Who was she kidding that she didn't care if that man chucked her out of his life?

Frowning, she plied her roller with fresh vigor. She should call him in a while and see how his day had been. Besides, it was only polite to thank him for the lovely evening on his houseboat. Uh-huh, and she was the Queen of Polite. A rueful smile stretched

Sam's lips. Funny how people made up excuses to do whatever they wanted to do. Oh, well, she'd call him anyway.

The phone in her office rang. Maybe that was Ryan now. She put down her roller and hurried to answer. Wouldn't it be nice if he missed her enough to be the one to call first?

She picked up the receiver on the third ring. "Hello."

"Hi, sweetie. You sound a bit breathless. What are you up to today?"

"Hello, Mom."

Her mother laughed. "That was enthusiastic. Did I call at a bad time?"

"Not at all." She leaned her back against the filing cabinet and crossed one ankle over the other. "I'm painting. I should finish by tomorrow, just in time for the flooring and the hazmat people to trip over each other on Tuesday and my equipment to arrive on Thursday."

"Oh, my! You're accomplishing a lot in a hurry. Are you sure you're not overdoing it?"

"I feel great, Mom."

"And no more strange happenings around there?"

"Other than a break-in, a missing cat and a freeway accident?"

Her mother gasped then sighed. "You! That wasn't funny."

No, it really wasn't. Her folks knew about the photos and the police search of her premises, but she ought to confess that she hadn't been kidding by her last remark. Only she'd rather be boiled in oil than cause her mother a moment's unnecessary anxiety. No unexplainable or dangerous things had happened in a while. Chances were any danger had blown right past her. She wasn't that sure about Ryan, though, with all the poking around he kept doing. Another reason to call him soon.

"Are you still there, honey?"

"Huh?" Sam shook herself and wandered over to her office chair. "Many apologies, favorite Mom of mine." She settled into the seat. "I'm a tad distracted, as you can tell. So what have you and Dad been up to?" She listened with half an ear to a description of the craft fair her parents attended yesterday.

She chatted with her mother a few minutes more, ended the call, and then punched in Ryan's business number. He'd given her his cell number, but she'd see if he was in the office first.

"Davidson Houseboats. How may I help you?"

"Hi, Larry. Is Ryan handy?"

"Nope. Sorry. He's gone for a week. Didn't he tell you?"

"Tell me what?" Sam tucked a strand of hair behind her ear.

"Hmmm. I assumed you and he had a deep discussion last night, and that was why he suddenly hared off to the Boundary Waters about six weeks earlier than usual and with no notice."

Her jaw dropped, but she quickly snapped it shut. "You mean up north on the border between Canada and the U.S.? Why would he go there?"

"Every fall, he takes off canoeing alone in the wilderness. Says it clears his head after a summer of nonstop people-pleasing."

"He goes alone? What if he has trouble or someone needs to contact him?"

"Ryan knows that area better than a lot of the park rangers, but he did take Jake with him this year." The sound of papers rustling came over the line. "Yep, here it is. Around noon today he faxed me his canoe route. He had to wait and see which entry portal to the Superior National Forest had an open slot for a single. They're pretty strict about how many people they let into the park at a time. Groups have to reserve months in advance to have a hope of getting in."

"Does he usually leave you his route?" Sam reached out and repositioned the vase Ryan had given her. The calla lilies were long gone, but she'd replenished it with a summery bouquet of daisies.

"You betcha. That way, if he doesn't come out of there as scheduled, we can send in the cavalry." Larry chuckled. "But don't worry. Ryan knows how to handle himself. If it'll make you feel better, I can give you the route. Got pen and paper?"

"No, uh, that won't be necessary. The directions wouldn't mean anything to me anyway."

"All right, but I figured maybe he had you in mind when he left this odd instruction."

"Odd?" She straightened.

"Yeah, when he called early this morning to let me know he was leaving, he told me whenever he got his route settled to go ahead and share it with anyone who asks."

"What *is* that man up to?"

"Beats me."

"Oh, sorry. I was talking out loud to myself."

Larry laughed again. "Just don't answer yourself, and you're okay."

Sam ended the call with thanks to Larry and his family for the nice time last night. She went back to her office and cradled the receiver, brow furrowed. No wonder Ryan hadn't been in church this morning. He'd fled the area. No, maybe she was looking at his actions all wrong. Hadn't Jesus been driven into the wilderness by the Holy Spirit for a time of fasting and prayer? Maybe he was doing some heavy soul-searching.

But why hadn't he at least phoned her and let her know he was leaving? That hurt a little. No, it hurt a lot, and it shouldn't. He didn't owe her anything. If he was out there getting right with God, she shouldn't complain. Still, an explanation would have been nice.

Oh, quit whining, girl, and get back to work.

A stupid, annoying knot hung around in the pit of Sam's belly as she returned to painting. Two more hours passed before she cleaned her paint gear and put it away. In the center of the large, empty work area, she stretched her arms over her head, worked a few kinks out of her back, and then did a 360-degree turn in place, admiring her handiwork. Another day should do it.

She went up to her apartment and fixed herself a tuna sandwich on whole wheat with lettuce and tomatoes. Bastian came out of hiding long enough to snap up a fresh dish of cat food, but he wouldn't tolerate petting, not even a scratch behind his ears. Sam shrugged. His loss.

Her door buzzer sounded as she licked the last of the mayo-laced tuna from her fingers. She rinsed her fingers over the sink, swiped them dry on the hand towel, and pushed the answer button. "Who is it?"

"Apple Valley police detective, Miss."

The police again? She didn't recognize this officer's voice. "What do you want?"

"We have information for you."

"Why didn't Detective Connell stop by with it?"

"Connell's on vacation, Miss."

Oh, great! The lead detective on Ryan's family's case was off to Tahiti. Well, maybe not that far afield on a policeman's salary. "I'll come down. Be prepared to show me your badge."

"No problem."

Sam clomped down the stairs. Bastian streaked past her on the way. She let him into the main building and closed the inner vestibule door. That cat was not escaping into the alley again. Then she pushed the proper buttons on the wall keypad to disable the alarm system. A peephole would be nice in her living quarters vestibule, but she'd have to get around to ordering a new door for that. Until then, she'd keep some of the good, old-fashioned features. She undid the deadbolt, but only opened as far as the chain would allow.

A stocky man of medium-tall height flipped open a PD badge with one hand. His other hand stayed planted in the pocket of a nondescript suit similar to Detective Connell's favorite mode of attire. Brown eyes stared soberly at her from behind glasses on a tanned face.

Sighing, Sam pushed the portal shut and undid the chain. Might as well find out what was up now? She opened the door.

Her visitor burst through and stuck something bulky in her

face. Sam stared cross-eyed down a pistol barrel, millimeters from her nose, while her heart performed unnatural contortions.

"Where's Davidson?"

The snarled question brought a little gasp from Sam, the only sound she could make through her closed throat. That hard brown gaze bored into hers, as if he could dig right into her head and extract information.

"Up." He gestured toward the stairs with the end of his pistol and shoved her in that direction.

Scrambling and falling to her knees then scuttling upward, she made it to her apartment, but the intruder was too close on her tail to shut the door on him. He grabbed her bicep and thrust her into a chair by the table. Sam's gaze darted around the room. Where was a weapon when she needed one? The knife she'd used to spread and cut her sandwich lay by the sink instead of on the table near her empty plate where it could have been of use. A butter knife against a gun wasn't fair odds, anyway.

Her captor leaned toward her, close enough that she smelled jalapeño breath. "I'll ask again. Where's Ryan Davidson?"

"I don't know." The words squeaked out. They were true, too. As she'd told Larry, the directions for the route Ryan had taken into the wilderness would be meaningless to her. Therefore, she couldn't pass on any specifics to this slime bucket. And she sure wasn't about to offer any generalities like Boundary Waters.

A cell phone began to play a syncopated tune, and the guy pulled one from the pocket where he'd tucked his fake badge—unless, of course, he was a real cop, but dirty. Sam swallowed, fear thoughts spurting through her brain, paralyzing her.

He flipped his phone open. "What did you find?... Excellent... Was anyone there when you got into his office?... Good. Make a copy of the map and leave the original on the counter where you found it. No one needs to know you were there... Are the birds with you?... *Stupido!* Go get them. Counselor will want regular updates. Then get over here and pick us up... Yes, I'm bringing along an insurance policy. If we have any trouble flushing Davidson out, a few yelps out of her should bring him running."

Sam's captor grinned down at her with very white teeth. Horror strangled her. She jumped up. He shoved her down.

"Be still." Panther-slow, he moved behind her.

The chill of his gun barrel grazed the back of her neck. A shiver shook her from top to toe. An odd sound like a plastic bag rattling came from his direction. Then a chemical-reeking cloth clamped across her mouth and nose.

Sam's shriek came out muffled. The pressure of his gun against her neck held her still.

"Nighty-night, *chica.*"

Blackness rolled over her and sucked her under.

TWENTY

Sam woke up to find herself in a twilit room lying flat on her back on a mattress that must have been stuffed with beans—really big, lumpy beans. And what was that smell? She licked dry lips. Ewww. Some rotten chemical.

Memory rushed back. She'd been kidnapped!

She lunged to a sitting position. Whoa! Her head whirled, and she sank back onto the lumps. Where had they taken her?

Gingerly, she rose onto her elbow and gazed around the room. From the dim light that filtered under a door, she made out bare wooden walls, a rough wood floor and no furnishings other than the cot on which she lay, a three-legged table against one wall and a bucket in the opposite corner.

Steps sounded outside the door, and a pair of foot-size shadows cut off part of the light. The lock rattled, and the door swung open.

The dark outline of a large man stood backlit—tall, broad and muscular. Not the guy who snatched her from her apartment. This was Mr. Atlas's bigger cousin. Sam's parched mouth became the Sahara. Boat-size boots clomped across the floor toward the table.

Now Sam made out a tray in his hands. The faint scent of food wafted from it. Sam's stomach roiled. He set the tray on the table and swiveled toward her. The light from the outer room fell across his ebony face. A nose ring and piercings in his ears glittered at her. His shaved bald head glowed nearly as bright. He didn't smile. If she could melt into the mattress she'd do it in a heartbeat.

"Stop intimidating the nice lady, Byce." The one who'd posed as a police detective came into the room, no longer attired in a suit, but jeans and a casual button-down shirt he hadn't bothered to tuck into his waistband. He stopped in front of her and held out a bottle of water. "Here. Byce forgot this." He pronounced his cohort's name in two syllables with long vowels.

Sam struggled to a sitting position and snatched the bottle, staring up into the Hispanic man's face. "People *will* miss me." Her statement would probably carry more weight if her voice didn't crack.

He shrugged. "Not until at least morning. By that time, we'll be in the air on the trail of your boyfriend."

"He's not my boyfriend, so I don't know what good you think taking me will do."

A tight smile crossed his face. "I like to hedge my bets."

"Speakin' a bets, Enrique, mon," the pierced giant spoke in Jamaican patois, "we got a game to finish."

The one called Enrique threw Sam a little wave then followed Byce. A telltale bulge beneath his shirt suggested a handgun tucked into the waistband of his jeans. The door closed and the lock clicked.

Sam worked at the cover of the water bottle. It was still sealed, so the contents probably weren't drugged. She took several rapid gulps then wiped her mouth with the back of her hand.

From Enrique's words it must be the same night she'd been kidnapped. Maybe not much time had passed. How soon could she expect to be missed? Not as soon as she'd like. She just talked to her mother, and her folks probably wouldn't contact her again for a couple of days. Jenna was still out of town at her convention, which didn't get over until Wednesday, and Hallie took off this morning for a three-day trip to Branson, Missouri. True, the floor layers and hazmat were scheduled for the day after tomorrow, but they were unlikely to call 9-1-1 if she wasn't there to let them in. No-show customers were probably a part of everyday business for them.

So if this was still the same night she'd been grabbed, how far could these lowlifes have taken her? The Minneapolis airport? No, she hadn't heard any jets passing overhead. Maybe a private airfield. Whoever was behind Ryan's family's death and all the strange things that had been happening to her and Ryan had to be a person of power and influence.

Her bones chilled, though the room was stifling. Against someone of that stature, how could she or Ryan hope to keep their lives?

God, You surefire are our only hope.

The small plane's drone vibrated through Sam, quivering her fear-jellied insides. Enrique flew the four-passenger Cessna she'd been shoved into at dawn after a long, sleepless night. A grim future and a lumpy mattress hadn't been the only culprits keeping her awake. Who could close their eyes for more than a second with a couple of goons outside the door who could burst in any time? They hadn't. She'd give them that much. They probably slept like babes. The jerks!

Sam gripped the edges of her seat. They hadn't tied her up. Why bother? She wasn't exactly going to jump out of the plane minus a parachute. Behind her, caged pigeons cooed, a small soothing note to her frazzle nerves. That and the constant prayers she sent heavenward. Too bad it felt like her pleas were bouncing off the plane's roof.

A pigeon cooed again. Had Bastian killed one of them? If so, that meant he'd come into contact with these people. Which one had been her burglar? Sam's skin crawled. If only she didn't have to imagine either of these creeps invading her first floor while she slept above.

"How we s'posed to find this Davidson dude wit' nothin' but a bunch a lines on a piece a paper, mon?" Byce waved what Sam assumed was a copy of the map Ryan faxed to Larry. "Only a word here, a word there. What's a Ka…wi…shi…wi?" He pronounced the syllables one by one, but Sam suspected he'd slaughtered the pronunciation of the Native American word. She probably would, too. "I don' see no towns, no roads, unless these blobs and squiggles—"

"They're lakes and rivers," Enrique snapped. "And quit worrying. The map's good enough that I could probably find Davidson by myself, but Counselor set us up with a tracker who knows the area."

Counselor? Her lead captor kept referring to their head honcho in a tone like the person was more than flesh and blood. Sam's brow furrowed. Where in this tangled maze of events had someone mentioned a counselor? Oh, yes. The last entry in Cassie's journal, the one she'd read just before these wise guys forced her and Ryan off the freeway.

A sharp intake of breath brought the scents of sweaty men and cheap cologne into her nostrils. It made sense. Cassie must have heard her dad mention Counselor to her mom, and assumed he meant counselor with a small *C*—someone a person sought for mental or emotional help. Hah! This particular counselor was hardly out to help anyone but himself and at any cost.

Evidently, the birds were his. Ryan was right when he said he needed to find out who was in the carrier pigeon club. Would she get the chance to share with him this new information, or were they doomed to unmarked graves?

Oh, Ryan, why did you take off all of a sudden? If she was going to smack anybody, it ought to be him for leaving her in the lurch.

Enrique began talking on the radio, and the plane's nose dipped. Sam gazed out her window onto wooded terrain dotted with lakes and twined with rivers sparkling beneath the morning sun. A distant clearing showed a flatbed truck the size of a thumbnail. A logging operation? They slid past that spot as the plane continued to descend. Sam gulped to open her ear canals.

Before them another clearing appeared with a fire lookout tower standing at its edge and what looked like a crude tarred airstrip flanked by several structures, one of them a log house. A few minutes later they bumped and lurched to the ground. The plane slowed nearly to a stop then turned and taxied to a tin garagelike building.

No one stepped out to greet them. Maybe the place was as deserted as the private strip they'd taken off from this morning. It was certainly even more secluded. So much for hollering for help.

Enrique opened his door, and warm, pine-laden air swept into the plane's cabin. "Wait here. I'll see if our host is ready. If I sense anything bogus about this setup, we'll take off like a shot. Keep an eye on our guest." He jerked his head toward her.

Byce peered around the back of his seat, and one corner of his ample mouth lifted. "She a-goin' no place in a hurry."

Enrique hopped out and headed for the log house across a lawn that hadn't been mowed in recent history. When he was about halfway there, the door opened and a white-haired guy in a long-sleeved shirt and jeans stepped out onto the porch. He walked up to Enrique, and they talked with some nodding and head shaking and gesturing. Then the older man ambled toward a heavy-duty pickup parked beside the house. A pair of canoes were tied across the cab.

Enrique returned to the plane and ordered them out. Byce unfolded his long legs and stepped down. Then he opened Sam's door. "Out ya go."

Sam ignored his outstretched hand and navigated to the ground by herself. Her legs still vibrated from the rocky plane ride. Or was that weak-kneed terror?

Wow! Sam lifted her nose and inhaled an enormous breath. That was the freshest air she'd ever smelled. Too bad present company destroyed her enjoyment of it.

The pickup roared up to their little group. A faded Superior National Forest logo was painted on the driver's door. The white-haired tracker stuck his head out the window, wrinkled face folded into a scowl. "Remember. I don't see nothin'. I don't know nothin'. This monkey business could cost me my job. I take you in, help you find this guy then take you out."

Enrique flashed an oily smile. "No problem. That's all Counselor hired you to do."

The oldster snorted. "That shark don't hire fellas like me. He collects his debts. And collects and collects."

Enrique frowned. "Well, now, I'm sure you don't want him to hear you've developed a bad attitude, would you?"

The tracker's leathery skin paled. "Get in. We got about a half-hour drive to the river. The lady rides up front with me. You gents pile in the back with the supplies and that bird cage."

"Sorry." The thug leader smiled. "The *chica* will fit nicely between us."

"Have it your way."

"Thank you. I always do."

Enrique opened the passenger door and motioned to Sam. With leaden limbs, she hoisted herself in and scooted over beside the tracker. Whew! What happened to the delicious air? The old guy smelled like he hadn't bathed since his lawn was mowed last. Enrique climbed in on her other side. Great! She was sandwiched between stinky and stinker.

A few minutes into the ride along a narrow, bumpy track between stands of birch and pine trees, Sam knew one thing: the shock absorbers in this truck were useless. About anything else, including survival for her and Ryan, she hadn't a clue.

TWENTY-ONE

Curses fouled the air as Enrique spun the canoe for the third time in less than a minute. In the bow of the craft, Sam bordered on vertigo.

"What the matter wit' you, mon?" Byce chuckled, gliding up beside them, canoe pointed in the right direction, while the nose of Sam's craft headed back the way they'd come—a whopping fifty yards of progress upriver from the launch point. "You don' know how to paddle a canoe? Jamaican's born wit' a paddle in they hands."

From the bow of Byce's canoe, the old tracker cackled. "You ready to let me drive that thing now, city slicker?"

With some more cursing, Enrique threw his paddle into the bottom of the boat, and they drifted backward at a sideways angle toward the bank.

Sam grinned. Thank goodness no one else could see her expression. Mr. Cool-and-In-Charge had a big, fat Achilles' heel—pride with a capital *P.*

A few minutes later, Sam perched in the bow of a canoe slicing through the crystal clear water under the propulsion of the old tracker's know-how, while Enrique sulked as Byce's passenger in the other boat. The morning sun heated Sam's skin. She'd have a fine burn before long. Of course, everyone but her was wearing long sleeves and a hat. But then, she hadn't been allowed to pack for the expedition. At least the old guy had brought high-powered bug lotion. With the insect population in the deep woods, that was a necessity.

Sam hid as much of her bare arms as she could beneath her paint-stained T-shirt and watched the amazing countryside pass. No wonder Ryan loved coming out here. A cooling breeze shushed through stands of spruce and cedar trees. Scents of wildflowers mingled with tree smells, a winsome spice in the pure air. She looked down into the clear, clean water. Eating-size fish darted away from the boat's shadow.

"God's country, miss," the old tracker said.

She glanced over her shoulder at him, and he grinned, displaying a black hole where several teeth had been on the left side of his mouth. "You can call me Chuck."

Sam turned away without responding. If she called him anything, it would be goodbye and good riddance. The beauty of the day dimmed as her chest constricted. All around, birds sang their hearts out. Why wouldn't they? They lived free in untamed wilderness.

God, I'd love wings to fly out of here right now, but if it's all the same to You, I'd just as soon they not belong to angels carrying me home quite yet.

A piercing cry rang out above, and Sam's head jerked up.

"Bald eagle," Chuck said.

Sam searched the sky. There, directly above the canoes, a great bird soared. The eagle cried out again and dipped toward them. Lower. Lower. Its shadow passed directly over Sam. "He covers me with his feathers," she murmured the words from Psalm 91. In the next second, the bird veered away and soon became a distant black speck in the cloudless sky. But it had left behind one very precious commodity—hope.

A couple of hours later, the party stopped in a clearing that was obviously an established campsite on this route. Stones ringed a blackened spot on the ground, and a pair of logs served as seats off the ground. Sam chose a perch as far away from the others as possible. Enrique raised a brow at her, but made no comment as he leaned a rifle with a scope against the log beside him.

Byce brought the cage of five pigeons and set them at his feet. "We gonna let fly now?"

"Not yet." Enrique shook his head. "When we reach Davidson's camping area, we'll send Counselor a message. Maybe we'll get lucky, and the target'll be in camp. Then we can finish the job on the spot. If not, we'll send word we've picked up the trail."

Byce shrugged. "You da boss."

Chuck started passing out bottles of water and sandwiches. "That bird thing is a real interesting way to communicate, seein' cell phones ain't too reliable out here."

"Counselor doesn't want us calling him on anything traceable. Not even a landline, if there was one." Enrique chomped a bite of his sandwich.

Sam nibbled hers then held it away and inspected the contents. Not a bad flavor, just different.

"Deer sausage, miss." Chuck let out a gravelly laugh.

Sam gobbled hers down and accepted another one. The fresh air had given her an appetite. Besides, she needed to keep her strength up in case she had an opportunity to run. Not that she had a candle's chance in a windstorm of finding her way out of these woods on her own, but she'd rather be eaten by a bear than murdered by dirt-sucking worms.

She licked her fingers free of crumbs and took a swig from her water bottle. "Are you the one who broke my vase?" She eyed Enrique.

"Ah, she speaks." He grinned.

"Pretty clumsy of you."

He sobered and drew up stiff. "It was Gracie here." He socked Byce in the arm.

"I didn't do it, mon. How was I to know that dumb cat follow me into the office? I'm mindin' my business, lookin' for the key, and it brush against my legs. Send me to the moon, mon! I try to shoo it out, and it jump on the desk." The Jamaican spread his hands in a gesture of innocence.

Enrique snorted. "Riiight. Then you get so rattled you chase the critter out a window you leave open and drive off without noticing it's in the back of the truck with the birds. *Stupido!*"

Byce muttered something nasty under his breath and pulled a pack of cigarettes from his shirt pocket.

Sam studied the cage. "So what did Bastian do? Transform himself thin as a cookie and slip between the bars?"

Byce bent and pressed one side of the cage. A door pushed inward. He let go, and the door snapped shut. "Easy to get in. Can't get out." He lit his cigarette and puffed out a cloud of smoke.

Sam shook her head. The jerk ought to get forty years to life for polluting the clean air.

"I had to drag him back there and make him mop up his mess." Enrique smirked. "You can thank me that we returned the cat. Byce wanted to break the nasty thing's neck as soon as he found it in the birdcage. But I figured it'd better show up on your premises somewhere so I had Byce stuff it in the vent instead. Had no idea where the ductwork led, but if the critter got stuck and died in there, so much the better. Stink up your place as a little payback for all the trouble."

Sam's fingernails dug into her palms. "Yes, I've noticed you're all compassion. Since you're trying to impress me, how about explaining how you got my fingerprint on that vase?"

"Simple." The man sat up straight and slapped his knee. "Your prints are all over your office. I found a real nice one on your desktop, lifted it with tape, and slapped it onto the glass of the new vase. Pain in the neck to replace that bouquet, but a brilliant touch. Confused you and the police. Made you look like the *loco* female, eh?" He *tsk*ed.

"You seem to know a lot about what's going on with the police. I can't figure out if you're a wannabe cop or a dirty one."

Enrique scowled and stood up. "Let's go. We're wasting time." Gaze boring into Sam, he hefted his rifle and patted the handgun bulge at his waistband. "Remember, *chica.* If we see anyone on our little vacation, keep your mouth shut. I will not shoot *you.* I will shoot *them.*"

Sam's insides went hollow.

In silence, the group hurriedly packed up. On the way to the canoes, Byce sidled over to Sam. "He flunk out the police academy years back," the Jamaican muttered with a dark scowl toward his leader's back. Then he stalked away.

Sam snorted. Such a huge failure would have been a major blow to Enrique's ego. And there was sure no love lost between this pair of crooks.

Back in position in the bow of the canoe, Sam pulled her arms close to her body and lowered her head, partly from inner chill, partly to protect her skin from the sun and partly to help herself concentrate.

Byce mentioned hunting a key. At the time of the break-in, her extra keys were in police custody, and this mystery boss would have known that from his contact inside the department. The key these bozos were looking for must not be in her bucket.

What other keys did she have? Her car keys? Those were out. She had obsolete keys to the dry cleaners, but they would have belonged to Abel Morris since time began. Access to her building was now controlled by keypads. Keypads! That concept opened a whole new bottomless pit of possibilities. There were lots of electronic gadgets people called keys. But she hadn't found anything like that in scouring the building. Well, except for stray hotel key cards, but she'd tossed those.

Besides, Ryan said his father and electronics weren't on the best of terms. So where would Mr. Davidson have put his secrets if not on his computer?

Man, she could give herself a headache trying to figure this out on her own. There was a lot to tell Ryan. Maybe he could make heads or tails of the fresh clues. Would she ever get the chance to share them?

By late afternoon, they'd paddled across several pristine lakes and up sparkling creeks. Occasionally they spotted another party on one of the lakes, but Chuck managed to make sure they never passed near them. Several times they came to portages where they stopped, unloaded and carried everything across dry ground, often rocky and steep, before entering another waterway. They traveled around and over beaver dams, and once they glided past a cow moose standing belly-deep in a lake, munching on water lilies. At last, they came to a small tributary off the main waterway.

"This is it!" The tracker headed the canoe into the side channel. "We're almost there. We've got a nasty little portage ahead. Some distance beyond that is where his camp'll be. This guy picked a real remote spot for himself."

"The better for our business with him."

Sam shivered at the snarl in Enrique's tone. The guy was reaching the end of his patience, and that couldn't be good for anyone. Within a few minutes, the creek petered out into a rocky swamp. They debarked and unloaded on the driest bit of land they could find.

Sam paced the rocks, stretching her legs, while Chuck strapped the gear down for portage. Enrique dug trail mix from a pack and passed the bag around. Byce grumbled that there was no beer to wash it down. Sam nibbled her peanuts and raisins and cast around in her mind for a conversation starter. Anything to delay their move into Ryan's proximity. Enrique enjoyed talking about himself. Maybe she could use his ego as an opening.

She forced herself to approach the man hunkered on his haunches with his snack. "Did you know the police have determined that the shooter in the Davidson case was a man who died the same night in a hit-and-run incident?"

Enrique rose, swiping his hands together. "Figured they'd get to that eventually."

"Were you the hit-and-run driver?"

The man laughed. "Would have been a lot more fun than dropping the dude off so he could pose as a jogger in the neighborhood, and then waiting to pick him up afterward. Saw it happen though."

"The hit-and-run was an actual accident?" She stared, wide-eyed.

Her captor chuckled harder. "Never considered that, did you? Some drunk tearing up the road at high speed, weaving all over the place. He jumped the curb and schmucked that high-brow hitter neat as you please. I got in there real fast, before the police came, and searched the body for the key the old Counselor was so desperate for, but didn't find a thing." Enrique shrugged. "Then I skedaddled, and the whole thing got dropped. Ten years later, we hear you found photos of the murders on your property, and he's hot after that key again."

"Let's get a move on," Chuck's call brought their heads around. "I'd like to make camp before nightfall."

Without further comment, the oldster flipped a canoe over his head and headed into the swamp, stepping from rock to rock.

Her captor snarled a nasty word then grabbed Sam's arm in a painful squeeze. "Here, Miss Chatty." He thrust a pack into Sam's hands. "It's our food and water. Don't drop it."

"I know. I've carried it at every portage."

He shook another pack at her. "Just be glad you don't get this one. It's twice as heavy, but I don't trust you with it." He stuck his face in hers. "Ammunition. Plenty of it." Cackling, he swung the pack onto his back, along with his rifle and picked up the cage of pigeons.

Byce was already hopping awkwardly after Chuck, the second canoe teetering on his head. Enrique motioned for Sam to precede him.

Head up, she stepped onto the first rock, then the next and the next. Many of them were moss-coated and slippery. At least, she'd been wearing tennis shoes with good tread when she was kidnapped.

Ahead of her, Byce yelped as one foot slipped from a stone. His leg sank up to the knee in watery muck. The canoe toppled from his head and splashed into the swamp. He retrieved the boat with a flurry of angry comments and stomp-squished onward. For twenty minutes they trekked, sometimes uphill onto dry ground, but always back down into swamp. Sam swatted biting flies and mosquitoes until she thought she'd slap herself silly. And then…

Magnificent! That was the only word for the bright aqua lake surrounded by lush vegetation that lay before them. If the trees and grasses were any greener, the color would hurt her eyes. A steady north wind brought welcome coolness and rippled the lake water into sparkling rills. Sam smiled and reveled in deep breaths of sweet air.

"Move along!" The harsh voice at her back jerked her to reality.

A few minutes later, they were again paddling in the canoes. They continued for fifteen minutes or so, and then Chuck slowed their boat and brought it next to Byce's. "According to the map, his site'll be around yonder bend. We can paddle past the place. Even if he's there, he won't know us from any other wilderness explorers."

Enrique pointed at Sam. "He will with her along."

"In that case, we'd better put in and leave her off."

"Not alone, and not with you. Byce will stay with the *chica*. You will paddle me over to Davidson's campsite. If all goes well," he said, grinning, "we can turn around and leave as fast as our paddles will carry us."

"No!" The word burst from Sam's lips. She'd had enough. She had to do something and do it now. "I won't let you." She glared at Enrique. "Ryan!" The scream echoed across the water. She lunged to her feet. "Run!" The craft wobbled wildly, and she toppled into the lake.

Cool wetness welcomed her. She sank with her eyes open. Sunbeams tinted the water gold, like liquid light. From above came splashes and angry shouts. Sam shook herself from the dreamlike state and swam with broad strokes away from the commotion. Silver flickers of fish darted out of her way.

Which direction was she going? Toward land or away from it? She came up for air. Oh, no, she was headed for the middle of the lake. A canoe cut across her vision, and she stared into the furious face of the leader of this deadly expedition. A telltale click said he'd cocked the pistol pointed her way.

"Get to the beach, and don't make another sound. Right now, I'd just as soon turn you into fish food."

Shortly, Sam lay on a rock, soaking wet and her mouth gagged with the tail of Enrique's shirt. Rope bound her ankles, and her hands were tied behind her back. Byce stood guard over her. Chuck and Enrique's canoe slid away in the distance toward the campsite Ryan had marked on his map. The craft went around a bend and was lost from sight.

Sam closed her eyes. *Please, God, let Ryan not be there.* Minutes ticked away. Sam breathed in…out…in…out—each breath a prayer.

Blam! Sam jerked. A flock of geese honked and burst up from the lake. *Blam!* Sam went limp, tears seeping from the corners of her eyes.

TWENTY-TWO

Enrique's canoe hove into view a minute later, but he and the old tracker didn't return to the rock where Sam lay. From the bow, Enrique waved toward Byce as Chuck guided their craft toward an inlet several hundred yards up the shoreline. The big Jamaican didn't look Sam in the eye as he loaded her into their canoe. Soon they joined the other two in a large clearing where Chuck had started building a fire and Enrique struggled with tent poles. Without a word, Byce toted Sam to a spot under the shade of a pine tree. He plopped her on the lumpy ground and left.

Numb inside and out, her gaze barely registered the camping preparations. The men talked, but mostly their words were eaten by the wind. She heard enough, though. Things like "fixed Davidson" and "dispose of him tomorrow."

Sam roused as Enrique took a pigeon from the cage and fastened a small tube to its leg. He was smiling as he did so. Gloating. Fury surged to Sam's extremities, and she fought her bonds, but to no use. Ryan's murderer released the bird, and it took off. All of them watched the pigeon shoot straight south. Enrique took out a second bird and did the same as for the first. Of course, the dirty rat had to insure that his message of triumph reached his master in case something happened to the first courier.

Chuck let out a low whistle. "If that ain't the crazy funnest thing I ever seen. Prob'ly have to get myself some a them pigeons now."

He turned away to tend his growing fire. After a while, he cooked something in a pot dangling from a makeshift spit, but Sam's stomach responded to the scents with nausea. The three men laughed and joked around the campfire while they ate. Finally, Chuck approached her with a plate and a bottle of water. He set the items down on the ground, helped her to sit up, and pulled the gag out of her mouth.

"Enrique's plenty mad about that stunt you pulled. Good thing everything turned out okay after all. He says I can feed ya."

She turned her face away. "Not hungry. It's just a last meal anyway."

Chuck shook his head. "Have it your way. At least drink a little water." He held the bottle toward her. She let him pour some between her lips.

A short time later, the sun began to set, and the bugs started getting bad. Byce picked her up and deposited her in a corner of the tent. Sam lay on the hard ground, staring into the dark. Why didn't they just kill her and get it over with?

After a while, the old tracker entered the tent, yawning. He tucked a small, inflatable pillow under her head and tossed a blanket over her. Then he turned away and rolled into a blanket next to her. Within minutes, light snores came from his still figure. Enrique slipped inside next, cuddling his rifle, and settled on the far side of the tent. The atmosphere was growing stuffy with all the bodies in close quarters. A tiny red glow bobbing outside and a faint whiff of tobacco smoke revealed that Byce was pacing back and forth in the clearing.

Other than the Jamaican's soft footfalls and Chuck's whiffled snores, Sam was left with only the night sounds of the forest. Rustles and squeaks of small nocturnal animals, the shushing of wind in the trees, and from the lake, a loon released its haunting trill. Before Byce's cigarette winked out, exhaustion claimed her, and she dozed off into fitful sleep. Discomfort woke her many times, but the need for forgetfulness quickly claimed her again.

Pop! Pop! Pop! Pop!

Sam sat up with a lurch, her body aching in protest. She winced against flashes of light that blazed through the thin tent shell. The men leaped up, shouting and swearing and bumping into each other. A foot kicked her in the shoulder. The sound of guns cocking accompanied the milling herd into the night. Staccato bangs continued, punctuated by men's shouts. Sam tugged and yanked at the bonds around her hands, but Byce had done his job well.

A ripping sound from the side of her tent brought her head around. Through a slice in the fabric a head poked through. Sam's breath caught, and her heart hammered against her ribs.

"Ryan?" she whispered. "I thought they shot you."

"Nah, they plugged my canoe, but explanations later, hon." He reached through with a knife and made quick work of the rope around her ankles. Sam swiveled and he did her hands, then grabbed her shoulders and hauled her out of the tent.

She looked toward the commotion and found the outlines of Enrique's and Byce's forms, crouching near the water's edge. Flashes continued from a shadowy craft on the lake, interspersed by answering gunshots from shore.

"Come on!" Ryan pulled her to her feet. "They're going to figure out any second that my homemade fireworks aren't bullets."

Sam staggered forward and folded. "My legs are numb."

Strong arms scooped her up, and Sam inhaled the scents of wood smoke and pine on her rescuer. Heavenly! Ryan hustled toward the trees with her.

A shout came from behind them, and a gun's report accented a bee-buzz past Sam's ear. Deep barking joined the fray, then a canine snarl followed by a male screech. "Get this dog offa me, mon!" A gun sounded again and the dog yelped.

Sam gasped, and Ryan's stride faltered, but then he picked up the pace, and the woods embraced them. Dark trunks of birch and fir flowed past her. Were Ryan's feet guided by radar or something? Oops, not quite. His stumble nearly deposited them both on the ground.

"Set me down," she hissed. "I'll make it now."

Her feet met terra firma, and Ryan grabbed her hand, tugging her onward with barely a moment for her to get her bearings. Sam stumbled behind him. She was slowing him down, but she couldn't help it. At least, he seemed to know where he was going. She sure didn't. For all she knew, the next step would take them off the edge of a cliff or into the lake.

Large bodies thrashed through the trees behind them. "Davidson!" Enrique's voice pursued them. He appended his shout with a furious comment on Ryan's lineage.

Sam and Ryan emerged from the trees on the lake's edge by the rocks where she had lain, thinking he'd been killed. Impending dawn tinted the darkness a rosy hue. A canoe sat waiting on the bank.

Ryan flipped the boat upright and pushed it into the lake. "Get in." She complied in an awkward scramble, and he hopped in behind her.

"I thought you said they shot your canoe."

"Not this one. No talking now."

Sam pressed her lips together and swallowed her heart back into her chest. Honestly, if she wasn't so overjoyed to see Ryan alive, she'd shove him into the water as payback for all the torment she'd suffered believing him killed, not to mention being kidnapped and terrorized on account of him dashing off into the wilderness. But first, they needed to get out of gunshot range as fast as Ryan could paddle, which appeared pretty fast. Sam watched the lake skim beneath them as continued vile shouts from the woods prickled the hairs at the base of her neck.

Whoof!

The bark from shore halted Ryan's paddle. Sam looked over her shoulder. She made out a dark blob perched on the rock they'd just left.

"We have to get him." Sam touched Ryan's shoulder, but he'd already begun turning the craft.

He skimmed the boat up to the side of the rock and did a squiggly little backpedal that interrupted forward momentum. The dog leaped, but clumsily and with a high whine on landing in the bottom of the canoe between Ryan and Sam. She reached down and touched the animal's flank. He yelped and her hand came away wet.

"He's bleeding," she told Ryan.

"My pack…is behind you." He spoke between grunts of effort at the paddle.

Sam turned and grasped the pack. Movement drew her gaze to the rock outcropping rapidly diminishing behind them. Enrique, by the size of the dark outline.

"Duck!" Sam minded her own words as a sharp report sounded.

The canoe skimmed faster. Another shot cracked and Sam heard a *plink* in the water wide right of them. The rifle spoke again, but without evidence of a bullet strike nearby. The murk must have swallowed them from view. Sam peeked up over the bow and could barely discern the outline of the shore, let alone the owner of the voice that still snarled unintelligible curses. She let out the breath she'd been holding and sat up.

"You're an Olympic rower, Davidson." She rifled in the pack and came out with one of his extra T-shirts.

"Adrenaline'll do that to you," he puffed back at her, and the canoe slowed the smallest degree.

Sam pressed the soft cloth to the dog's side. He whined, but didn't fight her.

"How bad is Jake?" Ryan asked.

"I can't tell. It's too dark. He's not gushing or anything."

The rhythmic *shirrrr* of his paddle answered her. Minutes dragged past, and the sky continued to lighten. "I think the bleeding's slowed."

"Good." The canoe slowed, as well. "We'll have to make this portage under rotten conditions."

Sam raised her head to find they were at the rocky swamp. Ryan got out and held the boat for her to debark. Old Jake crawled out after her, whimpering, then collapsed on the ground.

"I'll have to carry him." She looked up at Ryan. "I'm strong. I can do what I must."

"Don't I know it!" One side of his mouth lifted.

Sam stroked Jake's head while Ryan hastily prepared the canoe for portage. He slung his pack on one shoulder and a rifle on the other, and then hefted the boat. Sam gathered the dog in her arms. Jake was no miniature poodle, but at least he didn't thrash, just whined as she cautiously followed Ryan step by step across rocks she could barely see. Her ears stayed tuned for telltale noises of pursuit behind them.

"They'll come soon," Ryan said, as if reading her mind.

The portage took tortuously long, but at last they stood at the other end. Sam's arm muscles quivered by the time she laid the dog on the floor of the canoe. At least, the first rays of the sun had begun to peek over the horizon as Ryan took up the paddle and sent their craft upriver against a steady current.

Sam examined Jake's injury. "He's got a gash along his side that'll need stitches," she told Ryan, "and he's lost a lot of blood. He should be okay, though, if we get him medical attention soon."

"Just as quick as we can. Have to ditch our tails first. Do you hear?"

Sam held her breath and listened. Angry voices carried faintly on the morning breeze. Their pursuers were on the portage. Ryan didn't turn his head, just kept paddling. Sam watched the muscles strain and ripple beneath his shirt. Her heart pounded in rhythm with his strokes. He guided their craft around a bend in the river then headed it to the bank.

"What are we doing?" Sam climbed out behind him.

The dog made a weak effort to sit up. "Stay." Ryan pointed to the ground, then grabbed his rifle out of the boat. He laid a hand on Sam's shoulder. "Keep watch over Jake. I'll be right back." His head darted close, and he touched his lips to hers, then he was gone up a faint trail into the woods.

Sam pressed fingers to her mouth then shook herself and turned toward the suffering animal in the boat. She knelt and found Ryan's canteen in his pack, as well as a tin dish he must have been using to feed Jake.

"Have some water, boy. It'll do you good." Her voice shook as her ears strained for sounds of what might be happening. The dog lapped up the water like he might never see moisture again. She poured him more. "That should help put some fluids back in your—"

Blam! Sam jerked and slopped the water out of the dish. The same gun spoke again, answered by a report with the tone of the rifle she thought had shot Ryan. Enrique was returning fire. *Blam! Blam!* Those last two had to be Ryan's again. That meant he was still all right, but had he killed their pursuers? Under these circumstances, she wouldn't blame him, and neither would the law, but still she shuddered.

In silence she waited, heart pounding. At last, footfalls and panting breath came toward her from the trail. Sam stood as Ryan burst from the trees and came to a stop before her. He looked ragged with beard shadow on his cheeks and dark circles under his eyes, but his gaze was steady, his jaw set.

"Wh-what happened?" She gulped.

"I climbed a tree for cover and a good angle and returned the favor. Put a few slugs into their boat hulls." He grinned. "They're up a creek with plenty of paddles, but no canoes."

A giggle snorted through Sam's nose. "Sorry, I think I'm losing my mind here. We'd better get going before they catch up to us on foot."

"No rush. There's a big old swath of deadfall from the '99 windstorm between us and them. They can't get through anytime soon."

Her heartbeat hesitated then sped up. "You mean we got away?"

"We're home free." He spread his arms.

Laughing, she lunged into them, and then laughter turned to sobs.

"Shh-shh, honey." He squeezed her close. "I've got you." Was he planting gentle kisses on the top of her head? Oh, yes. And saying words that her heart echoed. "Thank you, Jesus! Thank you, Jesus!"

"We're not out of the woods yet, sweetheart. No pun intended." Ryan hunkered down beside Sam in the clearing where they'd stopped for midmorning break. She sat on a rock in the shade. He handed her an energy bar and a handful of dried fruit.

As she took the food, his gaze narrowed on the rope burns around her wrists. "I intended for them to come after me, but it never occurred to me that they'd bring you."

"What do you mean?" She blinked at him. "I thought you came out here to do some soul-searching."

Ryan let out a wry chuckle and settled onto the rock next to her. "I did that before I left. I had a phone call from Eldon Stahl. He and his wife are hiding out in some foreign country right now. He warned me to disappear because they'd be on my doorstep any minute. I prayed and asked God for an idea about what to do. All of a sudden it occurred to me that running up here was the perfect trap, as long as they found out where I was going."

"You used yourself as bait?" Sam nibbled a piece of fruit. "That was awfully risky."

Ryan shrugged and bit into an energy bar. "I know this place—those city boys don't. But how could they resist coming after me? I gave them a golden opportunity to dispose of me and let everyone assume I'd gotten lost in the wilderness and lunched on by wolves." He wagged the bar at her.

"Nasty picture."

"Sorry." He turned his head to hide his smile. "When I got up here, I set up a fake camp using old gear and a second canoe I portaged all by myself, two trips every time, thank you very much. Made myself another camp where I could watch whoever stopped by with bad intentions. I figured to catch myself a crook and make him tell me the name of his boss. But I didn't expect to put you in danger." He looked into those wide green eyes. "Part of the beauty of the idea was to draw them *away* from you."

The corners of her lips tilted upward. "It means a lot to me that you didn't just run off without telling me in order to put some distance between us. Part of me thought that."

"Never! Consider me Ryan 'Burr' Davidson where you're concerned. Could you handle that?"

"Hmmm. Let me think about it." She ducked her head and began unwrapping her energy bar, but not before he caught the little smirk on her face. "So Enrique put holes in your boat and figured that'd make you a sitting duck for them to hunt down. How were you able to use said boat for your fireworks display?"

Ryan chuckled. "The all-purpose male fix-it for every crisis known to humanity—duct tape. The tape wouldn't hold for any serious paddling, but it served my purpose."

"Very clever, Mr. Davidson."

"Very desperate, Miss Reid. I scrambled to turn my extra bullets into makeshift firecrackers and get everything in place for a predawn rescue. I couldn't leave you with them a minute longer than necessary. I'd recognize that ponytail anywhere." He reached over and tweaked it. "When I saw through my binoculars that those lowlifes had brought a certain woman with them, my heart nearly stopped." He stared at the ground. "I guess the inspiration wasn't from God after all because it put you in danger again."

Sam's hand rested on his knee. "I have no doubt that it was divine inspiration. Sure, I hated every second in those men's custody, but I found out a few things. Maybe something that will lead to the big boss."

Ryan looked up and slid a finger along her jawline. "I found out something, too. Catching the crook who ordered my family killed is important, but it's not top priority. When push came to shove, getting you to safety is what mattered, and like you told me, so is the future my family would want for me."

He picked up a small stick from the ground and twiddled it between his fingers. "I prayed for those things the whole night long like I've never prayed for anything in my life, and I felt like…well, like God became real to me. Not just an idea anymore, but a person who listens and cares. I'm going to be okay now. Spiritually, I mean." His cheeks warmed.

"I know you are." She leaned against his shoulder and munched another bite of her snack. "But aren't you the least bit curious what I found out?"

Ryan nudged her away from him. "Spill, woman."

She laughed. Oh, how he treasured the sound. He grinned in return, and from a spot under a Red Pine, Jake let out a woof. The old dog rose and padded gingerly toward them then eased himself down beside their rock.

She scratched behind his ears. "He's going to be all right. Now we just have to figure out who Counselor is."

"Counselor?"

"Enrique kept calling their boss that name. I think your sister overheard your dad talking about this guy to your mom. The reference was in her diary, but she misunderstood."

"Of course!" Ryan got to his feet and paced to the water, pulse thundering, a fresh recollection washing through his brain. "I think I know who Counselor must be. At least, I can narrow it down to one of two people." He turned toward Sam.

She stood and brushed crumbs from her fingers. "Who?"

"My dad had a lawyer friend who liked the nickname Counselor. I can't for the life of me remember the guy's real name. I've discovered that kids don't pay nearly enough attention to their parents' lives."

He stepped over to his pack and began shoving things into it. "When I visited Mrs. Stahl, I ran across a photo of my dad on the golf course with the lawyers who partnered in Mr. Stahl's firm over a decade ago. Eldon's not Counselor, I'm sure of that much, but it has to be one of the other two—Randolph Hanes, a district attorney who's running for state attorney general, or Warren Seiler, now a Minnesota Supreme Court justice. My money's on Hanes. Mrs. Stahl called him a barracuda."

Sam came to stand over him. "You could be right. Chuck called this Counselor guy a shark."

Ryan looked up at her while he zipped the pack. "Sounds like a match, but either one of these bigwigs would have the world to lose if they were proven a murderer."

"Proof," she said as he stood up. "Exactly what we need. We have to find the key."

"The key?" He stared at her.

"I don't know what it is yet, but together we'll figure it out. In the meantime, there are probably two pigeons heading toward Mr. Hanes or Mr. Seiler right this minute, telling him we're on the loose. What's to say Enrique and company are the only people he could send to do us in?"

TWENTY-THREE

"It's good to know we've got a team actively working on our side at last." Ryan slid his hand across the seat of his pickup and curled his fingers around Sam's.

As per common practice with those trekking into the Boundary Waters Canoe Area, he'd left his vehicle parked at the outfitter's in town and let them transport him to the entry site. But he was sure glad when they delivered it back to him this morning at the hotel in Ely. A guy felt a lot of freedom in having wheels at his disposal. At least they didn't have to ride in the cop car that was leading the way to the local PD office.

He smiled at Sam, and she squeezed his hand. She still looked tired but at least somewhat refreshed after a restful night in her own hotel suite with an officer stationed outside. He'd had one outside his door, too. Only the sunburn across Sam's cheeks and on her arms reminded him of the ordeal she'd been through on account of him. They both wore new jeans and matching BWCA T-shirts.

"It was so good to wake up in a comfortable bed and realize life could soon get back to normal," she said. "I even remembered to call the floor layers and the hazmat people and reschedule."

"What about Bastian?"

She laughed. "He'll be miffed about being left alone for so long, but he's got food and water and a bed in the workroom."

Ryan smiled. The woman had it all together.

"I hope Jake is all right at the vet's." She reached out to adjust the air-conditioning.

Ryan returned both hands to the wheel and negotiated the traffic that came with Ely's summer tourist season bonanza. "I called before we checked out of the hotel, and the old boy had a good night. Nothing to do but lie around and snooze and eat? I'd say Jakester is in his glory."

He pulled up beside their police escort outside the local PD building, but a lot more than locals waited for them inside. Ryan glanced at the lovely, capable woman beside him. "Those lowlifes made the mistake of their lives when they hauled their kidnap victim onto federal lands." When he and Sam reached a ranger station yesterday afternoon, the rangers had been extremely interested in their story, and they'd made phone calls. Agents of the Federal Bureau of Investigation had driven in from Minneapolis to hear the account for themselves. "Maybe Enrique and his crew have been rounded up by now and are singing like canaries."

Sam laughed. "Cooing like pigeons, you mean." She sobered. "Do you think they'll let us go home today?"

"Only if it's safe. I'm not taking any more chances with your life." He got out and walked with her inside, flanked by a pair of officers.

They were ushered into separate cubicles. After an hour's chat with an agent, Ryan and Sam were reunited in a larger room, where they went over their stories again with both agents. Their accounts had the men darting in and out of the room to initiate verifications.

The one who'd introduced himself as Special Agent Becker returned after his latest foray. "They found the plane that made the illegal entry into the BWCA at Charles Ferno's fire watch station. The description you gave of this man Chuck matches Ferno's." He nodded toward Sam, who was nursing a can of 7UP. "We're running the plane's registration now."

A knock sounded on the door, and it popped open to admit

the grizzled head of the local police chief. "Got one! They just brought in a big fellow who talks with a Jamaican accent. Found him stuck hip-deep in a mud hole, bawling like a newborn calf."

"Thanks," said the agent who'd given his last name as Grant. "Would you like to identify him, Miss Reid?"

Her gaze darted toward Ryan, who gave her a nod. "Um, sure, but can my friend come with me? He saw them, too, just not as close up."

Becker opened the door and waved them through.

"We'll let you go in and take a look one at a time so we get separate corroborations on him."

Ryan followed Sam up the hall then waited outside while she entered a cubicle with the agent. They emerged less than a minute later, Sam pale, her lips compressed into a thin line. Ryan touched her arm, then took his turn in the little room, where one-way glass looked into an interview chamber. Inside, a large, bedraggled, bug-bitten, mud-coated lump of humanity hunched at the table.

"That's Byce," Ryan confirmed to Agent Becker.

They left the cubicle and rejoined Sam in the hallway. She met Ryan's gaze. "Looks like the wilderness beat him up pretty good."

Ryan crossed his arms and rocked back on his heels. "Couldn't happen to a nicer guy."

Sam slapped her hand over her mouth, but Ryan still heard her snorted giggle.

Smiling, they returned to the conference room and found lunch waiting in foam boxes. The agents left, and Ryan tucked into his hot roast beef sandwich with gravy and mashed potatoes. Sam picked at hers.

He jabbed his fork her direction. "Not hungry?"

She sighed and met his gaze. "Enrique's the most dangerous one, and he's still out there."

"And he's no more capable of looking after himself in the wilderness than Byce."

"But he's with Chuck, and that man *does* know the BWCA."

"And we're sitting in a police station surrounded by dozens of cops, plus federal agents. The day is young, darlin', and the troops are just beginning to swarm. Have faith."

The tight lines around Sam's mouth smoothed away. "I like the way you talk. I'm being an idiot." She smiled and took a bite of her potatoes.

The afternoon drifted on while they batted around ideas of what the mysterious "key" could be and played Go Fish and Hearts with a deck of cards begged off the duty sergeant.

Around 3:00 p.m., Agent Grant stepped inside, a frown on his face. "Still no sign of Chuck Ferno, but a short time ago, a man fitting Enrique's description attempted to take a canoe from a couple of fishermen who happened to handle guns pretty well themselves. They exchanged shots. One of the fishermen is in critical condition in the hospital, but Enrique came out of the BWCA in a body bag. We hope to have a full identification on him soon. Perp like that's bound to have a rap sheet."

Sam paled. "How can I be thankful and sorry at the same time?"

The agent withdrew without comment.

Ryan pressed his forehead into his palms. He heard Sam move, and soon her hands closed around his shoulders from behind.

"You can't blame yourself for Enrique's vicious actions," she said.

"Tell that to the family of the hurt man."

A chair scraped away from the table, and Sam settled beside him. "Let's pray for his recovery."

Ryan lifted his head. "I'm too new at this. Not sure what words to use. You say the prayer, and I'll say 'amen.'"

They took hands and bowed their heads. Ryan inserted "amen" several times as Sam poured out her heart to the Almighty. She barely finished speaking when the door opened again.

Agent Becker entered the room holding a file folder and a piece of paper. "Just got a faxed report. Around noon, the home of Minnesota Supreme Court Justice Warren Seiler, known as 'Counselor' to his friends, was searched under warrant. A number of things turned up, including cages of carrier pigeons. Only one more thing I can share with you. Evidence was found that suggests Judge Seiler left the country this morning." He tucked the fax sheet into the folder. "It would appear you are safe to return home. We can talk to you quite easily as needed from the Minneapolis Field Office."

The photo of the genial-looking, round-faced Seiler passed through Ryan's mind. "He's the one Martha Stahl described as a nice guy and a great judge." He slammed his fist onto the tabletop and glared at the agent. "He ordered my family murdered, and no one knows why. And now he's on permanent vacation in Rio or wherever."

"Ah, Ryan."

Sam's gentle words wafted over him like a breath of compassion. He deflated. "Sorry." He stood and shook the agent's hand. "Thanks for what you're doing. I'm happy to be alive, and more than happy that Sam survived, but this bites." He strode out the door and up the hall.

In the fresh air he stopped on the sidewalk. Sam touched him, and he turned into her warm embrace. "Don't worry," he said. "I'll deal with this." He rubbed her back, and his palm passed over small ridges of scar tissue. Way to remind him that no matter what came at a person, life was precious and worth fighting for. "I meant what I said that I finally got it through my thick skull what's really important."

"That's awesome." She smiled up at him. "Let's grab Jake and head home, Mr. Davidson."

Sam dozed during the last leg of the trip home but roused when they reached the north end of the Twin Cities. Full dark had come by the time Ryan shut off the truck outside Sam's business. She drank in the brick building with her eyes. "Home sweet home at last," she murmured. "Seems like I've been gone a century, not two days."

Ryan chuckled. "Despite all the indications that we're safe, I won't be satisfied unless I go through your building top to bottom before I leave."

"And I won't be happy unless you do."

Ryan powered the windows down several inches. "Jakester should be all right in here for a few minutes now that the sun's down."

They got out and walked up the alley between the dry cleaners and the print shop until they reached the side door. Sam punched in the lock code on the keypad. The light flashed green and the latch clicked.

Ryan pushed past her into the darkness of the interior, and the lights came on in the big, bare workroom. Sam stepped over the threshold. Paint and turpentine smell greeted her. She waved a hand in front of her nose. Man, the fumes had accumulated from lack of ventilation.

The door closed behind them, automatically locking again, but Sam turned quickly to the blinking alarm panel, which would send an SOS to the security company if someone didn't punch in the code to let it know the proper owner was home.

Everything normal. Then why did she feel like she'd forgotten something?

Shrugging, she followed Ryan to the storage room. He opened the door and flicked on the light. They both peeked inside. Another empty area, except for a cluster of old solvent bottles on one shelf. He turned off the switch and headed up front.

"I wonder where Bastian's hiding?" Sam looked right and left, trailing in his wake. "Mad as a hornet and refusing to come greet me, no doubt. Probably crouched under the new counter. He's already laid claim to one of the niches. Little does his highness realize that his kingdom will diminish to our apartment after the business gets up and running. My employees and I can't have him underfoot while we're dealing with hot presses and steam cleaners."

"Funny cat." Ryan passed through the door into the customer area. "Where's the light switch out here?"

Sam came along behind him and turned it on.

"The remodel looks gooood." Ryan nodded at her then went toward the office.

Sam bent and inspected under the counter. "Bastian's not—"

"Where did this come from?"

The sharpness in Ryan's tone brought her head up. *Ouch!* Too fast. The back of her skull connected with the edge of the countertop.

She went to her office, rubbing her scalp. "What are you talking about?"

"This." He held out the trout paperweight. "It used to sit on my dad's desk. I gave it to him for his birthday one year. Bought it in Ely on one of our church canoe trips."

"The police had that and some other things in custody to check for prints and blood last time you were here. They gave the stuff back because they didn't find anything."

A mewl came from the direction of the closet. Sam's mouth fell open. "Not again! How—"

"My doing, I'm afraid."

The pleasant voice brought both of them around to face the doorway. A portly figure with a gentle, smiling face filled the space. Only the miniature pistol he pointed in their direction wasn't so friendly. And why was he holding an open jug of perc cleaning solvent?

TWENTY-FOUR

Ryan stood frozen, gaping at the man who ordered his family slaughtered.

"What a pity I didn't know that knickknack came from Michael Davidson's home office," Warren Seiler went on. "I have no idea how such an object might connect with the missing key, but I could have appropriated it from the police evidence room and found out. Perhaps we could all have been spared catastrophe."

This was not how Ryan had pictured meeting the killer after all these years. And certainly not how he'd imagined reacting. Cold. Blank. Nothing. Like every feeling had shut down.

"You're the murderer." He hardly recognized his own voice, so flat and toneless.

Seiler had the gall to lift his chin like he was offended. "The Honorable Judge Warren Seiler. I have never murdered anyone, though I've tried dozens of vicious killers."

Something sparked in the pit of Ryan's belly. "You ordered it done." Now there was heat in his tone.

"I ordered nothing of the kind. Your father threatened me. He told me if I didn't turn myself in, he would give the authorities the safety deposit key. Unacceptable! I merely sent a professional to reason with him, but of course, the stubborn man wouldn't listen."

"So it's my dad's fault they're all dead? You're sick!" His volume had gone up several notches. "Why? I have a right to know."

The man winced, but his gun's aim remained steady. "The reason doesn't matter now. Everything is ruined anyway."

Next to Ryan, Sam touched his sleeve and gave a miniscule shake of the head. "Judge Seiler." She turned her attention toward the other man. "You're a fool to be here in this country yet. There's a manhunt on for you. Maybe you should leave now."

"In due time we shall all leave." Seiler's mouth quirked upward, and he pulled the trigger. An inch of flame spurted, but that was all.

"Oh, no!" Sam gasped.

Ryan took a step forward. "You're holding us at bay with a lighter?" He charged.

Seiler flung up the arm carrying the jug, and a generous wave of the contents splashed onto Ryan torso. Chemicals and fumes seared Ryan's nostrils and stung his eyes and nose. Gasping and choking, he staggered backward and hit the corner of Sam's filing cabinet.

She screamed, and water struck Ryan's face. Blinking through a moist haze of tears and H_2O, he saw her holding the empty flower vase. She thrust a tissue box from her desk into his hands. Still clutching the fish paperweight—if this murderous scum was after it, he wasn't going to let the man have it—Ryan dabbed around his watering eyes with tissues.

Her back to Ryan, Sam moved between him and Seiler. "You've spread that solvent all over the building. Not enough to stink us out, but enough to accelerate a fire." The man tendered a half bow. She turned toward Ryan. "I'm so sorry. I should have realized that smell wasn't just turpentine. And I should have remembered that my alarm system was off when I was kidnapped. The judge had to reactivate it after he got in here somehow."

"Smart woman," Seiler said. "With the alarm deactivated, it wasn't hard to slip in through that antiquated window. But I debated long and hard what to do as I awaited you in the comfortable apartment upstairs. Leave it off and have you immediately become nervous when you returned and realized your electronic security was deactivated while you were gone? Or activate it and gamble you wouldn't remember it had been turned off? Apparently, I chose correctly." The man beamed, radiating benevolence.

Sam shook her head. "We were nervous anyway after all you've put us through."

Head still woozy from fumes, Ryan stepped around Sam…or tried to. He wobbled and she steadied him. Leaning on her shoulder, he lasered Seiler with a glare. What Sam had told him about those caught up in unrepented evil suddenly became crystal clear. If he could feel sorry for this guy and the eternity he faced, he would, but he wasn't that spiritual yet. "You haven't chosen anything right for years. You're a doomed man and don't have a clue."

"Ah, ah, ah!" The judge wagged the lighter pistol. "This thing can shoot flames several feet if I pull the trigger hard enough. Now back away, because you're a walking torch now, young man."

"So are you," Sam spoke up. "If you've been spreading this stuff around, your clothes are saturated with fumes. You took a big chance just flicking that pistol Bic a minute ago." She lifted her hands, palm out, in a placating gesture. "Now if you put down that jug and the lighter, we can all walk out of here alive."

Everything benign left Seiler's appearance as his face twisted, and his gray eyes sparked rage. "Do you think that's what I want? To walk away? To live my life in a foreign country, disgraced? My honor, my name is…*was* everything! Michael tried to take it from me, and I stopped him. But you two…" He paced forward, holding the jug in front of him, the pistol trained on it. "You couldn't leave it alone." He took another step away from the doorway.

Ryan grabbed Sam's hand, and she met his gaze. *I love you,* he mouthed. Then he released her hand, shoved her toward the door, and kicked upward at the solvent bottle. Was his aim good enough in his chemically induced high? His toe connected with something. Not the bottle. Something soft. Seiler's arm, the one that held the solvent.

The judge screeched, and the jug flew toward the far corner of the room, liquid splashing out of it onto the desk and the wall. Flame spurted in that direction.

"Run, Ryan!"

Sam's yell activated his feet, and he raced out the door after her just as heat struck him in the back. He reached down and ripped off his solvent-soaked shirt as he tore through the workroom on Sam's heels. A *whoomph* announced that other areas had begun to catch fire. From the front of the building, high-pitched screams trailed them.

They reached the side door, Sam first. She put her hand on the knob, but turned her head in the direction they had come. Ryan blocked her line of sight. "Don't look. Just go!"

She yanked open the door, and they stumbled into the alley. "Bastian. Oh, Bastian!" Sam moaned and fell to her knees. Ryan hauled her upright, sucking in great lungfuls of chemical-free oxygen. His head cleared more with every passing moment. Right now, this city air tasted even better than the BWCA's.

And what do you know? He still had a grip on his dad's paperweight. He shoved the fish end into his jeans pocket. The rock end was too big to fit. "Let's get to the truck." He tugged her up the alley while pulling his cell phone from his belt holder.

Screams from inside the building had ceased, but not the crackle of flames. The brick outside of the structure could withstand a lot of heat, but the interior was a big wooden tinderbox. Not much chance that Sam would salvage anything but a shell.

Déjà vu struck him as the 9-1-1 dispatcher answered, and he said, "Hello, this is Ryan Davidson..."

Sam reached the pickup across the street with Ryan beside her, talking on his phone. She looked back to see flames dancing in the glass-fronted customer area of the business she'd poured her sweat into. From the backseat of the truck, Jake began to whine.

"Fire trucks are on their way," Ryan said.

She gripped his arms. "We've got to go back for Bastian."

"Have you lost your mind? We can't go in there."

"Not inside the building. The alley. The vent." Her words came out in the same frantic spurts as her thoughts. She took a deep breath. "The screw holes were stripped on the inside cover in the closet so I just hung it back up loosely. Instead, I put one of those little rubber strips on the bottom of the closet door to keep the outside air inside the closet and not waste air-conditioning until I could get the whole thing plugged properly."

Ryan's eyes widened. "That door is thick and sturdy, almost as good as a fire door, and you've cut off fumes from getting into the closet space. There's a chance!" He headed for the rear of the pickup.

Sam followed him. "We need something long to reach into the ductwork and knock the vent cover off. If Bastian will hop up the mismatched boxes I stacked in there rather than reinstalling the shelves, he can crawl through to us."

"My fishing pole." He pulled a rod from the gear in the back and dashed toward the alley.

Sam didn't need any urging to keep up with him. "And for once that contrary cat better come when I call him."

Ryan halted abruptly, and she plowed into him. She bounced backward a couple of steps.

"Don't take the chance. Get Jake." He jerked his head toward the truck.

"Smart thinking." The knot in her chest began to ease. This might work. It had to!

She yanked open the pickup door. "Come on, Jakester. You've got to help save your BFFF." The dog seemed to understand because he jumped out with only a minor whimper over the strain to his stitches. "This way. Come on."

In her approach to the alley, she skirted in a wide arch away from the front windows that could blow out from heat at any time. If the firefighters were here already, they'd have apoplexy at these civilian antics.

She and Jake darted past her carport to where Ryan stood under the vent, calling, "Bastian! Come out, buddy! You can do it."

He turned at their approach, fishing pole in one hand, base resting on the ground. "The vent cover's off, and I can hear him caterwauling, but he hasn't responded to my voice."

Sam went quiet. Sure enough, above the dull rumble of fire in the main office, frantic meows came through loud and clear. Sam's heart leaped. "Bastian! Oh, your highness, please come to me now." The mewls cut off and scrambling sounds were heard, then ceased, and the meowing began again.

Ryan turned toward his dog. "Speak, Jake!"

His shout must have reached through the old dog's dim hearing, because he woofed. Then woofed again and again, while the humans called encouragement. Long seconds dragged past.

A feline head poked out of the hole in the brick wall, ears flat to its skull. *Mrrrrrrowwww!* Bastian made his outrage known loud and clear as Sam gathered the cat in her arms, laughter bubbling from her chest.

TWENTY-FIVE

Sam awoke the next morning to the gentle, rhythmic sway of a houseboat under her bed. Ryan had put her up in one of his rentals. Sunlight peeked around the edges of the blinds on the windows. She'd slept late and still felt like she could roll over and snooze some more, but haunting flashes of memory from the night before spurred her out of bed. Bruises and body aches put a hitch in her stride on the way to the bathroom…er, the head, as it was called on boats. She was getting to be a regular river rat.

What should she do today? For that matter, tomorrow? The rest of her life? She didn't have a business anymore. Strangely, that fact didn't put her under a black cloud of depression. The question of "what next" occupied her throughout a shower and donning the casual skirt and blouse Nancy had brought over, among other necessities, in the middle of the night.

She stepped out onto the deck and gazed across the water toward the next dock. Ryan waved to her from the rail of his boat. A smile bloomed on her face.

What a manifestation of God's grace that they had lived through the last few days. And what had he sort of said to her in her office right before he risked a fiery death to save her life? So the man who liked to keep relationships casual had a serious thing for her. The notion thrilled her to her toes. Did that mean she might feel a little bit the same way?

Hmmm. Yep. She had it bad.

He beckoned to her and then headed into his living quarters. Something was up.

Sam hustled down one dock and up another. As she stepped onto Ryan's boat, Jake and Bastian wandered around the corner from the starboard side of the deck. Bastian trotted over to her and twined around her legs, purring. She bent and scratched him behind his ears and then gave Jake a rub under his chin.

Her cat hadn't been this friendly to her in a long time. Must be Jake's influence. Evidently, Bastian was a dog kind of cat, not a people kind of cat. Anyway, she wouldn't be taking him home with her, whenever she determined where home was. Old Jake deserved his buddy with him for as long as he had left on this earth.

She entered Ryan's living quarters and found him sitting on his couch, staring at the fish paperweight on his coffee table. He looked up as she came in. No smile, but a warming in the blue gaze.

"Join me." He patted the cushion next to him. "I didn't want to do this without you present."

"Do what?"

"Open it."

She sank onto the couch. "There's some kind of trick to this paperweight?"

"That's why I bought it. My dad loved ingenious gadgets." He picked it up and showed it to her from every angle. "Looks solid, right? Even the police examining it for forensic evidence wouldn't be able to tell this was here."

He took a pin from the coffee table and stuck it into the trout's barely open mouth. A soft click sounded. Ryan twisted the base, and the fish came free. He held the base between them so she could see the hollow center about the circumference of a nickel. A torn scrap of yellow legal pad was rolled up inside of it.

With a tight little laugh, Ryan pulled it out. "Just like my dad. Write it down with pen and paper."

"Yes. Whatever 'it' is.'" Sam leaned in toward him as they read the neat block letters.

SECURENET
USER: MTDAVID
KEY: 0628R1122C

"I don't believe it." Ryan eased to his feet, staring at the paper as if mesmerized. "He used the computer after all."

"You've lost me."

He met her gaze, face alight. "Securenet is like an Internet security deposit box. You pay a rental fee to store data there. They're top of the line, have been since the midnineties. And the key for the data lock is Cassie's and my birthdays."

Sam's brows drew together. "That's a pretty elementary password. Warren Seiler should have been able to figure out that out without working up a sweat."

"Not if he didn't know where Dad put the information he was trying to hide. And anyone who knew Michael T. Davidson would never figure him to trust something important to an electronic brain."

Sam laughed. "Your father outthought his enemy by putting the information in the last place anyone would look for something he tucked away."

"But under duress he told the shooter that night where he hid the key to the information. He must have been promised some kind of mercy in exchange."

"An empty promise." She rose beside Ryan. "Let's go to your computer and find out why all this blood was shed."

A few minutes later, Sam perched in a chair beside Ryan while he booted up the computer in his office. She gnawed on her lower lip as he navigated through the Securenet system. A file came up that contained numbers and company names and a few lines of text here and there. Sam couldn't make heads or tails of the material, but Ryan scrolled through a few pages and then lowered his forehead to his computer desk.

"A measly insider trading scheme, and my dad found out about it."

Sam leaned toward the screen. "Why is Martha Stahl's name listed here at the bottom of the page?"

"Huh?" Ryan lifted his head and peered close. "I can't believe it!"

"What?"

"Mrs. Stahl had friends in key places. She was Seiler's source for the inside information, and she was in on the scheme with him."

Sam slumped back in her chair. "Oh, no! Eldon must have realized at some point what she was doing. She's who he's been protecting."

Ryan frowned and shook his head. "This offense wouldn't have rated more than a country-club stint in a minimum security prison, but the great and mighty Counselor with his eye on career advancement was willing to kill a whole family to protect his reputation."

Sam nodded. "And Martha and Eldon were willing to keep quiet about what they suspected regarding the murders rather than skewer their own reputations." She waved a hand at the data on the screen. "Are you going to turn this information over to the authorities?"

"Sure, it ties a bowknot on the case. However, the statute of limitations has run out. Martha won't even get even a slap on the wrist."

"Not from the human courts, but the scandal will sting more than a little."

Ryan cupped her face in his hands and leaned close. "I think we'd better pray for the Stahls. They have no idea of the eternal danger they're in."

Warmth overflowed from Sam's heart and spilled from her eyes. "I think, Ryan Davidson, that every member of your family would be proud of the Godly man you've become."

* * *

Six weeks later, Sam allowed Ryan to guide her out the door of The Meridian with a hand in the small of her back. The outside air held a hint of fall crispness, and she pulled the embroidered jacket of her matching dress closer around her. She glanced at her escort and smiled. He looked fabulous in a Western-style suit.

Ryan patted his tummy. "That *was* a 'fine dining experience,' just like the TV ad says."

Sam laughed as he opened the passenger door of his pickup for her. "Told you! Jenna is a master chef. I'm going to get fat living with her."

"Not as hard as you work." He handed her up to the seat.

"Helping Jenna at the restaurant and you with the houseboats has been loafing compared to all the effort I put into a business that may never be."

"I'd like to talk to you about that." He tapped the end of her nose, shut the door, and walked around to his side. When they got on the road, he looked over at her. "Everybody at church has been really supportive about you rebuilding."

Not a word about *him* sticking around to cheer her on. Sam stared out the window to hide the disappointment in her eyes. She would *not* pressure him to stay here this winter. "I'm grateful to my dad for talking me into taking out the maximum insurance. I could demolish the shell and rebuild brand-new with a little extra bank financing, but my enthusiasm for the project is in the basement." No way would she tell him why.

"Well, we'll just have to see what we can do about that." He grinned and did a little bounce in the seat.

She gave him a sideways look. He just chuckled and turned the pickup north on the freeway, instead of east toward their home areas. "Where are we going?"

"You'll find out."

"Secrets now, eh?" Lightness returned to her tone. She would enjoy being with Ryan every minute she could until he left for those long winter months.

"By the way, Detective Connell called again."

Sam snickered. "He's been exceptionally attentive these past weeks."

"The whole department was embarrassed that Judge Seiler had a pipeline into their records, and it was nothing more than the good-old-boy system. 'Keep me informed if anything comes up on this case. I knew the deceased.' Wink. Wink."

"So what did the detective want this time?"

"Real news. I didn't want to talk about death and killers over our meal, but they've identified the John Doe in the graveyard."

"Go, home team!" Sam smacked her hands together.

"Yeah, Connell was pretty pleased with himself that he thought to send the guy's prints to the FBI, who passed them along to Interpol. The Honorable Judge Seiler went overseas to recruit his talent. The shooter was some pro out of the Russian mafia with a name I'm not even going to try to pronounce."

They merged onto I-494 headed west, and Sam was truly mystified. "No hints about our destination?"

"I think you'll like it." He shot her a smug grin and would say no more on the subject during the next twenty minutes as they drove through moderate evening traffic.

"Lake Minnetonka?" Sam noted the huge, tree-lined lake on her left. The maples were in full ruddy color, and the water sparkled at her through the foliage. "We're not going for a swim this late in the season."

"Just a boat ride." He turned the pickup into a marina parking lot and pulled into an empty spot. A man locking up the office building waved at Ryan. He waved back, then went around and helped Sam out of the truck, shaking his head at the questions that kept popping out of her mouth. He led her by the hand past the building, down the sidewalk, and onto the docks.

Ryan halted them at a certain slip.

Sam gaped. "What is the *River King* doing here?"

"This is its new home. The *King*'s not going anywhere except dry dock when the ice starts forming."

"But—"

Ryan placed a finger over her lips. "I sold my business to Larry, who's only been summer help all these years and an odd-job carpenter in the winter. Going full-time with their own company is a dream come true for him and Nancy. And Derek's pea-green jealous that he has to return to school and not head south with them in a couple of weeks."

A sob escaped Sam's lips.

"You're crying?" Ryan's eyes widened. "Aren't you happy?"

Sam threw her arms around him. "I'm ecstatic," she blubbered.

"Oookaaay." He patted her back and let her bury her face in his lapel. "Um, I hope you don't mind if I keep busy this winter helping a certain wonderful woman put her business back together."

"I guess I could handle that." Her voice came out muffled against his jacket.

"Good, because I'm going to need something to do while the boat shop is constructing my charter yacht."

"Your yacht?" Sam lifted her head and stepped away from him, wiping at her eyes with her fingertips. She probably looked like a raccoon now from smeared mascara, but who cared?

Ryan swept his arm toward the vast body of water. "Lake Minnetonka is about to see the classiest floating facility for day trips, weddings, anniversaries, weddings, birthdays, weddings, graduations, weddings—"

She smacked him on the arm. "What is this 'wedding' fixation?"

His gaze searched her face. "Because one day, when the time is right, I'd like to talk about applying the word to us. Would you be open to that idea?"

If joy had a visible glow, she'd be a lighthouse. She ducked her head and turned away. "I might be persuaded to consider the prospect. But only if you promise me an awesome Boundary

Waters honeymoon." She swiveled back toward him. "I demand beautiful memories to replace the dismal."

Ryan's hearty laugh warmed the evening air. "I think that can be arranged."

He offered his arm and ushered her aboard his houseboat. They cast off as the setting sun spread shafts of pink and amber across the rippling water.

* * * * *

Dear Reader,

I hope you are inspired by the courage and perseverance of Samantha and Ryan as they wrestle with enemies of the heart and mind, as well as those who threaten their very lives. Thankfully, most of us will never face the awful loss to violet crime to the degree that these two characters do, but we can all relate to the confusion and temptation to bitterness that the death of a loved one or an undeserved wrong can thrust into our lives.

No, life will never be the same after such trauma, but can't it be good once more? Take heart that God is not only with us in sorrow, but stands ready to lift us out of grief and redeem the loss with fresh purpose and new direction. My own losses, which have been profound at times, have taught me that He indeed brings beauty from ashes and the oil of joy for mourning.

Write to me through my contact page at www.jillelizabeth-nelson.com if you have an encouraging story to share about new life after loss, and your testimony may be featured in my newsletter. I'm eager to hear from my wonderful readers!

Excellent blessings,

Jill Elizabeth Nelson

QUESTIONS FOR DISCUSSION

1. Past trauma has instilled in Samantha a heightened fear of intruders. For many years, this fear crippled her ability to move outside her personal safety zone. What fears do you possess that may be holding you back from your potential? How might you overcome them?

2. Because of catastrophic loss, Ryan no longer believed God cares about him. Many people are angry with God, and blame Him for the negatives in their lives. Why is this false reasoning, and how can people process their hurts without losing their faith?

3. Samantha is concerned about how appearances might affect her reputation and the success of her business. Keeping a good name is important in life, but where do we draw the line between maintaining a good reputation and doing the right thing, even though it might have a negative impact on how others perceive us? Does Samantha successfully strike this balance? How might her example apply to your life?

4. Ryan has decided that forming attachments to other people isn't worth the risk of losing them. Why is this ultimately more hurtful than taking a chance on investing in others?

5. Samantha is willing to risk her safety to maintain her hard-won independence. Do you agree with her decision to hold her ground in the face of threat? Why or why not?

6. Ryan began questioning his faith before his family was killed. Samantha assures him that God is not afraid of his questions. Does that statement make Ryan uncomfortable?

Why? Can questions be a legitimate part of the process of making faith personal?

7. The hallmark of character is integrity, which sometimes means owning up to wrongdoing and facing the consequences in order keep others from suffering needlessly. Which characters in the book display a lack of integrity in this way, and why do they choose the dishonorable path? Have there been times in your life that you've been faced with similar choices, though perhaps on a lesser scale? What did you choose? Why?

8. Some people will do anything to gain power and position and keep the esteem of society. What might be the root causes of that level of ruthless ambition? How can we keep our perspective when we see the abuse of power?

9. Unresolved issues between Ryan and his father have stolen his hope. How so? There are layers to this problem that are common to humanity. During Ryan and Sam's discussion on his houseboat, a new depth to this barrier is revealed. What is it, and does the realization free Ryan emotionally?

10. Samantha has an unusually compassionate attitude toward the criminal who devastated her life. What is it? By the end of the book, how does her hard-won wisdom help Ryan begin to walk free of bitterness?

11. At the conclusion of the book, what does Ryan give up in order to stay close to a person he has grown to love? Does he gain much more than he loses? Can you think of times in your life when you needed to let go of something in order to gain something else? Did the relinquishment ultimately benefit you?

12. By the final chapter, Samantha's focus is no longer on establishing an independent life as a successful businesswoman, but on her relationship with Ryan. Why are relationships always more important than accomplishments?

Turn the page for a sneak peek of RITA® Award-winner Linda Goodnight's heartwarming story, HOME TO CROSSROADS RANCH. On sale in March 2009 from Steeple Hill Love Inspired®.

Chapter One

Nate Del Rio heard screams the minute he stepped out of his Ford F-150 SuperCrew and started up the flower-lined sidewalk leading to Rainy Jernagen's house. He doubled-checked the address scribbled on the back of a bill for horse feed. Sure enough, this was the place.

Adjusting his Stetson against a gust of March wind, he rang the doorbell, expecting the noise to subside. It didn't.

Somewhere inside the modest, tidy-looking brick house, at least two kids were screaming their heads off in what sounded to his experienced ears like fits of temper. A television blasted out Saturday morning cartoons—SpongeBob, he thought, though he was no expert on kids' television programs.

He punched the doorbell again. Instead of the expected *ding-dong,* a raucous alternative Christian rock band added a few more decibels to the noise level.

Nate shifted the toolbox to his opposite hand and considered running for his life while he had the chance.

Too late. The bright red door whipped open. Nate's mouth fell open with it.

When the men's ministry coordinator from Bible Fellowship had called him, he'd somehow gotten the impression that he was coming to help a little old school teacher. You know, the kind that only drives to school and church and has a big, fat cat.

Not so. The woman standing before him with taffy-blond hair sprouting out from a disheveled ponytail couldn't possibly be any older than his own thirty-one years. A big blotch of something purple stained the front of her white sweatshirt and she was barefooted. Plus, she had a crying baby on each hip and a little red-haired girl hanging on one leg, bawling like a sick calf. And there wasn't a cat in sight.

What had he gotten himself into?

"May I help you?" she asked over the racket. Her blue-gray eyes were little too unfocused and bewildered for his comfort.

Raising his voice, he asked, "Are you Ms. Jernagen?"

"Yes," she said cautiously. "I'm Rainy Jernagen. And you are…?"

"Nate Del Rio."

She blinked, uncomprehending, all the while jiggling both babies up and down. One grabbed a hank of her hair. She flinched, her head angling to one side as she said, still cautiously, "Okaaay."

Nate reached out and untwined the baby's sticky fingers.

A relieved smile rewarded him. "Thanks. Is there something I can help you with?"

He hefted the red toolbox to chest level so she could see it. "From the Handy Man Ministry. Jack Martin called. Said you had a washer problem."

Understanding dawned. "Oh, my goodness. Yes. I'm so sorry. You aren't what I expected. Please forgive me."

She wasn't what he expected, either. Not in the least. Young and with a houseful of kids. He suppressed a shiver. No wonder she looked like the north end of a southbound cow. Kids, even grown ones, could drive a person to distraction. He should know. His adult sister and brother were, at this moment, making his life as miserable as possible. The worst part was they did it all the time. Only this morning his sister, Janine, had finally packed up and gone back to Sal, giving Nate a few days' reprieve.

"Come in, come in," the woman was saying. "It's been a crazy morning what with the babies showing up at 3:00 a.m. and Katie having a sick stomach. Then while I was doing the laundry, the washing machine went crazy. Water everywhere." She jerked her chin toward the inside of the house. "You're truly a godsend."

He wasn't so sure about that, but he'd signed up for his church's ministry to help single women and the elderly with those pesky little handyman chores like oil changes and leaky faucets. Most of his visits had been to older ladies who plied him with sweet tea and jars of homemade jam and talked about the good old days while he replaced a fuse or unstopped the sink. And their houses had been quiet. Real quiet.

Rainy Jernagen stepped back, motioned him in, and Nate very cautiously entered a room that should have had flashing red lights and a *danger zone* sign.

Toys littered the living room like Christmas morning. An overturned cereal bowl flowed milk onto a coffee table. Next to a playpen crowding one wall, a green package belched out disposable diapers. Similarly, baby clothes were strewn, along with a couple of kids, on the couch and floor. In a word, the place was a wreck.

"The washer is back this way behind the kitchen. Watch your step. It's slippery."

More than slippery. Nate kicked his way through the living room and the kitchen area beyond, though the kitchen actually appeared much tidier than the rest, other than the slow seepage of water coming from somewhere beyond. The shine of liquid glistening on beige tile led them straight to the utility room.

"I turned the faucets off behind the washer when this first started, but a tubful still managed to pump out onto the floor." She hoisted the babies higher on her hip and spoke to a young boy sitting in the floor. "Joshua, get out of those suds."

"But they're pretty, Miss Rainy." The brown-haired boy with bright blue eyes grinned up at her, extending a handful of bubbles. Light reflected off each droplet. "See the rainbows? There's always a rainbow, like you said. A rainbow behind the rain."

Miss Rainy smiled at the child. "Yes, there is. But right now, Mr. Del Rio needs in here to fix the washer. It's a little crowded for all of us." She was right about that. The space was no bigger than a small bathroom. "Can I get you to take the babies to the playpen while I show him around?"

"I'll take them, Miss Rainy." An older boy with a serious face and brown plastic glasses entered the room. Treading carefully, he came forward and took both babies, holding them against his slight chest. Another child appeared behind him. This one a girl with very blond hair and eyes the exact blue of the boy's, the one she'd called Joshua. How many children did this woman have, anyway? Six?

A heavy, smothery feeling pressed against his airway. Six kids?

Before he could dwell on that disturbing thought, a scream of sonic proportions rent the soap-fragrant air. He whipped around ready to protect and defend.

The little blond girl and the redhead were going at it.

"It's mine." Blondie tugged hard on a Barbie doll.

"It's mine. Will said so." To add emphasis to her demand, the redhead screamed bloody murder. "Miss Rainy."

About that time, Joshua decided to skate across the suds, and then slammed into the far wall next to a door that probably opened into the garage. He grabbed his big toe and set up a howl. Water sloshed as Rainy rushed forward and gathered him into her arms.

"Rainy!" Blondie screamed again.

"Rainy!" the redhead yelled.

Nate cast a glance at the garage exit and considered a fast escape.

Lord, I'm here to do a good thing. Can You help me out a little?

Rainy, her clothes now wet, somehow managed to take the

doll from the fighting girls while snuggling Joshua against her side. The serious-looking boy stood in the doorway, a baby on each hip, taking in the chaos.

"Come on, Emma," the boy said to Blondie. "I'll make you some chocolate milk." So they went, slip-sliding out of the flooded room.

Four down, two to go.

Nate clunked his toolbox onto the washer and tried to ignore the chaos. Not an easy task, but one he'd learned to deal with as a boy. As an adult, he did everything possible to avoid this kind of madness. The Lord had a sense of humor sending him to this particular house.

"I apologize, Mr. Del Rio," Rainy said, shoving at the wads of hair that hung around her face like Spanish moss.

"Call me Nate. I'm not that much older than you." At thirty-one and the long-time patriarch of his family, he might feel seventy, but he wasn't.

"Okay, Nate. And I'm Rainy. Really, it's not usually this bad. I can't thank you enough for coming over. I tried to get a plumber, but being Saturday..." She shrugged, letting the obvious go unsaid. No one could get a plumber on the weekend.

"No problem." He removed his white Stetson and placed it next to the toolbox. What was he supposed to say? That he loved wading in dirty soap suds and listening to kids scream and cry? Not likely.

Rainy stood with an arm around each of the remaining children—the rainbow boy and the redhead. Her look of embarrassment had him feeling sorry for her. All these kids and no man around to help. With this many, she'd never find another husband, he was sure of that. Who would willingly take on a boatload of kids?

After a minute, Rainy and the remaining pair left the room and he got to work. Wiggling the machine away from the wall wasn't easy. Even with all the water on the floor, a significant amount remained in the tub. This leftover liquid sloshed and gushed at regular intervals. In minutes, his boots were dark with moisture. No problem there. As a rancher, his boots were often dark with lots of things, the best of which was water.

On his haunches, he surveyed the back of the machine, where hoses and cords and metal parts twined together like a nest of water moccasins.

As he investigated each hose in turn, he once more felt a presence in the room. Pivoting on his heels, he discovered the two boys squatted beside him, attention glued to the back of the washer.

"A busted hose?" the oldest one asked, pushing up his glasses.

"Most likely."

"I coulda fixed it, but Rainy wouldn't let me."

"That so?"

"Yeah. Maybe. If someone would show me."

Nate suppressed a smile. "What's your name?"

"Will. This here's my brother, Joshua." He yanked a thumb at the younger one. "He's nine. I'm eleven. You go to Miss Rainy's church?"

"I do, but it's a big church. I don't think we've met before."

"She's nice. Most of the time. She never hits us or anything, and we've been here for six months."

It occurred to Nate then that these were not Rainy's children. The kids called her Miss Rainy, not Mom, and according to Will they had not been here forever. But what was a young, single woman doing with all these kids?

* * * * *

Love Inspired® SUSPENSE

TITLES AVAILABLE NEXT MONTH

Available March 10, 2009

POISONED SECRETS by Margaret Daley
An anonymous tip brought Maggie Ridgeway to her birth mother. Yet finding her led to more questions. Why did her parents abandon her? What's triggering the *multiple* burglaries in her new apartment? Can building owner Kane McDowell protect her? And once he finds out who she really is, will he still want to?

COLD CASE MURDER by Shirlee McCoy
Without a Trace
Loomis, Louisiana, holds no charms for Jodie Gilmore. Still, the novice FBI agent has a job to do, investigating the local missing person's case. But the job gets complicated when handsome forensic anthropologist Harrison Cahill uncovers a decades-old double homicide.

A SILENT TERROR by Lynette Eason
There was no motive for the murder—Marianna Santino's roommate shouldn't have died. Then Detective Ethan O'Hara realizes the deaf teacher was the *real* target. Ethan learns all he can about Marianna. Soon, he's willing to risk everything—even his heart—to keep her safe.

PERFECT TARGET by Stephanie Newton
The corpse in her path was the first warning. Next was a break-in at Bayley Foster's home. She's certain that the stalker who once tormented her has returned to toy with her again. Her protective neighbor, police detective Cruse Conyers, is determined to get answers—at any cost.

LISCNMBPA0209